As Dylan dre... catch her brea...

It seemed he was .... Except she wasn't sure she'd ever get her breath back again— that kiss was unlike anything she'd experienced before. In fact, if she just leaned forward a little, she could experience it again…

And then the enormity of the situation hit her.

She'd just kissed her boss.

Or he'd kissed her—she wasn't sure about the details of what had just happened. All she knew was she'd never been kissed with that much hunger. That much passion. That much mind-numbing skill. That it had been her employer, someone she shouldn't have been kissing in the first place, was a cruel twist of irony. If she'd screwed up her well-ordered plan, or caused him to not take her seriously, she'd never forgive herself.

"Faith," he said, his voice a rasp. "I'm sorry. That was completely out of line."

Honesty compelled her to point out the truth. "You weren't there alone."

* * *

Bidding on Her Boss is part of The Hawke Brothers trilogy: Three tycoon bachelors, three very special mergers…

BIDDING ON
HER BOSS

BY
RACHEL BAILEY

MILLS &
BOON

Published in Great Britain 2015
by Mills & Boon, an imprint of Harlequin (UK) Limited,
Eton House, 18-24 Paradise Road, Richmond, Surrey, TW9 1SR

© 2015 Rachel Robinson

ISBN: 978-0-263-25278-1

51-0915

Harlequin (UK) Limited's policy is to use papers that are natural, renewable and recyclable products and made from wood grown in sustainable forests. The logging and manufacturing processes conform to the legal environmental regulations of the country of origin.

Printed and bound in Spain
by CPI, Barcelona

Rachel Bailey developed a serious book addiction at a young age (via Peter Rabbit and Jemima Puddleduck), and has never recovered. Just how she likes it. She went on to earn degrees in psychology and social work but is now living her dream—writing romance for a living.

She lives in a piece of paradise on Australia's Sunshine Coast with her hero and four dogs, where she loves to sit with a dog or two, overlooking the trees and reading books from her evergrowing to-be-read pile.

Rachel would love to hear from you and can be contacted through her website, www.rachelbailey.com.

This book is dedicated to Sharon Archer, who is not only an amazing author, but is also a brilliant critique partner and very dear friend. Sharon, thank you for being on this journey with me.

ACKNOWLEDGMENTS

Huge thanks to Charles Griemsman for his editing and support with this book—Charles, it's always a pleasure to work with you. Also, thank you to Barbara DeLeo and Amanda Ashby for the brainstorming and help, and to John for always supporting my dreams.

One

Dylan Hawke had done a few things he regretted in his life, but he had a feeling this one might top the list.

The spotlight shone in his eyes, but he smiled as he'd been instructed and gave a sweeping bow before making his way down the stairs and onto the stage. Applause—and a few cheers that he suspected were from his family—greeted him.

"We'll start the bidding at two hundred dollars," the emcee said from the front of the stage.

Dylan sucked in a breath. *And so it begins.* Step one of rehabilitating his image—donate his time to charity. Now that his brother was marrying a princess, Dylan's own mentions in the media had skyrocketed, and he'd quickly realized his playboy reputation could be a disadvantage for his future sister-in-law and the things she wanted to achieve for homeless children in LA.

"What do I hear for Dylan?" the emcee, a sitcom actor, called out. "Dylan Hawke is the man behind the chain of Hawke's Blooms florists, so we can guarantee he knows about romancing his dates."

A murmur went around the crowded room as several white paddles with black numbers shot into the air. He couldn't see too much detail past the spotlight that shone down on him, but it seemed that the place was full, and that the waiters were keeping the guests' drinks topped off as they moved through the crowd.

"Two fifty, three hundred," the emcee called.

Dylan spotted his brother Liam sitting with his fiancée, Princess Jensine of Larsland. Jenna—who had been hiding incognito as Dylan's housekeeper before she met Liam—gave him a thumbs-up. This was the first fundraising event of the new charity, the Hawke Brothers Trust, which Jenna had established to raise money for homeless children. Now that she and Liam were to be married, they planned to split their family's time between her homeland and LA, and the trust would utilize the skills she'd gained growing up in a royal family. It would be the perfect project for her—she'd said it was something she could sink her teeth into.

Dylan believed in the cause and believed in Jenna, so his job tonight was to help raise as much money as he could. He just wished he'd been able to do it in a less humiliating way. Like, say, writing a check.

But that method wouldn't help rehabilitate his image.

Which had led him to this moment. On stage in front of hundreds of people. Being sold.

"Five hundred and fifty," the emcee said, pointing at a redhead near the side of the room, whose paddle said sixty-three.

Dylan threw Sixty-Three a wink, and then crossed to where a blonde woman held up her paddle. The emcee called, "Six hundred."

Dylan squinted against the lights. There was something familiar about the blonde… Then it hit him and his gut clenched tight. It was Brittany Oliver, a local network weather girl. They'd been out two or three times a few years ago, but she'd been cloying. When he found out that she was already planning a future and children for them, he'd broken it off. He swallowed hard and sent up a prayer that someone outbid her. Maybe the cute redhead with paddle sixty-three.

He dug one hand in his pocket and flashed a charming smile at the audience—a smile he'd been using to effect since he was fourteen. He was rewarded when a stunning woman with long dark hair and coffee-colored skin raised her paddle. He was starting not to mind being on stage after all.

"Six fifty," the emcee called. "Seven hundred dollars. Seven fifty."

He knew Jenna was hoping for a big amount from this auction to get their charity started with a bang, so he took the rosebud from his buttonhole and threw it into the crowd. It was a cheesy move, but then the bidding happened so quickly that all of a sudden it hit two thousand.

Dylan steeled himself and looked over at Brittany, and sure enough, she was still in the running. He had no idea whether she'd want to chew his ear off for breaking things off or try to convince him they should get back together. Either way, it would be an uncomfortable evening. He should have had a backup plan—a signal to tell Jenna to bid whatever it took if things went awry. He could have reimbursed her later.

"Three thousand four hundred."

It was the redhead. Dylan looked her over. Bright copper hair scraped into a curly ponytail on top of her head, cobalt blue halter top, dark eyes that were wide as she watched the other bidders, and a bottom lip caught between her teeth in concentration. She looked adorable. In his pocket where the audience couldn't see, he crossed his fingers that she won. He could spend an enjoyable evening with her, a nice meal, maybe a drive to a moonlit lookout, maybe a movie.

"Four thousand six hundred."

A flash bulb went off and he smiled, but he needed to get the bidding higher for the trust. He ambled over to the emcee and indicated with a tilt of his head that he had something to say. She covered the mic with her hand and lowered it.

"Make it three dates," he said, his voice low.

Her eyebrows shot up, and then she nodded and raised the mic again. "I've just received information that the package up for auction now consists of three dates."

Over the next few minutes, there was another flurry of raised paddles before the emcee finally said, "Going once, going twice, sold for eight thousand two hundred dollars."

Dylan realized he'd stopped following the bidding and had no idea who'd won.

"Number sixty-three, you can meet Mr. Hawke at the side of the stage to make arrangements. Next we have a sports star who will need no introduction." The emcee's voice faded into the background as Dylan realized the cute redhead had made the top bid. He grinned.

Maybe turning his reputation around and doing his bit for charity wouldn't be so bad after all.

Faith Crawford stood, adjusted the hem of her halter top over her black pants and slipped between the tables to where Dylan Hawke was waiting for her by the side of the stage.

Her belly fluttered like crazy but she steeled herself and, when she reached him, stuck out her hand.

"Hi, I'm Faith," she said.

Dylan took her hand, but instead of shaking it, he lifted it to his lips and pressed a kiss on the back. "I'm Dylan, and, on behalf of my family, I appreciate your donation to the Hawke Brothers Trust."

He gave her a slow smile and her insides melted, but she tried to ignore her body's reaction. Her body didn't realize that Dylan Hawke was a notorious charmer who had probably used that exact smile on countless women. Which was why her brain was in charge. *Well*, she thought as she looked into his twinkling green eyes, *mostly in charge*.

Dylan released her hand and straightened. "I have a few ideas about places we could go on our first date—"

Faith shook her head. "I know where I want to go."

He arched an eyebrow. "Okay, then. I like a woman who knows what she wants."

Oh, she knew exactly what she wanted. And it wasn't Dylan Hawke, despite how good he looked in that tuxedo. It was what he could do for her career. She'd just made a large investment in her future—having bid most of her savings—and she wouldn't let it go to waste.

He slid a pen out of an inside pocket of his jacket and grabbed a napkin from a nearby table. "Write down your address and I'll pick you up. How does tomorrow night sound?"

The sooner the better. "Tomorrow is good. But instead of picking me up, I'd rather meet you. Let's say in front of your Santa Monica store at seven?"

He grinned, but this time it wasn't a charmer's smile. It was genuine. She liked this one more—she could imagine getting into all sorts of mischief with the man wearing that grin.

"A woman of mystery," he said, rocking back on his heels. "Nice. Okay, Faith Sixty-Three, I'll meet you in front of the Santa Monica Hawke's Blooms store at seven o'clock tomorrow night."

"I'll be there," she said and then turned and walked along the edge of the room to the door, aware that several curious gazes followed her exit. Including Dylan Hawke's. Which was just how she needed him—with his full attention focused on her.

Now all she had to do was keep her own attention soundly focused on her career, and not on getting into mischief with her date and his grin.

Dylan pulled his Porsche into the small parking lot in front of his Santa Monica store. He tried to get around to all thirty-two stores fairly regularly, but given that they were spread from San Francisco to San Diego, it didn't happen as often as it used to, and he couldn't remember exactly when he was last at this one. It looked good, though, and he knew the sales figures were in the top quarter of all the Hawke's Blooms stores.

Movement near the door caught his attention. It was Faith. Her red hair gleamed in the window lights and bounced about her shoulders. She wore a halter-neck summer dress that was fitted in all the right places and flared out over her hips, down to her knees, showing shapely calves atop stylish heels. His pulse picked up speed as he stepped out of his car.

All he knew about this woman was that she liked halter tops, her hair could stop traffic, she was wealthy enough to have spare cash lying around to help out a new charity and her lips could set his blood humming. But damn if he didn't want to know more.

"Evening, Faith," he said, walking around and opening his passenger side door.

She didn't take a step closer, just stood at the shop door looking adorable and said, "We won't be needing your car tonight."

He glanced around—the parking lot was empty. "You have a magic carpet tucked away somewhere?"

"No need," she said brightly. "We're already here."

She dug into her bag and came out with a handful of keys looped together on what looked like plaited ribbons. As he watched in surprise, she stuck a key into the front door, and he heard a click. She stepped in, efficiently disabled the alarm and turned back to him. "Come on in."

Dylan narrowed his eyes, half expecting one of his brothers to jump out and yell "gotcha" because he'd fallen for the prank. But Faith was busy putting her bag behind the counter and switching on lights. Shaking his head, he set the keyless lock on his car, followed her into the store and closed the door behind them. He had no idea what she had planned or what she really wanted out of this date, but for some reason that didn't bother him. This woman was piquing his interest on more than one level—something he hadn't experienced in a long while—and he realized he was enjoying the sensation.

"Who *are* you, Faith Sixty-Three?" he asked, leaning back against the counter and appreciating the way her dress hugged her lush curves.

She faced him then, her cheeks flushed and her warm brown eyes sparkling. "I'm a florist. My name is Faith Crawford and I work for you in this store."

Faith Crawford? That name rang a bell, but he couldn't remember any specifics. He narrowed his eyes. "Mary O'Donnell is the manager here, isn't she?"

"Yep, she's my manager," Faith said over her shoulder as she turned the light on in the storeroom in the back of the shop.

He wrapped a hand around the back of his neck. This had gone past Woman of Mystery and was fast becoming ridiculous. Why would an employee want to spend a purseful of money on a night or three with the boss? Could she have an axe to grind? Was she hoping to sleep her way to a promotion?

He blew out a breath. "How long have you worked for me?"

She turned to face him, standing a little taller. "Six months, Mr. Hawke."

"So you know Hawke's Blooms has a no fraternization policy." A policy he wholeheartedly believed in. "Managers can't be involved with anyone who works for them."

She didn't seem fazed. "I'm aware of that, yes."

"Yet," he pressed, taking a step closer and catching a whiff of her exotic perfume, "you still paid good money for a date—well, three dates—with me."

A small frown line appeared between her brows.

"Nowhere was it specified that they were supposed to be romantic *dates* with the bachelors."

Dylan was about to reply, then realized he was losing control of the conversation. "Then what do you want from me?" he asked warily.

She grabbed a clip from her handbag and pulled her hair back. "I want you to spend the evening here with me."

"Doing what, exactly?" he asked as he watched her clip her red curls, which burst out the top of the clasp in copper-colored chaos.

"Watching."

He felt his eyebrows lift. "I have to warn you, kinky propositions still fall under the no fraternization policy."

Faith rolled her eyes, but he saw the corners of her mouth twitch. "I'll be making a floral arrangement."

Right. As if he didn't get enough of that in his average day. And yet, he thought, glancing at her pale, long fingers, there was something appealing about the idea of watching Faith at work. Her fingers looked as if they'd be gentle yet firm. He could almost feel them on his jaw, then stroking across his shoulders. His skin tingled…and he realized he was getting carried away. This was not a path he could take with an employee—which he'd only just explained to her.

Besides, his attraction was probably a result of being in the store at night, alone, cocooned in the area illuminated by the lights. It couldn't be more.

He rubbed a hand down his face. "Let me get this straight. I know what you're earning, so unless you have a trust fund, your bid was a decent amount of money to you. Yet you paid it to have me sit and watch you do the job that we normally pay you to do."

She beamed at him. "That's it."

"I've missed something," he said, tilting his head to the side. She was becoming more intriguing by the minute.

She opened the fridge door and pulled out buckets of peonies, lilacs and magnolias. "Have you ever had a dream, Mr. Hawke? Something that was all yours and made you smile when you thought about it?"

Dylan frowned. His career dreams had always been for Hawke's Blooms, but they were dreams he shared with his family. Had he ever had one that was his alone?

"Sure," he said casually, knowing it was probably a lie and unsure how he felt about that.

While looking at him, she began to strip the leaves from the flower stems. "Then you know how it is."

As he took in the glow on her face, his pulse picked up speed. "What's your dream, Faith?"

She smiled mysteriously. "I have many dreams, but there's one in particular I'm trying to achieve now."

He met her gaze and the room faded away. He could have looked at her all night. Then her eyes darkened. Her breathing became irregular. Dylan wanted to groan. She felt the chemistry between them as well. His body responded to the knowledge, tightening, heating. But he couldn't let that happen. This was dangerous. He frowned and swung away.

"Tell me about the dream," he said when he turned back around, this time more in control of himself.

After a beat, Faith gave a small nod. "To open the Hawke's Blooms catalog and see one of my designs there on the page."

This was all about the catalog? He leaned back against the bench opposite the one Faith was work-

ing on and crossed his ankles. "We have a procedure
in place for that."

"I know it by heart," she said, taking foam and a
white tray down from the shelf. "'Any Hawke's Blooms
florist may submit an original floral design to his or her
manager, accompanied by a completed, signed applica-
tion form. If the manager believes the design has merit,
she or he will pass it to the head office to be considered
for inclusion in the catalog of standard floral designs
used for customer orders.'"

Dylan smiled. She'd recited the procedure word for
word. "And," he added, "that process doesn't cost a single penny. Why didn't you go that route?"

"I did." She clipped the bottoms from a bunch of
peony stems. "About twenty times, in fact. After my
manager rejected number sixteen, I began to think that
way might not work for me." She smiled and her dimples showed.

He thought about her manager, Mary O'Donnell.
Mary was simpering to management, which was annoying, but he knew she ran a tight ship. Was it possible she was blocking her own staff from advancement?
"Are you making a complaint about your manager?" he
asked, serious.

She shook her head, and her hands slowed to a stop
as she met his gaze. "I'm a good florist, Mr. Hawke.
I take pride in my work, and take direction from my
manager. I do my best by our customers and have a
good group of regulars who ask for me by name. So I
don't think it's too much to ask to have just one of my
designs considered so I can move my career forward."

Dylan knew he was lucky—he'd grown up in the
family business, where his input had been not only lis-

tened to but also encouraged. But what if he'd been in Faith's shoes? An employee of a large company who was struggling to have her voice heard. He watched her place flowers in the foam, turning the arrangement with the other hand as she went. He'd like to think he'd have gone the extra mile, the way Faith was doing tonight.

"So you decided to get creative," he said, hearing the trace of admiration in his own voice.

"Seeing you were auctioning off a night of your time seemed like a sign." She glanced up at him, her long-lashed eyes earnest. "Do you believe in destiny, Mr. Hawke?"

"Can't say it's something I've ever paid much attention to," he said. Unlike, say, the way the side of her jaw sloped down to her neck, or the sprinkling of pale ginger freckles across her nose.

"Well, I do, and I'd just been thinking 'If only I could speak to someone in the head office myself' when the posters for the auction went up in the window. The very window where I work." She paused, moistening her lips. "You can see it was too strong a sign to ignore, can't you?"

He wasn't sure if he wanted to chuckle or to kiss those full lips her tongue had darted over. Instead, he murmured, "I suppose so."

"So I attended the auction, used a good portion of my savings, and here we are." She splayed her free hand to emphasize her point, and then picked up a roll of ribbon and went back to what she was doing.

Dylan shifted his weight. Something about this situation and her confidence was beginning to make him uncomfortable. After she'd spent that amount of money—which he'd reimburse now that he knew she was an employee trying to get a meeting with him—and she'd gone to this much effort, how would she react if he agreed with her manager?

"Tell me, Faith," he said carefully. "What happens if, after all this effort and expense, I don't like your design enough to put it in the catalog?"

She looked him in the eye again. There was no artifice, no game playing in her deep brown gaze. "Then I'll know I've given it my best shot, and I'll work harder to create an even better design."

Dylan nodded. She believed in herself but didn't have a sense of entitlement and was prepared to put in the work to improve her situation. He liked her attitude. In fact, there were a number of things he liked about Faith Crawford—including things he shouldn't allow himself to like now that he knew she worked for him. Such as the crazy hair that his fingers were itching to explore, and the way her sweet-shaped mouth moved as she spoke.

There was also a vibrancy about her that dragged his gaze back every time he looked away. How would it feel to hold all that vibrancy in his arms? Her kisses would be filled with passion, he just knew it, and in his bed… Dylan held back a groan and determinedly refocused on Faith's floristry skills.

Her movements were quick and economical but still flowed, almost as if her hands were dancing. He'd had a stab at displaying flowers in the past but hadn't pulled off more than rudimentary arrangements. It had been enough for the roadside stall his family had started the business with but hadn't come close to what a florist with training and flair could create. Yet having been around professional florists for his entire adult life, he was good at spotting skill in someone else.

He could already tell that Faith didn't just have the training all florists employed by Hawke's Blooms stores required. She also had that indefinable, creative *something* that differentiated the great from the good. Whether she'd harnessed that talent, and was able to use it to create designs of the standard needed to be included in the catalog, was yet to be seen.

But if nothing else, tonight Faith Crawford had achieved one thing she'd set out to achieve—she definitely had his full attention.

In fact, he was having trouble looking anywhere but at her.

Faith added another peony to the arrangement and tried to ignore the prickles on the back of her neck that told her Dylan was watching her again. Of course, that's what the whole night had been engineered to achieve, but he was only sometimes following what her hands were doing. At other times...

Heat rose in her belly as she thought about the way he'd been staring at her mouth a few minutes ago. She couldn't remember the last time a man had looked at her with that much hunger. Especially a man she'd been wanting to wrap herself around and kiss as if there was no tomorrow ever since he'd stepped out of his sex-on-wheels car.

And that it had to be Dylan Hawke, the CEO of the company? Well, that was fate playing a cruel joke on her. So she pretended that she wasn't wildly attracted to the man in front of her and that he wasn't sending her the same signals. She focused on the flowers. Which was working out fairly well, except for the prickles on the back of her neck.

But she needed to concentrate, to stop letting herself be distracted. Ruthlessly she reminded herself of what was at stake: getting this right could mean a fantastic boost to her career. She turned the arrangement with quick flicks of her wrist, checking for symmetry. Just a few stray leaves to trim. She snipped them away carefully. It looked good, balanced in color and form… but was it special enough to go into the catalog? She'd controlled her wilder artistic urges and gone for a safer conservative arrangement to impress. Butterflies fluttered mercilessly in her stomach. For the first time, she realized how much Mary's criticism had dented her confidence in her creativity.

She reached out to touch a crisp green leaf. This arrangement was finished—but still she hesitated.

"All done?"

She jolted at the sound of Dylan's voice so close to her ear. Last time she'd been aware of him, he'd been on the other side of the bench. She tried to move to the side. Her foot caught on something and she felt herself begin to fall. A hand closed around her arm, and her almost certain tumble was averted. She closed her eyes, and then opened them to find Dylan staring at her. The picture of him on the company website was nothing like the living, breathing man before her.

With him so close, no more than a hand span away, his scent surrounded her. It was dark and mysterious, surprising. She'd have expected something lighter, more recognizable, perhaps one of the expensive name-brand colognes. Yet this had undertones of a night in the forest—earthy, secretive and alluring. A shiver ran down her body to her toes. Dylan stilled.

Her breath caught in her throat. She could feel the heat from his body reaching out to envelop her. The world receded around her and all she could see, all she could feel, was Dylan. His eyes darkened and she swallowed hard. She should step away, not let her body lead her into temptation. But, oh, what temptation this man was. She could feel her pulse thundering at the base of her throat and saw Dylan's gaze drop to observe the same thing.

"Faith," he murmured, his breathing uneven.

She closed her eyes, fighting the effect of hearing her name on his lips, and when she opened them again, he was closer than before, his breath fanning over her face. Her hands found their way to his chest, so solid and warm.

A shudder ran down his body at her touch.

"Please—" she said, and before she could finish the thought his mouth was on hers. A small part of her mind told her to pull away, but instead, her hands fisted in his shirt, not letting him go.

He groaned as she opened her mouth to him, and his arms wrapped around her, holding her close while pushing her back against the workbench. His tongue was like nothing else as it stroked along the side of hers, leaving her wanting more. To be closer. So much closer.

She was lost.

Two

As Dylan drew away, Faith tried to catch her breath. It seemed as if he was doing the same. Except she wasn't sure she'd ever get her breath back again—that kiss was unlike anything she'd experienced before. In fact, if she just leaned forward a little, she could experience it again...

And then the enormity of the situation hit her, sending her knees wobbling.

She'd just kissed her boss.

No, not *her* boss—the *big* boss. She'd just kissed the man with ultimate responsibility for every single Hawke's Blooms store.

Or he'd kissed her—she wasn't sure about the details of what had just happened. All she knew was she'd never been kissed with that much hunger. That much passion. That much mind-numbing skill. That it had been her employer, someone she shouldn't have been kissing in the first place, was a cruel twist of irony. If she'd screwed up her well-ordered plan or caused him to not take her seriously, she'd never forgive herself.

"Faith," he said, his voice a rasp. "I'm sorry. That was completely out of line."

Honesty compelled her to point out the truth. "You weren't there alone."

"But I'm the one who's the boss." He winced. "It's my responsibility not to cross the damn line. You shouldn't feel pressured or uncomfortable in your workplace, and I apologize."

"I don't feel uncomfortable. Well," she amended, looking down at her hands, "I didn't feel uncomfortable or pressured *then*. I guess I'm uncomfortable now." She glanced back up, meeting his wary gaze. "But you should know, I wanted to kiss you. Then."

His head tilted to the side. "But not now?"

"No." Which was a lie. She definitely wanted to kiss him again. Wanted it more than almost anything. The key was the *almost*. She wanted a flourishing career more than she wanted to kiss Dylan Hawke again.

He blew out a breath. "That's a relief, but it's not enough. It was selfish of me to kiss you when you wanted me here for a completely different purpose. I give you my word it won't happen again."

"I appreciate that," she said, trying to conjure a professional facade.

He was silent for a couple of beats, his gaze assessing. "You seem quite certain, considering you just said you'd wanted me to kiss you only a few minutes ago."

She wasn't sure where he was coming from—it didn't look like flirting, but she couldn't read him well enough to know. Maybe he was testing her, wanting to ensure she wasn't going to change her mind and make waves in the company. Whatever it was about, she had to be absolutely clear so he understood her position.

She drew in a breath and lifted her chin. "Boyfriends and lovers aren't hard to come by, Mr. Hawke. What I need more than a man is someone to appreciate my talent. I hope this isn't offensive, but I want you professionally more than personally."

He flashed her a self-deprecating smile. "Understood. Which means I'd better have a look at this arrangement."

She stood back to give him some room. Everything she'd done recently, from making the plan to attending the auction to spending most of her savings to meeting Dylan here tonight, had led to this moment. It was the do-or-die moment, and all she could do was step back, cross her fingers and hope he'd still give an honest assessment after he'd kissed her.

Dylan dug his hands in his pockets as he faced her arrangement. He moved around, looking at it from several angles before straightening with a grimace.

"That bad?" she asked, her stomach in free fall. "You're grimacing."

"No, it's not bad." He leaned back against the bench and crossed his arms over his chest. "If I'm not smiling it's because I really wanted to put your arrangement in the catalog."

She felt the words like a slap. Tears pressed against the backs of her eyes, but she wouldn't let them form. "But you're not going to."

"I'm sorry, Faith," he said, his voice gentle. "Especially after…" He gestured toward the other end of the bench, where they'd been when he'd kissed her.

She bit down on her lip. She might feel bad, but she didn't want him to feel bad as well. He was only doing his job. "Don't apologize. If it's not good enough, that's my problem, not yours."

"The thing is, it's good, really good, but it looks a lot like the arrangements that are already in the book. If we add something new, then it needs to be unique. It has to offer our customers a genuine alternative to the options already there, and this arrangement, though beautiful, is—"

"Too much like what they can already choose," she finished for him, understanding his point, but still deflated.

He moved closer and laid a hand on her shoulder, his eyes kind. "But I'll reimburse the money you paid at the auction. You shouldn't have to pay to have an appointment with someone at the head office."

Her back stiffened. He wasn't going to wriggle out of this that easily. "I won't take the money back. I have two more *dates* left and I plan to use them."

There was no way she was giving up this direct line to the head of the Hawke's Blooms stores. It had been a good plan when she'd made it, and it was still a good plan…as long as she hadn't blown her chances by kissing him.

Sure, tonight hadn't been the raging success she'd hoped for, but there were two more dates yet. When she set her mind to something, she didn't give up until she'd achieved it. She'd impress him yet and get one of her arrangements in the catalog.

He dropped his hand and sighed. "The thing is, Faith,

I can't force you to take the money back, but it would be easier for me if you did."

"Perhaps," she said and smiled sweetly. "But it wouldn't be easier for me."

"Look, can I be honest?"

He thrust the fingers of both hands through his hair and left them there, linking them behind his head. This wasn't the same man who'd kissed her moments before, or the man who ran an entire chain of retail stores, or even the man who'd confidently strutted the stage at the auction. This one seemed more real.

She nodded. "Please."

"I'm in the process of trying to rehabilitate my image." He gave her half a smile, and she tried not to laugh at how adorable he looked now.

"From playboy to the future brother-in-law of a princess?"

He shifted his weight to his other leg. "Yeah, something like that."

"So to stop people seeing you as a playboy, you auctioned yourself off to the highest bidder?" She jumped up to sit on the bench, enjoying his discomfort more than she would have expected, but also enjoying seeing this private side of him.

He coughed out a laugh. "Yeah, when you put it like that, it sounds crazy."

Suddenly she was more than intrigued. This man was a mass of contradictions and she wanted to know more. To understand him. "Then how would you put it?"

"I'm throwing myself into our new charity. The auction was only the first step, but I'll be involved every step of the way."

"A respectable, upstanding member of the community." She could see him pulling it off, too. Going from a playboy to a pillar of the community.

"So you can see that the very last thing I need is a scandal involving a staff member, especially given that we have a policy about management being involved with staff."

A scandal? She frowned. What, exactly, did he think she wanted from those other two dates? "Dylan, I'm not expecting romance on the other dates any more than I expected it on this one."

He shrugged one shoulder. "But image is everything."

That was true. She cast her mind around for a solution. There was no way she was giving up her remaining dates without a fight. "What if no one knows? We could do them in secret."

"That boat pretty much sailed when the auction was covered by the media," he said and chuckled. Then he sobered and let out a long breath. "But it's more than that."

Understanding dawned. "Our kiss changed things." She said the words softly, as if acknowledging the truth too loudly would make a difference.

He nodded, his gaze not wavering from her eyes. "And it's very important that I see you only as an employee, and you see me only as a boss."

"I won't have any trouble with that. Are you saying you will?" She arched her eyebrow in challenge, guessing Dylan Hawke was a man who didn't shrink from a challenge.

One corner of his mouth kicked up. "If you can do it, I can."

"Then it looks like we don't have a problem, do we?"

Knowing he was trapped in the logic of it, she jumped down from the bench and grabbed the trash.

She felt him behind her, not moving, probably assessing his options. Then finally he took the trash can from her and began to sweep stem cuttings together with his free hand.

"It appears you've won this round, Faith Sixty-Three," he said from beside her.

She flashed him a wry smile. "Dylan, if I'd won this round, my design would soon be featured in the catalog. All I've done is kept the door open for another round."

"You know what?" he said, his voice amused. "Even though I know I shouldn't be, I'm already looking forward to the next round."

She turned and caught his gaze, finding a potent mix of humor and heat there—something closer to the real man she'd glimpsed earlier. Quickly she turned away. This was going to be hard enough without seeing him as anything more than the head of the Hawke's Blooms stores. And she had a sinking feeling it might already be too late for that anyway…

Two days later, Dylan pulled into the parking lot of the Santa Monica store. He hadn't done an all-day inspection for a while. It used to be part of his management style—show up in the morning unannounced, hang around in the background and help out where he could. Nothing beat it for getting a good feel for how a store was working and what needed improvement.

He'd been meaning to start doing a couple of these a month, so his office staff hadn't thought there was anything strange when he'd told them to clear his schedule for today. Of course, they weren't to know what he was trying to deny to himself—that he hadn't stopped thinking about one of the Santa Monica store's employees since the moment he'd dropped her home that first night.

Under different circumstances, there was no question he'd ask her out. That kiss had been beyond amazing and had been on an automatic replay loop in his mind ever since, but he'd also enjoyed her company. He never knew what she was going to say or do next, and that made her fun to be around.

He sighed and stepped from his car. No use wasting energy wanting what he couldn't have. She worked for him. End of story.

But that didn't stop him from wondering how this particular store was doing. Despite rejecting Faith's arrangement himself, he'd been left wondering if her manager was doing all she could for the advancement of her staff if Faith had put in twenty applications to the catalog of standard arrangements and not one had made it through to the head office.

Sure, he'd rejected the one he'd seen last night, but given Faith's enthusiasm and skill, a good, supportive manager should have found a way to guide her toward a more appropriate arrangement by now. Perhaps even submitted one or two just to encourage her. Yes, it was definitely time he had a closer look at how this store—and the other stores—were doing.

As he stepped through the front door and removed his aviator sunglasses, the manager, Mary O'Donnell, looked up and waved enthusiastically.

"Mr. Hawke!" she called, her voice obsequious. "So good to see you. Here, Faith, take over this arrangement. I need to talk to Mr. Hawke."

At the mention of his name, Faith froze, then looked

up like a deer caught in headlights. Her tongue darted out to moisten her lips, and he was assailed by memories of her mouth. Of how incredible it had felt under his. Of how it had opened to allow his tongue entry. Before he could forget all the reasons not to kiss her again, he determinedly drew his gaze to Mary O'Donnell.

"No need," he said. "I'm here for the day. Don't stop what you're doing—I just want to get a feel for the store."

"You haven't done an all-day inspection for quite a while." Mary shot a suspicious glance around the room. "Is there a problem?"

"Just continuing a procedure that worked well for us in the past. I've let it slip a bit as we've grown, but I'll be working my way around to all the stores in the coming months."

"And we're first?" she asked, pride beaming from her features.

"Yes, you are." He'd let her think it was a compliment. Plus, it was a much more professional reason than the fact that he hadn't been able to stop thinking about one of her employees.

"Well, in that case, let me introduce you to the team." She grabbed a middle-aged blonde woman by the wrist and dragged her over. "This is Courtney. She's our senior florist. If you want any bouquets made to take home at the end of the day, Courtney's your woman."

"Good to meet you, Courtney," he said, shaking her hand.

Courtney smiled openly. "Nice to meet you, too, Mr. Hawke. Though, if you don't mind, I need to finish this order before the courier arrives in a few minutes?"

"Of course," he said and watched her go back to

work on one of the long benches. She seemed efficient and nice enough, and the arrangement she was working on was good.

"And this is our other florist, Faith Crawford," the manager said, pointing in Faith's direction. He watched the reactions of the other two women closely, checking to see if they knew Faith was the person who'd won the bid at the auction, but neither gave anything away. Interesting. Faith obviously hadn't told them, and the company grapevine hadn't caught up with the news yet. Most of the staff from the head office had been at the auction the other night, but even if they'd managed to get a good look at Faith in the dim light, it seemed none had recognized her.

He glanced over at her now. She had a bright yellow Hawke's Blooms apron covering the halter top he could see peeking out from underneath. Her curly red hair was caught up in a clip on the top of her head. She looked up and he paused, waiting to see her reaction. Her eyes flicked to her manager, then back to him. He wasn't comfortable with an outright lie to his employees—it was probable that the information would circulate around the company at some point, and he didn't want to be caught in a lie—but that didn't mean he had to share all the details of their short history.

"Ms. Crawford and I have met before," he said as a compromise.

The manager's eyes darted between them, looking for snippets of information, so he cut her off at the pass. "Do you have an apprentice in this store?"

"Oh, yes. Sharon. But she's not in until lunchtime on Mondays."

He nodded and took off his sport coat. Instead of his

usual work attire of a business suit, today he'd worn a polo shirt and casual trousers—closer to the clothes the staff in-store wore. "Before she gets here, I'll do the sweeping and answering the phone. Wherever you need an extra pair of hands."

Unbidden, his gaze tracked to where Faith worked at her bench, and he found that she'd looked up at him at the same time. *Wherever you need an extra pair of hands...* He could still feel his hands in her hair, cupping her cheek, under her chin.

A pink flush crept up Faith's neck to her cheeks, and he knew she was remembering the same thing. He cleared his throat and looked away.

If he was going to make it through the day without letting everyone know he'd kissed his employee, he would have to do better at keeping his thoughts firmly under control.

It had been two hours since Dylan had appeared in the doorway, looking as if he'd just stepped off a photo shoot for a story entitled "What the Suave CEOs Are Wearing This Season." She'd spent those two hours trying to pretend he wasn't in the room, just so she could get her work done.

But every time he swept up the clippings from where she was working, or he handed her a slip of paper with an order that had come in over the phone, she lost the battle and was plunged back into those moments when they'd been in this very spot, at night, alone.

And occasionally, when their eyes met, she thought she saw the same memory lurking in his.

But she couldn't let herself be sidetracked. She needed to impress the businessman, Mr. Hawke, not the red-blooded Dylan who'd kissed her senseless. Men came and went, but this particular man could help her career. It was Mr. Hawke she needed to impress with what she could do.

They'd had a steady stream of orders in person, over the phone and on their website, and she was glad. It gave her an excuse not to talk to Dylan—no, Mr. Hawke—just yet. He'd sat with Courtney earlier and had a cup of coffee, asking her about her job and ideas for the store, and said he'd be doing the same with all the staff members.

The bell above the door dinged, and she looked up, smiling to see one of her favorite customers.

"Hi, Tom," she said, heading for the fridge. "How was your weekend?"

"Not long enough," he said ruefully. "Yours?"

Her eyes flicked to Dylan, who was thumbing through their order book, his dark reddish-brown hair rumpled, his sport coat gone and his tie loosened. His hand hesitated and his chest expanded as if he'd taken a deep breath.

"How about I go with *interesting*," she said, turning back to her customer.

Tom laughed. "Sounds as if there's a story there."

"My life is never dull." She reached into the fridge and drew out the assorted foliage she'd put to the side earlier. "I found some fresh mint at the markets this morning, as well as these cute little branches of crab apples. How does that sound?"

"Like a winner. Emmie loved the daisy and rosemary bouquet last week."

Out of the corner of her eye, she saw Dylan watching the conversation and then moving to her elbow. He put his hand out to Tom. "Hi, I'm Dylan Hawke, CEO of the Hawke's Blooms retail chain."

"Wow, the big boss," Tom said, winking at Faith.

Dylan turned to her. "You bought crab apples and mint yourself for this bouquet?" His tone was mild, but his focus had narrowed in on her like a laser pointer. "This sounds interesting. Can you talk me through the thinking behind your plan?"

Her stomach clenched tight. She'd wanted the attention of the businessman side of him, and now she had it, which was great. But if he thought what she was doing was too bizarre, then she might have lost her chance to win his approval. A second strike against her in a row might be too much to overcome.

All she could do was paste on a smile and do her job.

"Tom comes in each Monday to pick up some flowers for his wife," she said, her gaze on the work her hands were doing. "Emmie is blind, so I always put some thought into combinations that she can enjoy."

"You picked up the mint on your way in?" Dylan asked, his tone not giving anything away.

She nodded. "Monday mornings I leave home a bit earlier and drop in at the flower markets, looking for some inspiration. We usually go outside the standard range of flowers that the store stocks to get the right elements for Emmie's bouquet. I like something fragrant—" she picked up the mint "—and something tactile—" she pointed to the crab apple branch "—along with the usual assortment of flowers."

She cast a glance at the buckets bursting with bright blooms around them, looking for inspiration. *Something white, perhaps?*

Dylan raised an eyebrow and she hesitated. Maybe

he didn't like florists going this far off the beaten track? Her manager hadn't been particularly supportive and always complained if she tried to get reimbursement for the extras from petty cash, but Faith loved the challenge of something new each week, and the fact that Tom wanted to do this for his wife always melted her heart. Were there other men like Tom in the world? Men who were so dedicated to bringing a smile to the faces of the women they loved that they'd go the extra mile every single week? That sort of constancy was a beautiful thing to be a part of.

Perhaps Dylan Hawke didn't see the situation the same way. She held a sprig of mint out to him. "If that's okay, Mr. Hawke?"

"More than okay," he said, taking the mint and lifting it to his nose. "I think it's a great example of customer service."

Dylan's approving gaze rested on her, and her shoulders relaxed as relief flowed through her veins. But she was also aware that his approval was having more of an effect than it should...

As she worked, he blended into the background, but she felt his eyes on her the entire time she was making the crab apple, mint and white carnation arrangement. After Tom left, pleased with the results, Dylan cornered her near the cash register.

"Please tell me you get reimbursed for those extras you purchase on Monday mornings," he said, his voice low.

She maintained a poker face. Getting her manager into trouble was a quick route to reduced hours, but she couldn't lie, either. He could check the store's accounting books and find that she hadn't asked for reimbursement after the first few times, not since Mary had finally put her foot down and said she should use stock that was already in the store. And being caught in a lie by the CEO would be even less healthy for her career than not covering for her immediate manager.

"Sure, but sometimes I forget to hand the receipts in," she said in what she hoped was a casual, believable tone.

"I see," he said, and she had a feeling he really did see.

"I don't mind paying for those extras," she said quickly. "I know I should only use what we have in stock, but I get such a kick out of Tom's expression when he knows he's taking home something Emmie will love. It's like a present I can give them."

"It's your job, Faith. You shouldn't have to pay money to do your job." He crossed his arms over his chest. "Do you have the receipt from this morning?"

She picked up her handbag from under the counter and dug around until she found the crumpled bit of paper. "Here," she said, passing it to him.

Their hands brushed, and she couldn't help the slight gasp that escaped at the contact. Tingles radiated from the place they'd touched, and she yearned to reach out and touch him again. On his hand, or his forearm. Or— she looked up to his face—the cheek she'd stroked with her fingertips when they'd kissed. His eyes darkened.

"Faith," he said, his voice a rasp, "we can't."

"I know," she whispered.

"Then don't—"

"Anything I can help you with, Mr. Hawke?" Mary asked from behind them.

Without missing a beat, Dylan turned, his charming

smile firmly in place, where only seconds before she'd seen something real, something raw.

"I was just chastising your florist about not submitting her receipts for the extras she's been buying for that customer's weekly order." He handed over the receipt. "Ms. Crawford has promised she'll turn them in to you from now on, haven't you, Ms. Crawford?"

"Ah, yes," Faith said, not meeting her manager's eyes. "If you'll excuse me, I have another order to make up."

She slipped away and left them to their discussion, finally able to take a full breath again only when she was immersed in her next arrangement. This day couldn't end soon enough. He was too close here. In her space. Making her want him.

Yet even if he weren't the owner of the company, the last man she could give her heart to was a man whose love life had no stability. She'd heard the rumors about Dylan, that he changed female companions regularly, never seeming to form attachments. She couldn't fall for someone like that—she wouldn't do it to herself. She'd spend the entire time waiting for the moment he'd move on. Better to stay independent and create stability by relying on herself.

She repeated the words to herself over and over while she worked, the whole time trying to ignore her body's awareness of where he was in the room. And resisting the urge to walk over and touch him again.

Three

By late afternoon, Dylan was back in his office, staring out the window at the LA skyline. He had achieved what he'd set out to that morning—a detailed understanding of how the Santa Monica store was operating. He'd managed to sit down with all four employees during the day and chat about their perceptions and ideas, and had seen for himself that the customers were pleased with the floral arrangements being produced.

He'd also discovered one other thing—this fledgling attraction for Faith Crawford wasn't going to fade away. From the moment he arrived, he'd fought to stop his gaze traveling to her. Wherever she was in the store, he could feel her. And occasionally he'd caught her watching him with more than an employee's interest. His heart picked up speed now just thinking about it.

He'd cursed the Fates that he'd had to meet her while she worked for him.

He'd also noticed she was far from an average employee. He'd been taking orders over the phone and in person all day from people who wanted only an arrangement made by Faith. When he'd tried to suggest that another florist serve them, they'd said they'd wait. And he could see why. Her arrangements were spectacular. Why had she made such a conservative design the night she'd tried to impress him? When she was in her element, her work was original and beautiful. They were designs he wanted in the catalog so florists in the other stores were reproducing them.

And the bouquet she'd made using mint and crab apples for the man to give his blind wife had been the most cutting-edge design Dylan had seen in a long time. He liked it when staff went the extra mile for customers, adding that personal touch, and her customers seemed to appreciate it. In fact, just about everything about Faith impressed him. On every level, from the professional to the personal to the physical…

His skin heated.

Shaking his head, he focused back on the professional.

Faith Crawford was someone with a lot of potential. And he wanted to help her reach that potential for the benefit of Hawke's Blooms, and because he really wanted to see Faith get her just rewards. That manager of hers wasn't going to recognize her talents anytime soon, despite the overwhelming evidence under her nose.

He grabbed the phone on his desk and dialed Human Resources. "Anne, do you have a minute?" he asked when the head of HR picked up.

"Sure. What do you need, Dylan?"

"I did an impromptu inspection at the Santa Monica store today."

"Great," she said brightly. "You always bring back good feedback when you do one of those. What do you have for me?"

He dug one hand in his trouser pocket and looked out over the skyline. "One of the florists there has a lot of potential, and I want to do something about that."

"What was her name?"

"Faith Crawford," he said, ensuring his voice was even and didn't give away his reaction to her.

There was a pause, and he could hear fingers tapping on a keyboard as Anne brought up Faith's file. "What do you have in mind?"

"Her work is good. Really good. Original and creative. But in the interest of full disclosure, I should let you know that Faith is the person who bought the dates with me at the trust's bachelor auction."

"I was sorry to miss that night, it sounded like a lot of fun," Anne said, chuckling. "So how do you want to handle this from here?"

He rubbed a hand through his hair. "She's got a lot of potential, and I want to see Hawke's Blooms benefit from that, but I don't want any suggestion that she bought her way into a promotion. How about you get someone else to go out and assess her? Don't tell them that the idea came from me, just let them go to the Santa Monica store without any preconceptions and see her work."

"I'll see what I can arrange and let you know."

"Thanks, Anne."

He hung up the phone, feeling very satisfied with his day's work. The only thing that could make it better was to be the one who actually gave Faith the promotion, so he could be there when she found out about it. But he didn't want her to think this had anything to do with their kiss, so it was better that she had a fair and independent assessment first. He had no doubt that whoever did that would see what he'd seen and recommend her for something more senior.

But still, a good day's work indeed. He smiled, thinking about Faith's reaction. She was going to be over the moon.

As Faith picked out a long-stemmed apricot rose from the bucket at her feet, Mary appeared across the bench from her with a folded piece of paper in her hand.

"I've just had a call from head office about you," she said, her voice accusing.

Faith stopped what she was doing and looked up. "About me personally?"

Besides the initial paperwork when she'd started at the store, she hadn't had any direct dealings with the head office other than the impersonal pay slips. She wiped her hands on her apron and waited.

Mary planted her hands on her hips. "Have you been talking to the head office without my knowledge?"

"Of course not," Faith said, and then realized she'd been talking to Dylan on the weekend without her manager knowing. And would be talking to him again about their next two dates. But he had her phone number—he wouldn't be contacting her via her manager.

Hands still on her hips, Mary lifted her chin as she spoke. "It was Anne in Human Resources. They're offering you a promotion."

Faith's breath caught. *Hang on...*

"A promotion?" she repeated, trying to make sense of it.

"To the head office." Mary thrust the piece of paper at her. "They emailed the details."

Faith took the paper but didn't want to open it in front of the entire store. "I'll be back in a few minutes," she said and went out the back door to the lane. Then she opened the folded email printout.

It was a formal letter of promotion to the head office. To a desk job. She scanned the list of duties and found they were all things that didn't involve customers. Or flowers.

Frustration started simmering in her belly. She'd spent most of her life being told what would happen to her. Announcements would come that she'd be moving to another family member's house the next week, that she'd have to change schools, that her father would be visiting and taking her to a theme park, that he would be returning her to yet another relative afterward. The best thing about being an adult was that she was in charge of her own life.

So getting notice out of the blue saying she was being moved to a desk job that she hadn't applied for and certainly didn't want was particularly unwelcome.

She was ambitious, yes, but not for just any promotion. She had a very clear vision of what she wanted in her career, and this job—being stuck in a boring office, away from customers and the daily joy of working with flowers—wasn't it.

Besides, was this really out of the blue?

She'd kissed the CEO, and in less than a week he'd come to the store for a full-day inspection—something

the others said he used to do, but hadn't done since she'd
been working there. And now a promotion.

What was Dylan Hawke really up to?

The thought made her uneasy, so she went back
through the door and told Mary that she was declin-
ing the offer.

Dylan drove into the parking lot of the Santa Monica
store for the third time in a week, still not sure what to
make of the call he'd had from Anne telling him Faith
had turned down the promotion. With all her ambition,
he'd expected her to leap at the opportunity. So, surprised and intrigued, he'd jumped into his car to talk
to her face-to-face.

As he walked through the door, Mary dropped what
she was doing and headed for him, her face covered
in a fawning smile. Faith wasn't in sight, and he was
more disappointed than he should have been at not seeing an employee.

Then she walked in from the cold room, carrying
a bucket full of flowers. She was wearing black biker
boots that almost reached her knees and a bright purple dress that peeked out around the yellow Hawke's
Blooms apron. Her wild hair was caught up on top of
her head and sprang out in all directions. He only barely
resisted a smile—this woman was a force of nature.

Her step faltered when she saw him.

"Mr. Hawke!" Mary said when she reached him,
darting suspicious glances at Faith. "Twice in one week.
We're honored."

He paused before answering. He hadn't planned what
he should say here—how had the offer of the promotion gone down at the store level? Should he mention it

now, or play it cool for the moment? He glanced across at her as she pulled stems one by one from the bucket. His gut was telling him not to mention it until he'd at least spoken to Faith.

He smiled at Mary. "I just have a few follow-up questions from the other day."

"Well, I'm at your service," she said, untying the apron strings at her back. "Would you like to talk here, or perhaps at the café next door?"

"Actually, I'd like to talk to Faith if she has a few minutes."

Faith's hands stilled and her face grew pale. He was torn between wanting to reassure her and wanting to demand an explanation. Instead, he turned an expectant expression to Mary.

"Of course, Mr. Hawke. If that's what you want." But her face was sour. She really didn't like Faith getting more attention than her.

"Excellent." He smiled and rocked back on his heels. "You mentioned a café next door?"

Mary's mouth opened and closed again. "Er, yes. Courtney can finish that order. Faith. Can you come and talk to Mr. Hawke, please?"

"Certainly," Faith said, wiping her hands on her apron and removing it. The entire time, she kept her gaze down.

"Thank you," he said to Mary, and then opened the door for Faith and followed her out onto the pavement.

"Have I just made things difficult for you in there?" he asked.

She lifted her chin. "Nothing I can't deal with."

He was beginning to see how true that was. Faith Crawford was most definitely her own woman. From bidding on the CEO of her company at a charity auction to get his attention for her work, to turning down a promotion most of his staff would jump at and not bowing to the head office… The more he got to know this woman, the more he liked her.

They found a secluded booth at the café and ordered coffees.

"I heard you were offered a promotion." He leaned back and rested his arm along the top of the padded vinyl booth. "You turned it down."

The corners of her mouth twitched. "You *heard* I was offered the job? Are you sure you don't mean you *arranged* for me to be offered the job?"

He grinned. The fact that she spoke her mind was a very attractive feature. "Okay, I might have had a hand in it. After watching you in the store for a day, I realized your potential was being underutilized, and I implemented a plan to rectify that."

"Is that all it was?" She arched an eyebrow and waited.

"You think it's about more?" His gaze dropped to her mouth, and his pulse picked up speed. "You think you were being promoted because I'd kissed you?"

"Maybe it wasn't that straightforward, but we kissed, and suddenly the store has an all-day inspection and I get offered a job in the head office. Tell me that's not a coincidence." Her gaze didn't waver, challenging him to be honest.

"It's not a coincidence, but it's not direct cause and effect, either—there were steps in between. When you talked about your store and your designs not being submitted for the catalog, it made me wonder what was going on here, and I came to check it out. That's when I realized your potential."

She tapped her nails on the table, but the rest of her barely moved. "So it wasn't payback of some kind? Or a way to assuage your guilt about kissing an employee?"

"I don't work that way." He tried not to be insulted, given that she didn't know him very well, but it was good at least to have her concerns addressed now, before they had their other two dates. "I passed your name to HR with a suggestion that they check you out. They arranged a couple of people to come in as customers and ask for you so they could see your skills and how you interact with customers, and then one of the staff from the head office dropped in to see Mary and watched you while she was there. Her name was Alison—she chatted to you for a while on your break, apparently. You earned this completely on your own merits."

She looked into his eyes for a long moment and then nodded. "I believe you."

Their coffees arrived, and she tipped a packet of sugar into her cappuccino. He watched her hands as they worked—as efficient and graceful with a sugar packet as they were with flowers. What would they be like on his body? Fluttering over his neck and collarbone. Trailing a path down his chest, his abdomen.

He tore his gaze away and stirred cream into his own coffee. "Did you turn the job down because you thought you hadn't earned it?"

That fitted the emerging profile of this woman, but she shook her head.

"I don't want a desk job."

"But you want your career to go places," he pointed out.

"The places I want to go are filled with flowers and customers."

He took a sip of his coffee and replaced the cup on its saucer, giving himself a moment to think the situation through. "I honestly thought you'd want this job."

She frowned, her head tilted to the side. "If you'd wanted to do something nice for me, instead of doing something you thought I'd like, you could have done what I asked for in the first place."

"Put one of your designs in the catalog of standard arrangements." It seemed obvious now, but hindsight was twenty-twenty.

"Bingo." She lifted her coffee cup to her lips, smiling over the rim, her dimples peeking out.

He regarded her as she took a sip and then ran her tongue over her bottom lip to catch a droplet. In her vivid purple dress and with the smattering of pale freckles over her nose, she was the brightest thing in the whole café, as if her own personal beam of sunshine followed her around and shone down on her wherever she was. Yet the arrangement she'd made for him to consider had been as conservative as they came. It was a contradiction he wanted to understand.

He leaned back in the booth and interlaced his fingers on the table. "Why did you show me such a conservative design that night? It's not who you are."

For a brief second, her eyes widened. "Who am I?"

He thought back to the first time he'd met her, near the stage at the auction, to the night he'd kissed her, to the day he'd watched her work in his store. "You're crab apple, carnation and mint bouquets. You're mixing wild colors with flair that's uncommon. You're edgy and fresh." And so much more. "Why didn't you show me any of that?"

Her eyes lit from within. "I didn't think you'd want to see that. I thought you'd prefer more conservative designs, like the ones already in the catalog."

"But that's the point." He leaned forward, wanting her to understand this if nothing else. "We already have designs like that. We don't have *your* designs. Hawke's Blooms needs your vision."

An adorable pink flush stole over her face, from her neck up to her cheekbones. "So, you're not mad I turned the job down?"

"Mad? No." He rubbed two fingers across his forehead. "It was my fault—I leapt ahead without talking to you. With any other employee, I would have researched first, found out what they wanted before making a decision."

"So, why didn't you?" she asked, her voice soft.

Good question—one he'd been asking himself. And she deserved the real answer. "To be honest, you've had me off center from the start."

She gave him a rueful smile. "I know how that feels."

He smiled back, and their gazes held for one heartbeat, two. Part of him was glad he wasn't the only one off kilter—that it was the result of some inconvenient mutual chemistry—but another part of him wished it had been more one-sided. That he could justify to himself that reaching across the table for her now would be an unwelcome advance, and reinforce that he had to keep his hands to himself.

What they needed was a new start. He drew in a deep breath and pushed his cup to the side. "How about we forget the promotion and you continue working in this

store for now. I know the customers here will be glad
to keep you."

"I'd like that," she said with a quick nod.

She glanced in the direction of her store, and a
thought suddenly occurred to him. This wouldn't be a
new start for her—he already suspected Faith's manager might resent her, and now she'd be heading back
into that same environment after turning down a promotion. That could get awkward fast. He'd made a complete mess of this from start to finish.

"You know," he said, thinking on his feet, "another
option is to move to a different store. I can think of a
few managers who'd welcome someone with your skills
and ability to form rapport with customers."

"Thank you, I appreciate the offer but I'm happy
here." She turned her wrist over and checked her watch.
"Speaking of which, I'd better get back."

He resisted a chuckle. Many of his employees would
try to drag out their one-on-one time with him, especially if they'd already spent money on an opportunity
to impress him. Not Faith. "You realize you're out with
the person in charge of the entire chain of stores, right?
You're not playing hooky."

She shook her head, unmoved by his reasoning. "We
have a lot of orders to fill before I clock off."

"What time do you finish today?" he asked, an idea
forming in his head as he said the words.

"Three o'clock."

"That's in two hours. How about I pick you up then
and we go on our second date?" Since she wouldn't let
him buy the dates back from her, it was probably better to get them out of the way as soon as was practical.

"Sure," she said as she stood. "But do me a favor and

don't come back to the store. It won't help my popularity in there."

It was a reasonable point. He liked that she thought that way. She could have used the opportunity to gain points against her manager, perhaps engage in a game of one-upmanship, but he'd come to see that wasn't the way Faith operated.

He pushed a paper napkin across the table and took a pen from the inside pocket of his jacket. "Give me your address and I'll drop by your place at about three-thirty."

She leaned over and wrote her address on the napkin before pushing it back to him and leaving.

He watched her walk out, taking in the sway of her hips as she moved, and then looked down at the napkin in his hand. After her address, she'd written four words. *I like the beach.*

A grin spread across his face. He was already looking forward to this afternoon way too much.

Four

By three-twenty, Faith was waiting at her front door. She wanted to be ready to dash down the front steps when Dylan arrived because the last thing she needed was him knocking on her door. Being alone with him would lead to the possibility of her dragging him inside and repeating that kiss. And knowing there was a bed in the next room couldn't be good in that situation…

The beach suggestion had come from the same train of thought—she knew they had to go somewhere public. Though she'd also wanted it to be informal so she had a chance to question him casually and get more insight into what he was looking for with the catalog, to make her next attempt more likely to succeed. She had high hopes of getting the information while sitting next to him on the sand and not having to look him in the eye.

At three twenty-seven, his Porsche convertible drew

up, and she pulled her front door shut behind her, hiked her beach bag higher on her shoulder and jogged down the concrete stairs to the road. She loved the idea of owning a convertible, of having the wind in her hair as she drove, but the sheer expense of the model Dylan owned simply served to reinforce the differences between them.

"Have you got your swimsuit in that bag?" he asked as she slid into the passenger seat.

Was he kidding? Being half-naked in his presence could be disastrous. And seeing him in board shorts, his bare chest dripping with water…? Yeah, that was only going to lead to trouble. Whether they'd be in public or not, her willpower had its limits.

Though, she thought as she glanced over and took in the red-and-white-striped T-shirt that bunched around his biceps and stretched across his shoulders, perhaps his covered chest wasn't going to be much easier to cope with.

She faced the windshield and shrugged. "I was thinking more along the lines of sitting on a towel with the sand between my toes."

"That sounds safer," he said as he pulled away from the curb.

So he was still having trouble, too. Interesting. They talked about the weather and made other small talk until he found a park and they stepped out into the sunshine.

He looked down at her Hawaiian print bag. "Did you bring a towel, or should I get the picnic blanket?"

"You keep a picnic blanket in your car?" She couldn't help the smile—it seemed such a sweet thing for a playboy like Dylan to do. Although maybe he used it to seduce women under the stars…? Her smile faded.

"My brother Liam and I took his daughters, Bonnie and Meg, for a picnic a couple of weeks ago. The blanket is still in the back."

Her smile returned. She'd read the newspaper stories about Liam Hawke's engagement to Princess Jensine of Larsland—everybody had—and seen the photos of Liam's tiny baby, Bonnie, and Jenna's daughter, Meg, who was only a few months older than Bonnie. She just hadn't quite imagined Dylan actually interacting with the little girls. Which was probably unfair—by all accounts, the three brothers were close.

She hitched the bag over her shoulder. "No, I have a towel."

He nodded and set the keyless lock. They found a spot on the white sand to spread out her towel. The beach was fairly quiet, so there was no one else close enough to hear them, but there were still people around—people swimming in the sparkling blue Pacific, a couple of guys throwing a Frisbee back and forth, couples on towels farther away, occasional joggers.

Dylan slipped off his shoes and rolled up his chinos before sitting at the other end of the towel, leaving plenty of space between them. She wasn't facing him, which was supposed to be safe, yet her attention seemed to be located on his bare ankles, which she could see out of the corner of her eye. Why had she never noticed how attractive men's ankles were before? Or was it something special about this man's?

She swallowed hard and brought her focus back to her career. These dates were for her career.

"Mr. Hawke, you—"

"Dylan," he said, interrupting her. "'Dylan' is fine when we're alone."

"Are you sure?" A light breeze toyed with the hair that had escaped her clip, so she tucked it behind her ear. "If we become personal, won't we risk…?" She didn't know how to end that sentence, so she left it hanging.

He pulled his legs up and rested his forearms on his bent knees. "I hardly think using my first name will lead to me leaping on top of you here on the towel. Besides, 'Mr. Hawke' is too formal for the beach."

As soon as he'd said the words *me leaping on top of you*, she had trouble drawing breath. For a long moment, she couldn't get past the image of him above her, feeling his weight pushing her into the sand. She bit down on her bottom lip, hard. It seemed that he was right—using his first name wasn't the problem since she hadn't said it yet.

"Okay. Dylan." She gathered a handful of towel and the sand beneath it and gripped tight, as if she could draw strength from the beach itself. "You mentioned that the catalog didn't have anything like the designs you saw me do when you were at the store."

"That's true," he said, his voice deep and smooth. "We don't have anything like them."

She twisted around a little so she could see his eyes, but more importantly, so he could see hers and know she was serious about this. "Will you give me another chance to submit a design? One that's more…*me*?"

A slow smile spread across his face, and he nodded once. "I was hoping you'd still want to submit. Hawke's Blooms needs at least one Faith Crawford design between the covers of its catalog."

"Thank you," she said, excitement building inside. She'd been pretty sure he'd be open to looking at another arrangement, but even so, she hadn't wanted to

count her chickens before they hatched. This time she'd
blow his socks off.

"But," he said, "explain this to me, because I still
don't understand. You're ambitious enough to use your
savings to get access to me, yet you don't want a promotion." His expression was curious. It didn't feel as
if the man who'd offered her the promotion was asking
this time—it was more like a friend asking.

She looked out over the blue Pacific Ocean, the
sound of the waves crashing on the shore lulling her
into feeling at ease. "I like working with flowers. Flowers make people happy. They make *me* happy."

"So, what do you want out of your career, Faith?"
His voice was soft near her ear, but she didn't turn, just
watched the rhythmic pounding of the waves.

"I want to keep growing as a florist, to move on to
new experiences and places, to be doing bigger and
better arrangements all the time." She risked a glance
at him, wondering if she dared tell him the size of her
dreams. She'd never told a soul—had always been
scared people would laugh at her.

"There's more, isn't there?" he asked, his gaze encouraging.

There was something about him looking at her like
that. He could ask her anything and she'd probably tell
him. She nodded. "One day, my arrangements will
grace important places, large-scale events—they'll
reach hundreds, maybe hundreds of thousands of people and bring them happiness."

One side of his mouth pulled into a lopsided grin.
She looked back at the waves crashing on the shore
and the children building sand castles. "You probably
think that's silly."

From her peripheral vision she saw him reach out as if to run a hand down her arm, but he let it drop a moment before he touched her. She felt his gaze, however, remain trained on her. "I think it's amazing."

"You're not teasing?" she asked, turning to him, hardly daring to breathe. She wanted so badly for him to be telling the truth.

"I've heard a lot of reasons that people have chosen floristry before, and most of them were really good. But I think yours is my favorite." His voice was soft, intimate. Despite sharing the beach with countless other people, it was as if they were completely alone on the towel. From a distance, they might look like any couple together for an afternoon, and the idea was exhilarating.

"Thank you," she whispered.

There was silence for a long moment when all she could hear was her own breath. Then Dylan rubbed a hand down his face and sat a little straighter. "So is there a destination for your life's plan? Somewhere in particular you're headed?"

She picked up a handful of sand and let it fall through her fingers. "Not really." In fact, the idea of reaching a destination made her uneasy. "I guess I'm more comfortable staying on the move."

"Hmm… There's more to that answer, isn't there?"

She looked up, startled that he'd seen through her. Again. Then she nodded. "I've moved so much in my life, changing everything each time, that I've become something of a rolling stone."

"That makes me wonder, Faith Sixty-Three." He raised an eyebrow. "Are you moving all the time because you want to, or are you worried that if you stop, you'll sink?"

She laughed softly. "That's ridiculous. I move because I want to. I like my life this way."

But was that true? Something inside her tensed at the thought. Perhaps she was more comfortable choosing to move on, being a step ahead of anyone who might make her leave. That little girl who was always waiting for the axe to fall was still inside her. A cold shiver ran down her spine. Honestly, she was only comfortable if she decided to move on her own terms—jumping before she was pushed. If she jumped, she was in control of the situation, so since she'd become an adult, she'd been jumping from place to place. So far she'd avoided being pushed away.

Not that she'd ever admit that to Dylan Hawke—she'd pretty much reached her limit on sharing. Yet this was still the most open she'd been with anyone, and it didn't scare her the way it usually did. Why was that, exactly?

She took in his strong profile, his dark hair that was moving in the gentle breeze, the day-old stubble that covered his jaw. She felt safe with him.

"You know," she said, feeling this was something that he *should* know. "I haven't told anyone this before. About being a rolling stone."

His green eyes softened. "Thank you for sharing it with me." His forehead crumpled into lines and he swallowed. "And it seems only fair that I repay your honesty in kind."

"Yes?" she said and held her breath.

"The night we met, you asked if I'd ever had a dream of my own." His voice was stilted, as if he hadn't put these thoughts into words before. "I didn't answer you, but the truth is, no. The only dreams I can remember having are the dreams I have in common with my family for our business." His gaze was piercing, looking deep within her. "Are you shocked?"

She swallowed hard to get her voice to work. "I'm honored you shared that with me."

"And if we're being completely honest," he said, his chest rising and falling faster than it had only minutes ago, "I have to tell you that I've never wanted to kiss a woman more than I do in this moment. But I can't let myself."

She squeezed her eyes shut against the truth, but he deserved to know he wasn't alone. Deliberately she opened her eyes again and met his gaze. "I've never wanted to kiss a man this much, either. Ever since the moment our lips first touched, I've been thinking about doing it again."

He groaned and let his head fall into his hands. "I'm not sure if I prefer knowing that, or if it was easier not thinking you felt the same."

She sighed, understanding how he felt. "You're not the only one feeling the chemistry. But I don't want to act on it, either."

Without looking up, he reached across the towel and intertwined their hands. The slide of his skin against her fingers made her breath hitch. Holding his hand was such a poor substitute for what she really wanted, but it would have to be enough.

Dylan refused to look down at where his fingers were wrapped around Faith's. If he acknowledged it, he'd have to break the contact.

What were they doing at the beach, anyway? She'd been clear from the start that she'd bought the time with him to help her career. Since this was their second date, he should be doing something for her career now.

Reaching a decision, he released her hand and jumped to his feet. "Come on. There's somewhere I want to take you."

She looked up at him warily. "Where?"

Her meaning hit him—he'd said he wanted to kiss her and then held her hand. It was natural she would think that next he might push the boundaries further. "It's job-related, I promise."

He held out his hand again, but this time it was to help her up. She took it and he pulled her up to stand in front of him. She was so close he could feel her body heat. She smelled of flowers, which was no surprise given that she'd been handling them all day, but also of strawberries. His gaze dropped to her lips, which had a slick of red gloss coating them. She was wearing strawberry lip gloss. His pulse spiked, imagining the flavor when he kissed her.

Abruptly she released his hand and stepped back. "You said we were going somewhere job-related?"

He picked up the towel and shook it with more force than was necessary before answering. "I want you to see the Hawke's Blooms flower farm."

Her eyes lit with the same passion she'd shown when she talked about her future. "I'd love that!"

As they walked back to the car, then drove out of LA to San Juan Capistrano, where the farm was located, she peppered him with questions about the farm's capacity and stock.

"Have you always had it out here?" she asked once they drew close.

He nodded. "We moved here when I was a kid. My

parents had been farmers, so when they came out to California, they tried their hand at growing flowers. They wanted something that would give their three sons opportunities and thought this was the way to do it."

"From your success, I'd say they were right." Her voice held no trace of flattery. It was an honest observation, and it had more weight for it.

"Yeah," he said, allowing satisfaction about the business he'd built with his family to fill his chest. He owed his parents more than he could ever repay. Not that they wanted anything other than to see their sons happy and thriving, but he'd find a way to show them how grateful he was one day.

"So, whose idea was it to sell the flowers as well as grow them?" Faith asked.

"We had a roadside stall when we started." He smiled at the memory. "Dad would sell to the flower markets, but every weekend, Adam and I would go with Mom and sell whatever we had left."

"What about your other brother?"

He chuckled. "Liam prefers plants to people, so he'd stay home with Dad. And it's a good thing he did—it was Liam's breakthroughs with new flowers that put us on the map."

"I was really impressed with his Midnight Lily. The customers have been loving it."

"It's a great flower," Dylan said, feeling a surge of pride. The new blue lily had been launched a couple of months earlier and had been selling like crazy ever since.

She lifted one foot up, rested it on the seat and wrapped an arm around her knee. "So you and your other brother were stuck selling by the roadside?"

"There were three of us there, but the sales came down to our mom and me. Adam always saw himself in a more…managerial role." Adam had set himself up behind the stall in what Dylan and his mother had called "Adam's office."

Out of the corner of his eye, he saw her cock her head to the side. "How much management does a road-side stall need?"

"Even though I teased him about trying to get out of work, he probably worked harder than any of us. He made posters and put them on stakes by the road, ex-perimented with price points and kept a chart of the sales so he could work out what to stock. During the week, he was always doing something to our stall, too. Either painting it a different color to see if that attracted more people, or constructing new benches for the flower buckets from wood he salvaged."

"Sounds like quite the entrepreneur." There was a smile in her voice.

"He is," Dylan said with no small measure of affec-tion. "That's why Liam and I let Adam run the over-all company. Liam's happier with his plants, anyway."

"And you?" Her voice grew soft. "What do you pre-fer?"

He shrugged one shoulder. "I'm more of a people person. I like the buzz of retail. The colors of it. I like talking to staff and customers—interacting."

"I can see that about you," she said, her tone pensive.

"When we opened our first store, my mother and I staffed it." They'd been amazing times, full of energy and excitement. "Liam and Dad were back home grow-ing the plants and drawing scientific charts of plant breeding, and Adam was in his room, making spread-sheets and plans. My job was more fun."

"To you. But I'll bet to them, your job sounded like hell."

He grinned. "Actually, yes. Being in a room full of people has been known to make them both yearn for their charts and spreadsheets."

He pulled into the drive to Liam's place and went through security. It had been tightened now that Liam was engaged to a princess, and Dylan was glad for the little girls' sakes.

"This looks more like a private residence," Faith said warily.

"Liam still lives on-site. It's the same house we grew up in, actually, though he's had so much work done to it, you'd never know."

"But there was a specific farm entrance before this driveway," she said, pointing.

"If I came all the way out here and didn't tell him, he'd kill me. Well," he amended as he thought about what he'd said, "he probably wouldn't notice, but his fiancée definitely would kill me. We'll only be there a minute or two—just passing through."

"Hang on—" she put her hands on the dashboard as if she could slow their approach "—you're taking me to meet his fiancée?"

"If that's okay with you," Dylan said, glancing over at her. He hadn't thought she might be uncomfortable—Faith always seemed as if she was ready for any adventure life threw at her.

Her mouth opened and closed again before she replied. "She's a princess!"

"As it turns out, yes." He wanted to smile at the awe

in her voice, but he restrained himself. He'd known Jenna before he'd found out she was a princess, so he hadn't had a chance to be overwhelmed by her royal status. However, he understood that this was probably an intimidating situation for Faith to be thrown into with no warning. He had confidence that she'd cope—he couldn't imagine anything overwhelming Faith for long.

Her expression was still uncertain as he pulled up in front of the house. But he wasn't driving out here without at least saying hello to little Bonnie and Meg.

He walked around to open her door. "Are you coming?"

"Are there protocols about what I should say?" she asked as she climbed out.

He shrugged one shoulder casually. "I'd go with complimenting their daughters and being particularly nice to me."

"You?"

"What can I say? The princess is fond of me."

She narrowed her eyes at him as she realized he was teasing, but she'd lost the slightly awed look, which was what he'd been aiming for.

Jenna met them at the door, twelve-month-old Meg on her hip. "Dylan," she said in her lilting Scandinavian accent, "what a nice surprise."

He kissed her cheek, took Meg from her and held her up in the air until he elicited a giggle, and then kissed her cheek as well. "I'm not here long. We're on our way down to see Liam and stopped by to say hello first."

"Liam's in his office, working on his latest project. In the meantime," she said, taking Meg back, "why don't you introduce me to your friend?"

"Jenna, this is Faith. She's a florist at our Santa Monica store." He didn't need to emphasize the point. Jenna knew as well as any of them that he couldn't get involved with one of their florists. "Faith, this is my future sister-in-law, Jenna."

Jenna held out her hand. To Faith's credit, she hesitated only a moment before accepting it. "Lovely to meet you," Faith said.

Jenna smiled, and he could see her brain working overtime, trying to work out if there was something going on between them. She was far too insightful. "Would you like a drink before you set out?"

Faith shook her head, and he wanted to get moving and focused on work again before Jenna could corner him with awkward questions. "We're fine."

"Do you mind if we come with you? Bonnie is still napping, and our housekeeper can keep an ear out for her. I haven't been outside the house all day, and I'd like Meg to get some fresh air and see something other than me."

"That would be great." And it would keep him on his best behavior. None of those intimate moments they'd accidentally had at the beach.

Five minutes later, they were walking out the back door.

"It's huge," Faith said, looking out across the fields of brightly colored blooms. "Do you use them all?"

"The main purpose is to stock our own shops," he said as he opened the small gate that marked the edge of Liam's yard, "but we sell the excess to other stores at the flower markets."

They followed a paved path to a building off to the side—Liam's pride and joy. The Hawke's Blooms research facility.

When they went through the sliding doors, Jenna lifted Meg from the stroller and carried her in her arms, and Dylan spoke to a woman at the front desk. "Can you let Liam know that I'm here to see him, please?"

She put a call through, and then looked back to him. "He's on his way down."

Dylan dug his hands into his pockets and glanced over at Faith as she made baby talk with Meg. He had another plan in mind to help her career, and this time he'd be sure to take it slow and check that she was on board first. But despite his caution, he had a very good feeling about this particular plan. And that made him happier than he should have been comfortable with.

Five

Faith was aware that Princess Jensine of Larsland was studying her, and she had to resist squirming. It seemed almost surreal that a small-town girl who'd spent her entire childhood being shunted from one relative to another should find herself face-to-face with a member of royalty.

"You look familiar," Jenna eventually said. "Have we met before?"

Dylan cleared his throat. "You might have seen her at the auction," he admitted. "Faith had the winning bid on a date with me."

Jenna's eyes widened. "This is a date? You brought a *date* to a research lab?"

"It's not like that," Faith said quickly. "Besides, even if we wanted to, we couldn't have a real date because of company policy."

She covered her mouth with two fingers. Had she just admitted she would have liked to date Dylan if the situation had been different? No one else seemed to have taken it that way. But she needed to stay on her guard because, deep down, there wasn't much in the world she would want more than for Dylan to kiss her again, and she didn't want anyone—especially Dylan—guessing that.

"Ah, yes," Jenna said. One corner of her mouth turned up. "That old fraternization policy. I know it well."

Liam pushed through the door into the waiting room and beamed when he saw his fiancée. He took Meg from her, swung her around onto his hip and kissed Jenna softly. "Hi," he said.

"Hi, yourself," she said back and kissed him again.

Dylan coughed loudly. "Hey, other people present."

Liam looked up but pulled Jenna under his arm. It was only then that he seemed to register there was a stranger in the room. He released Jenna and stuck out a hand. "I'm Liam Hawke, since it seems my brother isn't going to introduce us."

"I'm Faith Crawford," she said, straightening her spine as she shook his hand. "I work for you."

"You do?" Liam asked, his head cocked to the side.

Dylan took a step closer to her elbow. She could feel his body heat. "Faith is a florist at the Santa Monica store."

"Okay, good to meet you," Liam said.

Jenna looked up at her man, her eyes full of mischief. "Faith won Dylan at the auction."

Dylan held up a hand. "She didn't win me." His gaze darted to Faith before turning back to his brother. "She had the winning bid on some *time* with me."

"Three dates," Jenna supplied helpfully.

"They're not dates, just time," Dylan clarified. "In fact, this is some of that time now. Faith has a lot of creativity in her designs, and we've identified her as someone with potential. So I wanted to show her around the building."

"Sure," Liam said casually, holding Dylan's gaze. "The public areas?"

"Up to you," Dylan said just as casually.

Faith looked from one to the other, trying to work out what they were really saying. It was obvious something else was being discussed, but what?

"You'll vouch for her discretion?" Liam asked.

Dylan nodded. "I'm willing to bet on it."

"Then you're about to." Liam looked up at Faith and smiled. "Welcome to my world. Let me show you around."

It seemed she'd passed some kind of test on Dylan's say-so, but she had no idea what it had been for. They spent the next twenty minutes walking through the research rooms, and Faith was enthralled with all the projects they had going on. Crossbreeding for stronger scent or bigger flowers, rooms full of benches with lines of pots containing grafted plants. Excitement buzzed through her blood at seeing the powerhouse behind the business.

Then they reached a locked door. Liam caught her gaze. "Past this door is my personal project. Very few people know what's in here, and even fewer have seen it. If we go inside, I need your word that you won't leak the information."

"You have my word," she said without hesitation.

Liam looked to Dylan, who nodded, and opened the door.

The room was like many of the others in that it had

benches with rows of pots, each containing plants at different stages of growth. But the flower that many of the pots had was like nothing in the other rooms. Or anything she'd seen before. Faith knew flowers. She knew the conditions they preferred and their shelf lives. She knew which flowers were in season at any given time in which area of the country. She knew what colors each variety came in. But she'd never seen anything like the flower in those pots.

She stepped closer. It was an iris, but it was a rich red. She wanted to touch it but was unsure, so she looked up at Liam. "May I?"

He nodded his permission. With her fingertip, she touched the petal of one of the more advanced flowers. "It's beautiful," she breathed.

"Thank you," Liam said.

Dylan moved to her elbow. "How do you think it will go with the customers?"

She lifted her head and found his deep green gaze. "I think we'll be stampeded." She meant it. There was nothing like this flower on the market, and it was stunning. Already she could imagine how perfect it would look in a bridal bouquet or dramatic table decoration. Its crimson bloom would be the center of attention.

"Tell me, Faith," Dylan said, crossing his arms over his broad chest, "what would you put with it to showcase it?"

"The design would need to be simple. It's so beautiful, it doesn't need much adornment. Perhaps something with soft white petals, like old-fashioned roses. Maybe a touch of silver foliage."

Dylan gave her an indulgent smile and dug his hands in his pockets. "Do you want a chance to try?"

"Make an arrangement with one of these?" she asked, her heart racing with excitement. "Now?"

Dylan lifted an eyebrow at Liam, who nodded. "Yep, now. We'll wait here while you go out to the farm. Collect whatever you want. Then come back and make us an arrangement."

Chest almost bursting, Faith nodded and threaded her way back to the door.

As soon as Faith was gone, Dylan looked to his brother. "Thanks."

"If you believe in her, then that's enough for me. But," he said, his voice becoming serious, "do you know what you're doing? She's an employee."

Dylan arched an eyebrow. "That didn't stop the two of you."

"It did for a little while," Jenna said, grinning up at Liam.

Liam returned the grin and then said, "It was different for us. Jenna was working for me personally, not the company."

Dylan leaned back on the bench. He'd had enough of this topic of conversation. The last thing he needed was for them to discover he'd crossed the line in a spectacular fashion on the very first night by kissing her.

He shook his head once. "There's nothing to worry about. I'm just being a good boss and giving opportunities to someone with potential."

"Sure you are," Jenna said and winked.

"How are Bonnie and Meg?" Dylan asked, hoping the new topic would sidetrack them both for the short while it took Faith to return.

"They're just perfect," Jenna said, a dreamy look of contentment on her face.

Dylan asked Jenna a few more questions about the girls and suggested Liam find some floral tools for Faith to keep them occupied. Finally there was a call from the front desk, and Liam told them to let Faith back through.

She entered with her arms full of flowers, her bright red hair falling from the clip she'd used to try to tame her curls. Dylan jumped up to help, taking some of the blooms and spreading them across a vacant bench.

"Here, you might need these," he said, passing her the box of tools. As their fingers brushed, he felt a tingle of electricity shoot up his arm, but he did his best to ignore it. This was a professional situation, and even if it weren't, she was still an employee, as Liam had just pointed out.

After recapturing her hair in the clip, Faith began to work with the flowers, trimming the thorns and leaves from the white roses, using floral wire on the blush-pink gerbera daisies and arranging them together. Liam cut three of his red irises and handed them to her.

The expression in Faith's eyes, of awe and honor, made Dylan's heart swell in his chest. Her passion was contagious—he felt alive, as if every cell in his body was waking up.

"Thank you," she said as she took the flowers from Liam, her voice breathless. Then she wove the other flowers around them, creating a design that was elegant in its simplicity, yet stunning.

When she was finished, she held the bouquet out to Dylan. He smiled as he took it and then showed it to Jenna and Liam.

"What do you think?" he asked his brother and soon-to-be sister-in-law. They knew what he was really ask-ing—they'd begun talks already about launching the new flower on the market with an event, in the same way they'd launched the Midnight Lily a few months ago. Jenna had been the brains behind that and it had been a roaring success. They'd already started on pre-liminary plans for the second launch, and Jenna had asked him to supply a florist from his staff to work on it part-time.

Jenna turned to Liam, one eyebrow raised, and he nodded. Then she turned to Faith.

"Faith," she said, her musical voice soft. "What would you say to working part-time with me on the launch of the new iris? I need a florist to handle the ar-rangements and a few other duties, and we think you'd be perfect."

Faith looked from Jenna to Dylan, eyes wide. Wary about pushing her into a job she didn't want again, he explained further. "If you want to do it, we'll work your hours at the store around this. You could do part-time at each until the launch, then go back to full-time at the store."

"Then I'd love to," she said, her warm brown eyes sparkling, and Dylan felt the satisfaction of a good plan coming together.

Jenna grinned. "Great. I have to take Meg back up to the house, but I'll be in touch about the details."

As they drove away a short while later, Dylan glanced over at Faith. He wanted to make sure this was really what she wanted, especially after he'd botched things the last time he'd tried to help her career.

"Faith, I want you to know that this is totally up to you. If you'd enjoy the work, we'd love to have you on the project. But you can still change your mind, and it won't affect your job at the Santa Monica store."

She gave him a beaming smile. "Honestly, I can't thank you enough. The opportunity of doing large arrangements that will be seen by hundreds of people is a dream come true. And Jenna seems lovely—I think I'll enjoy working with her."

As he stopped at a red light, he glanced over and found Faith looking at him as if he'd hung the moon. His heart clenched tight. He had a bad feeling that, despite everything, he'd do whatever it took to keep that look on her face. The light turned green, and he trained his gaze on the road ahead, shoring up the strength to do the right thing.

One week into her new working life, Faith looked up from the arrangement she was making to find Dylan letting himself in through the door of the secure room where they were keeping the new flower a secret from the world.

As he crossed over to her, she bit down on a smile, unwilling to let it escape. He was earlier than expected, and that made her happier than it should have. Of course, every time she saw him—no, every time she even thought about him—it made her happier than it should. And yet it also made her sadder, since this was one man she shouldn't be thinking about, or daydreaming about, in the first place. Her reactions to him were stronger than they should have been to a boss, and somehow she had to find a way to contain that.

This week she'd been designing arrangements with the new iris for the Hawke's Blooms promotions team to use for posters and media releases after the official launch. To give them enough lead time for their own design work, she'd agreed this would be her first priority. It hadn't been a problem to work quickly—she was bursting with ideas. She'd even suggested they call the new flower the Ruby Iris, and everyone had liked the name. She loved that this flower would permanently have a little piece of her attached to it.

And this afternoon, a panel of the three Hawke brothers and Jenna would choose the two arrangements to send the publicity team from six Faith had made. Her stomach had been filled with butterflies all day.

"Hey, Dylan," she said when he reached her. "I didn't expect you for another hour, when the rest of the panel is coming."

He dug his hands into his trouser pockets. "I had a bit of time on my hands and thought I'd stop by in case you needed any last-minute help."

"You've already been a huge help."

He'd dropped in a couple of times already this week. She'd taken advantage of that time, peppering him with questions about the launch of the Midnight Lily, looking for details that would give her clues about what they'd be looking for this time. Dylan had answered all her questions. She wondered, though, if he was also keeping an eye on her—he'd suggested her for this job, so if she messed it up, it would reflect badly on him.

He made himself busy clearing the bench where she'd been working.

"You don't have to do that," she said, her gaze on the white iris in her hand. "I've left enough time to clean up before the others arrive."

He flashed her a smile. "But I'm here. I may as well do something to help."

She paused, watching him clearing the bench with bold, sweeping movements, fixing things. Making things better for her. Dylan Hawke was a mystery in many ways. She'd worked for several florists and had quite a few bosses over the years, but never had she found any who were happy to roll up their sleeves and get their hands dirty. They usually preferred to have their underlings do the menial tasks.

She popped the flower back into the jug of water and turned so she could see him more clearly. "Why is it that you're the only boss I've ever had who was willing to do this?"

His broad shoulders lifted, then dropped, as if it were no big deal. "Someone's got to do it. Don't see why it shouldn't be me."

"Because your time is more valuable." He opened his mouth, and she could tell there was a denial on his tongue, so she held up a hand. "Seriously, your hourly rate must dwarf mine."

"I might get paid more, but I can't create something like that," he said, gesturing to the design she had almost finished. But there was something else in his eyes, something he wasn't admitting to.

She crossed her arms under her breasts. "Tell me what the rest of that story is."

"Don't you have work to do?" He tried to frown, but the corners of his mouth were twitching.

"Conveniently, someone just cleaned up my work area, so now I have a few extra minutes to play with. And I'd like to spend them hearing the real story behind the line you just tried to feed me."

"A line?" His hand went to his heart. "You wound me."

"Wow," she said, hoisting herself up to sit on the

bench. "You really don't want to talk about this, do you?"

He arched an eyebrow, leaning on the bench only a hand span away. "You really want to know the truth?"

"Yeah, I really do."

Something changed in his face, his demeanor. She couldn't quite put her finger on it, but she knew without a doubt that he was baring himself to her. Trusting her. The knowledge squeezed her heart tight.

"Truth is," he said, his voice deep, "lately I've been thinking about the buzz I used to get, setting up the original stores. Working with customers and having a new challenge were what got me out of bed in the mornings."

"Your job now must have challenges." Being the head of the Hawke's Blooms stores sounded as if it would be pretty much all challenge.

"Sure. But there was a joy back then that doesn't exist now." He ran his hands through his already rumpled hair. "I'm not sure how to explain it exactly, but in the old days, when my family was first starting the company, we never knew what each day would bring. I can glimpse that excitement again when I watch you work."

Dylan looked into Faith's trusting brown eyes. There was another part to the answer that he dared not say aloud—he found that excitement again not only by watching her work but also by being around her. He never knew what she'd say or do next, and it was the most refreshing thing he'd experienced in a long time.

A knock on the door drew him out of his thoughts. He looked up to see his oldest brother, Adam, poking his head around the door. He suddenly realized how close he was standing to Faith and took a step to the side.

As Adam made his way over to them, his face was blank, but after a lifetime of knowing him, Dylan could read the question in his eyes.

"Liam and Jenna aren't here yet," Dylan said by way of a greeting—he'd spoken to Adam a couple of times today already, so a greeting seemed superfluous.

"That's okay," Adam replied. "It gives me a moment to meet our star florist."

Again, Adam's outward facade—politeness this time—didn't match what was going on underneath. He had sensed something and had every intention of getting to the bottom of it. Dylan squared his shoulders.

"Adam, this is Faith Crawford. Faith, this is Adam, the CEO of Hawke's Blooms Enterprises, which is the overall company that encompasses the stores, the farm and the markets."

Faith stuck out her hand, and Dylan didn't think his brother noticed the slight tremble as she shook his hand. "Good to meet you, Mr. Hawke."

"You'll have to call me Adam, or this meeting is going to get very confused with the three Mr. Hawkes together at once."

"Oh, of course." Her eyes darted to Dylan. "Thank you, Adam."

Dylan looked back at the bench and realized Faith wasn't quite finished with the last arrangement—he'd made her lose precious minutes. He swore under his breath.

He turned to his brother. "How about we give Faith a few minutes to make the last touches before the others arrive?"

"Sure. There are a few things I wanted to discuss with you, anyway."

As they headed for the door, Dylan threw Faith a smile over his shoulder, and she mouthed "thank you" back to him. Knowing her, even once she'd added the final couple of flowers, she'd want a few minutes on her own to get her head together without worrying about a new Hawke brother watching her.

Once the door closed behind them, Adam said, "Coffee?"

"Excellent plan."

The staff room was empty, and Dylan headed for the coffee machine, making an espresso each for himself and Adam.

"So, what's the deal with you and Faith?" Adam asked bluntly as he grabbed the sugar jar.

Dylan handed his brother a coffee. "Just helping an employee with potential to advance her career."

Adam sighed, but there was a smile lurking in his eyes. "Dylan, I've known you your entire life. I saw you when you had your first crush, and I drove you to the movies on your first date. Don't try to bullshit me. Your interest in that woman is more than an employer's."

Dylan leaned back on the counter. "It's really that obvious?"

"Maybe not to everyone, but to me? Yes." Adam moved closer and clapped him on the back. "What are you going to do?"

"I've got it under control."

"You call this under control?" Adam rolled his eyes to heaven as if appealing for help. "What happened when you kissed her?"

Caught off guard, Dylan felt as if he'd been sucker punched. "How do you know I kissed her?"

Adam's eyebrows shot up. "I didn't until you just confirmed it."

Realizing his mistake too late, Dylan groaned. "What you have to understand—"

"Oh, good. Stories that start this way are always juicy."

Ignoring him, Dylan started again. "What you have to understand is that we didn't meet at work. Well, not exactly."

Adam sipped his coffee. "You ran into an employee socially?"

"Remember that bachelor auction Jenna organized for our charity? The one you managed to wriggle out of being involved with?" he asked pointedly.

Uncharacteristically, Adam's gaze dropped to the floor. "I was, uh, busy that night."

"Sure you were," Dylan said, not believing it for a second. "Anyway, Faith placed the winning bid on me."

"You were bought by one of your florists?" Adam said, horrified.

"She bought some of my *time*," Dylan clarified.

Adam's expression didn't soften. "You've been out on a date with an employee?"

"No, she didn't want dates."

"What did she want?" he asked, his eyes narrowing.

"She asked me to meet her at the Santa Monica store and made a submission for the catalog."

"Did you accept it?"

"Nope."

"Her design wasn't even good enough for the book,

yet you have her here working on the most high-profile event in our history?"

"Her work is good. She deserves this spot, no question. The design she showed me that night was what she thought I wanted. When she does her own work, she's amazing."

"You said you wanted to rehabilitate your image. This won't help."

"It won't hurt, either, because nothing is going to happen."

"Sure. Let's get back to you kissing an employee."

"Yeah, I'd rather not. I'm trying to forget it."

"How's that working out for you?"

"Not as well as I'd like."

"Dylan," Adam said, shaking his head. "This is dangerous."

"I know."

"Do you? She seems nice, but if this goes badly for her, she can sue you. Hell, she can sue all of us because we have a policy that you've violated, but you're especially vulnerable."

"She's not like that. She wouldn't."

"You haven't known her long enough to be sure. You're the head of the chain of stores she works for, so she's been on her best behavior."

"I have no doubt that I've seen the real her."

"Now I'm even more worried. Is this woman really worth risking your career over? Exposing the entire company to legal action and a potential scandal?"

Liam poked his head around the door. "I thought I might find you two in here, stealing my coffee."

Dylan raised his mug. "You should have cookies in here, too."

Liam snorted a laugh. "Faith is ready if you are. Jenna's already in there."

Adam didn't move. "Come in here a minute and close the door."

Liam took the extra step inside the room and shut the door behind him. "What's up?"

Adam gestured in Dylan's direction. "Did you know about him kissing his florist?"

"Yes. Wait, no." He turned to Dylan. "You kissed her?"

"He kissed her," Adam confirmed, rocking back on his heels. "I'll brief the lawyers this afternoon in case we need to take preemptive action."

Dylan groaned. "Glad we're not overreacting."

Liam blew out a breath. "Look, I know things were different with me and Jenna, but I kissed her—heck, I made love to her—while she worked for me, and the world didn't end."

Dylan chuckled. "You sure acted as if it had ended there for a while. Remember that day we came over and—?"

Liam hit him upside the head. "I'm trying to help you, idiot."

"Uh, thanks?" Dylan said, rubbing his head.

Adam narrowed his eyes at them both. "You were lucky with Jenna. Most women in that situation would have reacted differently. Would have taken what they could get."

Dylan frowned at Liam. "Since when did he get so jaded about women?"

Liam shrugged a shoulder. "Many years ago. I always figured someone had broken his heart."

Adam threw up his hands. "I'm standing right here."

"Good point," Liam said. "So tell us who broke your heart? Was it Liz in college?"

"Nope," Dylan said. "He left her. I had to talk to her when she started calling the house, brokenhearted. Maybe it was—"

"Stop," Adam said in his oldest brother voice. "We're not discussing my dating history. We're talking about Dylan and the here and now."

"Actually," Liam said, "we're talking about which arrangements we want on the publicity materials. And two people are waiting for us." He opened the door and indicated the hallway with a hand. "Shall we?"

Adam straightened his tie, gave a last pointed look to Dylan and headed out.

"Thanks," Dylan said to Liam.

Liam nodded. "Just don't mess this up and get us into legal problems."

"I'll be careful," Dylan said and followed his brothers out the door, hoping like all hell he *was* capable of being careful around Faith Crawford.

Six

From the corner of Liam's research lab, Faith watched the three Hawke brothers and Jenna as they walked around the designs she'd been working on all week. She'd been nervous the night she'd made the first arrangement for Dylan, but this was more intense. There was so much more riding on this verdict.

Finally Adam looked up and said, "Is everybody ready to make a decision?" The others nodded, so he continued. "I like number three. It's simple enough to work well in publicity, it keeps the focus on the iris and it's elegant, which will appeal to the public."

"Agreed," Liam said. "It's one of my top two choices as well."

They quickly settled on that arrangement and then had a robust discussion about the second choice, since the vote was split between two options.

As Faith watched the conversation, the excitement began to outweigh her nerves—the four of them were so animated about her designs. Her personal favorite hadn't been mentioned at all, and now that she'd heard the reasoning for their other choices, she could assume that her favorite was too cluttered to be effective in the posters. It was fascinating to hear the opinions of people more experienced than she was in this side of the flower business. In such a short time, she'd learned so much.

Once the decisions were made, all four of the panel members complimented Faith on her work, though it was Dylan's praise that made her heart swell. She tried not to watch him as the others spoke, tried to keep her reaction to him veiled, but there was a charisma that surrounded him, a magnetic force that drew her gaze back against her will.

Then Adam excused himself to rush off to a meeting, and Liam turned to Dylan. "Are you still okay to take them to the photographer's studio?"

"Sure," Dylan said. "I drove here in one of the refrigerated delivery vans. Faith, did you want to come to the photo shoot?"

Faith jerked her head up. She'd known they'd booked the photographer for this afternoon and that the chosen designs would be taken straight to the studio, but she'd been able to concentrate only on her part. She hadn't thought further than the panel arriving and assessing her work. Now, though, she could barely contain her enthusiasm about seeing the two successful designs photographed.

"I'd love to," she said, trying not to bounce on her toes. "If that's okay."

Jenna smiled. "Seems only fair that since you created them, you get to see it through."

"Then I'm in. I'll grab my bag."

While she gathered her things, Liam and Dylan sealed the two chosen arrangements plus a few single stems in boxes—since the new iris was still a secret—and carried them out to the delivery truck.

"What about my car?" Faith asked once the flowers were all loaded.

Dylan's green gaze flicked from her to her car. "Since your place is near the studio, how about I drop you home afterward, then bring you back out here in the morning for work?"

Jenna nodded. "This parking lot is secure overnight—the security gates will be shut and monitored."

"Okay, that sounds good then. Thank you."

"Not a problem," Dylan said as he opened her door for her. Her arm brushed his hand as she climbed in, sending a buzz of awareness through her body. He held her gaze for an instant, showing that he'd felt it, too. She pulled her seat belt over her shoulder and tried to pretend the moment of connection hadn't happened.

Once they'd set off on the road, he flashed her a grin. "So how did your nerves hold out? That must have been trying for you."

She tucked her legs up underneath her on the seat. "I have to admit, I was pretty tense while you were all judging, but it was thrilling, too. Thank you again for this opportunity."

"No, thank you," he said as he changed lanes to overtake a station wagon. "Even Adam liked your work, and he's hard to impress."

Her thoughts drifted back to seeing the three brothers together. They all looked so alike—tall and broad-shouldered, with thick, wavy hair the color of polished mahogany—yet so different at the same time. There was something…*more* in Dylan. An energy down deep in his soul, a passion for life that shone through in everything he did. In every move he made.

"I found Adam difficult to get a read on."

"That's Adam for you. He's what our mother calls 'self-contained.' Doesn't like sharing parts of himself if he can avoid it."

Curiosity made her turn to face Dylan. "Even with you and Liam?"

"Liam and I have found ways over the years to nudge him until he cracks." Dylan's expression changed—there was a touch of devilish mischief in the way his mouth quirked. "Some less fair than others."

"Like what?" she asked, intrigued.

"Oh, we just know what buttons to push." He grinned. "But we try to use our powers for good instead of evil. Most of the time we succeed."

Faith laughed. "Your powers are truly scary. I think I should be more careful around you."

There was silence for several heartbeats, and she felt the mood in the car—no, between *them*—change. Deepen.

"Pushing buttons isn't the reason you should be careful around me, Faith," he said, his voice like gravel.

Her skin heated. Even though she knew she shouldn't, she asked, "Why is it, then?"

"Because I start to lose perspective around you." He didn't look at her; his gaze remained focused on the road ahead, but she felt as if he was whispering in her ear.

"Sometimes I think you could crook your finger at me and I'd forget the company rules."

The breath caught in her throat. She was on the edge of a precipice, desperately wanting to fall, to let go, but she knew she couldn't. She swallowed hard and tried to make light of his comment. "Don't worry, I've never been able to master whistling, skipping or crooking a finger."

He laughed, but it sounded tight and unnatural. "Then we won't have a problem."

They talked about less loaded topics for the rest of the trip back to LA until they finally pulled up at the studio. They carried the boxes of arrangements and single stems to the front door, where the photographer was waiting for them.

"Come on in," she said. "The others are already here."

Dylan leaned over to whisper to Faith, "A couple of the publicity team members from Adam's office are meeting us here."

Once they were inside, the shoot seemed to move forward like clockwork. Dylan introduced her to the women from Hawke's Blooms' publicity team. Then she found a chair a few feet behind the camera and tried to stay out of the way.

Dylan, however, seemed to be the center of everything. His people management skills were on display, and in a charming, relaxed way, he was in total control of the photo shoot. She couldn't take her eyes off him. He exuded confidence, charisma and power. He raised an arm and everyone turned to see what he was pointing at. He called for assistance with something and several people rushed to help. He looked at her with his simmering gaze, and she practically swooned.

One of the publicity staff members, Amanda, took a seat next to her. "I can't wait to see how the photos turn out. You did some great work with those arrangements."

Faith felt the blush moving its way up her neck and was grateful that Amanda was watching the work in front of them and wouldn't notice. "Thank you. I'm looking forward to the photos as well."

"You're so lucky, getting to work with Dylan. All the girls in our office have a bit of a crush on him."

Faith tensed. Did Amanda know? Was she fishing? But the other woman still hadn't spared her a glance—if she'd been fishing, she would have been watching for a reaction.

Faith drew in an unsteady breath. "You all work for Adam, don't you?"

"Yep, and don't get me wrong. We love Adam, too. He's a great boss. But Dylan? He could charm the pants off just about anyone if he put his mind to it."

Faith felt the blush deepen and creep up to her cheeks. She didn't doubt that assessment in the least. Fortunately, Amanda didn't seem to be waiting for a reply.

"There's something about the way that man moves," Faith's new friend said. "You can tell he'd be a great lover."

Faith's heart skipped a beat. Just at that moment, Dylan glanced their way. He must have seen her looking a little flustered because he mouthed, "You okay?"

Amanda's words replayed in Faith's head, and she imagined lying naked with Dylan Hawke. Touching him without reserve. Being touched. Her mouth dried. Dylan frowned, taking a step toward her, and she realized she hadn't replied to him yet.

Summoning all her willpower, she found a smile and nodded, and he went back to overseeing the shoot. Amanda was called away and Faith tried to focus on something, anything that wasn't Dylan. Luckily, several people stopped to comment on her arrangements, so that gave her a ready-made distraction.

By the time the photographer said she had enough shots and called a halt, Faith had successfully avoided looking at Dylan since he'd asked her if she was okay. So when he appeared in front of her, tall, dark and smiling, she lost her breath.

"You ready to go?" he asked.

She blinked. "Yeah. You sure you don't mind dropping me home? I can catch a cab."

"Actually, I was thinking we should do something to celebrate the success of your designs first."

"Like what?" she practically stammered. *Celebration* and *Dylan* were two words that could be dangerous when paired together.

He ran a hand over his jaw. "A fine champagne should do it."

She looked around. "Here?" Maybe it wouldn't be so dangerous if the others were involved as well.

"I need to drop these flowers off at my place so the delivery van can be picked up—the iris is still under wraps, so I can't let them go anywhere else. But there's a bar downstairs in my building. How about we drive over, I'll race the arrangements upstairs and then we can have a bottle of their best champagne in the bar before I drop you home?"

The plan sounded harmless—he hadn't suggested she go up to his apartment with him, so they'd be surrounded by people the whole time. They couldn't get carried away the way they had at the store on their first meeting. And truth was, she was too buzzed about the day's events to go home just yet. This would be the perfect way to end the day: a small celebration with the person who understood how much making those arrangements and having them photographed for the publicity posters meant to her.

"I'd love to," she said.

They set the flowers back in the boxes and carried them out to the delivery van, said their farewells and set off for Dylan's building. Once they got there and parked, he went around to the back of the van and opened the doors.

"How about you grab us a table while I take these up," he said as he drew out the boxes. "I'll only be a couple of minutes."

"Sure," she said. Part of her wanted to go with him and see his apartment, and the other part knew how dangerous that would be. Best to stay to public areas.

It was still fairly early, and the bar mainly had the after-work crowd, not the evening revelers yet, so she didn't have any trouble finding a booth. She was perusing the cocktail list on the wall behind her when she heard the sound of fabric moving over vinyl. Dylan slid onto the bench seat across from her. His sculpted cheekbones and sparkling green eyes seemed to make the whole world brighter.

"Would you prefer a cocktail?" he asked.

It wouldn't be very smart to drink stronger alcohol when she was alone with this man. "No, I think you're right. Champagne is perfect to celebrate."

"Good, because I just ordered a bottle." His grin just about had her melting on the spot. And over the course of a couple of glasses of champagne each, the effect of Dylan Hawke on her system only intensified.

His cell beeped and he fished it from his pocket. "That was quick," he said as he thumbed some buttons. "The photographer has sent some preliminary shots over."

Her pulse jumped. "Can I see?"

He turned the cell screen to her, but the images were small, so she couldn't see much detail on how the individual iris looked at the center of the shot. "I can't tell much," she said.

He turned the cell back to himself and rotated it as he swiped the screen, flicking through the photos. "We could run up to my apartment and look at them on my computer screen."

He'd made the suggestion almost absent-mindedly, not lifting his gaze from the photos on his phone, and she wondered if he realized the enormity of the possible consequences of his offer.

"Is that wise?" she asked and laced her hands together in her lap. "We agreed it was best to stick to public places."

He stilled. Then his gaze slowly lifted to meet hers. She was right—he hadn't thought it through. He blew out a breath and shrugged. "It'll be fine. It would only be a few minutes, and we'll be focused on the flowers. Then I'll bring you straight back down and drop you home."

She chewed on her bottom lip. She really did want to see those photos, and since the flower was a secret, she wouldn't ask him to forward them to her own email address, so this was the only chance she'd have to get a sneak peek before the posters were produced. Surely she could control her reaction to this man for a few minutes. In fact, when she thought of it that way, her caution seemed crazy—she wasn't ruled by her lusts. Of course she could keep her hands to herself.

Decision made, she nodded. "I'd appreciate that."

She followed him out of the bar, then down a short corridor to a bank of elevators. One was waiting and he ushered her inside, then punched in a code before hitting the *P* button, which she assumed stood for *penthouse*.

They were silent as they stood side by side in the small space, both watching the doors. Perhaps this had been a bad idea after all. Even these first few moments of being alone were filled with tension. A feeling of leashed anticipation.

She opened her mouth to suggest they skip this and he drop her home when the doors whooshed open. He held out a hand to let her precede him into another hallway, and she hesitated.

"Is something wrong?" he asked.

Her mouth was suddenly dry, so she swallowed before speaking. "I guess I'm having second thoughts."

"You know," he said, reaching out to hold the lift doors, "we've been alone quite a bit of time, if you think about it. In the car, the delivery van, the room where you've been working at Liam's. And not once in those times did I lose control and leap on you."

But each of those times there had been the threat of someone entering the room or people in other cars looking through the windows. This time they'd be utterly alone. She moistened her lips.

"If it helps," he said, one corner of his mouth turning up, "I swear to keep my hands to myself."

She believed him. In the time she'd known him, he'd proved to be a man of his word. So she nodded, but as he unlocked his door, she admitted to herself that it wasn't *his* control she was worried about…

Dylan pushed open his door and hoped like hell he could keep the promise he'd just made.

"Do you want anything? A drink? Water?"

She shook her head. He closed the door behind her, then led the way through his living room to a study off to the side. As he booted up the computer, he pulled a second chair over to the desk, but Faith was still in the doorway, standing at an angle, looking out into his living room. He moved to her side, curious to see what she was looking at. Following her line of vision, his gaze landed on the flower arrangements she'd made only hours before.

"You did a really good job," he said, his voice low. "They're beautiful."

She didn't move. "Mainly due to Liam's work creating the Ruby Iris."

"No, mainly due to you. You forget what line of work I'm in." With a gentle finger, he turned her chin to him so he could see her eyes. So she could see his and know he meant this. "I've seen beautiful flowers rendered awkward by a bad arrangement. You, however, have enhanced the Ruby Iris's beauty."

Her eyes darkened. He realized she was close enough that he could lean in and kiss her again. Hell, how he wanted to. But he'd made her a promise to keep his hands to himself. So he dropped his hand and stepped back.

He cleared his throat to get his voice to work again.

"Speaking of your skill, let's have a look at those photos."

He held a chair out for her, then sat in his and opened the email.

There was a tiny gasp from beside him, and he turned to watch her reaction. "What do you think?" he asked.

"I've taken snapshots of my arrangements before, but I've never seen professional photos of them." Her voice was soft, as if she wasn't even conscious she was speaking.

"The photographer has done a good job." He passed the mouse to her so she could flick through the photos at her own pace.

"The lighting is amazing," she said as she scrolled. "And the angles…"

He was sure the lighting and angles were out of this world, but he didn't even glimpse them. His attention was firmly focused on Faith. Her eyes shone with unshed tears—were they of pride? Or joy? As one of those tears broke away and made a track down her cheek, he brushed it away with his thumb.

She turned to him, eyes shocked, lips slightly parted.

"Dylan—"

He withdrew his hand and sat on it and his other hand for good measure. "I'm sorry. I promised not to touch you, and I won't."

Her chest rose and fell more quickly than it had only a few minutes before. "You cross your heart?"

"Yes. I give you my word."

She sucked her luscious bottom lip into her mouth, obviously considering something. Finally she released her lip and met his gaze again. "Then do you mind if I do something?"

"Whatever you want," he said and meant it.

She lifted her hand and cupped the side of his face, running her thumb along his skin, the roughness of his jaw. "I've been dreaming about doing this, but I knew if I did, it would start something neither of us wanted. But since you've promised, then I just wanted to see…"

His pulse had spiked at her touch, and now it raced even faster.

"Faith," he said, his voice ragged. "Have a little mercy."

"Just a moment more," she whispered as her other hand joined in the exploration of his face.

Dylan tensed the muscles in his arms, trying to retain control over them, but he kept sitting on his hands. He didn't dare move. Then her index finger brushed over his lips, and he couldn't stop his tongue darting out to meet it. She pressed a little harder into his bottom lip, and he caught the tip of her finger between his teeth. She moistened her own lips and watched his mouth as if there was nothing she wanted more than to kiss him. He knew exactly how that felt.

"Faith," he said as her fingers moved to his throat. "This is a dangerous game."

"I'll stop in a moment." But her fingers continued their path, moving from his throat up to thread through his hair. "I've been thinking, daydreaming about doing this, and I'll never get another chance."

He groaned. She'd been daydreaming about him? About touching him?

All the blood in his body headed south. He adjusted his position on the chair but didn't release his hands.

"It seems as if it's been forever since our kiss," she continued as her hands traced a path down his throat again, but this time not stopping, instead spreading over his chest. "And even though this can't go anywhere, I've sometimes thought I'd die if I never touched you again. So I just want to make a memory to keep."

"You'll be the death of me." His head dropped back—he couldn't handle her touch combined with the sight of her a moment longer. Though some devil inside him made him ask, "Tell me what else you daydreamed."

There was a pause and he thought she wasn't going to answer, until in a soft voice she said, "You were touching me as well."

"I've thought about that." A lot. And he was thinking about it now. There was something about this woman who made him feel more alive than he had in a long time. Being around her when she worked, laughing with her, having her hands on him.

"Dylan?" she whispered, her voice close to his ear.

Her breath was warm on his earlobe, and he could barely get enough brain cells working to answer. "Yes?"

"What would it take to get you to break that promise?"

A shudder raced through his body. "Faith," he warned.

"Would you touch me if I begged?" Her hands trailed down his arms to rest on his wrists—as far as she could go while he was still sitting on his hands.

His arms trembled but he didn't move, couldn't speak. Then her hands cupped either side of his face and brought his gaze down to land on her. The air from her lungs fanned across his face.

"Please," she whispered against his lips, and then leaned in the last inch and kissed him.

And his last thread of control snapped.

Seven

Faith knew she was being reckless, but the moment Dylan's mouth closed the tiny space to reach hers, she didn't care. She'd been craving this since the last time they'd kissed. Had been craving *him*.

As she gently landed in his lap, his tongue pushed between her parted lips. She couldn't have contained the sound of satisfaction that rose in her throat if she'd tried. And she definitely didn't want to try. She could talk for an hour about the reasons they shouldn't cross the line again, but this, *this* felt too right. She speared her hands through his hair, reveling in the slide of it over her sensitive fingers.

His arms closed around her, holding her close, but it wasn't close enough. She dug at his waistband until she worked his shirt free, then skimmed her hands underneath, over his abdomen and up as high as she could reach with the fabric restraining her hands. His light chest hair tickled, and she dug her nails in.

"Faith," he said as his head dropped back, but his arms didn't relax their grip an inch.

His arousal pressed against the underside of her thighs, and she wriggled against it. A groan seemed to be ripped from him, and he lifted his head to meet her eyes. "I knew you'd be the death of me."

She smiled and kissed him. He tasted of champagne and heat, and she'd never tasted anything so decadent. After minutes, or hours, her lungs screamed for air, so she pulled back, gasping, but he didn't miss a beat. He scraped his teeth across her earlobe, and electric shivers radiated out across her body. She'd never been this desperate for any man. There was something about Dylan Hawke that drove her to the brink of insanity.

"If we're doing this—" he said, gasping between words.

Before he could finish his sentence, she said, "Oh, we're doing this."

He grinned against her mouth. "Then let's move somewhere more comfortable."

He stood, taking her with him and setting her on her feet, and began to walk her backward, through the living room and down the hall, expertly guiding her so that she didn't hit anything, his mouth not leaving hers the entire time.

Once they reached his bedroom, she had no interest in looking around except to ensure there was a bed. Her gaze found a large one with a dark wood headboard and a navy blue comforter and pillows. Perfect. Dylan flicked on a lamp, and its soft yellow light joined the last rays of the sunset filtering through large windows that overlooked downtown LA. The sunset was stunning, but nothing compared with the man before her.

His hands explored her shape through her clothes, but she had less patience—she slid her hands under his cotton shirt so that she could feel his skin again. It had been only minutes since she'd touched his bare chest, but she missed the sensation. She worked up from the ridges of his abdomen, higher, until she found the crisp hair that covered his pecs. It still wasn't enough, so she unbuttoned the shirt and began the journey again, this time with more freedom.

He groaned and pulled her closer, trapping her hands between them, and with palms cupping her bottom, he lifted her until she was standing on her toes, pressed against him. The ridge of his arousal pressed at the juncture of her thighs, the pressure only teasing and nowhere near enough. There was an ache deep inside her and it was only intensifying.

With a hand flat on his chest, she pushed him back. She reached out and unbuckled his belt, pulling it through the loopholes until it came free in her hands, and then dropped it over her shoulder. It clattered on the polished wood floor, and Dylan let out a laugh.

"Seems like you have flair in more than one area of your life, Faith Sixty-Three."

"Seems like you're a smooth talker in more than one area of your life." She undid the button at the top of his trousers and slowly lowered the zipper. With thumbs tucked into the sides, he gave the trousers a nudge and they fell to his ankles, along with his underwear.

He continued to walk her backward to the bed, but she put her hands on his shoulders, stilling him. "Give me a moment to appreciate you."

Obligingly he nodded, but almost immediately he cradled her face and kissed her again. She moved in, closing the distance between them, feeling the heat of his naked body through his clothes. So much, but not enough.

When she didn't think she could take it another second, he stepped backward until he hit the side of the bed and then sank down, bringing her with him to straddle his lap. She pushed up on her knees to give herself a little extra height and took control of the kiss. He ran his hands along her exposed thighs, up underneath her skirt, and then wrapped them around her hips. Her heart beat so strongly, she could feel the resonant thud through her entire body.

"Dylan," she breathed between kisses. She'd never wanted a man this badly before. Couldn't imagine ever wanting someone this badly again.

One by one, he undid the buttons on her blouse, and then peeled the fabric back to reveal her blush-pink demicup bra. He traced a finger around its lacy edges and over the slope of her breasts just before they disappeared into the cups. "So beautiful," he breathed. "Every inch of you is just so beautiful, Faith."

He hooked a finger into one of the cups, pushing down, seeking, and ran the back of his nail over her nipple. She shuddered. The corner of his mouth quirked up, and he did it again, eliciting the same response. Then he pulled the lace down, exposing her breast, and her back arched.

His mouth closed over her nipple and she shuddered. He wrapped an arm around her back, holding her to him as his teeth scraped her skin, followed by his tongue licking her. Through the fog of desire, she was only barely aware of his free hand working deftly behind her to undo the catch on her bra. He finally pulled it down her arms and threw it to the side.

The knowledge that they wouldn't have to stop before they were carried away this time created an intimacy that stole her breath. After all the wanting, finally being together without the barriers between their skin was almost too much to comprehend.

She pushed his open shirt over his shoulders, kissing the skin she'd exposed. The muscles of his shoulders bunched and tensed as first her lips made contact, then her tongue. The scent of his skin was intoxicating.

He fell back against the covers, taking her with him. She was still straddling his hips but now leaning her weight against his torso. She had a semblance of control, but her options for touching him were limited because most of him was either covered by her or hidden against the comforter. He, however, had full access and was taking most delicious advantage, his hands exploring her back, her sides, wherever he could reach.

Her skin was scorching, everything inside her so hot she thought she might explode into flames. And if that happened, so be it—being with Dylan would be more than worth it.

Then he rolled them over so that she was beneath him, his glorious weight pushing her into the mattress. But before she'd had a chance to appreciate the sensation fully, he moved down the bed, lifting her knee as he went. He ran his lips along the inside of her calf, stopping to press a kiss and then to bite lightly at the sensitive back of her knee. Electricity shot along her veins. His hands moved higher, capturing her skirt as he went, taking the fabric with him as his fingers skimmed over her thighs, her hips, until it bunched at her waist.

His fingers hooked under the sides of her pale pink underwear, pulling it inch by inch down her legs. Once it was removed, he covered her with one hand, applying delicious pressure, moving in patterns that were designed to take her to the brink.

Without pausing his hand, he moved back up her body to find her gaze and placed a tender, lingering kiss on her lips. "I feel as if I've wanted you forever. I can't believe you're really here."

"I can barely believe I'm here, either." Her heart squeezed tight at his expression. "It's like a dream."

"It's no dream," he said with a wicked grin. "Let me show you how real this is."

Breaking contact, he disappeared for excruciating moments before reappearing with a foil packet. He ripped it open, but before he could put the condom on, she took it from him and rolled it down his length. When it was on, she circled him with her hand and, taking her time, let herself learn his shape, his secrets. Air hissed out from between his teeth.

Abruptly, and with a pained expression on his face, he grabbed her wrists, freed himself and knelt between her legs. As he lifted her hips, she held her breath. Then he guided himself to her and filled her bit by bit until she gasped.

"Okay?" he asked, his brow furrowed.

She smiled. "More than okay."

He returned the smile and then began to move. She met each stroke, wanting to make the most of every last sensation. But as the tension inside her climbed, she forgot to move, forgot everything but Dylan above her.

His rhythm was driving her slowly out of her mind. She gripped frantically at his back, trying to find purchase, but it felt as if the world was slipping away and all that remained was Dylan moving above her, within her.

Heated breaths near her ear drove her higher, his whispered words telling her she was beautiful, higher still.

His hand snaked down to where their bodies joined, and as he applied pressure with his thumb, she called out his name and exploded into a thousand little pieces, every single one of them filled with bright, shining light. He groaned, and a few strokes later he followed her over the edge before slumping his weight on top of her. She welcomed the heaviness as if it could keep her grounded here on Earth while her soul wanted to fly away.

Whispering her name, Dylan rolled to the side, taking her with him, holding her close. She nestled against his chest, feeling more safe and secure than she could ever remember.

Faith woke slowly and stretched, deep contentment filling her body, down to her bones. And before she was even fully awake, she was wary. It was the contentment that made her suspicious—she'd learned young not to trust the feeling.

The night before came back to her in snatches, then in its entirety. The sensation of Dylan's hand caressing her face, the taste of him in her mouth, the sound he'd made at the back of his throat when he'd found his release.

She'd made love with Dylan, and it had been glorious. And dangerous.

High moments had always preceded her lowest moments, and last night had been a huge high, meaning there was a low—just as huge—coming, whether she was ready or not.

She opened her groggy eyes to the early morning light and found Dylan lying a hand span away on the thick white sheets, watching her. No chance of sneaking away or not facing the consequences of what they'd done.

"Good morning," he said. His voice was sleep-roughened and his hair rumpled, but his expression was guarded. She couldn't get a read on him.

"Good morning," she replied and gathered the sheet a little higher to reach her neck, as if that could give her a buffer between what they'd shared last night and the reality of the morning after. They'd gone too far this time and crossed a line that couldn't be uncrossed. She'd slept with the boss.

He arched an eyebrow and looked pointedly at the sheet she was clutching. "It's a little late for that, don't you think?"

Memories assaulted her—of seducing him, of begging him to touch her. Even as her skin heated with desire, she recognized that this mess they were in was her fault, and she had to find a way to fix it.

"Dylan—" she began, gripping the sheet more firmly.

Before she could say anything else, he interrupted with a false smile stretched across his face. "I'll make us some coffee."

He swung his legs out from the bed, the sheet dropping away to reveal six feet of toned perfection. Her breath caught high in her throat. Dylan in the early morning light was just as impressive as Dylan in the lamplight in the middle of the night. Her hand demanded a chance to touch, but that was what had gotten her into this situation in the first place, so she resisted. Barely.

He found a pair of jeans in his closet, slipped them on and then pulled a charcoal T-shirt over his head before turning back to her.

He indicated a door to the left that she remembered from last night was the bathroom. "Feel free to use the shower or whatever you need."

"Thanks," she said, not releasing the sheet even an inch. She would have loved a shower, but more than that, she wanted to be home, safe and cocooned. Away from temptation that could ruin everything and these messy feelings that Dylan seemed to evoke in her.

After he left the room, she jumped up and grabbed her clothes from the floor where he'd dropped them after he peeled them off her. Maybe once she was dressed she'd feel more in control, though she had a sneaking suspicion it wouldn't be enough.

She'd been becoming more concerned about her attachment to this man every time she saw him. But in her experience, attachments didn't last. Her family had shown her that no matter how sincere people appeared, they'd drop you like a hotcake when someone better came along. And Dylan had had a reputation as a playboy before they met.

Her aunt had promised that she loved her and would always be there for her, but as soon as she'd gotten pregnant, she'd shipped the eleven-year-old Faith off to her grandparents.

Her aunt had been apologetic, saying she just didn't think she could cope with a new baby as well as a child in the house, and Faith had understood that. She'd never blamed her aunt. Instead, she'd just felt stupid that she'd let herself believe this time it might be different. Had let herself hope.

Hope was dangerous.

After the way she'd felt in his arms last night, it was clear that if she let herself begin to hope with Dylan, it would end up devastating her when he left. She'd allowed herself to feel too much.

By reputation, Dylan Hawke was the last man whose commitment she could depend on. No matter how sweet he was being to her now, she'd never be able to hold his attention for long. Better they step back from each other now, before she was hurt by his straying attention later.

As she found her way down the hallway to the kitchen, the scent of freshly brewed coffee hit her senses, promising that everything would be better after she was caffeinated.

She rounded the corner and found Dylan leaning back against the counter, tapping his fingers in a rapid tattoo. He looked about as confused as she felt, and that gave her the confidence she needed.

"I think we need to talk," she said, hoping her voice didn't wobble.

Dylan nodded and handed her a mug of coffee. "I'm sorry about last night."

"If anyone's going to apologize, it should be me." She looked down into her steaming mug. "You held to your word longer than I did."

"Nevertheless, I shouldn't have given in at all." He rubbed a hand up and down his face, clearly annoyed at himself.

"Dylan, I don't want to get into the blame game. I'd rather we look at where we go from here." She leaned a hip on the counter across from him. "First, I think we crossed a line."

He coughed, almost choking on his coffee. "That's pretty safe to say."

At least they agreed on that. However, what to do about it was another matter entirely. She prayed for the strength to see this through. To avoid giving in and dragging him back to the bedroom now.

Interlacing her fingers in her lap, she focused on the cabinet over his shoulder as she spoke. "Crossing lines is becoming something of a habit for us."

"A habit?" He coughed out a laugh. "More like an addiction."

"And like all addictions, it's not healthy," she said reluctantly. "But clearly, I don't know how to stop."

He gave her a wry smile. "I guess that's the exact reason why people struggle with addictions. The how to stop part is hard."

Taking a deep breath, she met his gaze squarely. "So what do you think we should do?"

"There's only one solution. Cold turkey." There was a slight wince in his features as he said the words.

"That sounds final." And severe. Her body tensed just thinking about it. She imagined her reaction the next time she saw him, having to lock down her need as if they hadn't shared the deepest of connections. "How would cold turkey work?"

He put his empty mug in the sink and was silent for a long moment, his gaze trained on the view out the window. When he spoke again, he didn't turn back. "You're still working on the project, so we'll be seeing each other at meetings and at Liam's lab. But in general, we give up spending time alone."

"We haven't gone out of our way to spend time alone up until now. It's just kind of happened." When said aloud, it sounded feeble, but since that first night, when she'd realized they had a problem, they'd both tried to be careful. Yet they'd still ended up in his bed.

He turned back to her, crossing his arms over his chest, a tiny frown line appearing between his eyebrows. "New rules, new level of caution. I'll stay away from the Santa Monica store. If the opportunity arises to, say, attend a photo shoot together, one of us declines."

She nodded slowly. "We become extravigilant."

"Exactly." But he didn't meet her eyes as he said it.

It seemed surreal to be talking about this, to be more attracted to someone than she'd ever been but discussing ways to not act on it. Though it was the strength of that attraction that was the exact problem.

Hope was dangerous.

"So," she said, seeking to disarm some of the tension that had grown between them in the last ten minutes, "I guess standing around in your kitchen early in the morning is probably not something we should be doing, either."

"Nope," he said, his lips curving in a tight smile. "Especially with the way my thoughts are heading, seeing you leaning against my cabinetry."

She stepped away from the counter, which only brought her closer to him. In two steps, she could be in his arms again…

She bit down on her lip. He was right—there was no safe way to spend time alone together.

"Okay," she said, feeling as if she was signing her own death warrant. But she wouldn't give up this job or the opportunities Hawke's Blooms could offer her at this stage in her career. And if she wanted the job, she couldn't sleep with the boss. "I agree to your new plan."

He held out a hand for her mug, and as she gave it to him, his hand closed around hers for a long moment. "Even though we're trying to avoid repeating it, I want you to know I've enjoyed every moment I've spent with you, Faith Sixty-Three."

A ball of emotion rose up and lodged itself in her throat, and she had to swallow to get her voice to work. "I've enjoyed the time I've spent with you, too."

"Come on," he said, his voice rough. "I'll drive you out to get your car."

He grabbed his keys from the end of the counter, and she followed him out, stopping only to pick up her handbag and, one last time, to look around the apartment where she'd glimpsed heaven.

Eight

Dylan knocked on the door of Faith's ground-floor apartment and stepped back to wait. It had been almost a month since the night she'd stayed at his place. The night that had rocked him to his core. In that time, they'd seen each other at Liam's research lab and in meetings about the launch, but, as agreed, they hadn't spent any time alone together. And every day it had been a little more difficult than the day before to keep himself from calling her.

But that third date had been weighing on his mind. It was a loose end that needed clearing up, and it was time he did just that. The closure would help him move forward. Maybe he was grasping at straws, but nothing else had worked so far to help him forget her and move on.

The apartment door opened to reveal Faith in shorts and a T-shirt, her face makeup-free and her curling hair loose around her shoulders. She stole his breath.

"Dylan," she said, her voice betraying her surprise.

"Sorry for the unannounced visit." He smiled and dug his hands into his pockets. "Do you mind if I come in for a couple of minutes?"

She blinked and then opened the door wider. "Sure."

Once inside, he turned to take in the decor. Or lack of decor. The place was beyond minimalist—it was practically bare. There was an old sofa, a coffee table and a TV. The coffee table had a small pile of floristry magazines sitting haphazardly on it, and an empty mug. No bright cushions on the sofa, no colorful paintings on the walls. No collections of eccentric odds and ends, no surprises at all. It was like the anti-Faith apartment.

There was a kitchen beside the living room, with a counter acting as a divider between the rooms. Except for a chrome toaster and a mismatched wooden knife block, the kitchen counters were bare, echoing the interior design of the living room. He'd expected flair. Color. Personality. Faith.

"Can I get you a drink?" she asked, her features schooled to blank.

He shook his head and brought his attention back to the reason he'd come. "No, I won't be here long."

"Even so, maybe we should have this conversation outside." She headed out through the door she'd opened for him and stood in the small courtyard at the front of the apartment block. There were a few dry-looking shrubs enclosing a paved square that was heavily shaded by the building, and it looked about as wrong for her as the interior did.

"Is there a problem with the launch?" she asked, crossing her arms under her breasts.

The launch was only a week away and plans were

in full swing, but it was running as smoothly as could be expected. But it was connected to why he'd knocked on her door this morning.

He cleared his throat. "We need to talk about the auction and our last date."

He'd wanted to bring it up again for a while now, but it didn't seem right to talk about it when they were at work. Where he was the boss and she was his employee. Those roles didn't disappear simply by talking to her here, obviously, but at least by discussing the situation when they were on her turf, it felt a little more equal.

She snapped off a leaf from a nearby shrub and crumpled it in her fingers. "I've told you we can let that slide. I've already got more than I expected from the auction with this assignment working with the Ruby Iris."

That sounded fine in theory, but he needed the closure, so he ignored her objection. "And I've told you that I won't let it slide. You paid to have me look more closely at your floristry skills and I did, but I want to make sure you've had the opportunity to say all you need to about where you see yourself in the company." He offered her a smile. "Since we're both going to the launch anyway, I thought we could go together and it could serve as our final date."

She shifted her weight from one leg to the other. "I seem to remember we decided to keep our distance. To go cold turkey. In fact, those rules pretty much exclude you even being here today."

"It's been almost a month without incident. I think we're fine." Well, *she* seemed fine, anyway. He was still kept awake at night, replaying memories of their night together. Of the feel of her skin, the touch of her lips as she kissed him in desperation.

She, however, seemed unaffected, which was more than a little annoying.

"So how would you see this working?" she asked, sounding unconvinced.

"I'll pick you up, like a date. We've never had any problems being alone in a car together, so that should be fine. Then we'll attend the launch together. Perhaps dance, but since we'll be in public, surrounded by Hawke's Blooms staff and management, there won't be any chance to get carried away. Then I'll drop you home."

"That last point sounds like a danger area," she said as she ran her hands over a branch near her shoulder.

"Good point." In theory, it would only be the same level of temptation that they had right now, but on the night of the launch, they'd both be wearing their finest, would have danced, perhaps would have had a glass or two of champagne. "I'll arrange a limo to drop you home. It will be on standby so you can leave when you want to. Alone."

She screwed up her nose as she considered. "Okay, that sounds harmless enough. And then we'll be square?"

"Then we'll be square," he confirmed. Of course, he was going to reimburse her the money she'd paid for the dates as soon as they'd had the last one, despite her earlier protests. Eight thousand two hundred dollars was a lot of money for someone on her wage.

And speaking of money, there was one other aspect of this last date that needed addressing. "Also, I'd appreciate it if you'd let me buy you a dress for the launch."

She shook her head. "You don't have to buy me a dress, Dylan."

He'd expected opposition, so it didn't faze him. He rocked back on his heels and laid out his reasoning. "You admitted that you spent almost all your savings at the auction, so yes, I do. Will it help if I promise not to buy you a corsage?"

"Dylan—" she began, but he interrupted.

"Humor me. Let me buy you a dress, we'll have the date, and then we can properly go back to being a boss and an employee."

"You want to take me shopping?" She arched an eyebrow. "Alone?"

Alone would be crazy. Luckily, he'd already come up with a solution. "I've arranged a personal shopper who will take us to a store after closing time. We'll not only have private access to the store and advice but also be chaperoned."

She didn't say anything, but he wanted this closure, so he smiled and said, "Just say yes, Faith."

She blew out a breath. "Okay, sure."

Good. Part of him was glad he'd been able to get her to agree. After this he'd be able to move on. Another part of him was wondering if he'd stepped out of the frying pan into the fire.

Faith pulled up in the parking lot of the upscale clothing store and let out a sigh. She was looking forward to spending time with Dylan far more than she should, and that worried her.

Pretending to be unaffected by him in her apartment had almost cost her her sanity. If he hadn't promised to have a personal shopper here tonight, she would never have agreed. Though he'd seemed remarkably unaffected when he'd made the offer, which was hardly fair. If she was struggling, then it would boost her ego if he'd been struggling right along with her.

Perhaps he'd moved on already? Her stomach dipped at the thought, but it would be for the best. Yes, indeed. It was exactly what they needed to happen. If only it didn't feel like the end of the world to contemplate…

His Porsche pulled up beside her. Dylan stepped out and paused to set the keyless lock. He wore jeans and a white polo shirt—it was the only time she'd seen him in jeans besides the morning after they'd made love. She gripped the steering wheel tighter. The memory threatened to overwhelm her with sensation, so she pushed it to the back of her mind and focused on the here and now. However, the fact that the here and now consisted of Dylan's rear end outlined by soft denim wasn't helping her gain control much.

"Evening, Faith," he said as he opened her car door. The deep, sexy drawl sent a shiver up her spine. She stepped out and Dylan closed the door.

"Hello, Dylan," she said. Then, before she could give herself away, she smiled and locked her car. "Is the personal shopper here already or do we need to wait?"

"She's inside."

"Let's not keep her waiting, then," she said and set off for the entrance.

Dylan was beside her in two strides. "You know, you seem a lot more keen about this than I expected."

Actually, she was keen to have another person in the mix and avoid being alone with him, especially in a dimly lit parking lot. If he'd moved on, she wasn't letting him know she was still back where she'd been the night they'd made love. She straightened her spine.

"The sooner we start, the sooner it will be over," she said over her shoulder.

A middle-aged woman wearing a designer pantsuit, her hair in a sleek silver bob, opened the door for them. "Dylan and Faith?" she asked.

"That's us," Dylan said, holding out his hand.

"I'm Julie." She shook Dylan's hand and then held her hand out to Faith. "As I understand it, we're looking for an outfit for Faith to wear to an event?"

"Yes," Faith said. "So, something formal."

"Lovely. The formal section is this way." She moved away, and Faith turned to Dylan.

"You don't need to hang around," she said brightly. "Or if you want to stay, you could wait over by the doors? You'll get bored looking at women's clothes." The last thing she wanted was to be trying on clothes with him within touching distance.

He grinned. "Not a chance. I'm staying to make sure you don't weasel out."

"What if I promise—"

Dylan cut her off. "I'm staying, Faith, so you may as well catch up with Julie."

"Sure," she said on a sigh. She'd come to learn a thing or two about this man, and she could tell this wasn't a battle she was going to win. She followed the path Julie had taken to the formal wear section, very aware of Dylan's gaze on her as he tagged along.

Once they arrived, Julie made a sweeping gesture with her arm to point out the options. "Did you have anything in mind? Some guidelines so I know where to start?"

Faith chewed the inside of her cheek, trying to come up with some ideas. She'd been too worried about being here with Dylan to think about the actual dress.

"Something bright," Dylan said. "Vibrant."

"Okay, good." Julie nodded. "Anything else?"

Dylan rocked back on his heels. "Perhaps something quirky. She looks great in halter necks, but then, she looks great in everything, so that shouldn't limit you."

Faith watched the exchange, a little stunned. Dylan glanced over and caught her expression. "What? I've been paying attention."

He certainly had. Suddenly this situation they were in tonight felt even more uneven than it had earlier. She lifted her chin. "So what are you planning on wearing to the launch?"

He shrugged. "A suit, I guess."

"White shirt and a random tie from your closet?" she asked sweetly.

"Probably."

She shook her head in mock disappointment. "Conservative choice."

One corner of his mouth twitched. "Is that so?"

"New deal." She planted her hands on her hips. "You get to stay and have input into what I wear if I can choose something for you to wear."

He blinked slowly. "You're changing the rules?"

"I am." She stood a little taller. "You got a problem with that?"

"Nope. I've always liked your attitude. Deal." He turned to Julie. "We'll need time in the menswear section as well."

They walked around both sections of the store for twenty minutes, each handing garments to Julie to take to the other's changing room. By the time they were finished, there were probably more clothes in there waiting for them than left on the shelves.

"We're done," Dylan said.

Julie nodded. "Okay, follow me."

She led them into a room the size of a small store in itself. It was circular, with mirrored doors along the outer wall and a round sofa in the middle. On one side of the room was a long chrome stand on wheels that was full of the dresses Faith had agreed to try on, and on the other side of the room was a matching stand with the clothes for Dylan. There was also an ice bucket on a stand, with champagne chilling.

Julie lifted the bottle. "How about we start with a glass of bubbly?"

Faith glanced at Dylan, and he raised an eyebrow, leaving it to her. The night they'd lost control had started with champagne… But tonight they were chaperoned, and she was having fun, so the champagne would be nice.

She nodded at Julie. "Thank you."

Julie poured two glasses and handed them over. Dylan clinked his to Faith's. "Here's to an interesting night."

"Cheers," she said and took a sip before handing her glass back to Julie and heading for her changing room. There were so many dresses, she didn't know where to start, so she grabbed the first one her hand landed on and slipped through the door.

It was an electric-blue velvet, floor-length number. As she was zipping up, Julie called out, "How's it going? Need any help?"

"I'm fine, thanks. The zip is on the side."

She adjusted the dress and looked in the mirror. The color was amazing on her, and the dress itself made her look more elegant than she'd anticipated. As she opened the door, Dylan stilled, his hand freezing on the shirt cuff he'd been adjusting.

He cleared his throat. "Stunning. But it's not the right one."

Faith looked down at the dress. "I like it."

"I like it, too. But it's not the right one."

She was about to argue when she caught sight of the rack full of dresses still to try. No point becoming attached to the first one, anyway. "Turn around and show me what you're wearing."

He held his arms out and turned, letting her see. He'd chosen the most conservative of all the options— a cream shirt with a black suit and charcoal tie. The colors set off his tan, but she smiled and said, "I like it, but it's not the right one."

Julie jumped up from the sofa. "Good, we're narrowing it down. Next! I'll take those two outfits back into the store when you have them off."

Faith grabbed another dress and slipped back into the changing room. For the next five changes, Dylan's eyes heated with approval, but he said each wasn't the right one, so she kept going, wondering what he was waiting for.

And for each of those five changes, she'd also rejected his outfits. Seeing him in a fitted white shirt that accentuated the breadth of his shoulders and his toned biceps had made her mouth dry, but she was waiting for something a little bit different.

She emerged wearing the sixth dress, a light-as-air

confection in mint green that shimmered like mother-of-pearl and seemed to float and sparkle as she moved.

Dylan's eyes darkened when he saw her. "Now we're getting somewhere." He reached out to touch the sleeve, and the warmth of his hand seeped through the light fabric. "This is more how I see you."

"What do you mean?" she asked, looking down at the dress.

"Let me ask you a question instead." He lifted her chin with a crooked finger. "I've seen your heart. When you make flower arrangements, your heart is on display. Crab apple and mint, the Ruby Iris with pale pink blooms and crystals. You're unique, you're creative and you're effervescent. So why is your apartment so plain that it's practically military issue?"

She moved away, giving herself a moment to think. They'd agreed not to spend time alone together, so where did that leave soul-baring admissions? Maybe it would be best not to get too deep for exactly the same reasons.

She shrugged. "I just haven't gotten around to decorating yet. It doesn't seem as if I've been there long enough."

"It's more than that," he said, moving back into her field of vision. "It's part of not wanting to put down roots, isn't it? Being a rolling stone?"

This man saw through her far too easily. She let out a long breath and told him more than she'd ever told a living soul. "There was one time when I was nine. I was living with my grandparents, and I'd thought I was finally settled, that I'd finish growing up at their house." She'd begun to hope. "I looked through magazines and ripped out posters of bands and actors that my little nine-year-old heart was crushing on, and I covered my walls with them. It was more than just putting posters up. It was about marking my territory. That room was mine, you know?"

"Yeah, I do," he said softly, his green eyes intense.

"I spent ridiculous amounts of time arranging who to put where and who could be side by side with someone else. I was so proud of that damn wall when I was finished that I would lie on my bed and just stare at it."

He ran a hand up and down her back, hypnotizing her into a sense of calm. "What happened to the wall, Faith?"

"Nothing. The wall was fine." She swallowed hard. "But my father called one night and said he was picking me up in the morning to take me out to a theme park. Once we were on the road, he told me he was dropping me off with my mother afterward. She wanted to give parenthood another go."

Dylan's body tensed, but his voice remained even. "What about your things?"

"My grandparents had packed my clothes while I was having breakfast—I didn't have a lot—and they were already in the back of the truck." The betrayal of their not giving her advance warning, of always keeping her in the dark, still stung. "Part of me was happy my mother wanted me, but part of me was thinking about my wall. About where I'd begun to feel settled."

"Oh, baby," he said on a sigh. "You had it all ripped out from under you again."

"I never put anything up on a wall again. And the next time I went back to my grandparents' to live— after my aunt handed me back when I was eleven— I ripped down every one of those pictures and threw them in the trash." She rubbed at her breastbone. That damn memory still had the power to hurt, even after all these years.

"Hey, come here," he said, and wrapped his arms around her.

She just stood in his embrace, not relaxing. "I'm okay."

"I know you are," he said gently. "But I'm going to hug you anyway."

It was the perfect thing to say, and she let herself lean against his solid chest to soak up his strength for just a moment. Then she chuckled—of course it was the perfect thing to say, since he was a known charmer.

He dipped his head. "What's funny?"

"You know, I was warned about your way with words," she said, biting down on a smile and stepping back.

His eyebrows shot up. "Who said that?"

She shrugged a shoulder innocently, enjoying his surprise. "One of Adam's staff members at the photo shoot. She also said the girls in Adam's office have a crush on you."

"Really?" he asked, grinning.

She smacked him on the shoulder. "Yes, really. She also said that you could charm the pants off anyone if you tried."

His gaze slowly made its way from her face to her toes. "Lucky you're wearing a dress, then."

"Somehow," she said, her breath coming a little faster, "I don't think choice of clothing would affect your success."

The green of his eyes grew dark, became full of promise. "There's only one thing that's stopping me from trying right now."

She swallowed. "Our personal shopper?"

"No, she's easy to deal with." His fingertips toyed with the neckline of her dress, sending sparks through her bloodstream.

"Oh." And here she'd thought the chaperone was protecting them. "Then what is it?"

He moved closer, surrounding her with his body heat. "We made a decision. In my kitchen."

"We did." She moistened her lips, and he watched the action as he spoke.

"And nothing has changed in the factors that led us to make that decision." His head dipped to kiss a spot just below her earlobe.

It took several heartbeats for her to remember what they were talking about, since his lips were working magic, drawing her into a haze of desire. "They haven't," she agreed, reaching her arms around his neck.

He kissed one corner of her mouth, then the other, his lips brushing hers, featherlight, in between. "So I won't be trying to charm your pants—or dress—off you. I won't be trying anything."

When his lips brushed past hers again, she opened her mouth, intoxicated by him, and he took the invitation, kissing her once, twice.

"Then why are you kissing me?" she asked, using the last brain cell left working in her head.

He pulled away and looked at her with heavy-lidded eyes. "That's a very good question. One I don't have a logical answer for."

She already missed his touch even though his mouth was only inches away. "Do you have an illogical answer?"

"Several," he said with a smile that melted her insides. "Starting with how you look in that dress."

"You don't look so bad yourself." He wore a lavender shirt and a silver tie that Julie had matched with it. "Speaking of our clothes, where is our personal shopper?"

"She slipped out of the room right about when I started touching the sleeve of this dress."

Faith blinked. "She's been gone all this time? She must be getting bored."

"I'll pay her a bonus for her discretion—it will be worth it." He leaned in and placed a kiss on the curve of Faith's jaw. "It's been a long, difficult month."

It had been a difficult month for him, too? "I thought that was just me."

"Why would you think that?" he asked, his voice low.

How far into her mind was she willing to let him see? She sucked her bottom lip between her teeth. There probably wasn't a point in holding back now. "You seemed so together when you came to my apartment, while I was falling apart from wanting you."

His eyebrows lifted. "I thought the same about you. You seemed unaffected, and I was having trouble keeping my hands to myself. In fact, I was getting annoyed that you were so calm."

"Not even close." She smoothed her hands over the lapels of his jacket. "In fact, I thought you must have moved on."

He let out a wry laugh. "I haven't even been able to contemplate another woman since that first night at the Santa Monica store, when you pretty much ambushed me so I would watch you work."

For a long moment she considered just staying here in

this little world they'd created. It would be like heaven. Well, until it was ripped away. Places she wanted to be were always ripped away in the end. And the longer she let herself become used to this, the worse it would hurt when it was over.

"It's been the same for me," she said. "But we've already discussed this, and standing here, so close, isn't helping any."

He drew in a sharp breath and moved back. "You're right." He scrubbed a hand through his hair and didn't meet her eyes as he said, "I'll find Julie."

Nine

The night of the launch, Faith was a jumble of excitement and nerves as she sat beside Dylan in the back of the limousine. Going on a date with this man felt like standing at the edge of a cliff and hoping she didn't fall.

He glanced over and squeezed her hand. "Did I say you look beautiful?"

"Twice," she said, smiling. "But I don't mind."

The limo driver pulled over a short distance from the hotel. "Apparently I need to drop you here so you can walk the red carpet," he said over his shoulder.

Faith turned to Dylan. "Red carpet?"

Dylan grinned. "After the success of the Midnight Lily launch, and since Jenna has come out as Princess Jensine, we were able to attract a few more celebrities this time."

A thought suddenly occurred to her. "Will it be a

problem if you're seen on the red carpet with an employee?"

"Not in the least." He stroked his thumb over the back of her hand. "It's perfectly natural that I'd escort the florist who made the arrangements for tonight."

Put that way, it seemed reasonable, so she let out a breath and smiled.

The driver opened their door and Faith stepped out, taking in the scene around her. Paparazzi lined the street and a crowd had gathered, hoping to catch a glimpse of someone famous. The atmosphere was like nothing she'd ever experienced before and was a little intimidating.

Then Dylan was at her elbow, with a warm hand on the small of her back, grounding her. Keeping her centered.

"I don't know how Jenna lives like this," she whispered.

"Most of the time, she doesn't," he said. "She spends the majority of her days with Meg, Bonnie and Liam."

The image of a little family rose in Faith's mind—the stability, the love. Only in her mind, it wasn't Jenna's family. It was Dylan surrounded by a bunch of kids with her curly red hair and his green eyes. The image was so perfect, so unattainable, her chest ached.

"Dylan," a voice called once they reached the carpet. "Can we get a quote?"

Dylan smiled and waved, then leaned to Faith's ear. "Ebony is from a local morning show. They sometimes do a gardening segment, and I've been talking to them about doing something with us, so I need to talk to her. Can you—?" He paused, then grabbed an arm a few feet away. "Adam, I need to do a bit of media. Can you walk in with Faith? You're here alone, aren't you?"

Adam offered Faith a smile before nodding to his brother. "Sure."

He put a hand under her elbow and they walked through the door, making small talk about the weather. Once inside, he dropped her arm and asked, "Can I talk to you privately about something?"

She resisted taking a step back as his expression changed. There was something serious on his mind. Something he wasn't happy about. But he was the CEO of Hawke's Blooms Enterprises, which covered the farm, the stores, the markets and R&D, above even Dylan, so she said, "Of course," and smiled politely.

He glanced around and then led her through a door marked Staff Only into what appeared to be an office.

Then he turned and faced her squarely, face stony. "I need to ask. What do you want out of this involvement with my brother?"

Her blood turned cold at the implication about her morals. Then she crossed her arms under her breasts and matched his stance.

"What does a woman normally want out of an involvement with a man?" she asked, heavy on the sarcasm.

Without missing a beat, he began to make a list, raising a finger for each item. "Money, promotion, prestige, access to something, an opportunity to sue or blackmail. I could go on."

She coughed out a laugh, more amazed than insulted by his cynicism. "Please don't."

"If you're planning to use whatever it is between you and my brother to get ahead, it won't end well for you."

She cocked her head to the side, examining Adam's face. It was amazing how similar he looked to Dylan, yet how little they were alike. She'd seen a range of expressions on Dylan's face before but nothing this hard, this remote. Adam's green eyes were the cold arctic sea, whereas Dylan's sparked with life and energy. There was no doubt in her mind that Dylan was the better man, and she wasn't going to let his brother push her around.

She narrowed her eyes and poked her index finger into his chest. "Are you always this suspicious of people's motives?"

He looked a little less certain. "I've found it pays to be."

"Well, let me put your mind at rest." She took a step back and folded her arms again. "Hawke's Blooms has been good to me. I would never do anything to hurt the company. And Dylan? He's a good man. I would never hurt him, and anyone who wanted to would have to go through me to do it."

Adam frowned, apparently taken by surprise by her answer. "So you are planning on a future with him?"

"Actually, I'm not. But here's a question for you. How much of this—" she waved a finger, taking in the room he'd corralled her in "—is about the company and how much is about protecting your little brother?"

Adam opened his mouth to answer but then hesitated, frowned and closed his mouth again. Before he was able to find any words, Dylan burst through the door.

"What the *hell* is going on here?" His voice was tightly controlled but his gaze was clearly full of irritation aimed at his brother.

"I was just—" Adam began, but Faith had had enough and stepped in front of him.

"Your brother was grilling me about my intentions. Turns out he was worried I'd sue the company. Or was it blackmail that you were more concerned about?" she asked, moving to stand beside Dylan and smiling brightly at Adam.

Dylan's face turned red. "You said *what* to her?"

Adam held his hands up in surrender as Dylan took a step forward. "It was a reasonable concern."

"Adam, I'm warning you, get out of this room." Dylan planted his feet shoulder width apart and glared at his brother. "Now."

Adam's eyebrows shot up. "Okay, sure," he said and headed for the door. "Look, I'm sorry—"

"Not the time," Dylan said, his voice tight and fists clenching at his sides.

"Right then." Adam disappeared completely from view.

Dylan kicked the door shut behind him and then turned to Faith and blew out a breath. "I can't believe he did that. Sorry doesn't seem enough."

He seemed so tense that she laid a hand on his arm, wanting to reassure him. "No harm done. I was handling it."

One corner of his mouth quirked up. "Actually, when I opened the door, the expression on his face did seem a bit lost."

"Good," she said, satisfied she'd been able to hold her own. "You know, I think he was more worried about us as your brother than he was as the CEO."

A frown line appeared across his forehead. "What do you mean?"

"He's protective of you." Heat radiated through Dylan's

suit coat to her hand, and she rubbed his upper arm, always wanting a little more when she was near him.

He let out an exasperated breath. "He should be more worried about himself."

"Why?" The dynamics between Dylan and his brothers were endlessly fascinating to her, but then again, anything about Dylan fascinated her.

"I can't remember the last time I saw him in a relationship. Or with a woman who made him happy. I don't know why he thinks he's in any position to sort out anyone else's love life."

Her throat was suddenly tight, and she had to swallow before she could get her voice to work. "We don't have a love life. We've put a lot of effort into ensuring that."

"That's true," he said, his eyes pained. "I still love this dress on you, by the way."

She looked down at the shimmering green dress. "Thank you again. It's a lovely present." Then, unable to help herself, she looked back at him, taking in the lavender shirt and silver tie. "And I like you in that suit."

His eyes darkened. "Someone with great flair picked it out for me."

She ran a hand down the front of the shirt, remembering what it felt like to touch him without fabric between them. Without reserve.

He sucked in a sharp breath. "If we're going to leave this room, we'd better go now."

She dropped her hand and took a step back. "I think you're right."

He opened the door and gestured for her to go past, and they walked into the ballroom as if nothing had happened.

* * *

Dylan looked out over the crowd of the fashionable and famous mingling and drinking champagne in honor of Hawke's Blooms. He was still annoyed at his brother but was trying not to let it affect him. He just wanted Faith to have one perfect night to remember, and he wouldn't let Adam ruin it.

She'd bought three dates at the auction—she'd spent the first making flower arrangements at the Santa Monica store and the second making flower arrangements at Liam's research facility. Was it too much to ask that he be able to give her one night when she wasn't working, without his stupid brother ruining it?

He glanced down at Faith and pulled her a little closer against his side as they made their way through the ballroom. They were stopped by several people he knew in the industry, and he introduced Faith each time as the florist who had created the designs that adorned the room. The guests were full of praise, and although Faith didn't say it, he could feel her pride in her work. He smiled inside, knowing he'd become attuned to her feelings.

"Thank you," she whispered just below his ear once they'd moved on from another person who'd been impressed by her work.

He took a moment to appreciate the warmth of her breath on his neck before asking, "For what?"

"I told you once that my dream was to create arrangements that reached lots of people. To spread joy on that larger scale." She moistened her lips. "You've made it happen."

His chest expanded at the expression in her eyes, but he couldn't take the credit. "No, you've made it happen. I might have arranged the opportunity for Jenna, Liam and Adam to see your ideas for the Ruby Iris, but you're the one who impressed them."

"As you said, you arranged the opportunity," she said, clearly unwilling to let it drop.

"Ah, but you were creative enough in your approach to attend the auction and get my attention in the first place." He smiled down into her eyes. "You're one of a kind, Faith."

His mother appeared at his elbow, wineglass in hand. "Here you are, Dylan. I've been looking everywhere for you."

He leaned down and kissed her cheek. "Did you need something?"

"Just to check on you. Adam said something cryptic about wanting me to make sure you're all right. What happened?"

Dylan smiled tightly, not wanting to get into it with his mother. "Just big brother pushing too far."

"Don't be hard on him," his mother said indulgently. "His heart is always in the right place."

Dylan didn't say anything, letting his silence speak for him.

"Okay," his mother said, chuckling. "Sometimes he does take things too far. Now, introduce me to Faith. I've heard such good things about your work from Jenna."

Obediently, he glanced back down at his date. "Faith, this is my mother. Mom, this is Faith Crawford."

Faith smiled and held out her hand. "Lovely to meet you, Mrs. Hawke."

"You, too, Faith. But call me Andrea." She shook her

hand. "The floral arrangements are gorgeous. You've worked miracles with them."

The two women looked over at the closest arrangement, and Faith smiled. "Thank you. I made these final versions this morning out at Liam's facility, so this is the first time I've seen them under the ballroom lights."

The crystals interspersed among the blooms caught the sparkling light and refracted it into little sunbeams across the ceiling. All the guests were commenting on the effect.

"Oh, I meant to say—" Dylan's mother turned to him "—Jenna was looking for you. She wanted you to meet a journalist before you go up on stage. You go and find her and I'll keep Faith company."

Dylan looked from one woman to the other, uncomfortable about leaving them together but not completely sure why. He looked down at Faith and she patted his arm. "Go. I'll be fine."

He released her elbow and threaded his way through the crowd, restricting himself to only one last look back over his shoulder.

Faith watched Dylan walk away with the same wrench in her chest that she always felt when he left.

Women stopped him constantly, sometimes with a hand on his forearm, sometimes by putting themselves in his path. Even from a distance, she could tell he was charming them and then moving on.

"He's good with people," his mother said from beside her. "They like him."

"Yes," Faith said, turning back to face Andrea with a polite smile. "They do."

"Interesting thing is, his brothers are easier to read

than he is. It might look as if Dylan is more open than them, but he manages to keep more of himself hidden. He wears a mask of openness, which tricks people, if that makes sense."

Faith thought about conversations they'd had and the hidden depths he'd revealed. "It does make sense."

"Although he seems different with you," Andrea said casually, and then took a sip of her wine.

Butterflies leapt to life in Faith's belly. First Adam and now their mother—what was it with Dylan's family fishing for information? "You only saw us together for about ten seconds," she said, matching the other woman's casual tone.

Andrea waved the objection away with a flick of her wrist. "A mother can read between the lines. Also, I know my son, and his face is different when he speaks about you."

"He speaks about me?" Faith asked before she could think better of it.

Andrea grinned. "He's mentioned you a few times when giving me an update on this launch and your work with the Ruby Iris."

Faith could see the expectation in the other woman's eyes, the excitement that her son had found someone to settle down with. But it wouldn't be her, and that hurt more than she could let on.

She took a breath and chose her words carefully to ensure there was no misunderstanding. "I feel I need to tell you that nothing is going to happen between Dylan and me."

"Huh, that's funny. I seem to remember hearing the same story from Liam and Jenna a while ago." Her expression said Andrea wasn't deterred in the slightest. "Is this because you work for him?"

"Yes, partly. But it's more than that." Would a woman with a loving, close family even understand Faith's issues with love if she told her? Regardless, this was Dylan's mother, and it was up to him to share the parts of his life with her that he wanted.

"I'll leave it alone, then." Andrea looked up at the stage, where the tech guys were switching on microphones and getting ready. "I think the speeches are about to start."

Faith turned so that she could see the stage, her eyes easily finding Dylan in the group. He glanced up and caught her watching him, a slow smile spreading across his face. Then Jenna tapped him on the shoulder and he turned away.

"Nope," Andrea whispered. "Nothing going on between you two at all."

Faith bit down on her lip to stop the smile and watched the stage. Jenna began by welcoming everyone and gave the crowd a short history of the new flower. When she was done, Liam took the microphone and spoke of his vision in creating the Ruby Iris. Then he handed the microphone to Dylan.

Faith drank him in as he stood tall and confident at the center of the stage, but with that mask of openness, which made it seem he was sharing something with the people gathered. He was a natural, and even before he spoke, the audience was responding to him.

"Hi, everyone," he said, giving them his charmer smile. "I'm Dylan Hawke and I'd like to say a few words on behalf of the Hawke's Blooms stores. We're looking forward to working with this new flower—we think our customers will be excited to have it in their bouquets, and I know our florists are keen to create arrangements that people will love."

He walked a few steps along the stage, ensuring he was including the entire audience in his gaze. "I'd like to thank everyone who's played a part in bringing the Ruby Iris to this point, but I'd especially like to thank one of our florists, Faith Crawford, for working behind the scenes and creating these stunning arrangements we have in the room tonight. Faith, can you come up here for a moment?"

He shielded his eyes from the spotlight with the hand that still held the microphone, then raised his other hand in her direction as a round of applause flowed through the room.

Faith's pulse jumped. She hadn't expected this, but she was touched that he'd think to mention her. His mother gave her a little prod, and Faith began making her way through the crowd until she reached the two steps that led up to the small stage. Dylan reached out to steady her and moved to the side to join in the clapping.

Faith looked out over the crowd and, although the majority of people were strangers, they were smiling at her with approval. They liked her work. She'd achieved another step in her career plan—she'd reached a large group of people with her designs. She'd made them smile. She caught Dylan's gaze and mouthed, "Thank you." He nodded, his eyes sparkling.

Giving Faith's arm a little squeeze on the way past, Jenna took the microphone from Dylan and wound up the proceedings. As the music started again and the people on the stage descended to the ballroom floor, Faith was still on cloud nine. So when Dylan said, "Dance with me," she didn't hesitate.

He took her hand and led her out onto the small dance floor, where a few couples were moving to the music, and then pulled her into his arms. The clean scent of him surrounded her, and she wanted nothing more than to lean into him, to lose herself in his heat. Would she ever be able to be near him and react as if he was any other man? Or would he always have this power over her?

She needed to get her mind onto a normal topic of conversation. She cast around for an idea, then remembered that Jenna had wanted him to talk to someone earlier. "How did it go with the journalist?"

"He was from the same morning show as the woman outside. I've made an appointment to see them both tomorrow, so cross your fingers for me."

"I will." Though she was sure he wouldn't need it. Everything Dylan touched turned to gold. Except her—when he touched her, she turned to flames.

His hand on her back traced a path up, then down, leaving a trail of tingles in its wake. Faith hesitated. "Should we be doing this?"

"It's a date—our last one—and people dance on dates." He pulled her a couple of inches closer. "Besides, there are hundreds of people here. We're in no danger."

"It feels dangerous." Which was possibly the understatement of the night.

"I'll admit that it's lucky I have that limo waiting outside to take you home." His Adam's apple slowly bobbed up and down. "I don't think I could kiss you on your cheek at the door and leave tonight."

She couldn't imagine letting him walk away from her

door tonight, either. In fact, she was starting to think she would have just as much trouble leaving him here and getting into the limo.

"Speaking of the limo," she paused, moistening her lips, "I'm thinking it's probably time I went home."

"Now?" he said, coming to a standstill in the middle of the dance floor. "We haven't been here that long."

In some ways, any amount of time on this date was always going to be too long, especially now when they were touching again.

She drew in a breath, pretending this wasn't going to wrench her in two. "I was here for the speeches, I saw my arrangements in the ballroom full of people and I've danced with the most eligible bachelor in the room. What more could the night possibly bring?"

He grinned and his eyes sparkled with promise. "More dancing with that eligible bachelor."

"Yeah, that's what I'm worried about."

He chuckled. "Fair call."

The music segued from one song to another, which seemed like a natural place to end things. She stepped back, away from the circle of his arms. "Thank you for tonight. You've made it magical."

"You brought the magic," he said, his voice low.

It was too much. Being this close to him, knowing she couldn't have him, was too much. She couldn't breathe. She turned and wove her way through the crowd until she reached the door and could fill her lungs again. Dylan followed and spoke to the doorman. Within moments, the limo had pulled up in front of the door, and with a last chaste but lingering kiss on his cheek, she slipped into the backseat and left the launch—left him—behind.

Ten

Faith sat bolt upright on the studio sofa, waiting for *The Morning Show* to start again after the ad break. Her palms were sweaty—a combination of the hot lights and a case of nerves that just might kill her—so she tried to wipe them discreetly on her skirt.

"Hey," Dylan said beside her. "Are you all right?"

"Well, I've forgotten my name. Will that be a problem?"

He chuckled and rubbed a hand up and down on her back. "They have your name written on the autocue for the host, so that doesn't matter. Just tell me you remember how to arrange flowers."

"I can do that in my sleep." Then she winced as she imagined herself fumbling. "Well, as long as I don't drop the flowers with my sweaty hands."

A man wearing a microphone headpiece waved an arm. "And we're back in three…two…one…"

The host, Lee Cassidy, a woman in her early thirties with black hair pulled tightly back from her face, scooted back into the seat at the last moment and smiled at the camera. "We have a treat for you now. Dylan Hawke, one of the brothers behind the Hawke's Blooms, and head of their hugely successful chain of florist stores, is here in the studio to tell us about a brand-new flower they launched a couple of days ago, the Ruby Iris. And he's brought along one of his florists, Faith Crawford." The host turned to them and smiled her megawatt smile again. "Welcome to the show. How are you both this morning?"

Dylan looked at Faith, giving her the chance to speak first. She opened her mouth to reply but no words came out. She closed her mouth, swallowed and tried again. Nothing. Prickles crawled across her skin.

Dylan smoothly picked up the ball. "We're both great, thanks, Lee. In fact, we're still buzzing after the launch of the Ruby Iris on the weekend. It was quite a night."

"It sounds as if it was fabulous." The host turned to the camera, giving her viewers the full benefit of her smile. "In fact, we have some photos."

The big screen behind them suddenly flashed with images from the night, including one of Faith taking Dylan's hand as she stepped up onto the stage. She was gazing up at him with her heart in her eyes. Would anyone else recognize that? Would Dylan be able to read that expression?

"So, Faith," Lee said, "tell me why you love the Ruby Iris so much. What's special about this new flower?"

Faith steeled herself. She had to answer this time.

She needed words. Any words would do. "Well, Lee, it's red."

Lee raised her eyebrows as if to say, *Is that really what you want to go with?*

Dylan leaned forward. "Of course, there are many red flowers, but there haven't been any red irises before now." He nodded at Faith, encouraging her to pick up the thought and run with it.

"That's true," she said, aware she was probably speaking too fast, but at least her vocal cords were working now. "The most popular iris has been the traditional purple, and a customer favorite is the white, and there has been pink—"

"Okay," Lee said cutting her off, "how about you show us more about this flower. We have a few things over here waiting for you."

"I'd love to," Faith said, relieved she could finally do something she was comfortable with instead of mindlessly listing flower colors.

The guy with the microphone headpiece waved at her to stand and pointed to the counter he'd shown her earlier. Lee followed him over, and the cameras panned to track their progress.

Faith stood behind a gleaming white counter with all the flowers and tools they'd brought along with them neatly laid out, and sent up a silent prayer that she didn't mess this up. Hawke's Blooms was counting on her. Dylan was counting on her.

Lee was at her side. "What are you going to make for us today?"

Faith's nerves were rising, threatening to take over; she tried to breathe through it, but it wasn't working. Then Dylan appeared at her other elbow and passed her a single white carnation. Faith took the flower, and the moment it was in her hand, she relaxed. She could do this.

As she trimmed the base of the stalk, she smiled at Lee. "I'm doing a simple arrangement that anyone at home could try. I'm going to use the Ruby Iris, but you can substitute your favorite flower—say, daffodils or tulips."

For the next few minutes, she worked on the arrangement, bringing the vision in her mind to life, giving a couple of easy jobs to Lee to do so the segment was more interesting.

When Faith was done, Lee called Dylan back into the shot and thanked them both for coming in. Then the guy with the headphones told them they were on an ad break. Lee rushed back to the sofa to be ready for the next segment, a girl with a ponytail guided Dylan and Faith off the set and within minutes, they were in Dylan's car.

Faith blinked. It was over. She'd made her first-ever TV appearance and it had consisted of her freezing and generally messing it up. Her head was still spinning.

"I'm so sorry, Dylan," she said as he slid into the driver's seat.

He started the car and glanced over at her. "What for?"

"You worked so hard to get that segment and I ruined it."

"You were great," he said cheerfully as he leaned over and squeezed her knee. She'd never met someone as skilled at manipulating the truth. If she hadn't been in the studio herself to see the train wreck, she might have believed him.

She raised an eyebrow at him and he grinned. "Okay, so you stumbled a couple of times, but your demonstration was great. You were professional, yet you explained things in ways the viewers would understand, and your love for your work shone through."

"I've let Hawke's Blooms down," she said, trying not to grimace as she said it. She didn't want pity. She wanted to apologize. "Let you down."

"Hey, you did us proud." Before he could say anything else, his cell phone rang in its cradle on the dashboard and he thumbed the Talk button. "Dylan Hawke."

"Dylan, it's Ben Matthews from *The Morning Show*. Thanks again for coming on today."

"Thank you for inviting us." Dylan pulled out to overtake a car without missing a beat in the conversation. "Anytime you want someone from Hawke's Blooms back, let us know."

"I was hoping you'd feel that way. I've just been talking to a producer from our network office in San Diego. I'd asked them to watch out for your segment today and they were impressed."

"That's good to hear," Dylan said, sliding Faith a grin.

"They've been considering a weekly gardening segment, but now they're interested in making it about flowers instead. Maybe how to arrange them, keeping them alive longer, that sort of stuff. What would you think about Hawke's Blooms doing that segment? If it goes well, we could talk about other guest spots on our LA show then."

Dylan squeezed the steering wheel harder, but his voice remained easygoing. "We'd be very interested in doing that, Ben."

"There's only one condition they've laid down. You need to have that woman from today's segment as the florist. Our social media went crazy for her when she was on air."

Faith gasped and then covered her mouth with her hand in case Ben could hear her in the background. The producers had liked her enough to make her involvement a condition? It was surreal. And people watching had liked her enough to comment about her?

"I'll talk to her and let you know," Dylan said.

"Well, talk quickly. They want you down there for tomorrow's show. You'll need to be in the studio by five a.m."

"I'll get back to you within the hour." Dylan ended the call and threw Faith a grin. "I guess you didn't ruin it."

"They want me," she said, the awe she felt coming out in her voice.

He laughed. "They sure do. What do you think? Interested?"

"Absolutely." This was the biggest thing ever to happen in her career—in her *life*—and nothing could make her let the opportunity pass.

"Then we'd better start making plans." He turned into her street. "I'll ring Ben Matthews back and work out the details. I'll also have my personal assistant book us flights and rooms in San Diego for tonight. We'll catch a late flight down and one back after the show in the morning."

His voice had been so calm, planning the details it would take to get them there, that at first she missed the significance of what he'd said. Then it hit her.

"A hotel?" she said as she wrapped one arm around herself. "Us?"

Gaze still on the road, he nodded. "They want us on set at five a.m., and I don't want to take any chances on delays. It would be much better if we're already in town."

"But we agreed…" She let her words trail off, wondering if she was making too big a deal out of this since he didn't seem worried at all.

"Don't worry about it," he said, his voice a notch lower than it had been only a minute earlier. "I'll get rooms on different floors. We'll be fine."

Okay, that seemed reasonable. Different floors should be enough distance if they were both on their best behavior.

He pulled up in front of her house. "You pack a bag and I'll let you know the time of the flight."

"Sure," she said and climbed out. As he drove away, she sighed and hoped she could trust herself to be on her best behavior if Dylan Hawke was sleeping in the same building.

The flight to San Diego was uneventful, and as soon as they arrived at the hotel, Faith excused herself to her room. She told Dylan she needed some quiet time so that her head was together for the show tomorrow, and that she'd order room service for dinner and read the book she'd brought.

But it wasn't that she needed quiet so much as a break from the tension of being with Dylan. Or, more precisely, being with him and not touching him as her body was screaming out to do. That particular tension was going to drive her insane.

And going insane just before going on live TV representing Hawke's Blooms would not help anyone. She tried to drag in a full breath but it felt as if there was an iron band around her ribs, stopping her lungs from expanding. It might have been okay to mess up last time, but tomorrow had higher stakes. It was the first of what could become a regular segment. The expectations would be higher. The crew would be anticipating someone professional. Could she be that professional?

Her cell rang, and the sudden buzzing made her jump. She checked the screen and Dylan's name flashed up. She took a breath and thumbed the Talk button. "Hey, what's up?"

"Just wanted to make sure you're okay."

Even over the phone, his voice had the power to send a shiver down her spine. "I'm fine. I've stayed in hotels before."

"About tomorrow," he said, and she could hear the smile in his voice. "You freaked out a little bit last time."

She sank down to the edge of the bed. "I'm older and wiser now."

His voice dipped, became serious. "Honestly."

"Okay." She blew out a breath. "I'm probably not wiser. Though I'm not freaking out."

"Promise?"

She lay back over the hotel bed and covered her eyes with the inside of her arm. "Maybe freaking out just a little bit. But nothing to worry about. I'll have it under control in a moment."

"Try and minimize it in your mind," he said, his voice like warm honey. "It's no big deal."

She snorted. "It's probably not a big deal for you.

You've spoken in public heaps of times. This is still big and intimidating for me."

"If you worry about it all night, you'll have yourself in a state by morning."

"Is it too late to cancel?" she asked, only half joking. "Or fly someone else up here?"

"You're the one they want."

There was something in the way he said the words that made her think he wasn't just talking about the TV spot or about business. It was in the way he said *want*, as if he was on this bed beside her, whispering the word in her ear. Her pulse picked up speed. Part of her was longing to whisper it back. Longing to walk the corridor and stairs to his room and whisper it in person. But they'd made a decision, and she needed to be strong. She pulled herself up to sit against the headboard, piling the pillows behind her, trying to focus back on the real reason for this conversation. Having her eyes closed when talking to Dylan Hawke was probably not the best way to stay focused on work.

"But if I ruin this, it's Hawke's Blooms that will suffer," she said, shifting her weight against the pillows, unable to get comfortable.

"You won't ruin it. I have every faith in you."

He meant it, too. She could tell. What she wouldn't give to have him here beside her right now, sharing his strength, his self-assurance. She always felt more anchored when he was near. Unfortunately, having him near would also kick her libido into action. What she needed was to stay on topic.

"You said yourself I'll have myself in a state by the morning. Maybe I'm not cut out for this. I'd be better off standing behind the counter back in Santa Monica."

"Think about something else." His voice was cajoling, like the devil inviting her to sin. "Go to your happy place."

"My happy place?" she asked warily.

"A memory or thought that always makes you happy. Do you have one of those that you can use?"

Her breath caught high in her throat. *Him.* "Yeah, I can think of something."

"What is it?"

"It doesn't matter," she said, attempting to sound breezy. "I've got one."

"If you tell me, I can talk you through it. Work with me here. I'm trying to help."

"Okay, it's...um...the flower markets."

"The flower markets?" he asked, skepticism heavy in his voice.

Seemed she wasn't as good at manipulating the truth as he was. Maybe more detail would help. "In the mornings, like at about two or three a.m., when they first open."

"Faith, I don't doubt you like the flower markets. But that's not the happy place you decided to use."

"Sure it is."

"Faith," he said, his voice low. "What is your happy place, really?"

"I can't tell you." She hoped that would be enough to make him drop the subject but had a sinking feeling nothing would make him do that now.

"Why?" It was a simple question, merely a word, but when it was him asking, it became more potent, and she lost her will to resist.

"Because it's you," she said on an anguished breath. "You're my happy place."

A groan came down the line. "Hell."

There was a knock on the door, and she wasn't sure if the interruption was good timing or bad. "Hang on, someone's at the door."

"I know," he said, and as she opened the door, she saw him leaning in the doorway as if he'd been there a while, his cell still at his ear, his eyes blazing.

"You're here," she said. She'd never wanted him more than in that moment. She disconnected the call and threw her cell in the direction of a table, but she missed and it fell to the floor. She left it.

Instead of answering, he reached out with his free arm and dragged her to him, his mouth landing on hers with a comfortable thud. Or maybe that sound was his cell phone dropping to the floor. He stepped forward, so she stepped backward, and he kicked the door behind them closed, blotting out all sound except breathing and the rub of fabric on fabric as they moved.

She grabbed the front of his sweater and pulled him to the bed. The pillows were still bunched in a pile at the headboard, so she maneuvered him to lie diagonally across the crisp white cover. Then she followed, not worrying about grace and finesse, just needing to touch him, to be as close to him as she could.

His leg wrapped around hers, pulling her against him, and she almost melted, but she didn't stop her frantic touching, exploring wherever she could reach. It was as if a fire burned deep inside every cell, and the only thing that could relieve the burn was Dylan. Her fingertips brushed over his jaw, his throat, needing to feel the stubble of his evening beard as if the roughness held the secrets of the universe.

As they moved, his fingers worked at her buttons

until the sides of her top fell apart. She shrugged out of it without missing a beat and was rewarded when his large palm covered a breast. She was rendered motionless, absorbing the sensations, the heat, the pure beauty of the moment.

"Dylan," she said without even realizing she was speaking.

He pulled her bra aside and leaned down, covering the peak of her breast with his mouth, using his tongue, his teeth, to make her writhe.

When he began to undo the button and zipper on her trousers, she lifted her hips, glad he was the one doing it, because operating a simple zipper was probably beyond her. Once the trousers were off, she relaxed her hips, but his hand smoothed over the front of her and her hips bucked straight back up again.

"I've been dreaming of touching you again," he said, his voice urgent. His fingers caressed her over the thin fabric, then moved underneath. At the first contact with her skin, an electric current shot through her body and she shivered.

"I've been dreaming of it, too." Fantasizing, hoping, even though she knew she shouldn't.

She tried to wriggle out of the underpants but there were hands and intertwined legs in the way, so she made no progress until he grabbed the sides and pulled them down her legs. Then he moved down her body and rested his face on her hip, his fingers toying with her, driving her crazy. His warm breath fanned over her, and the world narrowed to just this moment. She felt the weight of his head lift from her hip a moment before his mouth closed over the center of her. She gasped and moaned his name.

He moved her leg to accommodate his shoulders, and she offered no resistance—couldn't have if she'd wanted to, since every single bone in her body seemed to have dissolved. His tongue was working magic, and she was on the edge of something powerful, something glimmering in the edges of her vision. When it hit, he rode it out with her, holding her tight, his face pressed against her stomach.

Then he was gone and she heard his clothes dropping on the carpet, his belt buckle clinking as it landed, the heavy fabric of his sweater making a more muffled sound as it hit the ground. The mattress dipped as he came back into view, already sheathed, crawling over her, hovering, his features pulled taut with tension. She looped her arms around his neck and pulled him back to her, reveling in the feel of his body against hers, leg to leg, hip to hip, chest to chest.

She scraped her nails lightly across his back, eliciting a shudder, so she did it again. He reared back, lifting himself above her, and stilled. "I'm not sure I'll ever get enough of you."

A faint sense of misgiving twinged in her chest—she suspected no matter how much time she had with him, it would never be enough. She pushed the thought away. She'd take the time with him that she could get.

He began to move again, guiding himself to her, and she raised her hips to meet him. Then as he slid inside her in one smooth thrust, he held her gaze. His eyes were so dark she couldn't see the green, just an intensity she'd never known. She was trapped by it, could only move in sync with his strokes, becoming more and more lost as if pulled deeper by an exquisite undertow.

He changed his angle and the friction increased,

becoming too much, not enough. He was above her, around her, inside her. Everything was Dylan. When the fever within her peaked impossibly high, she burst free, her entire body rippling with the power of it. And while she was still flying, Dylan called her name and shuddered, joining her, holding her close.

Minutes later, she was still in his arms, trying to catch her breath. After her experience of being with this man twice now, she'd come to the realization that making love with him was nothing short of explosive.

"We did it again," she said, opening one eye to look at him.

He reached for her hand and interlaced his fingers with hers. "Perhaps it was unreasonable to stay in the same hotel and expect to keep our hands to ourselves."

She thought back over the evening, at her attempts to resist. "We almost made it."

He laughed. "We nowhere near made it. But at least you're relaxed now."

"You're right," she said and stretched. "And if I tense up in the studio, my happy place is happier than ever."

"Tense up? Then you're not relaxed enough. How about I do something about that…"

He reached for her again and, smiling, she went to him.

Eleven

Dylan had fallen asleep, sprawled across both the bed and her, but Faith was wide awake. She wouldn't let herself fall asleep with him. She'd glimpsed heaven with him tonight, and it had made her face something.

He wasn't just her happy place. He was more than that.

She was in love with him.

Sleeping in his arms was her idea of paradise, which was why it would be emotionally reckless. How could she stay ahead of the eight ball and protect her heart if she indulged herself in sleeping beside Dylan's warm body? She couldn't let her guard down and lose her independence in whatever it was they had between them.

From the experience of her childhood, she knew she had a tendency to become attached more often and more deeply than other people did, and she'd done it again by falling in love with Dylan. He would be moving on at some point—people always did—and in the meantime the idea of coming to rely on him for anything, including letting herself fall into a routine of sleeping beside him, frightened her witless. Anytime in her past that she'd started to feel that she belonged somewhere, it had all been ripped out from under her. The path toward letting herself relax and get sucked into the belief that this could be permanent held only heartache.

She slipped out from under his arm—pausing when his breathing changed and he rolled over—and picked up her clothes. After she was dressed, she grabbed her purse and, with one last look at his sleeping form half draped by the covers, quietly slipped out of the hotel room.

She checked her watch. Ten past two a.m. The flower market would be open. She headed down to the lobby and caught a cab. Checking out the San Diego flower market had been on her list of things to do while she was here—perhaps not this early in the morning, but she was grateful for this way of keeping her mind off the man sleeping in her hotel room. The man she loved.

An hour later, she had a call on her cell from Dylan.

"Where are you?" he asked, his voice raspy from sleep but with an edge of concern.

She covered her other ear with a hand to hear better. "Down at the flower market."

"On your own?" Suddenly he sounded fully awake. "Jesus."

"I wanted to check them out."

There was scuffling on the line as if he was dragging on clothes. "Why didn't you wake me? I would have come with you."

Because that would have defeated the purpose of finding some breathing space. "I'm fine, and you needed the sleep."

"I'll come down there." From his tone, he was already set on his course of action.

"No need," she said quickly. "I was just about to leave." It was true anyway—she was about done, and she wanted some time back at the hotel before having to head to the studio.

"Hang tight. I'll send a car for you."

"I can catch a cab."

"The car will be there in a few minutes. I'll call you back as soon as I've ordered it, and we'll stay on the line till you're back here."

"You know," she said wryly, "this isn't my first visit to a predawn flower market."

"Indulge me."

She sighed. He wasn't going to give up, and in all honesty, it was nice that he was trying to ensure her safety. "Okay."

By the time she made it back to the hotel, Dylan was waiting in the lobby. He hauled her into his arms and held her until she could barely breathe.

"Hey," she said. "I need a little air."

He loosened his grip and led her to the bank of elevators. "Sorry. When I woke and couldn't find you… and then found you were out in the city in the middle of the night…" He punched the Up button and the doors swooshed open. Once they were inside and he'd hit the button for her floor, he gathered her against him again. "I can't remember the last time I was that scared."

She'd had no idea that he'd be so worried. That he cared that much. She rested her head against his shoulder and let him hold her. "I'm sorry. I didn't mean to worry you."

"Tell me honestly." He tilted her chin up so she met his gaze. "Why did you go down to the markets?"

It was as if she could see the universe in the depths of his green eyes, and in that moment she couldn't lie, not even to protect herself. "I needed a little space."

A bell dinged and the doors opened. Neither of them said a word until they were in her room again. Dylan headed straight for the minibar and grabbed two orange juices. He handed her one, then took a long drink from the other bottle before asking, "Space from me?"

"From us," she said, choosing her words with care. "Sometimes when I'm with you, it's intense."

He thought about that, putting his juice down and taking hers as well. Then he found her hands and interlaced their fingers. "What if we decided to give this thing between us a go? What would you think about that?"

Her pulse jumped. He cared enough to try? Although it was impossible, it meant so much that he wanted to. "We can't." She lifted one shoulder and let it drop. "The fraternization policy."

"Screw the policy," he said without hesitation.

She coughed out a laugh. "It's your company. You can't be that cavalier."

"What's the point of being one of the owners if I can't?"

"You want to change a policy that's doing some good in creating a safe workplace and protecting staff from unwanted advances, just because you want to get involved with an employee?"

"Okay, it doesn't sound good when you put it like

that. But I want to spend more time with you. I want us to be together." His eyes were solemn as he cupped the side of her face with his palm. "Is that what you want?"

Was it what she thought was in her best interests? No. What she thought would last? No. But he'd asked what she wanted. And she wanted nothing more than to be with the man she loved, so before she could stop it, a whispered "yes" slipped from between her lips.

He stepped closer and kissed her forehead tenderly. "Then we'll find a way."

Her heart squeezed tight. He sounded so determined that she didn't have the heart to say it didn't matter. She'd be moving on. Or he would be. One of them would leave; it was the way these things worked.

But maybe she could enjoy the time they had together? Just because she couldn't have forever didn't mean she couldn't have for now.

So she decided to ignore the consequences, and instead nodded and smiled and said, "I'd like that."

Five weeks later, and Faith's life was going well. Almost too well. When things fell into place this easily, it often preceded a fall, so part of her was on guard. The San Diego job was amazing—she'd become relaxed in front of the camera, and had been getting great viewer feedback on her segments. And spending more time with Dylan was her very favorite part of each day.

She was just shoving a vegetable lasagna in the oven when her cell rang. Dylan was due in about half an hour for dinner, so it was probably him letting her know he was leaving the office. Since the first trip to San Diego, they'd fallen into a pattern of spending more time together, usually at his place. They'd order takeout, maybe watch a movie, then make love, and she'd slip out and head home afterward, determined to keep her vow of not getting used to sleeping next to his warm body.

Tonight was the first time she'd agreed to have him visit her apartment. Things had been going so well, she'd let her guard slip and agreed when he'd suggested it. Her stomach was a tight ball of nerves as she wondered how she'd cope when she couldn't leave during the night. Which, of course, was probably why Dylan had suggested it...

She pulled the oven mitts off and grabbed her cell, but it was an unknown number on the screen.

"Hello?"

"Hi, is that Faith Crawford?"

Seven minutes later, Faith disconnected the call and fell onto the sofa.

She'd just been offered a job. A dream job. A nationally syndicated gardening variety show in New York had been looking for a florist to add to their team of gardeners and landscapers, and they'd seen her work on the San Diego show. Her role would be to teach people about flower arranging in a regular segment, but also to travel with a producer and record stories on high-profile floral arrangements—the ones found in the White House, in cathedrals, at big events. She'd be paid to study up close the very designs she hoped to be making one day, make contacts and share her love of flowers with a huge audience.

Yet she'd hesitated. The producer had given her a day to think about it—if she wasn't interested, they needed to know soon so they could approach someone else.

The job was full-time and in New York. She'd have to move across the country. Leave Dylan. A white-hot pain pierced her chest and she had trouble drawing a breath. Could she do it? It was unthinkable. But what if she turned the job down and stayed? When this thing with Dylan fizzled out, she'd be left without him and the dream job. And in the meantime, she'd still be working for him, so they'd have to keep sneaking around so no one guessed they were breaking company rules.

Outside, his car pulled up. She stood, tucking her hair firmly behind her ears and trying to pull herself together. What would she say to him? She'd never been more torn in her life. She might love Dylan, but her career had been her constant, the rock in her life. She *had* to take the incredible job offer in New York. To do anything less would be cheating herself and banking on a dream that could never come true.

She pulled open the front door and was confronted by the only man who'd ever touched her heart. He leaned down and kissed her and she sank into him, trying to create a memory, because she had no idea how he would react once she told him.

When they finished dinner, Faith gathered the plates and headed for the kitchen, almost as if she was escaping. Dylan followed, determined to find out what was on her mind, since she'd avoided his prodding while they ate.

"You've been distracted all through dinner," he said, standing behind her at the sink and massaging her shoulders. "Which is a shame, because that was the best vegetable lasagna I've had—and I'm not sure you even tasted it as you ate."

She turned in his arms, searching his gaze. "There's something I need to tell you."

"I'm right here." He smiled indulgently and smoothed a bright red curl back from her face.

"I had a job offer today." Her gaze didn't waver—she was watching for his reaction.

He rubbed her arms up and down, wanting to reassure her. He didn't own her. The businessman side of him hoped she'd stay at Hawke's Blooms, but the man in a relationship with her just wanted her to be happy.

"I'm not surprised. You've been doing high-profile work—one of our competitors was bound to headhunt you at some stage."

"It isn't one of your competitors," she said, sucking her bottom lip into her mouth.

He raised an eyebrow, curiosity piqued. "Who was it?"

She named the show and he let out a long whistle. "Isn't that recorded in New York?"

"The job is located there. I'd have to move."

His gut clenched as her words hit home. "What did you tell them?"

"That I'd think about it." She looked at the counter as she spoke.

He withdrew his hands and dug them into his pockets, not liking where this was headed. "And have you thought?"

She hesitated, then said, "There are so many factors to consider. I don't know what to do."

He let out a relieved breath and pulled her against his chest. "If you're not sure, then don't take it."

"Why?" she asked, her voice partly muffled by his shirt.

"I think we have something special here. Between us. If you stay, we can see where it goes." In fact, this conversation had been something of a wakeup call. He'd been happy enough going along, spending time together, making love when they could, but now that the possibility of separation had been raised, he was completely aware of how much she meant to him. He wasn't letting her go.

"Dylan," she began, but he cut her off.

"Don't decide just yet." He leaned in and placed a trail of kisses along the line of her jaw. "Give us a chance." He moved to her earlobe. He tugged it gently with his teeth and then pulled it into his mouth. She gasped and he smiled against her skin. What they had was too strong—she wouldn't leave him. And he'd never leave her.

Digging his fingers into her wild curls, he tipped her head back and claimed her mouth. Even though it had been less than twenty-four hours, it felt like forever since he'd kissed her, and he made up for the lost time. Weeks of having her in his bed at night hadn't slaked his desire for her; if anything, they had increased it. Whenever his mind wandered at work, it was always Faith it went to. The sound of her laugh, her dimples, the warmth of her mouth on him, the way her hips moved when she walked.

Her arms snaked around his waist, grabbing fistfuls of his shirt at the back, holding him in place. He loved the way she wanted him as fiercely as he wanted her.

He spun them around, away from the counter, and pressed her against the wall, kissing her, relishing the feel of her curves against him. He hooked a hand under her knee and lifted, pulling her pelvis closer, and he groaned at the delicious pressure. No woman had ever affected him this deeply or made him want this hungrily.

When her fingers worked on the buttons of his shirt, fumbling in her haste, his heart beat so hard against his ribs that she must have felt it under her hands. Finally she made it to the last button and pushed aside his cotton shirt, spreading her palms over his chest. It was as if her hands were magic; everywhere she touched she left a path of sparks, drawing him further under her spell.

Her top had a bow behind her neck, and when he pulled the end, the knot came undone. She wasn't wearing a bra, so as he peeled the front of her top down, he bared her breasts to his gaze. He cupped them with reverent hands, lifting them to meet his mouth, making her writhe against him and murmur his name. His blood heated, his pulse raced, he was helpless and she was everything.

As she undid the top button on his trousers and dipped her hand inside his pants and encircled him, he hissed out a breath between his teeth, then again as she slowly moved her hand up and down. He dropped his head to her shoulder. He was hers. No question, she owned him. After tonight, he'd make sure they were always together.

Suddenly unable to wait a moment longer, he grabbed the condom from his pocket and took off his trousers and boxers before doing the same with her underwear, not bothering to remove her skirt, just lifting it out of the way. She took the condom from him and rolled it down his length, wrapping a leg around his waist again. This time he lifted her hips, supporting her weight so that she could wrap her other leg around him as well, and then brought her down on top of him. Her sharp intake of breath mirrored his, and he paused to take in the beauty of the moment, of the sensations she evoked in his body and in his heart.

Tensing her legs, she moved up and slowly down again, and he whispered raggedly, "I love you."

The only sign that she'd heard was that her movements became faster, and he met her stroke for stroke, telling her how beautiful she was, loving the way the flesh of her bottom filled his hands. He grew more frantic, loving her, feeling the rising tension in his entire body.

He was near the edge, so close to falling over, but he held on, hovering, unwilling to go alone. He reached down between them, found her most sensitive spot and caressed until she exploded, moaning his name, contracting around him so tightly that he couldn't hold a moment longer. He let go, calling out the name of the woman he loved.

When Faith woke the next morning, she was alone. She reached out to feel the other side of her bed and found it rumpled but cold. Rising quickly, she slipped on a robe and padded through the apartment, finding no trace of Dylan.

A small part of her was relieved. She'd made a decision during the night to take the job and didn't think she could face telling him just yet. She knew that was cowardly—of course it was—but how could she face the man she loved and tell him she was leaving? Instead, when they'd made love, she'd said goodbye with her touch. In every silent way she could.

Maybe tomorrow, or once she was packed and her

flight was booked, she would drop in to see him and try to explain. Maybe by then she'd have found the words.

She pulled on some clothes and dragged the boxes she always kept on standby out of the hall closet. It wouldn't take long—being wary of putting down roots meant she liked to be ready to pick up and travel when the need struck, so packing was easy.

She was on her living room floor, surrounded by sealed and half-packed boxes, when Dylan returned. In one hand he held a takeout tray with two coffees and a pastry bag, and in the other, a bunch of flowers. But his expression…his expression was going to haunt her dreams.

Dylan froze on the threshold to Faith's apartment, feeling as if he'd been sucker punched.

When he'd woken this morning, he'd been so damn filled with love and optimism, all he could think about was waking like this every morning. Of spending the rest of his life with her. He'd slipped out without waking her to hunt down the perfect engagement ring. He knew it couldn't be a standard diamond for Faith, and he'd found a purple diamond in a platinum setting in a window and convinced the owner to open early for him.

He'd been on cloud nine, seeing a rosy future in front of them, seeing everything he'd never known he wanted all wrapped up in one gorgeous woman. Faith. Telling her he loved her last night had felt right, deep in his soul. She might not have said the words back, but he was in no doubt that she loved him. Not after the way she'd been touching him last night.

He'd hoped she'd still be asleep when he got back with breakfast and the ring, but it had taken a little longer than he'd planned. Still, the last thing he'd expected to see was her getting ready to flee.

Again.

Especially after spending a night together that had rocked his world. It was as if all the air in the room—in his life—had been sucked out, leaving him in a vacuum.

"Going somewhere?" he asked mildly.

"Uh, yes."

He took a step inside but couldn't bring himself to sit down or even cross the room. Not when she was surrounded by those damn packing boxes. "You're taking the job, aren't you?"

"It's an incredible opportunity." Her voice was laced with guilt, and she wouldn't meet his eyes. It seemed that they weren't on the same page about this relationship at all.

"When did you decide?" he asked, not 100 percent sure he wanted to know the answer. "Just now, or had you already made up your mind last night?"

She was silent, which pretty much answered his question. He wanted to throw up.

"So you'd made up your mind and were obviously hoping to skip out this morning while I wasn't looking. Were you planning on ever telling me? Or perhaps the plan was a quick call from New York after you'd arrived?"

"I was definitely going to talk to you." She finally looked up and met his gaze, and he could see that much was true. Shame about the rest.

"So," he said and drew in a breath, steeling himself, "telling you last night that I love you doesn't mean anything to you?"

"Of course it does, but love isn't enough, Dylan. It's

not steadfast." She moistened her lips, her beautiful brown eyes pained. "You have to understand that my career is the only thing I've ever been able to count on."

Suddenly Dylan was angry. She was giving up because she didn't think she could count on them? On him? He dropped the flowers on the coffee table and slid the takeout tray down beside the bouquet. Then he reached into his pocket, found the little velvet box, held it up and opened it.

"How's this for steadfast?" he said, forcing each word out past a tight jaw. "I was willing to commit my life to you."

She flinched. "I'm sorry. But you say that now—"

"I said it last night, too," he pointed out, setting a clenched fist on his hip.

She brushed at a tear as it slid down her cheek. "Thing is, I believe you. I promise I do. But once the novelty wears off, you'll be gone. It was never going to last."

"Explain that to me," he said, not caring that his exasperation was coming through in his tone. "Explain how you know what I'll do."

She collected her hair up in her hands, and then let it drop as she sat back on her heels. "One thing I've learned is that love is fickle. All my life I've seen the proof of people's attraction to the next bright, shiny thing. *I* was never enough. My aunt who loved me for a year then gave me up when she got pregnant. My mother who loved me but was always leaving for the next big adventure. My grandparents who loved me but were always relieved when someone else took me in. My father who loved me but wouldn't arrange a job on land so I could live with him. You might love me, Dylan," she said, her voice cracking on his name, "but something else will come along, snag your attention and drag you away. I will never allow myself to be in the position of thinking I'm not enough again."

He'd known she had a rough childhood and that made trust difficult for her, but he couldn't believe she thought their relationship wasn't worth fighting for. Wasn't worth giving a chance. She didn't think he was worth taking a risk on. Weariness suffused every cell in his body.

"You know, you say people leave, but you're the one leaving. It's always you leaving, either sneaking out of my place after we make love, or leaving early from the launch, or going to the flower market at two in the morning."

Then he dropped the ring on the hall stand and glanced over his shoulder. "Ever heard the phrase 'Be careful what you wish for'? You've been expecting me to leave since day one, and here I go."

He walked out the door and across the small courtyard to his car without once looking back.

Twelve

Faith sat on a plastic chair at the window of her tiny New York apartment, chin in her hands as she looked down at the street below. She'd been here for only two weeks, so it wasn't strange that it didn't feel like home yet…though when had anyplace ever felt like home?

She loved the new job, but deep in her soul she'd been numb from the moment she'd arrived. No, before. She'd always been alone, but this loneliness was different—it was a yearning for one person. A tall, flirtatious man with sparkling green eyes and hair like polished mahogany.

Since she'd learned the hard lessons about life as a child, she'd always been emotionally self-sufficient, but something had changed. She'd developed relationships. She'd never let a person get as close to her, under her guard, as Dylan had. But it wasn't just him—she'd become friends with Jenna.

Jenna had called to congratulate her when she'd heard about the job, and they'd kept in touch since she moved. They'd spent a lot of time together while organizing the launch of the Ruby Iris, but at the time, Faith had thought of them as colleagues working together. Now she realized what Jenna had known then—they'd become friends.

Somewhere along the line, Faith had learned to believe in people again.

Desperate to hear a friendly voice, she picked up her cell and dialed Jenna's number.

Jenna picked up on the first ring, her lilting voice a little breathless. "Hi, Faith."

"Is this a bad time?" Faith asked. She was acutely aware that Jenna had two babies and her time was often not her own.

"Now is good. We're out back in the double stroller, walking along the flower beds. As long as I keep pushing them, I can talk to you until snack time."

Faith's mind drifted to when she'd worked on-site at the flower farm and could wander along those same flower beds during her lunch break, sometimes chatting with Jenna or carrying one of the babies on her hip. "Give them both a cuddle from me when you get a chance."

"Will do. How are you?"

"It's all good here." Faith smiled as she said it, hoping it would make her voice sound happy. "Just home from work and felt like a chat."

There was a pause. "Have you talked to Dylan lately?"

By an unspoken rule, they'd never spoken about Dylan, and Faith wasn't sure how much Dylan had told his sister-in-law of what had happened between them. "Um, no. I don't think we've had a chance to touch base since I arrived."

"A chance to touch base? That sounds as if you're talking about an acquaintance."

"Dylan and I worked together," she said carefully.

Jenna laughed. "You're not honestly going to try to tell me that nothing happened between you two. I haven't pushed you on it because I realize things must have been messy, but I've never seen two people who looked at each other the way you guys did. It was intense."

Faith's eyes stung with tears that she wouldn't let fall—they *had* been intense. She swallowed before she could reply. "So Dylan hasn't said anything?"

"No, which isn't like him. I can usually wheedle information out of him, but when your name comes up, he clams up. Come on," she said, her voice ultrasweet, "tell Aunty Jenna what happened. You know you want to."

Jenna was right—having no one to talk to about it had made her heart feel even heavier. "But Dylan is your family…"

"Don't worry about that. If he's treated you badly, I'll be mad at him, but he'll always be Bonnie's uncle and soon he'll be Meg's uncle too. There's nothing you can say about Dylan that will ruin my relationship with him. Tell me what he did."

"He didn't do anything," Faith admitted. "It was me." She curled her legs up underneath her on the hard chair and told Jenna the whole story.

"So," Jenna said when Faith was done, "Dylan loves you but you won't trust him to stick around?"

Already feeling raw from reliving everything that

had happened, the words hit her hard. "It's not about trusting him—it's about relationships in general. I... have trouble believing in them."

"Faith, Dylan is the most steadfast man you're ever likely to meet. He's devoted himself to his family's business since he was a child. He's always there for his brothers, for his parents, for me. You might have trouble believing in relationships, but if Dylan offers a commitment, he means it."

The floor was falling away from under her feet, and all Faith could do was squeeze her eyes shut. He'd been prepared to commit to her as well, but she'd thrown it away. Had she made the biggest mistake of her life?

A man who was committed to all the things in his life that were important to him was nothing like her own family, yet she'd been expecting him to behave the way they had. She'd taken her issues with her family out on him.

She hadn't been fair to either one of them. Her stomach clenched and dipped.

Unfortunately, even if it was a mistake, it was too late. After their last morning together, he wouldn't ever want to see her again. The pain in his eyes when he'd seen her packing her things had felt like a slap.

He would never trust her again, and she couldn't blame him.

Dylan sat in a wingback in his pristine white-on-white living room and swore. Then he took another mouthful of the beer he'd been nursing for a good ten minutes. This room was mind-numbingly dull. How had he never noticed that before? The interior designer who'd done the place had told him it would look modern, crisp and fresh. But it looked bland.

Like his entire life.

When Faith left, she'd taken all the damn sunshine with her. He hadn't found the energy to get excited about—or even interested in—anything for weeks. Maybe he never would again.

He took another swig of the beer.

Regardless, he shouldn't be giving her another thought. She'd given up on what they had, on their future. Hell, she'd left the state without a second thought. The best thing he could do was forget her. Which, naturally, was easier said than done.

There were voices at his door, and then the sound of people letting themselves in. Only his housekeeper, parents and brothers had their own keys. His parents had enough manners not to use them, and it was his housekeeper's day off. Which left his brothers. He sighed. He was in no mood to see them or anyone.

"I'm not home," he called out.

Ignoring him, Adam and Liam headed through the entryway, straight for him.

"So this is your answer," Adam said, shaking his head. "Drinking on a Saturday morning."

"I'm not *drinking*. I'm having a beer and watching football."

Liam made a point of looking around the room. "Are you doing it telepathically? Or hadn't you noticed the TV isn't on?"

"Not yet, smartass. I was about to switch it on when you barged in here. Also, I want the keys back."

Adam crossed his arms over his chest. "We're worried—this isn't like you. Tell us what you're going to do about your relationship."

Dylan looked away. "I don't have a relationship."

"With Faith," Adam said with exaggerated patience.

Dylan pointed a finger at his brother. "I seem to recall you were the one constantly telling me not to get involved with her."

"True." Adam nodded, seemingly unperturbed. "And my word should be law to my younger brothers. Yet you ignored me and went ahead anyway. What does that tell you?"

"That you're deluded about the extent of your power over us?" Dylan looked down at his beer. There was only half left. He was going to need a lot more alcohol to make it through this conversation.

Liam dropped onto a sofa across from him. "That's a good point, and we'll return to that later. But Adam's right. You broke company policy for this woman. I wouldn't have believed it if I hadn't been there watching the whole thing unfold."

"I made a mistake," Dylan said and took another swig of his beer, hoping they didn't see through him, because he'd make that same mistake again in a flash if it meant more time with Faith.

Adam blew out a breath. "I saw the way you and Faith defended each other at the launch. You're in love. Both of you. So why are you drinking here alone?"

Dylan flinched. That was a hell of a question, but not one he wanted to get into with his brothers. "She's gone. Feel free to follow her lead, and make sure you close the door on the way out."

Propping one ankle on a knee, Liam leaned back in the sofa. "Did you ask her to stay?"

Did he ask her to stay? What sort of idiot did they take him for? He drew in a measured breath before replying. "Of *course* I asked her to stay. I even bought her a damn ring."

Liam rubbed a hand over his jaw. "I've come to know Faith, and I think I understand her."

Adam and Dylan both turned disbelieving eyes to him.

Liam shrugged. "Okay, Jenna understands her. But still, she told me a couple of things."

Adam sighed. "If Jenna had some ideas, out with it."

"Faith didn't need a ring," Liam said, leaning forward and resting his forearms on his knees. "She needed you, you moron. Words have always come easy to you, and she knows that, so how would she know what to believe?"

Dylan frowned. "Jenna called me a moron?"

"No, that part was me. But listen up. You have to do something to *show* her that you're in it for the long haul. That you'll stand by her." Liam's eyes narrowed. "You are in it for the long haul, aren't you?"

"Would I have bought her a ring if I was going to bail out?"

Adam nodded. "So if you want her back, you won't be able to rely on your gift of gab. You can't just talk—you'll have to show her."

For a long moment, Dylan was speechless. They were right. He'd known her childhood had been full of promises that had quickly been broken—how had he not realized he'd need to do something more?

People had loved her in the past only when she fitted into their lives, and he'd pretty much asked her to say no to a new job for him. He rubbed his hand down his face. Hell, he'd asked her to give up a great opportunity because he lived in LA—to fit in with his life.

Adam dug his hands into his pockets. "Final question, then we'll leave. Is what you had with Faith worth fighting for?"

Dylan stilled. Was it too late to show her that his love didn't depend on anything else? That he'd take her on her own terms? And how would he show her? He'd have to make a change in his life *for* her. So she wouldn't simply have to fit in with him ever again.

He reached for his cell. "Let yourselves out," he said without looking at his brothers. "And leave your keys. I was serious about that."

He didn't have to look up to know his brothers were smiling, but he ignored them and made a call. He had several calls to make and was impatient to get going. The sooner he started on the plan that was forming in his mind, the sooner he could see Faith.

Excitement bubbling away in her belly, Faith checked the address again and looked up at the building. Yes, the gorgeous apartment building on the edge of Central Park was the right place.

Jenna had called a couple of days ago, saying she'd be in New York for a few days visiting a friend and would love to meet up, and Faith had jumped at the offer.

A doorman asked if he could help, and Faith said she was visiting a friend in 813. The doorman smiled and said she was expected, and then ushered her to the elevator.

Once she'd found the right floor, she buzzed the button outside apartment 813 and waited. But when the door swung open, it was Dylan on the threshold, not Jenna. He looked so tall and solid and gorgeous and *Dylan* that Faith's throat tightened too much to speak. So she just stood there and drank in the sight of him.

After what seemed like an eternity, he cleared his throat. "Come in," he said.

Still without speaking, she walked in, and he closed the door behind her. Such simple actions, but weighted with so much meaning. Expectation. Hope.

The apartment was empty of furniture, but it was beautiful—huge, filled with light, and with great views of the park through floor-to-ceiling windows. But as soon as Dylan was in front of her again, she couldn't look at the room. Or speak.

"Hi," he said eventually, his voice raspy.

"Hi," she whispered back.

Being this close again, it seemed natural, necessary even, to reach out and touch him…but she didn't have that privilege anymore. He'd offered it to her and she'd declined it. She'd left, just as he'd accused her of doing.

She dropped her gaze to the floor. "I came to see Jenna."

"I know." But he didn't make any move to summon Jenna or do anything else. The tension in the room was thick enough to press down on her, make her want to run. But she wouldn't leave this time, not when she had this chance to be near him, if even for a few minutes.

She took a breath, steeled herself and looked at him again. "How are you?"

He lifted one shoulder and then let it drop. "As well as can be expected. You?"

"Good," she said, but her voice cracked, so she added, "I'm good." Her hands trembled with the intensity of seeing him and not touching him, not being able to speak freely. Of being alone with him. "Is Jenna here?"

"No," he said simply.

Suddenly the strangeness of the situation hit her. Seeing Dylan again had fried her brain, so she hadn't put two and two together right away. "Whose apartment is this?"

"Yours." His expression didn't change, giving nothing away.

She took a step back. "What do you mean?"

"I've had a contract for this place drawn up in your name—" he gestured to some paperwork on the kitchen counter through an archway "—but if you'd rather have a different apartment, we can tear this contract up and keep looking."

"I already have a place to live," she said warily.

"It's a present. Although," he said, casting a quick glance around, "if you wanted, this place is big enough for both of us."

"Both of us?" she repeated, not daring to believe he meant what she thought he was saying.

He nodded, his beautiful green eyes not sparkling now—they were too somber. "If you'll have me. Or you can have it for yourself if you choose not to invite me back into your life. No strings attached. A parting gift. Completely your choice."

"My choice?" She circled her throat with a hand. He really wanted her back?

"Or if you don't like the city," he said with a casual shrug, despite his entire body being tense, "we could move farther out, and you can commute for your job. Whatever you want, I'll make it work."

She paused as the pieces of what he was saying

clicked together. "Hang on. You're willing to move to New York?"

"In an instant," he said without hesitation. "If that's what it takes."

It was so unexpected, she couldn't get her head around it. "What would you do here? Your company is on the West Coast."

He rubbed his fingers across his forehead. "I've been thinking that I could open some Hawke's Blooms stores on the East Coast. It makes business sense."

She checked his expression more closely and realized he was sincere. "That's quite a change in your role—moving away from managing the existing stores to starting small again."

"We can employ people to oversee the existing stores to free me up to start the new ones. I've realized that's what I love doing—the buzz and excitement of starting something new. You gave me that by pushing me to think about my own dreams." He reached out and cradled the side of her face in his palm. "Have I thanked you for that?"

She leaned into his palm and laid her hand over his, pressing in, making the contact more solid. "You just offered me an apartment, Dylan. I don't think you need to do anything else."

He took a small step closer. He was so close, she could feel his body heat. Her lungs struggled to find enough air. She released his hand from her cheek, and he let it fall to his side.

"Loving you means I like to do things for you."

"You know," she said looking up at him from under her lashes, "all of this is a big risk for you, given you don't even know if I love you back."

One corner of his mouth turned up in a cocky grin. "Are you going to deny it?"

She was immediately sorry she'd teased. She sucked in her bottom lip between her teeth, trying to think of the best thing to say. She couldn't lie, but it didn't feel like the right time to tell him that she loved him for the first time. It should be special.

His grin stretched wide. "No need to say it. I already know you love me, despite your unwillingness to admit it."

"You always were confident." She wanted to chuckle, but a thick ball of emotion had lodged in her throat and she was worried that if she tried to laugh, she'd cry instead.

He took her hands and held them between their bodies. "You can keep leaving, Faith, but as long as you love me, I'll keep following, even if I have to open stores in every damn state."

His words were the last straw—she burst into tears, and Dylan drew her against his body. Everyone in her life before had found a loophole to get rid of her. By leaving, she'd given Dylan a huge loophole—and he simply went around it to follow her. Jenna was right— he was the most steadfast man she was ever likely to meet. He was a man she could trust to stand by his word.

She pulled back so she could see his eyes, still hiccupping as the tears pressed in on her. In his gaze, she saw his love, his commitment, and she knew she could finally completely trust that he really wanted to be with her and would stay for the long haul.

"I love you, Dylan Hawke," she said, her heart full to bursting.

He lifted her off her feet and spun her around. "I can't tell you how glad I am to hear you say that."

"Hey," she said on a surprised laugh, "I thought you said you already knew."

He gently set her down and tucked her hair behind her ears. "I did, but it's still nice to hear it said aloud."

"I'll be sure to say it often, then." Her voice was barely more than a whisper.

He leaned in and kissed her. She wrapped her arms around his neck, pulling him closer. Weeks of not seeing him, not touching him, not kissing him, had built into a need that she was finally free to let loose.

When he pulled back, his breathing was heavy, but he was smiling. "Do you still have the ring I left on your hall stand in LA?"

She reached down to grab her purse where she'd dropped it, and then dug around before producing the precious little velvet box. "I've had it with me every day."

She passed it to him with an unsteady hand. When he'd left it in her apartment, she'd closed the box and hadn't opened it again, so she'd had only the one fleeting glance at the ring from across the room when he'd shown it to her in anger. She might have carried it with her ever since, but she hadn't given in and peeked inside. Technically it was still Dylan's ring, and she'd known she should give it back, but she hadn't been able to bring herself to do it.

He took the box from her, opened it and retrieved the purple diamond ring.

"More than anything in the world," he said, his voice low, "I want to be your husband and you to be my wife. Faith Crawford, will you marry me?"

"I want that so badly." She swiped at the tears still rolling freely down her cheeks. "Yes, I'll marry you."

He slid the ring onto her finger and then kissed her slowly, reverently. As he pulled away, he whispered against her mouth, "I think this is the start of our biggest adventure yet."

* * * * *

She closed her eyes, and for the merest, most exquisite millisecond, she thought she felt the brush of his lips over hers.

But she told herself she'd only imagined it.

The crowd had dispersed, caught up in another song, another dance, another moment. But Gracie couldn't quite let this moment go. And neither, it seemed, could he. When he began to lower his head toward hers— there was no mistaking his intention this time—she didn't know how to react. Not until his mouth covered hers completely. After that, she knew exactly what to do.

She kissed him back.

The feel of his mouth was extraordinary, at once entreating and demanding, tender and rough, soft and firm. By the time he pulled back, her brain was so rattled all she could do was say the first thing that popped into her head. "I thought you didn't like me."

He nuzzled the curve where her neck joined her shoulder. "Oh, I like you very much."

"You think I took advantage of your father."

"I don't think that at all."

"Since when?"

* * *

Only on His Terms
is part of The Accidental Heirs duet:
First they find their fortunes, then they find love.

ONLY ON
HIS TERMS

BY
ELIZABETH BEVARLY

Published in Great Britain 2015
by Mills & Boon, an imprint of Harlequin (UK) Limited,
Eton House, 18-24 Paradise Road, Richmond, Surrey, TW9 1SR

© 2015 Elizabeth Bevarly

ISBN: 978-0-263-25278-1

51-0915

Harlequin (UK) Limited's policy is to use papers that are natural, renewable and recyclable products and made from wood grown in sustainable forests. The logging and manufacturing processes conform to the legal environmental regulations of the country of origin.

Printed and bound in Spain
by CPI, Barcelona

Elizabeth Bevarly is a *New York Times* bestselling and award-winning author of more than seventy novels and novellas. Her books have been translated into two dozen languages and published in three dozen countries, and she hopes to some-day be as well traveled herself. An honors graduate of the University of Louisville, she has called home places as diverse as San Juan, Puerto Rico and Haddonfield, New Jersey, but now writes full-time in her native Kentucky, usually on a futon between two cats. She loves reading, movies, British and Canadian TV shows, and fiddling with soup recipes. Visit her on the web at www.elizabethbevarly.com, follow her on Twitter or send her a friend request on Facebook.

For Wanda Ottewell.
With many, many thanks
and even more fond memories.

Prologue

Gracie Sumner came from a long line of waitresses. Her mother worked for a popular chain restaurant for three decades, and her grandmother manned the counter of a gleaming silver diner on the Great White Way. The tradition went all the way back to her great-great-great-grandmother, in fact, who welcomed westward-ho train passengers to a Denver saloon. Gracie may have brought a bit more prestige to the family trade by finding work in a four-star, Zagat-approved bistro, but the instinct and artistry of waitressing was pretty much encoded on her DNA, the same way her tawny hair and brown eyes were.

And that instinct was how she knew there was something more to the silver-haired gentleman seated at table fifteen of Seattle's Café Destiné than a desire to sample the pot-au-feu.

He had come in at the end of the lunch shift and asked specifically to be seated in her area, then engaged her in conversation in a way that made her feel as if he already knew her. But neither he nor the name on the credit card he placed atop his check—Bennett Tarrant—was familiar. That wasn't surprising, however, since judging by his bespoke suit and platinum card, he was clearly a man of means. Unlike Gracie, who was struggling to pay her way through college, and who, at twenty-six, still had three semesters left before earning her BA in early childhood education.

"Here you go, Mr. Tarrant," she said as she placed the server book back on the table. "I hope you'll visit Café Destiné again soon."

"Actually, Miss Sumner, there's a reason why I came here today."

Her gaze flew to his. Although she always introduced herself as Gracie to her customers, she never gave out her last name. Warily, she replied, "The pot-au-feu. Yes, it's the most popular item on our menu."

"And it was delicious," Mr. Tarrant assured her. "But I really came in to see you on behalf of a client. I inquired for you at your apartment first, and your landlady told me where you work."

Good old Mrs. Mancini. Gracie could always count on her to guard absolutely no one's privacy.

Mr. Tarrant withdrew a silver case from inside his suit jacket and handed her a business card. Tarrant, Fiver & Twigg, it read, and there was a New York City address. Bennett Tarrant's title was President and Senior Probate Researcher. Which told Gracie all of nothing.

She looked at him again. "I'm sorry, but I don't understand. What's a probate researcher?"

"I'm an attorney. My firm is one of several appointed by the State of New York when someone passes away without a will, or when a beneficiary named in someone's will can't be found. In such circumstances, we locate the rightful heirs."

Gracie's confusion deepened. "I still don't understand. My mother died in Cincinnati, and her estate was settled years ago."

Not that there had been much to settle. Marian Sumner had left Gracie just enough to cover four months' rent and modestly furnish a one-bedroom apartment. Still, she had been grateful for even that.

"It's not your mother's estate my firm was appointed to research," Mr. Tarrant said. "Did you know a man by the name of Harrison Sage?"

Gracie shook her head. "I'm afraid not."

"How about Harry Sagalowsky?"

"Oh, sure, I knew Harry. His apartment was across from mine when I lived in Cincinnati. He was such a nice man."

For a moment, she was overrun by warm memories. Harry had been living in the other apartment on the top floor of the renovated Victorian when Gracie moved in after her mother's death. They had become instant friends—he filled the role of the grandfather she never had, and she was the granddaughter he never had. She introduced him to J. K. Rowling and Bruno Mars and taught him how to crush the competition in *Call of Duty.* He turned her on to Patricia Highsmith and Miles Davis and taught her how to fox-trot at the Moondrop Ballroom.

She sobered. "He died two years ago. Even though I haven't lived in Cincinnati for a while now, when I come home from work, I still halfway expect him to open his front door and tell me how he just got *The African Queen* from Netflix or how he made too much chili for one person." Her voice trailed off. "I just miss him. A lot."

Mr. Tarrant smiled gently. "Mr. Sagalowsky thought very highly of you, too. He remembered you in his will, which was just recently settled."

Gracie smiled at that. Although Harry's apartment had been crowded with stuff that was both eclectic and eccentric, nothing could have been worth much. After his death, she helped their landlord pack it all up, but no one ever came to claim it—Harry had never spoken of any family, so she'd had no idea whom to contact. Their landlord finally decided to toss it all, but Gracie offered to rent a storage unit for it instead. It had meant tightening her belt even more, but she hadn't been able to stand the thought of Harry's things rotting in a dump. She was still paying for the unit back in Cincinnati. She brightened. Maybe Mr. Tarrant could help her get it all into the hands of Harry's next of kin.

"I'm afraid it took me a while to find you," he continued.

She stiffened. "Yeah, I kind of left Cincinnati on a whim about a year and a half ago."

"Without leaving a forwarding address?"

"I, um, had a bad breakup with a guy. It seemed like a good time to start fresh. My mom and Harry were gone, and most of my friends from high school moved after graduation. I didn't really have many ties there anymore."

Mr. Tarrant nodded, but she got the feeling he wasn't too familiar with bad romance. "If you have some time today," he said, "we can discuss Mr. Sagalowsky's estate and the changes it will mean for you."

Gracie almost laughed at that. He made Harry sound like some batty Howard Hughes, squirreling away a fortune while he wore tissue boxes for shoes.

"There's a coffee shop up the street," she said. "Mimi's Mocha Java. I can meet you there in about twenty minutes."

"Perfect," Mr. Tarrant told her. "We have a lot to talk about."

One

As Gracie climbed out of Mr. Tarrant's Jaguar coupe in the driveway of the house Harry had abandoned fifteen years ago—the house that now belonged to her—she told herself not to worry, that the place couldn't possibly be as bad as it seemed. Why, the weathered clapboard was actually kind of quaint. And the scattered pea-gravel drive was kind of adorable. So what if the size of the place wasn't what she'd been expecting? So what if the, ah, overabundant landscaping was going to require a massive amount of work? The house was fine. Just fine. She had no reason to feel apprehensive about being its new owner. The place was…charming. Yeah, that was it. Absolutely…charming.

In a waterfront, Long Island, multi-multi-multi-million-dollar kind of way. Holy cow, Harry's old house could host the United Arab Emirates and still have room left over for Luxembourg.

In spite of the serene ocean that sparkled beyond the house and the salty June breeze that caressed her face, she felt herself growing light-headed again—a not unfamiliar sensation since meeting Mr. Tarrant last week. After all, their encounter at Mimi's Mocha Java had culminated in Gracie sitting with her head between her knees, breathing in and out of a paper bag with the phrase Coffee, Chocolate, Men—Some Things are Better Rich printed on it. To his credit, Mr. Tarrant hadn't batted an eye. He'd just patted her gently on the back and told her everything was going to be fine, and the fact that she'd just inherited fourteen billion—yes, *billion,* with a *b*—dollars was nothing to have a panic attack about.

Hah. Easy for him to say. He probably knew what to do with fourteen billion dollars. Other than have a panic attack over it.

Now that they were here, he seemed to sense her trepidation—probably because of the way her breathing was starting to turn into hyperventilation again—because he looped his arm gently through hers. "We shouldn't keep Mrs. Sage and her son and their attorneys—or Mr. Sage's colleagues and their attorneys—waiting. I'm sure they're all as anxious to get the formalities out of the way as you are."

Anxious. Right. That was one word for it, Gracie thought. Had the situation been reversed, had she been the one to discover that her long-estranged husband or father, a titan of twentieth-century commerce, had spent his final years posing as a retired TV repairman in the blue-collar Cincinnati neighborhood where he grew up, then befriended a stranger to whom he had left nearly everything, she supposed she'd be a tad anxious, too. She just hoped there weren't other words for what Vivian Sage and her son, Harrison III, might be. Like *furious*. Or *vindictive*. Or *homicidal*.

At least she was dressed for the occasion. Not homicide, of course, but for the formal reading of Harry's will. Even though Harry's will had already been read a few times, mostly in court, because it had been contested and appealed by just about everyone he'd known in life. This time would be the last, Mr. Tarrant had promised, and this time it was for Gracie. She looked her very best, if she did say so herself, wearing the nicest of the vintage outfits that she loved—a beige, sixties-era suit with pencil skirt and cropped jacket that would have looked right at home on Jackie Kennedy. She'd even taken care to put on some makeup and fix her hair, managing a fairly convincing French twist from which just a few errant strands had escaped.

She and Mr. Tarrant moved forward, toward a surprisingly modest front porch. As he rapped the worn knocker, Gracie could almost convince herself she was visiting any number of normal suburban homes. But the humbleness ended once the door was opened by a liveried butler, and she looked beyond him into the house. The entryway alone was larger than her apartment back in Seattle, and it was crowded with period antiques, authentic hand-knotted Persian rugs and original works of art.

She began to take a step backward, but Mr. Tarrant nudged her forward again. He announced their names to the butler, who led them through the foyer and down a hall to the left, then another hall to the right, until they were standing in the entryway of a cavernous library. Gracie knew it was a library because three walls were virtually covered by floor-to-ceiling bookcases filled with exquisite leather-bound collectors' editions. They matched nicely the exquisite leather-bound furnishings. And there were floor-to-ceiling windows that looked out onto the gleaming water. She might as well have fallen through the looking glass, so grand and foreign was this world to her.

Her breathing settled some when she realized the room was full of people, since that would make it easier for her to be invisible. Mr. Tarrant had cautioned her that there would be a veritable army of attorneys present, along with their clients—Harry's former business associates and family members. It had come as no small surprise to hear that Harry had left behind a widow and two ex-wives, along with three daughters by the exes and a solitary son by his last wife. Gracie had no idea how to tell one person from another, though, since everyone was dressed alike—the men in suits and the women in more suits and a couple of sedate dresses—and they represented a variety of age groups.

One of those suited men hailed Mr. Tarrant from the other side of the room, and after ensuring that Gracie would be all right for a few minutes without him, he strode in that direction. So she took a few steps into the fray, relieved to be able to do it on her own.

See? she said to herself. This wasn't so bad. It was just like working a wedding-rehearsal dinner at Café Destiné for some wealthy Seattle bride and groom. Except that she would be in the background at one of those events, not front and center, which would be happening here all too soon. Not to mention that, at a rehearsal dinner, she'd be sharing 18 percent of a final tab worth a couple of thousand dollars with two or three other waiters, and here, she would be receiving 100 percent of almost everything.

Fourteen billion—yes, *billion* with a *b*—dollars.

She felt her panic advancing again, until a gentle voice murmured from behind her, "How can you tell the difference between a bunch of high-powered suits and a pack of bloodthirsty jackals?"

She spun around to find herself gazing up—and up and up some more—into a pair of the most beautiful blue eyes she had ever seen. The rest of the man's face was every bit as appealing, with straight ebony brows, an aristocratic nose, a sculpted jaw and lips that were just this side of full. Not to mention a strand of black hair that tumbled rebelliously over his forehead in a way that made him look as if he'd just sauntered out of a fabulous forties film.

She took a quick inventory of the rest of him, pretending she didn't notice how he was doing the same to her. He had broad shoulders, a slim waist and the merest scent of something smoky and vaguely indecent. Gracie couldn't have identified a current fashion label if her life depended on it, but it was a safe bet that his charcoal pinstripes had been designed by whoever had the most expensive one. He looked like one of the high-powered suits in the riddle he'd just posed and nothing like a bloodthirsty jackal. She couldn't wait to hear the answer.

"I don't know," she said. "How can you tell the difference?"

He grinned, something that made him downright dazzling. Gracie did her best not to swoon.

In a voice tinted with merriment, he said, "You can't."

She chuckled, and the tension that had wrapped her so tightly for the last week began to ease for the first time. For that, more than anything, she was grateful to the man. Not that she didn't appreciate his other, ah, attributes, too. A lot.

"But you're one of those suits," she objected.

"Only because professional dictates say I have to be."

As if to illustrate his reluctance, he tugged his neck-tie loose enough to unbutton the top button of his shirt. In a way, he reminded her of Harry, someone who knew there was more to life than appearances, and there were better ways to spend time than currying the favor of others.

"Would you like some coffee?" he asked. "There's an urn in the corner. And some cookies or something, too, I think."

She shook her head. "No, thanks. I'm good." She didn't add that the addition of even a drop of caffeine or a grain of sugar to her system would turn her jitters into a seismic event. "But if you'd like some—" She started to tell him she'd be right back with a cup and a plate, so automatically did her waitress response come out.

But he offered no indication that he expected her to get it for him. "No, I've had my quota for the day, too."

The conversation seemed ready to stall, and Gracie was desperate to hold on to the only friend she was likely to make today. As a result, she blurted out the first thing that popped into her head. "So…this house. This room. This view. Is this place gorgeous or what?"

Her question seemed to stump him. He glanced

around the library as if he were seeing it for the first time, but he didn't seem nearly as impressed as she. "It's all right, I guess. The room's a little formal for my taste, and the view's a little boring, but..."

It was a rare individual who wouldn't covet a house as grand as this, Gracie thought. Although she had no intention of keeping it or much of anything else Harry had left her, since fourteen billion—yes, *billion* with a *b*—dollars was way too much money for a single individual to have, she still felt a keen appreciation for its beauty.

"Well, what kind of place do you call home?" she asked.

Without hesitation, he told her, "Bright lights, big city. I've lived in Manhattan since I started college, and I'm never leaving."

His enthusiasm for the fast-paced setting didn't seem to fit with how he'd reminded her of Harry earlier. But she tried to sound convincing when she said, "Oh. Okay."

She must not have done a very good job, though, because he said, "You sound surprised."

"I guess I am, kind of."

"Why?" He suddenly seemed a little defensive.

She shrugged. "Maybe because I was just thinking how you remind me of someone I used to know, and he wasn't a bright-lights, big-city kind of guy at all."

At least, he hadn't been when Gracie knew him. But Harry's life before that? Who knew? Nothing she'd discovered about him in the past week had seemed true to the man she'd called her friend for years.

Her new friend's wariness seemed to increase. "Old boyfriend?"

"Well, old, anyway," Gracie said with a smile. "More like a grandfather, though."

He relaxed visibly, but still looked sweetly abashed. "You know, the last thing a guy wants to hear when he's trying to impress a beautiful woman he's just met is how he reminds her of her grandfather."

He thought she was beautiful? Was he trying to impress her? And was he actually admitting it? Did he know how one of her turn-ons, coming in second after a bewitching smile, was men who spoke frankly and honestly? Especially because she'd known so few of them. Really, none other than Harry.

"I, uh…" she stammered. "I mean, um, ah…"

He seemed to take great pleasure in having rendered her speechless. Not arrogantly so, but as if he were simply delighted by his success. "So you're not a big-city type yourself?"

Grateful for the change of subject—and something she could respond to with actual words—she shook her head. "Not at all. I mean, I've lived in big cities all my life, but never in the city proper. I've always been a suburban girl."

Even though she'd never known her father and had lived in an apartment growing up, her life had been no different from her friends' who'd lived in houses with yards and a two-parents-and-siblings family unit. Her mother had been active at her school and the leader of her Brownie troop. And even with her meager income, Marian Sumner had somehow always had enough for summer vacations and piano and gymnastics lessons. As a girl, Gracie had spent summers playing in the park, autumns jumping into leaf piles, winters building snowmen and springs riding her bike. Completely unremarkable. Totally suburban.

Her new friend considered her again, but this time, he seemed to be taking in something other than her physical appearance. "At first, I was thinking you seem like the city type, too. The suit is a little retro, but you'd still be right at home in the East Village or Williamsburg. Now, though…"

His voice trailed off before he completed his analysis, and he studied Gracie in the most interesting—and interested—way. Heat pooled in her midsection, spiraling outward, until every cell she possessed felt as if it was going to catch fire. The entire room seemed to go silent for an interminable moment, as if everyone else had disappeared, and it was just the two of them alone in the universe. She'd never experienced anything like it before. It was…unsettling. But nice.

"Now?" she echoed, hoping to spur his response and end the curious spell. The word came out so quietly, however, and he still seemed so lost in thought, that she wondered if he'd even heard her.

He shook his head almost imperceptibly, as if he were trying to physically dispel the thoughts from his brain. "Now I think maybe you do seem like the wholesome girl next door."

This time, it was Gracie's turn to look abashed. "You know, the last thing a girl wants to hear when she's trying to impress a beautiful man she's just met is how she reminds him of a glass of milk."

That, finally, seemed to break the weird enchantment. Both of them laughed lightly, but she suspected it was as much due to relief that the tension had evaporated as it was to finding humor in the remark.

"Do you have to go back to work after this thing?" he asked. "Or would you maybe be free for a late lunch?"

In spite of the banter they'd been sharing, the invitation came out of nowhere and caught Gracie off-guard. A million questions cartwheeled through her brain, and she had no idea how to respond to any of them. How had her morning gone from foreboding to flirtatious? Where had this guy come from? How could she like him so much after only knowing him a matter of moments? And how on earth was she supposed to accept an invitation to lunch with him when her entire life was about to explode in a way that was nothing short of atomic?

She tried to reply with something that made sense, but all that came out was "Lunch…? I…? Work…?"

He was clearly enjoying how much he continued to keep her off-kilter. "Yeah, lunch. Yeah, you. As for your work, which firm do you work for?" He glanced around the room. "Maybe I can pull some strings for you. I've known most of these people all my life. A couple of them owe me favors."

"Firm?" she echoed, the single word all she could manage in her growing confusion.

"Which law firm, representing which one of my father's interests?" For the first time since they began chatting, he sobered. "Not that they're my father's interests anymore. Not since that trashy, scheming, manipulative gold digger got her hooks into him. Not that my mother and I are going down without a fight."

It dawned on Gracie then—dawned like a two-by-four to the back of her head—that the man to whom she had been speaking so warmly wasn't one of the

many attorneys who were here representing Harry's
former colleagues. Nor was he one of those colleagues.
It was Harry's son, Harrison Sage III. The man who
had assumed he would, along with his mother, inherit
the bulk of his father's fortune. The one whom Gracie
had prevented from doing just that. The one she had
earlier been thinking might be furious, vindictive and
homicidal.

Then his other remark hit her. The part about the
trashy, scheming, manipulative gold digger. That was
what he thought she was? Her? The woman whose
idea of stilettos was a kitten heel? The woman who
preferred her hemlines below the knee? The woman
who'd nearly blinded herself that morning with a mas-
cara wand? The woman who intended to give away
nearly every nickel of the fourteen billion—yes *billion*
with a *b*—dollars with which Harry had entrusted her?

Because even without Mr. Tarrant's having told her
about Harry's wish that she give away the bulk of his
fortune to make the world a better place, Gracie would
have done just that. She didn't want the responsibility that came with so much money. She didn't want
the notoriety. She didn't want the pandemonium. She
didn't want the terror.

Maybe she'd been struggling to make ends meet before last week, but she had been making them meet.
And she'd been happy with her life in Seattle. She had
fun friends. She had a cute apartment. She was gain-
fully employed. She was working toward her degree.
She'd had hope for the future in general and a sunny
outlook for any given day. Since finding out about her
inheritance, however, she'd awoken every morning
with a nervous stomach, and had only been able to

sleep every night with a pill. In between those times, she'd been jumpy, withdrawn and scared.

Most people would probably think she was nuts, but Gracie didn't want to be a billionaire. She didn't even want to be a millionaire. She wanted to have enough so that she could make it through life without worrying, but not so much that she spent the rest of her life worrying. Did that make sense? To her, it did. To Harry's son, however…

She searched for words that would explain everything to Harrison Sage III quickly enough that he wouldn't have time to believe she was any of the things he'd just called her. But there was still so much of it she didn't understand herself. How could she explain it to him when even she couldn't make sense of it?

"I, um, that is…" she began. She inhaled a deep breath and released it, and then shifted her weight nervously from one foot to the other. She forced a smile she was sure looked as contrived as it felt and tried again. "Actually, I mean… The thing is…"

Gah. At this rate, she would be seeing Harry in the afterlife before she was able to make a complete sentence. *Just spit it out,* she told herself. But all she finally ended up saying was "Um, actually, I don't have to go back to work after this."

Well, it was a start. Not to mention the truth. *Go, Gracie!*

Immediately, Harrison Sage's expression cleared. "Excellent," he said. "Do you like Thai? Because there's this great place on West Forty-Sixth that just opened. You'll love it."

"I do like Thai," she said. Still being honest. *Forward, Gracie*, she told herself. *Move forward.*

"Excellent," he said, treating her again to that bewitching smile. "I'm Harrison, by the way," he added. "Harrison Sage. If you hadn't already figured that out."

Gracie bit back a strangled sound. "Yeah, I kinda did."

"And you are?"

It was all she could do not to reply, "I'm the trashy, scheming, manipulative gold digger. Nice to meet you."

"I'm—I'm Gracie," she said instead.

She was hoping the name was common enough that he wouldn't make the connection to the woman he probably hated with the burning passion of a thousand fiery suns. But she was pretty sure he did make the connection. She could tell by the way his expression went stony, by the way his eyes went flinty, by the way his jaw went clinchy...

And by the way the temperature in the room seemed to drop about fourteen billion—yes *billion* with a *b*—degrees.

Two

Harrison Sage told himself he must have misheard her. Maybe she hadn't said her name was Gracie. Maybe she'd said her name was Stacy. Or Tracy. Or even Maisey. Because Gracie was a nickname for Grace. And Grace was the name of the woman who had used her sexual wiles to seduce and manipulate a fragile old man into changing his will to leave her with nearly every nickel he had.

This was that woman? he thought, taking her in again. He'd been expecting a loudmouthed, garishly painted, platinum blonde in a short skirt, tight sweater and mile-high heels. One who had big hair, long legs and absolutely enormous—

Well. He just hadn't expected her to look like something out of a fairy tale. But that was exactly the impression he'd formed of this woman when she first walked into the room. That she was some fey, other-worldly sylph completely out of her element in this den of trolls. She was slight and wispy, and if she was wearing any makeup, he sure couldn't see it. Stray tendrils of hair, the color of a golden autumn sunset, had escaped their twist, as if all it would take was a breath of sorcery to make the entire mass tumble free.

And when had he become such a raging poet? he asked himself. Golden autumn sunset? Breath of sorcery? What the hell kind of thoughts were those to have about a woman who had robbed his family of their rightful legacy? What the hell kind of thoughts were those for a man to have, period? Where the hell had his testosterone got to?

On the other hand, he was beginning to see how his father had been taken in by her. Obviously, she was the kind of grifter who got better results as a vestal virgin than a blonde bombshell. Harrison had almost fallen into her trap himself.

It didn't matter *how* she'd conned his father. What mattered was that she'd swindled one of the last century's most savvy businessmen and convinced him to turn his back on everyone and everything he'd loved in life. Well, as far as his father *could* have loved anyone or anything—other than his fortune, his commercial holdings and his social standing. But then, what else was there to love? Money, power and position were the only things a person could count on. Or, at least, they had been, before everything went to hell, thanks to this, this…

Harrison took a step backward, and met Grace Sumner's gaze coolly. "*You're* the trashy, scheming, manipulative gold digger?" he asked. Then, because something in her expression looked genuinely wounded by the comment—wow, she really was good—he tempered it by adding, "I thought you'd be taller."

She mustered a smile he would have sworn was filled with anxiety if he hadn't known she was a woman who made her way in the world by conning people. "Well, I guess zero out of five isn't bad."

Harrison opened his mouth to say something else, but Bennett Tarrant—another thorn in the Sage family's side for the last two years—appeared next to Gracie, as if conjured by one of her magic spells.

"I see you've met Mr. Sage," he said unnecessarily.

"Yep," Grace said, her gaze never leaving Harrison's.

Tarrant turned to Harrison. "And I see you've met Miss Sumner."

"Yep," Harrison said, his gaze never leaving Grace's.

The silence that ensued was thick enough to hack with a meat cleaver. Until Tarrant said, "We should head for our seats. We'll be starting shortly."

Instead of doing as Tarrant instructed, Harrison found it impossible to move his feet—or remove his gaze from Grace Sumner. Damn. She really was some kind of enchantress.

In an effort to make himself move away, he reminded himself of everything he and his mother had been through since his father's disappearance fifteen years ago. And he reminded himself how his mother would be left with nothing, thanks to this woman who had, by sheer, dumb luck, stumbled onto an opportunity to bleed the last drop out of a rich, feeble-minded old man.

Fifteen years ago—half a lifetime—Harrison had

gone down to breakfast to find his parents seated, as
they always were, at a dining-room table capable of
seating twenty-two people. But instead of sitting side
by side, they sat at each end, as far apart as possible.
As usual, his father had had his nose buried in the
Wall Street Journal while his mother had been flip-
ping through the pages of a program for Milan Fashion
Week. Or maybe Paris Fashion Week. Or London Fashion Week. Or, hell, Lickspittle, Idaho, Fashion Week for
all he knew. So he'd taken his regular place at the table
midway between them, ensuring that none of them
was close enough to speak to the others. It was, after
all, a Sage family tradition to not speak to each other.

They'd eaten in silence until their butler entered
with his daily reminder that his father's car had arrived to take him to work, his mother's car had arrived
to take her shopping and Harrison's car had arrived
to take him to school. All three Sages had then risen
and made their way to their destinations, none saying
a word of farewell—just as they had every morning.
Had Harrison realized then that that would be the last
time he ever saw his father, he might have…

What? he asked himself. Told him to have a nice
day? Given him a hug? Said, "I love you"? He wasn't
sure he'd even known how to do any of those things
when he was fifteen. He wasn't sure he knew how to
do any of them now. But he might at least have told his
father…something.

He tamped down a wave of irritation. He just wished
he and his father had talked more. Or at all. But that
was kind of hard to do when the father spent 90 percent of his time at work and the son spent 90 percent
of his time in trouble. Because Harrison remembered

something else about that day. The night before his father took off, Harrison had come home in the back-seat of a squad car, because he'd been caught helping himself to a couple of porno magazines and a bottle of malt liquor at a midtown bodega.

Five months after his father's disappearance had come the news from one of the family's attorneys that he had been found, but that he had no intention of coming home just yet. Oh, he would stay in touch with one of his attorneys and a couple of business associates, to make sure the running of Sage Holdings, Inc. continued at its usual pace and to keep himself from being declared legally dead. But he wouldn't return to his work life—or his home life—anytime soon. To those few with whom he stayed in contact he paid a bundle to never reveal his whereabouts. He'd come back when he felt like it, he said. And then he never came back at all.

Harrison looked at Grace Sumner again, at the deceptively beautiful face and the limitless dark eyes. Maybe two judges had decided she was entitled to the personal fortune his father had left behind. But there was no way Harrison was going down without a fight. He would prove once and for all, unequivocally, that she wasn't entitled to a cent. He'd been so sure the appeals court would side with the family that he hadn't felt it necessary to play his full hand. Until now. And now…

Soon everyone would know that the last thing Grace Sumner was was a fey, unearthly creature. In fact, she was right at home in this den of trolls.

Gracie wanted very much to say something to Harry's son before leaving with Mr. Tarrant. But his expression had gone so chilly, she feared anything she offered by way of an explanation or condolences would go unheard. Still, she couldn't just walk away. The man had lost his father—twice—and had no chance to make amends at this point. His family's life had been turned upside down because of Harry's last wishes and what he'd asked her to do with his fortune. She supposed she couldn't blame Harrison III for the cool reception.

Nevertheless, she braved a small smile and told him, "I doubt you'll believe me, but it *was* nice to meet you, Mr. Sage. I'm so sorry about your father. He was the kindest, most decent man I ever met."

Without giving him a chance to respond, she turned to follow Mr. Tarrant to the other side of the room, where chairs had been set up for everyone affected by Harry's will. They were arranged in two arcs that faced each other, with a big-screen TV on one side. She seated herself between Mr. Tarrant and two attorneys from his firm, almost as if the three of them were circling the wagons to protect her.

Gus Fiver, the second in command at Tarrant, Fiver & Twigg, looked to be in his midthirties and was as fair and amiable as Harrison Sage was dark and moody— though Gus's pinstripes looked to be every bit as expensive. Renny Twigg, whom Mr. Tarrant had introduced as one of their associates—her father was the Twigg in the company's name—was closer in age to Gracie's twenty-six. Renny was a petite brunette who didn't seem quite as comfortable in her own pinstripes. Even with her tidy chignon and perfectly manicured hands, she looked like the kind of woman who would be happier working outdoors, preferably at a job that involved wearing flannel.

Everyone else in the room was either connected to Harry in some way or an attorney representing someone's interests. Seated directly across from Gracie—naturally—were Harry's surviving family members and their attorneys. In addition to Harrison Sage III, there was his mother and Harry's widow, Vivian Sage, not to mention a veritable stable of ex-wives and mistresses and a half-dozen additional children—three of whom were even legitimate. As far as professional interests went, Harry had had conglomerates and corporations by the boatload. Add them together, and it totaled a financial legacy of epic proportion. Nearly all of what hadn't gone back to the businesses was now legally Gracie's. Harry had left a little to a handful of other people, but the rest of his fortune—every brick, byte and buck—had gone to her.

Oh, where was a paper bag for hyperventilating into when she needed it?

Once everyone was seated and silent, Bennett Tarrant rose to address the crowd. "Thank you all for coming. This meeting is just a formality, since Mr. Sage's estate has been settled by the court, and—"

"Settled doesn't mean the ruling can't be appealed," Harrison Sage interrupted, his voice booming enough to make Gracie flinch. "And we plan to file within the next two weeks."

"I can't imagine how that's necessary," Mr. Tarrant said. "An appeal has already supported the court's initial ruling in Miss Sumner's favor. Unless some new information comes to light, any additional appeal will only uphold those rulings."

Harrison opened his mouth to say more, but his attorney, a man of Mr. Tarrant's age and demeanor, placed a hand lightly on his arm to halt him. "New information will come to light," the man said.

Mr. Tarrant looked in no way concerned. "Mr. Landis, it has been twice determined that Harrison Sage, Jr., was of sound mind and body when he left the bulk of his personal estate to Grace Sumner. Another appeal would be—"

"Actually, we'll disprove that this time," Mr. Landis stated unequivocally. "And we will prove that not only did Grace Sumner exert undue influence over Mr. Sage of a sexual nature, but that—"

"What?" This time Gracie was the one to interrupt.

Mr. Landis ignored her, but she could practically feel the heat of Harrison Sage's gaze.

Mr. Landis continued, "We'll prove that not only did Grace Sumner exert undue influence over Mr. Sage of a sexual nature, but that he contracted a sexually transmitted disease from her which rendered him mentally incapacitated."

"What?" Gracie erupted even more loudly.

She started to rise from her chair, but Gus Fiver gently covered her shoulder with his hand, willing her to ignore the allegation. With much reluctance, Gracie made herself relax. But if looks could kill, the one she shot Harrison Sage would have rendered him a pile of ash.

Especially after his attorney concluded, "She used sex to seduce and further incapacitate an already fragile old man, and then took advantage of his diminished state to convince him to leave his money and assets to her. We're hiring a private investigator to gather the necessary evidence, since this is something that has only recently come to light."

"I see," Mr. Tarrant replied. "Or perhaps it's something you've pulled out of thin air in a vain last-ditch effort."

Unbelievable, Gracie thought. Even if she'd known Harry was worth a bundle, she never would have taken advantage of him. And she certainly wouldn't have used her alleged *sexual wiles*, since she didn't even have *a* sexual wile, never mind sexual *wiles*, plural. True friendship was worth way more than money and was a lot harder to find. And incapacitated? Diminished? Harry? Please. He'd been full of piss and vinegar until the minute that damned aneurysm brought him down.

Mr. Tarrant met the other attorney's gaze levelly. "Harrison Sage, Jr. changed his will in person, in the office of his attorneys, two of whom are seated in this room. And he presented to them not only a document from his physician stating his excellent health, both mental and physical, but his physician was also present to bear witness in that office. Your father's intent was crystal clear. He wished for Grace Sumner to inherit the bulk of his personal estate. Two judges have agreed. Therefore Miss Sumner *does* inherit the bulk of his personal estate.

"Now then," he continued, "on the day he amended his will for the last time, Mr. Sage also made a video at his attorneys' office that he wanted Miss Sumner and his family and associates, along with their representatives, to view. Renny, do you mind?"

Renny Twigg aimed a remote at the TV. A second later, Harry's face appeared on the screen, and Gracie's stomach dropped. He looked nothing like the Harry she remembered. He was wearing a suit and tie not unlike the other power suits in the room, a garment completely at odds with the wrinkled khakis and sweatshirts he'd always worn in Cincinnati. His normally untidy hair had been cut and styled by a pro. His expression was stern, and his eyes were flinty. He looked like a billionaire corporate mogul—humorless, ruthless and mean. Then he smiled his Santa Claus smile and winked, and she knew this was indeed the Harry she had known and loved. Suddenly, she felt much better.

"Hey there, Gracie," he said in the same playful voice with which he'd always greeted her. "I'm sorry we're meeting like this, kiddo, because it means I'm dead."

Unbidden tears pricked Gracie's eyes. She really did miss Harry. He was the best friend she'd ever had. Without thinking, she murmured, "Hi, Harry."

Every eye in the room fell upon her, but Gracie didn't care. Let them think she was a lunatic, talking to someone on a TV screen. In that moment, it felt as if Harry were right there with her. And it had been a long time since she'd been able to talk to him.

"And if you're watching this," he continued, "it also means you know the truth about who I really am, and that you're having to share a room with members of my original tribe. I know from experience what a pain in the ass that can be, so I'll keep this as brief as I can. Here's the deal, kiddo. I hope it didn't scare the hell out of you when you heard how much I left you. I'm sorry I never told you the truth about myself when I was alive. But by the time I met you, I was way more Harry Sagalowsky than I was Harrison Sage, so I wasn't really lying. You wouldn't have liked Harrison, anyway. He was a prick."

At this, Gracie laughed out loud. It was just such a Harry thing to say. When she felt eyes on her again, she bit her lip to stifle any further inappropriate outbursts. Inappropriate to those in the room, anyway. Harry wouldn't have minded her reaction at all.

He continued, "That's why I wanted to stop being Harrison. One day, I realized just how far I'd gotten from my roots, and how much of myself I'd lost along the way. People love rags-to-riches stories like mine, but those stories never mention all the sacrifices you have to make while you're clawing for those riches, and how a lot of those sacrifices are of your morals, your ethics and your character."

Gracie sobered at that. She'd never heard Harry sound so serious. He grew more so as he described how, by the time he'd left his old life, he'd become little more than a figurehead for his companies, and how unhappy his home life had become, and how all he'd wanted was to escape. So he left his work, his family and his "big-ass Long Island estate," returned to the surname his ancestors had changed generations ago and moved back to the blue-collar neighborhood in Cincinnati where he grew up.

At this, Gracie glanced across the room at Vivian and Harrison and saw them looking at the television with identical expressions—a mixture of annoyance, confusion and something else she couldn't identify. She tried to be sympathetic. She couldn't imagine what it must be like for them, being ignored by their husband and father for fifteen years, and then being disinherited by him. She supposed they were justified in some of their feelings toward Harry.

But maybe they should take a minute to wonder

why Harry had done this. He hadn't been the kind of man to turn his back on people, unless those people had given him a reason to do it.

Harry spoke from the video again, bringing Gracie's attention back around. "Vivian and Harrison, this part is for you. Billions of dollars is way too much for anyone to have. Gracie Sumner is the kind of person who will understand what an awesome responsibility that much money is, and she'll do the right thing by it. She won't keep it for herself. I know her. She'll get rid of it as quickly as she can, and she'll make sure it gets into the hands of people who need it."

At this, Gracie braved another look across the room. Vivian Sage, her hair silver, her suit gold, her fingers and wrists bedecked in gemstones of every color, looked like she wanted to cry. Harrison, however, was staring right at Gracie. But his expression was unreadable. He could have been wondering where to eat lunch later or pondering where to hide her body. She hadn't a clue.

Thankfully, Harry's mention of her name gave her a reason to look back at the TV. "Gracie, this part's for you. I could have given my money to worthy causes myself and saved you a lot of trouble. But being a better person than I am, you'll know better than I would what to do with all my filthy lucre. But listen, kiddo. This last part is really important. Keep some of the money for yourself. I mean it. Buy yourself one of those ridiculous little cars you like. Or a house on the water. Go to Spain like you said you wanted to. Something. You promise?"

Again, Gracie felt every gaze in the room arc toward her. She had no idea what to say. It just felt wrong to take Harry's money, even a modest sum. After that first meeting with Mr. Tarrant, Gracie had gone home and headed straight for Google. In every article she'd read about Harrison Sage, Jr., he'd been defined by his wealth. "Billionaire Harrison Sage, Jr.," he'd invariably been called. Even after his disappearance, when the word *recluse* had been added to his descriptions, it had still always been preceded by the word *billionaire*. In his old life, Harry had been, first and foremost, rich. Anything else had been incidental. Gracie didn't want to be one of the people who saw only dollar signs in conjunction with his name, and she didn't want to be one of the ones who took from him. Especially after he'd given so much to her.

"Promise me, Gracie," he said again from the big screen, obviously having known she would hesitate.

"Okay, Harry," she replied softly. "I promise."

"That's my girl," Harry said with another wink.

He said his farewells, and then the TV screen went dark. Again, Gracie felt tears threatening. Hastily, she fished a handkerchief out of her purse and pressed it first to one eye, then the other.

Across the room, Harrison Sage began a slow clap. "Oh, well done, Ms. Sumner," he said. "Definitely an award-worthy performance. I can see how my father was so taken in by you."

"Were I you, Mr. Sage," Bennett Tarrant interjected, "I would be careful what I said to the woman who owns the Long Island mansion my mother calls home."

It hit Gracie then, finally, just how much power she wielded at the moment. Legally, she could indeed toss Vivian Sage into the street and move into the Long Island house herself. That was what a trashy, scheming,

manipulative gold digger who'd used her sexual wiles
to take advantage of a fragile old man would do.

So she said, "Mr. Tarrant, what do I have to do to
deed the Long Island house and everything in it to Mrs.
Sage? This is her home. She should own it, not me."

Harrison Sage eyed Gracie warily at the comment,
but he said nothing. Something in Vivian's expression,
though, softened a bit.

"It's just a matter of drawing up the paperwork,"
Mr. Tarrant said. "Today being Wednesday, we could
have everything ready by the end of next week. If you
don't mind staying in the city for a little while longer."

Gracie expelled a soft sigh. Harry's Long Island
estate had to be worth tens of millions of dollars, and
its contents worth even more. Just shedding that small
portion of his wealth made her feel better.

"I don't mind staying in the city awhile longer,"
Gracie said. "It'll be fun. I've never been to New York
before. Could you recommend a hotel? One that's not
too expensive? The one I'm in now is pretty steep, but
I hadn't planned to stay more than a couple of nights."

"It's New York City, Gracie," Mr. Tarrant said with
a smile. "There's no such thing as *not too expensive*."

"Oh, you don't want to stay in the city," Vivian said.
"Darling, it's so crowded and noisy. Spend the time
with us in the Hamptons. It's beautiful in June.
We've been having *such* lovely evenings."

Harrison looked at his mother as if she'd grown a
second head. "You can't be serious."

Gracie, too, thought Vivian must be joking. A minute ago, she'd looked as if she wanted Gracie to spontaneously combust. Now she was inviting her to stay

at the house? Why? So she could suffocate Gracie in her sleep?

"Of course I'm serious," Vivian said. "If Grace—you don't mind if I call you Grace, do you, darling?—is kind enough to give me the house, the least I can do is make her comfortable here instead of having her stay in a stuffy old hotel in the city. Don't you think so, Harrison?"

What Harrison was thinking, Gracie probably didn't want to know. Not if the look on his face was any indication.

"Please, Grace?" Vivian urged. "We've all gotten off on the wrong foot. This just came as such a shock, that's all. Let us make amends for behaving badly. You can tell us all about how you met my husband and what he was like in Cincinnati, and we can tell you about his life here before you met him."

Gracie wasn't sure how to respond. Was Vivian really being as nice as she seemed? Did she really want to mend fences? Or was there still some potential for the suffocation thing?

Gracie gave herself a good mental shake. She'd been a billionaire for barely a week, and already she was seeing the worst in people. This was exactly why she didn't want to be rich—she didn't want to be suspicious of everyone she met.

Of course Vivian was being nice. Of course she wanted to make amends. And it *would* be nice to hear about Harry's life before Gracie met him. She'd always thought the reason he didn't talk about himself was because he thought she'd be bored. His life must have been fascinating.

For some reason, that made Gracie look at Harrison

again. He was no longer glowering at her, and in that moment, she could see some resemblance between him and his father. They had the same blue eyes and square jaw, but Harrison was a good three inches taller and considerably broader in the shoulders than Harry had been. She wondered if he had other things in common with his father. Did he share Harry's love of baseball or his irreverent sense of humor? Did he prefer pie to cake, the way his father had? Could he cook chili and fox-trot with the best of them?

And why did she suddenly kind of want to find out?

"All right," she said before realizing she'd made the decision. "It's nice of you to open your home to me, Mrs. Sage. Thank you."

"Call me Vivian, darling," the older woman replied with a smile. "I'm sure we're all going to be very good friends before the week is through."

Gracie wasn't so sure about that. But Vivian seemed sincere. She, at least, might turn out to be a friend. But Harrison? Well. With Harrison, Gracie would just hope for the best.

And, of course, prepare for the worst.

Three

Gracie awoke her second day on Long Island feeling only marginally less uncomfortable than she had on her first. Dinner with Vivian last night—Harrison was, not surprisingly, absent—had been reasonably polite, if not particularly chatty on Gracie's part. But she still felt out of place this morning. Probably because she was out of place. The bedroom in which Vivian had settled her was practically the size of her entire apartment back in Seattle. Jeez, the bed was practically the size of her apartment back in Seattle. The ceiling was pale blue with wisps of white clouds painted on one side that gradually faded into a star-spattered twilight sky on the other. The satiny hardwood floor was scattered with fringed flowered rugs, and the furniture and curtains could have come from the Palace at Versailles.

How could Harry have lived in a house like this?

It was nothing like him. His apartment had been furnished with scarred castoffs, and the rugs had been threadbare. His walls had been decorated with Cincinnati Reds memorabilia, some vintage posters advertising jazz in Greenwich Village and a couple of paint-by-number cocker spaniels. And Harry had loved that apartment.

There had been no ocean whispers drifting through the windows in the old neighborhood. No warm, salt-laden breezes. No deserted beaches. No palatial homes. There had been tired, well-loved old houses crowded together. There had been broken sidewalks with violets growing out of the cracks. There had been rooms crammed with remnants of lives worked hard, but well spent, too. Life. That was what had been in her and Harry's old neighborhood. Real life. The sort of life she'd always lived. The sort of life she'd assumed Harry had lived, too.

Why had a man who could have had and done anything he wanted abandoned it all to live in a tiny apartment in a working-class neighborhood six hundred miles away? Harry Sagalowsky, alleged retired TV repairman, had turned out to be quite the mystery man.

For some reason, that thought segued to others about Harry's son. Harrison Sage was kind of a mystery, too. Was he the charming flirt she'd first met in the library yesterday? Or was he the angry young man who was convinced she had taken advantage of his father? And why was it so important that she convince him she wasn't like that at all?

Today would be better, she told herself as she padded to the guest bathroom to shower. Because today she and Harrison—and Vivian, too—would have a chance to get to know each other under better circumstances. They would get to know each other period. It was a new day. A day to start over. Surely, Harrison Sage would feel that way, too. Surely, he would give her a chance to prove she was nothing like the person he thought she was.

Surely, he would.

Harrison was deliberately late for breakfast, hoping that by the time he showed up, Grace Sumner would have left, miffed to be shown so little regard now that she was richer and more important than 99 percent of the world. Instead, when he ambled out to the patio, freshly showered and wearing a navy blue polo and khakis more suitable for playing golf than for being intimidating, he found her sitting poolside with his mother. Even worse, the two women were laughing the way women did when they realized they had some shared experience that had gone awry.

And damned if Grace Sumner didn't have a really nice laugh, genuine and uninhibited, as if she laughed a lot.

His mother sat on one side of the table, still in her pajamas and robe. Grace sat on the other, looking nothing like a gold digger and very much like a girl next door. At least, she looked like what Harrison figured a girl next door was supposed to look like. It was the way girls next door always looked in movies, all fresh and sweet and innocent. He'd never seen an actual girl next door who looked like that, since the girls he'd grown up with who lived next door—a half mile down the beach—had always looked...well, kind of like gold diggers, truth be told.

But not Grace Sumner. Her burnished hair was in a ponytail today, the breeze buffeting a few loose strands around her nape and temple in a way that made Harrison itch to tuck them back into place, just so he could watch the wind dance with them again. Her flawless face was bathed in late morning sunlight, making her skin rosy. The retro suit of the day before had been replaced by retro casual clothes today—a sleeveless white button-up shirt and those pants things that weren't actually pants, but weren't shorts, either, and came to about midcalf. Hers were spattered with big, round flowers in yellow and pink. Her only jewelry was a pink plastic bracelet that had probably set her back at least two dollars. Maybe as much as three.

Had he not known better, he could almost believe she was as innocent of conning his father as she claimed. He would have to stay on guard around her. Would that his father had been as cautious, none of this would be happening.

"Oh, Harrison, there you are!" his mother called out when she saw him. "Come join us. We saved you some caviar—mostly because Gracie doesn't like caviar. Can you imagine?"

No, Harrison couldn't imagine a woman who had just swindled herself billions of dollars not liking caviar. But it was an acquired taste for some people. She'd get the hang of it once she was firmly entrenched in the new life she'd buy with his family's money.

"And there's still some champagne, too," his mother continued. "Gracie doesn't like mimosas, either."

Neither did Harrison. Still, he would have expected someone like Grace to lap up champagne in any form from her stiletto. The thought made his gaze fall to her feet. She wore plain flat shoes—pink, to match the flowers on her pants.

Okay, that did it. No woman could be as adorable and unsullied as Grace Sumner portrayed herself. It just wasn't possible in a world as corrupt and tainted as this one. He stowed what little sentimentality he had—which, thankfully, wasn't much—and armed himself with the cynicism that was so much more comfortable.

Yeah. That felt better.

"Good morning," he said as he took his seat between the women.

"It *is* a good morning," his mother replied. "I slept so much better last night, thanks to Gracie."

Gracie, Harrison repeated to himself. His mother had tossed out the diminutive three times now. It was the sort of nickname any self-respecting girl next door would invite her new best friends to use. Great. His mother had fallen under her spell, too.

"You missed a wonderful dinner last night," she added. "Gracie is giving us the Park Avenue penthouse and everything in it, too. She's already called Mr. Tarrant about it. Isn't that nice of her?"

Harrison's gaze flew to Grace, who was gazing back at him uncomfortably.

"Really," he said flatly.

His tone must have illustrated his skepticism, because Grace dropped her gaze to the fingers she'd tangled nervously atop the table. The plate beside them held the remnants of a nearly untouched breakfast. In spite of her having looked like she was enjoying herself with his mother, she was clearly uneasy.

"It's the right thing to do," she said, still avoiding

his gaze. "Harry would have wanted his family to keep the places they call home."

"The right thing to do," Harrison told her, "would be to return everything my father left you to the family who should have inherited it in the first place."

That comment, finally, made Grace look up. "Harry wanted me to give his money to worthy causes," she said. "And that's what I'm going to do."

"When?" Harrison asked.

"As soon as I get back to Seattle. I want to meet with a financial consultant first. I have no idea what to do at this point."

Of course she wanted to meet with a financial consultant. She needed to find out how to bury that much money so deep in numbered and offshore accounts that no one would be able to find it after the new appeal ruled in the Sages' favor. Which reminded him…

Harrison turned to his mother. "I spoke with our attorney this morning. He's hired the private detective we talked about, to explore this new…avenue."

Vivian said nothing, only lifted the coffeepot to pour Harrison a cup. Grace, however, did reply.

"You're wasting your money," she said. "Not only is this…new avenue…pointless, but I'll be happy to tell you anything you want to know about me."

He studied her again—the dark, candid eyes, the bloom of color on her cheeks, the softly parted lips. She looked the same way she had yesterday when she first caught his eye, the moment she walked into the library. He couldn't remember ever reacting to a woman with the immediacy and intensity he had when he'd met her. He had no idea why. There had just been…something…about her. Something that set her apart from everyone else in the room.

At the time, he'd told himself it was because she wasn't like anyone else in the room. His joke about the pack of bloodthirsty jackals hadn't really been much of a joke. That room had been filled with predators yesterday, which anyone who'd spent time with Park Avenue lawyers and socialites could attest to. And Grace Sumner had walked right into them like a dreamy-eyed gazelle who hadn't a clue how rapacious they could be. It was that trusting aspect that had gotten to him, he realized now. Something in that first moment he saw her had made him feel as if he could trust her, too.

And trust was something Harrison hadn't felt for a very long time. Maybe he never had. Yet there she had been, making him feel that way without ever saying a word. Now that he knew who she really was…

Well, that was where things got even weirder. Because even knowing who Grace Sumner really was, he still found himself wishing he could trust her.

He quickly reviewed what he'd discovered about her on his own by typing her name into a search engine. Although she had accounts at the usual social networking sites, she kept her settings on private. He'd been able to glean a few facts, though. That she lived in Seattle and had for a year and a half. That before that, she'd lived in Cincinnati, where she grew up. He knew she'd been working as a waitress for some time, that she was attending college with an early childhood education major—always good to have a fallback in case conning old men didn't work out—and that she never commented publicly or posted duck-face selfies.

It bothered him that her behavior, both online and

now in person, didn't jibe with any of his preconceived ideas about her. An opportunistic gold digger would be a braying attention-grabber, too, wouldn't she? Then he reminded himself she was a con artist. Right? Of course she was. Naturally, she would keep her true self under wraps. That way, she could turn herself into whatever she needed to be for any given mark. Like, say, a dreamy-eyed gazelle who made a mistrustful person feel as if he could trust her.

"All right then," he said, deciding to take her up on her offer. "Have you ever been married?"

"No," she said. But she didn't elaborate.

So he did. "Have you ever been engaged?"

"No," she replied. Again without elaboration.

"Do you have a boyfriend?"

"There's no one special in my life," she told him. Then, after a small, but telling, hesitation, she added, "There never has been."

Her reply was ripe for another question, this one way more invasive than she could have considered when telling him he could ask her anything. And had it not been for his mother's presence at the table, he might very well have asked it: *Does that mean you're a virgin?* It would have been perfect. If she replied no immediately after saying there had never been anyone special in her life, she would have sounded like a tramp. Had she answered yes, at her age, she would have sounded like a liar. Win-win as far as a court appeal was concerned.

Funny, though, how suddenly he wasn't asking because he wanted to use her status against her. He wanted to know about her status for entirely personal reasons. *Was* Grace Sumner a liar and a con artist? Or was she really as sweet and innocent as she seemed? And why was he kind of hoping it was the latter? Not only would it give him the upper hand if he *could* prove she was conning them all, but it would make her the kind of person he knew how to deal with. He knew nothing of sweetness and innocence. No one in his social or professional circles claimed either trait.

"Do you have any brothers or sisters?" he asked, trying a new tack.

She shook her head. "I'm an only child."

"Mother's maiden name?"

"Sumner."

The same as Grace's. Meaning… "No father?" he asked.

At this, she smiled. "Um, yeah, I had a father. Everyone does. Were you absent from health class that day?"

He refused to be charmed by her irreverence—or her smile. Instead, he asked, "What was your father's name?"

Her answer was matter-of-fact. "I don't know."

"You don't know who your father was?"

She shook her head, something that freed another tantalizing strand of gold from her ponytail. "My mother never told me. On my birth certificate, he's listed as unknown."

Okay, this was getting interesting. It wouldn't be surprising to anyone—like, say, a probate appeals judge—to discover that a young woman whose father had been absent when she was a child would, as an adult, turn to conning old men. Even if she hadn't set out to become a professional grifter when she was a little girl, should an opportunity for such present itself when she was older, it wasn't a stretch to see how a woman like that would take advantage of it.

Maybe she was right. Maybe he wouldn't need a private investigator after all.

"What about your grandparents?" he asked.

"I barely remember my grandmother," she said. "She died before I started school."

"And your grandfather?"

"He died when my mother was in high school. My grandmother never remarried."

Oh, this was getting too easy. A pattern had developed of male role models being completely absent from the life of little Gracie Sumner. It didn't take Freud to figure this one out.

Unable to help himself, he spoke his thoughts out loud. "So. Major daddy issues. Am I right?"

"Harrison!" his mother exclaimed.

Whether her reaction was due to anger at his invasive question or worry that it would make Grace change her mind about giving her back her homes, he couldn't have said. Still, he supposed maybe, possibly, perhaps, he had overstepped there.

"Sorry," he apologized. Almost genuinely, too. "That was out of line."

"Yeah, it was," Grace agreed.

Surprisingly, though, she didn't seem to take offense. Certainly not as much as Harrison would have, had he been asked the same question.

"No, Mr. Sage, I do not have daddy issues," she continued evenly. "I come from a long line of smart, independent women who didn't need the help of anyone—least of all a man—to get by."

He was surprised by the splinter of admiration that tried to wedge itself under his skin at her cool reply.

Until she added, "But you should probably talk to someone about your own issues."

He grinned at that. "What issues?"

"The one you have about strong, independent women."

"I don't have issues with women," he told her. "I have issues with *a* woman. A woman who took advantage of my father."

He could tell by her expression that there was more she wanted to say on that matter. Instead, she said, "If you'll both excuse me, I thought I'd take the train into New York today to do some sightseeing, since I may never have the chance again."

Harrison bit back a comment about the private jet and the yacht she owned, thanks to his father, and how she could go anywhere in the world she wanted, whenever she felt like it. Instead, he sipped his coffee in silence and tried not to notice the wisp of dark gold hair that was curling against her nape in a way that made him unwillingly envious. If she were any other woman, he would have reached over and coiled that strand of silk around his finger, then used it to gently pull her face toward his so he could—

So he could nothing, he told himself. Grace Sumner was the last woman he wanted to touch with affection. Or anything else. Even a ten-foot pole.

"That's a lovely idea," his mother said. "You should do some shopping, too. A young girl like you—" She smiled in a way that was kind of astonishing in light of the fact that she'd just encouraged a stranger to go out and spend money that should belong to her. "A young *rich* girl like you," she amended, "should have a closet full of beautiful things to wear. Beautiful *new* things."

The emphasis on the word *new* obviously didn't escape Grace's notice. She glanced down at her outfit, one that looked like something from a sixties flick titled *Beach Blanket Barbie*. Strangely, she didn't seem to think there was anything wrong with it. For a moment, she looked as if she wanted to explain her wardrobe choices, and then seemed to change her mind. Good call, Harrison thought. His mother never kept clothes past the season and year for which they'd been designed.

"Timmerman can drive you to the train," Vivian told her. "Just remember to be back by eight, because Eleanor is making something special for dinner tonight. In your honor."

Somehow, Harrison kept from rolling his eyes. His mother was becoming such a suck-up.

After Grace left, he finished his coffee, downed what was left of the bacon and toast and listened for the car to pull away from the house. Then he headed for his Maserati and made his way to the train station, too.

So Grace wanted to see the sights of New York City. Right. All along Fifth Avenue, he'd bet. Starting with Saks and ending with Tiffany, allowing just enough time for a late lunch at Le Bernardin. Luckily, he'd given himself the rest of the week off—he could do that, being the owner of his own company—to deal with The Sumner Problem, so he had no obligations today.

None except exposing a con artist who was so good at what she did, she could make a man long for things he knew he would never have.

* * *

It was some hours later that Harrison discovered how right he'd been in his suspicions—Grace Sumner did go shopping and treat herself to a late lunch. But only after seeing sights like the Empire State Building, Rockefeller Center and Times Square. And even though that last left her within walking distance of Fifth Avenue, she took the subway to go hopscotching all over Brooklyn. Specifically, through the thrift stores of Brooklyn. And instead of Le Bernardin, she bought her lunch from a Salvadoran food truck.

Grace Sumner was either a con artist of even greater sophistication than he'd thought, or she knew he was following her. And since he was confident he hadn't revealed himself, he was going for the former. Unless, of course, her intentions toward his father's money were exactly what she claimed, and she would be giving it all away, meaning she was on a major budget that prohibited things like Fifth Avenue shopping sprees.

Yeah, right. And maybe tonight, while he was sleeping, the Blue Fairy would fly into his room and turn him into a real boy.

What the hell kind of game was she playing? And how long was she going to play it? Even if—no, when—his detective discovered the truth about her, and an appeals court finally found in the Sages' favor, for now, his father's money legally belonged to her. It could be weeks, even months, before Harrison had the evidence he needed to win the return of his father's fortune. It would take even longer for another appeal in court. In the meantime, she was within her rights to spend every dime.

So why wasn't she doing that? And why was she

staying with his mother on Long Island, away from Bennett Tarrant and his colleagues, who were the only support she had? There was more going on here than a simple con. There had to be. Harrison just needed to figure out what it was. And he would have to do it within a week, since Grace would be leaving after the paperwork was complete to return the estate and the penthouse to his mother. Just who was Grace Sumner—wicked woman or good girl?

And the toughest question to answer of all—why was Harrison kind of hoping it was the latter?

Four

Until she saw it in action, Gracie never would have guessed how closely the New York Stock Exchange after the ringing of the bell resembled the kitchen of Café Destiné after the eighty-sixing of the béchamel sauce. Absolute mayhem. And she wasn't even *on* the floor. She was with Harrison in the gallery above it, looking down as millions of dollars' worth of commodities, futures and options—and, for all she knew, lunches, Pokémon cards and Neopets—were traded, bought and sold in a way she would never, ever understand. Not that Harrison hadn't tried to explain it to her. He'd used every minute of their drive from Long Island doing just that—probably because it kept him from having to talk to her about anything else.

It had been Vivian's idea that he should bring Gracie into the city again today, but for a different kind of sightseeing. Last night, over dinner, when Gracie and Harrison had been gazing suspiciously at each other across the table and responding to Vivian's attempts at repartee with little more than awkward mumbling, his mother had suggested the two of them should spend more time together so that each could get to know the other's version of the man they shared in common.

Gracie figured it was more likely, though, that Vivian was worried about the antagonism that could potentially mushroom between Gracie and Harrison, and how Vivian would then be left homeless.

So Gracie and Harrison had risen extra early to make it to Wall Street in time to hear the Friday opening bell. Early enough that Gracie only had time to consume a single cup of coffee. That had given her just enough presence of mind to at least pretend she understood all the stuff Harrison said about SEC, PLC and OTC—and the stuff about yearlings and bulls and bears, oh my—but it hadn't constituted much in the way of breakfast. Now her UGI was growling like a bear, her mood was fast depreciating and her brain was beginning to liquidate.

Hmm. Maybe she'd understood more of what he'd said than she thought. Despite the downturn of her current market…ah, she meant, body…she tried to focus on what he was saying now.

"My father had a real gift for trading," he told her.

Harrison fit in this world nicely with his dark slate suit and dove-gray dress shirt, but his necktie, with its multicolored dots, was a tad less conservative than the staid diagonal stripes and discreet tiny diamonds on the ties worn by the other men. Although Gracie had tried to dress for business, too, the best she'd been able to do was another vintage suit—the second of the only two she owned. This one was a dark ruby with pencil skirt and cinch-waisted jacket with a slight peplum. She'd thought she looked pretty great when she got dressed. Seeing the other women in their dark grays and blacks and neutrals, she now felt like a giant lollipop.

"His initial fortune," Harrison continued, "the one he used to buy and build his companies, was all earned in the stock market. He never went to college. Did you know that?"

There was something akin to pride in his voice when he spoke of Harry's lack of formal education. It surprised Gracie. She would have thought Harrison was the kind of man who wouldn't want anyone to know about his father's lack of education because it would be an embarrassment to the family name.

"I did know that, actually," she said. "But he told me it was because he couldn't afford to pay for college."

"He couldn't. Not after he graduated from high school, anyway."

"Harry never graduated from high school."

The moment the words were out of her mouth, Gracie regretted them. Not because she worried they would be an embarrassment to the Sage name, too, but because Harrison's expression made clear he hadn't known that. And now he was finding it out from someone he'd just met who had obviously known it for some time.

Nevertheless, he said, "Of course my father graduated from high school. Findlay High School in Cincinnati. Class of fifty-three."

"Harry never even made it to his junior year," Gracie told him. "He dropped out when he was fifteen to work in the Formica factory. He lied about his age to get the job and join the union."

Harrison gazed at her blankly. "Why would he do that?"

Oh, boy. There was obviously *a lot* he didn't know about his father's early life. And Gracie didn't want to be the one to let the cat out of the bag, which, in Harry's case, would be more like freeing a Siberian tiger from the Moscow Zoo.

Gently, she said, "Because by then, Harry's father was drinking so much, he couldn't hold down a job, and his mother was caring for his little brother, so she couldn't work, either. Harry had to be the one to support the family."

At the word *brother*, Harrison's eyes went wide, and Gracie's heart dropped to her stomach. Surely, he'd at least known his father had a brother.

"My father had a *brother*?"

Okay, maybe not. "Yeah. You didn't know?"

Although Harrison's gaze was fixed on hers, she could tell by the emptiness in those blue, blue eyes that his thoughts were a billion miles away. Or, at least, a few decades away. Or maybe he was just trying to decide whether or not to even believe her. But Gracie had seen photos of Harry's family. The old pictures were with his things in the storage unit.

Harrison shook his head lightly, honing his icy blue gaze—which somehow, suddenly, seemed a little less icy—on Gracie again. "But I always thought... I mean he told me... Well, okay he never really *told* me, but I always assumed..." When he realized he wasn't making sense, he inhaled a breath and released it. "I always thought he was an only child. By the time I was born, his parents were both dead, and he never mentioned any other family. Hell, he barely mentioned his parents."

Gracie tried to tread lightly as she told him, "Benjy—that was his little brother—had polio. He died when he was thirteen, and Harry was sixteen. It hit him pretty hard. His mother, too. She left home a year or so later, and Harry never saw her again. He took care of his dad for a couple more years, until he died, too, of cirrhosis. Then Harry left Cincinnati and didn't come back until after he retired from his job as a TV repairman.

"Well, that was what he told me, anyway," she quickly amended. "That he made his living in New York as a TV repairman. Obviously, that part wasn't true. But the rest of it was. When I packed up his things after his death, I found photos and some old diaries that belonged to his mother. I'll be sure everything is sent to you and Vivian once I get back to Seattle."

Harrison eyed her thoughtfully. A little too thoughtfully for Gracie's comfort. He was doing that thing again where he seemed to be trying to peer into her soul. And was succeeding. All he said, though, was "What else did my father tell you about his childhood?"

"He said that after his father died, he took what little money he'd saved and went to New York. TV was just starting to become popular, and he got a job in a little appliance shop and taught himself everything he could. After a while, he opened his own repair business in Queens and lived and worked there until he retired."

"He never mentioned getting married?" Harrison asked. "Three times, at that? Never mentioned having kids? Seven of us?"

She shook her head. "Never. I mean, I always won-dered. He never said he *didn't* marry or have a family. But I didn't want to pry. He just told me that after he retired, he started missing Cincinnati, so he moved back to his old neighborhood."

Harrison said nothing in response to that, but he continued to look at Gracie in that way that made some-thing hot and gooey eddy in her belly, melting bit by bit until it warmed her all over. How could he make her feel like that? He'd made no secret of the fact that he didn't trust her. He didn't even like her. Except for their initial meeting, the time the two of them had shared together had been combative at worst and un-comfortable at best. There should be no hot gooeyness in a situation like that.

But maybe that was the problem. Not the unpleas-ant times since the two of them met. But the handful of moments when the two of them had first encoun-tered each other in the library. Something had defi-nitely blossomed between them in those moments, and it had been anything but unpleasant. Those moments had been some of the sweetest Gracie had ever known. She'd never had a reaction to a man like she'd had to Harrison. Why couldn't the two of them hit Rewind and start over? Go back to that first second when her eyes met his, and she felt as if the pieces of her life that had been ripped apart in the days since meeting Mr. Tarrant had suddenly fallen back into place?

When Harrison still didn't respond to anything she'd told him, she asked softly, "You didn't know any of that stuff about his parents or brother, did you?"

He shook his head.

"What did your father tell you about his childhood?"

"Not much. That he grew up in Cincinnati. That his mother was a teacher and his father worked in a factory. That he used money he saved from a paper route to come to New York after high school."

His expression suddenly changed, moving from quietly preoccupied to fiercely keen. "After his arrival in New York, though, I heard all about that. Over and over again."

"Guess it didn't have anything to do with a TV repair shop, huh?"

He chuckled, but there was nothing happy in the sound. "No. It was all about how he found work as a runner for a brokerage in Manhattan and worked his way up, investing what he could where he could whenever he had a spare nickel. How he made his first million when he was twenty-five. How he bought his first business at twenty-seven. How, at thirty, he was worth tens of millions of dollars. At forty, hundreds of millions. Easy as pie. He had things fall into his lap and then was smart enough to exploit them for all they were worth. Hell, he berated me for not earning my keep when I was a kid. He may have gone into his office every day to keep an eye on things, but as far as actual work? He never worked a day in his life as an adult."

Gracie couldn't help the sound of disbelief that escaped her. "Oh, please. I never met anyone who worked harder than Harry Sagalowsky."

Harrison threw her another one of those dubious looks. "You said he was retired when you met him."

"Yeah, but he was active in his church, he volunteered at the veterans hospital, he served meals at a homeless shelter most weekends and he coached Little League."

She could tell Harrison stopped believing her with the first sentence—he even started shaking his head before she finished speaking. "My father never went to church, he was never in the military, he thought poverty was a scam and he hated kids."

"Your father sang in the choir," Gracie countered. "And he felt a debt to people in uniform because he grew up during a time when a lot of them never made it home from war. I'd think by now you'd realize how he feels about poverty, since he wants me to give away all his money to worthy causes. And I never saw him happier than he was when he was with his team. I bet you didn't even realize what a huge Reds fan he was, did you?"

Now Harrison was the one to utter an incredulous sound. "This just proves I can't trust anything you say. Nothing you've said about my father rings true. Nothing."

"And nothing you've said about him rings true for me, either."

She still couldn't understand how the Harry she'd known could have been a big-shot corporate mogul or abandoned a wife and son. There must have been a reason for it. He'd said in his video that his home life had become unhappy, but that should have made him determined to stay and fix whatever was wrong. Harry really was the finest man Gracie had ever met. So how could he have done things that weren't fine at all?

The tentative moment of…whatever it was she and Harrison had begun to share was gone. And really, did it matter how they felt about each other? Two judges had awarded Gracie Harry's fortune, and she was duty-bound to disburse it in a way that would honor his wishes. It didn't matter if Harrison Sage believed her. It didn't matter if he trusted her. It didn't matter if he liked her. And it didn't matter how he felt about his father, either, since it was too late for any attempts to make amends there. Harry's death had ensured that his son would never have a chance to understand the man beneath the high-powered pinstripes who had walked out on his family fifteen years before. There would be no resolution for that relationship. Ever.

Or would there?

Gracie studied Harrison again, remembering the way he'd been in the library, before their formal introductions. He had reminded her of Harry, she recalled. He had smiled like his father. He'd been as charming. As easy to talk to. He had the same blue eyes and, now that she paid more attention, the same straight nose and blunt jaw. Had circumstances been different, had Harry not been a titan of industry, had he spent more time with his family and given more freely of himself to them, things might have turned out differently for father and son. They might have recognized they had a lot in common. They might have even been friends.

"You didn't really know him, either, did you?" Gracie said softly.

Harrison deflated a little at the question. "The man I knew was nothing like you describe."

"Maybe while he was your father, he wasn't," she conceded. "And that's a shame."

Now Harrison stiffened. "Why is that a shame? My father was one of the most successful men of his time. How can there be anything shameful in that?"

"Because he could have been a successful father,

too," Gracie said. "I wish you'd known the man I did. The Harry I knew was a good guy, Harrison."

It was the first time she had called him by his first name, and it surprised her how easily it rolled off her tongue, and how good it felt to say it. Harrison seemed surprised, too. He opened his mouth to say something, then evidently changed his mind and glanced away. When he did, something—some odd trick of the light—shadowed his eyes, turning the anger to melancholy.

She tried again. "You know, there's a lot of your father in you. I recognized it right away, when you and I were talking in the library the other day."

He turned to look at her again, more thoughtfully this time. "That was who you meant when you told me I reminded you of someone."

She nodded.

"But he and I had nothing in common."

"You look like him."

"Not surprising, since we come from the same gene pool."

"You told me a joke, right off the bat. That was just like something Harry would do."

"That was just like something a lot of men would do if they were trying to impress a—" He halted abruptly, then said quickly, "That was just like something a lot of men would do."

"It still reminded me of Harry."

Harrison returned his attention to the trading floor. "He brought me here when I was a kid," he said quietly. "Once. I was six or seven. He wanted to show me how fortunes were made and lost. He said this—" he gestured down at the chaos below "—was what made

the whole world work. He told me money was more important than anything, because it could buy anything.
Not just material possessions, but *anything*. Adventure.
Culture. Intelligence. It could buy friends. Allies. Even
governments. Not to mention things like respect and
dignity and love."

Gracie wanted to deny that Harry could have ever
been that cynical or said anything that cold. Especially
to a child. Especially to his own son. The man she'd
known had thought money was what caused all the
world's problems, not solved them. And he'd known it
was a person's actions, not their income, that garnered
respect and dignity and love.

"You can't buy love," she said softly.

Harrison looked at her. "No?"

She shook her head.

He glanced back down at the floor. "Maybe not. But
you can buy something that feels like it."

"No, you can't," Gracie countered. "Maybe you can
lie to yourself until you believe that, but…"

When he looked at her this time, she was the one
to glance away.

"But what?" he asked.

She shook her head again. "Nothing."

He studied her so long without speaking that it
began to feel as if he were trying to insert a little piece
of himself inside her. What was weird was that a piece
of him should feel like a pebble in her shoe. Instead,
it felt more like more a ray of sunshine on her face.

"You must be hungry," he finally said.

There was a huskiness in his voice when he spoke
that made something in her stomach catch fire. She
didn't dare look at him for fear that those blue eyes

would be burning, too. How did he do that? How did he make any given situation feel almost…sexual? He'd done it in the library that first morning, and again at breakfast yesterday. The man was just strangely potent.

"A little," she said, hoping her stomach didn't decide to punctuate the statement with the kind of growl that normally preceded a lunge to the jugular.

"My mother suggested I take you to my father's club for lunch," he said. "By the time we get there, they should be ready to serve."

"Lunch sounds great," she told him.

Even if lunch actually sounded like another opportunity for the two of them to find something to be at odds about. At least food would quiet the wild animal that seemed to have taken up residence in her belly.

Now if she could just figure out how to quiet the wild thoughts suddenly tumbling through her brain.

Harrison watched Grace from the other side of the table at the Cosmopolitan Club, doing his best to not notice how, in this place, surrounded by all its Art Deco splendor, she looked like some seductive film-noir siren. Her form-hugging suit, the color of forbidden fruit, was buttoned high enough to be acceptable in professional circles, but low enough to make a man— to make Harrison—want to reach across the table and start unbuttoning it. She'd worn her hair down today, parted on one side to swoop over her forehead, something that only added to her Veronica Lake, femme fatale appearance. All she needed to complete it was some raging red lipstick. As usual, though, she didn't seem to be wearing makeup at all. Meaning she was once again that combination of sexpot and girl next door that made him want to—

Okay, so it probably wasn't a good idea to think further about what her appearance made him want to do. Probably, it was better to look at the menu and figure out what he wanted. Besides Grace, he meant.

How could he want someone who had almost certainly taken advantage of his father and pocketed the family fortune? On the other hand, what did ethics and morality have to do with sex? It wasn't as if Harrison hadn't slept with other women who were ethically and morally challenged.

Wait a minute. Hang on. He replayed that last sentence in his brain. It wasn't as if he hadn't slept with *other* women like that? Meaning that somewhere in his subconscious, he was thinking about sleeping with Grace? When did that happen? Then again, why shouldn't he sleep with Grace? He might as well get something out of this arrangement.

"What's good here?" she asked, bringing his attention back to the matter at hand.

"If you like light, go with the brie salad. If you like sandwiches, try the club. It you want something more exotic, the curried shrimp."

"Oh, that does sound good," she said. She scanned the menu until she found a description, then uttered a flat "Oh."

"What?" Harrison asked.

"There aren't any prices listed on this menu."

He still couldn't decide whether or not she was pretending to be something she wasn't. If this was all an act, then she really did deserve an award. If it wasn't, then she was a pod person from outer space. No one could be this naive.

"You don't know what it means when prices aren't listed on a menu?" he asked skeptically.

"Of course I know what that means," she said. "No one's that naive."

"Then what's the problem?"

"I can't afford a place where the prices aren't listed. The money your father left me isn't mine."

"It is until you give it to someone else." And he still wasn't convinced she would do it.

"But—"

"Look, it's my treat," he interrupted. "I'm a member here, too."

"Oh," she said again. Only this time it wasn't a flat *oh*. This time it was a surprised *oh*. As in "Oh, you have your own money?"

"I do have a job, you know," he replied before she could ask.

"I didn't mean—"

"You thought I was just some lazy, entitled player who never worked a day in his life, didn't you?"

"No, I—"

"I actually have my own business," he said, hoping he didn't sound as smug about that as he felt, but figuring by her expression that he probably did. Oh, well. "Sage Assets," he continued. "We're consultants in financial risk management."

She clearly had no idea what he was talking about, a realization that nagged again at his conviction that she was driven only by money. "Which means what?" she asked.

"We advise businesses and investors on how not

to lose their shirts in times of financial crisis. Or any other time, for that matter. I started the company right after I graduated from Columbia, and it took off right away," he added modestly. Well, sort of modestly. Okay, not modestly at all. "That being a time of financial crisis. And my father wasn't the only one in the family with a gift for trading." Then, because he couldn't quite keep himself from saying it, he added, "I made my first million when I was twenty-three. I was worth tens of millions by the time I was twenty-seven."

Beating his father's timetable on those achievements by years. At the rate he was going, he'd be beating that hundreds-of-millions thing, too, by a good five years. Not that his father had ever realized—or would ever realize—any of those things. Not that that was the point. Not that Harrison cared. He didn't.

Grace didn't seem as impressed by his achievements as Harrison was. Then again, she had fourteen billion dollars. He was a lightweight compared to her.

"Well, for what it's worth," she said, "I didn't think you were a lazy, entitled player who never worked a day in your life."

"No?"

She shook her head. "I figured you had a job."

Only when she punctuated the statement with a smile did he realize she was making a joke. He refused to be charmed.

"Then you did think I was an entitled player."

Instead of answering, she glanced back down at her menu and said, "You know, I do like a good club sandwich…"

Their server came and took their orders, returning with their drinks. Grace reached for the sugar caddy and used the tongs to pluck out four cubes for her tea. After stirring, she took a sip, and then tonged in two more. As if Grace Sumner needed any more sweetness.

It didn't help that she kept glancing around the room as if she'd just fallen off the turnip truck. Of course, the place was pretty impressive. The Cosmopolitan had been built in the Roaring Twenties by a group of rich industrialists so they and all their equally wealthy friends would have a sumptuous sanctuary to escape the wretched refuse of New York. The furnishings were as rich, extravagant and bombastic as they'd been, all mahogany and velvet and crystal, and the current owners spared no expense to maintain that aura of a bygone era. He and Grace might as well have been lunching with Calvin Coolidge.

"I don't think I've ever been in a place like this before," she said. She grinned again before adding, "Unless you count the Haunted Mansion at Disney World."

Harrison smiled back, surprised to discover it felt genuine. Not sure why, he played along. "I wouldn't count that. They let in all kinds of riffraff at the Haunted Mansion, and the dress code is way too relaxed."

She gave the room another assessment and sighed. "I can't imagine Harry here. His favorite place for lunch was Golden Corral. And I never saw him in a suit."

"I don't think I ever saw him in anything but a suit," Harrison said. "When I was a kid, he was always already dressed for work when I got up, and he usually didn't get home until after I went to bed."

"What about on weekends?" she asked. "Or vacations? Or just relaxing around the house?"

"My father never relaxed. He worked most weekends. The only vacations I ever took were with my mother."

She shook her head. "Everything you tell me about Harry is just so not Harry. What happened to him, that he was so driven by work and money for so long, and then suddenly turned his back on all of it?"

Harrison wished he could answer that. Hell, he wished he could believe everything Grace had said about his father was true. But none of it sounded like him. Not the part about having a sick little brother, not the part about his dropping out of school and definitely not the part about coaching Little League or serving meals to the homeless. *Was* she a con artist? Or had she been as much a target of his father's caprice as the rest of them?

"If what you said about my father's childhood was true—"

"You don't think I was telling the truth about that, either?" she interjected, sounding—and looking— wounded.

"I don't know what to believe," he said honestly.

He still wasn't convinced she was as altruistic as she claimed. The return of his mother's house and the Manhattan penthouse were only drops in the ocean when it came to the totality of his father's wealth. She would still have billions of dollars after shedding those. And she hadn't committed any of those billions to any causes yet.

"But if what you said is true," he continued, "then it's obvious why he was driven by money. Anyone who grew up poor would naturally want to be rich."

"Why is that natural?" she asked.

He didn't understand the question. "What do you mean?"

"Why do you think the desire to be rich is natural?"

He was still confused. "Don't you think it is?"

"No. I mean, I can see how it might have motivated Harry, but not because it was natural. A lot of people are content with what they have, even if they aren't rich. There is such a thing as enough."

"I don't follow you."

At this, she leaned back in her chair and sighed with unmistakable disappointment. "Yeah, I know."

He was about to ask her what she meant by that, too, when their server returned to deliver their selections, taking a few moments to arrange everything on the table until it was feng shui-ed to his liking. After that, the moment with Grace was gone, and she was gushing about her club sandwich, so Harrison let her comment go. For now.

"So where else does Vivian want you to take me?" she asked.

"To one of my father's businesses and a prep school whose board of directors he sat on. And tonight one of his old colleagues is having a cocktail party. I was going to blow it off, but my mother is going and insists you and I come, too."

A flash of panic crossed her expression. "Cocktail party?"

"Is that a problem?"

"Kind of. I didn't bring anything to wear to a cocktail party."

"Fifth Avenue is right around the corner."

Her panic increased. "But Fifth Avenue is so—"

When she didn't finish, Harrison prompted, "So…?"

She looked left, then right, to make sure the diners on each side of them were engrossed in their own conversations. Then she leaned across the table and lowered her voice. "I can't afford Fifth Avenue."

Harrison leaned forward, too, lowering his voice to mimic hers. "You have fourteen billion dollars."

"I told you. That's not mine," she whispered back.

Seriously, she was going to insist she couldn't afford a dress? He leaned back in his chair, returning to his normal voice. "My father told you to take some of the money for yourself," he reminded her.

She sat back, too. "I refuse to pay Fifth Avenue prices for a dress when I can buy one for almost a hundred percent less in a thrift shop."

Harrison turned his attention to his plate, where a gorgeous swordfish steak was just begging to be enjoyed. "Yeah, well, I'm not traipsing all over Brooklyn again, so you can forget about going back there to shop."

The pause that followed his statement was so pregnant, it could have delivered an elephant. When he looked at Grace again, she had completely forgotten her own lunch and looked ready to stick her butter knife into him instead.

Very softly, she asked, "How did you know I went to Brooklyn yesterday?"

Crap. Busted.

He scrambled for a credible excuse, but figured it would be pointless. "I followed you."

"Why?"

Resigned to be honest, since she seemed like the kind of woman who would sniff out a lie a mile away, he said, "Because I wanted to see if you would go out

and start blowing my father's money. On, say, Fifth
Avenue."

"Why won't you believe me when I tell you I intend
to give away your father's money the way he asked
me to?"

"Because it's fourteen billion dollars. No one gives
away fourteen billion dollars."

"I'm going to."

Yeah, well, that remained to be seen. Instead of continuing with their current topic, Harrison backpedaled
to the one before it. "Don't worry about the dress. I'm
sure we can find a store you like nearby. I'll ask the
concierge on our way out."

Which would doubtlessly be the highlight of the
concierge's month. Someone at the Cosmopolitan asking where the nearest thrift shop was. The club would
be talking about that one for weeks.

Five

Gracie couldn't believe she was standing at the front door of an Upper East Side penthouse, about to ring the bell. How could she have insisted earlier that Harrison go ahead of her to the party so she could shop for something to wear? She was never going to be allowed into a place like this without him. She still couldn't believe the doorman for the building had opened the door for her in the first place—even tipping his hat as he did—or that the concierge hadn't tried to stop her when she headed for the elevator, or that the elevator operator had told her it wasn't necessary when she fumbled in her purse for the invitation Harrison had given her to prove she had been invited into this world. He'd just closed the doors and pushed the button that would rocket her straight to the top, as if that were exactly where she belonged.

This was the kind of place that wasn't supposed to allow in people like her. Normal people. Working people. People who hadn't even had the proper attire for this party until a couple of hours ago, and whose attire still probably wasn't all that proper, since she'd bought it at a secondhand shop.

She couldn't remember ever being this nervous. But then throwing herself into a situation where she had no idea how to behave or what to talk about, and didn't have a single advocate to cover her back, could do that to a person. Even if being thrown into situations like that had been Gracie's entire day.

After leaving the Cosmopolitan Club, she and Harrison had gone to the prep school where Harry had, once upon a time, sat on the board of directors. Interestingly, it was also the school Harrison had attended from kindergarten through twelfth grade, for a mere sixty-three thousand dollars a year—though he'd told her tuition was only forty-eight thousand when he started, so a big "whew!" on that. The kids had worn tidy navy blue uniforms, they'd walked silently and with great restraint through the halls, their lunches had consisted of fresh produce, lean meats and whole-grain breads trucked in from Connecticut and their curriculum had focused on science, mathematics and the classics. Art and music were extracurriculars that were discouraged in favor of Future Business Leaders of America and Junior Achievement.

It had been such a stark contrast to Gracie's public school education, where the dress code had been pretty much anything that wasn't indecent, the halls had been noisy and chaotic during class changes, the lunches had overwhelmingly been brown-bagged from home and filled with things factory-sealed in plastic and the curriculum had been as busy and inconsistent—in a good way—as the halls, with art and music as daily requirements.

So not only had Harry told his son that money was the most important thing in the world, but he'd also proved it by spending all his time making money and sending Harrison to a school more intent on turning its students into corporate drones than in guiding them into something constructive and fulfilling. What the hell had he been thinking?

The headquarters of Sage Holdings, Inc., where Harry had once been the man in charge, had been no better: all antiseptic and barren, in spite of being filled with workers. Workers who had spoken not a word to each other, because they'd all been confined to cubicles and hunched over computers, tap-tap-tapping on their keyboards with the diligent dedication of worker bees. How could Harry have made his employees work in such soul-deadening surroundings?

And would this party tonight reinforce her anti-Harry Sagalowsky feelings as much as the rest of today had?

Gracie inhaled a deep breath and released it, telling herself everything was going to be fine. She was fine. Her attire was fine. She'd been enchanted by the dress the moment she saw it, a pale mint confection of silk with a frothy crinoline underskirt, a ruched neckline and off-the-shoulder cap sleeves. She'd found accessories at the shop, too—plain pearly pumps and a clutch and a crystal necklace and earrings, along with a pair of white gloves that climbed midway between wrist and elbow. And she'd managed to twist her hair into

a serviceable chignon and applied just enough blush
and lipstick to keep herself from being as pale as…
well, as pale as a woman who was about to enter a situation where she had no idea how to behave or what
to talk about.

With one final, fortifying inhale-exhale—*for God's
sake, Gracie, just breathe*—she pushed her index finger against the doorbell. Immediately, the door opened,
and she was greeted by a smiling butler. Though his
smile didn't look like a real smile. Probably, it was a
smile he was being paid to smile.

Wow. Harry was right. Money really could buy anything.

No, it couldn't, she immediately reminded herself.
Money hadn't been able to buy Gracie, after all. Not
that Devon Braun and his father hadn't tried once upon
a time.

Wow. Where had that memory come from? She
hadn't given a thought to those two scumbags for a
long time. And she wouldn't think about them tonight,
either. This party would be nothing like the one that
set those unfortunate events in motion.

She opened her purse to retrieve her invitation, since
butlers were obviously way too smart to allow someone entry just because she was wearing a vintage Dior
knockoff and a serviceable chignon. But even though
the purse was roughly the size of a canapé, she couldn't
find what she was looking for. Just her lipstick and
compact in case she needed to refresh her makeup,
her driver's license in case she got hit by a bus, and
the paramedics needed to identify her body, and her
debit card in case Harrison shoved her out of the car
in a sketchy part of town and she needed to take a cab

back to Long Island, which could happen, since he still didn't seem to believe her intentions toward Harry's fortune were honorable. But no invitation.

She must have dropped it in the elevator when she was fumbling to get it out of her purse the first time. She was about to turn back that way when the same dark, velvety voice that had rescued her from the crowd at the reading of Harry's will saved her again.

"It's all right, Ballantine," Harrison said from behind the butler. "She's with me."

She's with me. Somehow, Harrison made it sound as if she really was *with him.* In a romantic, intimate sense. A tingle of pleasure hummed through her.

Although Gracie had had boyfriends since she was old enough to want one, none had ever been especially serious. Well, okay, that wasn't entirely true. There had been one a while back who'd started to become serious. Devon Braun. A guy she'd met at a party she attended with a friend from school. A guy who'd taken her to a lot of parties like this one, since his family had been rich. But Devon had been sweeter and less obnoxious than most of the guys who came from that background. At least, Gracie had thought so then. For a couple of months, anyway.

But she wasn't going to think about that—about him—tonight. She'd done extremely well shoving him to the back of her brain since leaving Cincinnati, and she wasn't about to let him mess things up now. Tonight she was with Harrison. He'd just said so. And even if they went back to their wary dancing around each other tomorrow, she intended to avoid any missteps tonight.

Unfortunately, she was barely two steps past Ballantine the butler when she began to wonder if she'd been premature in her conviction. Because the minute Harrison got a good look at her, his smile fell. Somehow, Gracie was positive his thoughts just then were something along the lines of how he couldn't believe she'd shown up dressed the way she was.

When she looked past him into the room, she realized why. Although all the men were dressed as he was—in dark suits and ties—none of the women was dressed like her. Nearly all of them were wearing black, and although there were one or two bursts of taupe, there wasn't any clothing in the entire room that could have been called colorful. Or frothy. Or a confection. Except for a bubbly bit of pale mint silk on a woman who looked and felt—and was—completely out of place.

She forced her feet forward, manufacturing a smile for Ballantine as she passed him that was no more genuine than his, and made her way toward Harrison, whose gaze never left her as she approached.

Although she was pretty sure she already knew the answer to the question, she greeted him by asking, "Is there something wrong?"

He gave her a quick once-over, but didn't look quite as stunned this time. She decided to take it as a compliment.

"Why do you ask?" he replied.

She lifted one shoulder and let it drop. "You look like there's something wrong."

Instead of giving her the once-over this time, he simply studied her face. "You look…"

Here it comes, Gracie thought, bracing herself.

"…different," he said.

It wasn't the word she'd expected. Nor did she understand why he chose it. She hadn't done anything different today from what she'd done every other day he'd seen her. Maybe she'd put on a little more makeup and expended more effort on her hair, but what difference did that make?

"Good different or bad different?" she asked.

He hesitated, then slowly shook his head. "Just… different."

"Oh. Should I leave?"

At this, he looked genuinely surprised. "No. Of course not. Why would you even ask that?"

"Because you seem to think—"

"Gracie, darling!"

The exclamation from Vivian Sage came just in time, because Harrison looked like he wanted to say something else that was probably better left unsaid. Vivian looked smashing, her black dress a sleeveless, V-necked number that was elegant in its simplicity and sumptuous in its fabric. She carried a crystal-encrusted clutch in one hand and a cocktail in the other. She stopped in front of Gracie, leaning in to give her one of those Hollywood air kisses on her cheek before backing away again.

"Darling, you look absolutely adorable," she said. "You could be me when I was young. I think I had a dress just like that."

Of course she did. Except Vivian's would have had a genuine Dior tag sewn inside it, instead of one that *looked* like it said, Christian Dior Paris, but, upon close inspection, really said, Christina Diaz, Paramus. But Vivian had uttered the compliment sincerely, so maybe the evening wouldn't be so horrible, after all.

Then she had to go and ruin that possibility by turning to her son and saying, "Doesn't she look beautiful, Harrison?"

But he surprised Gracie by saying, "Uh, yeah. Beautiful."

Unfortunately, he dropped his gaze to the floor before saying it, thereby making it possible that he was talking about their host's carpet selection instead. Which, okay, was pretty beautiful, all lush and white, like the rest of the room.

This time, when Vivian leaned in, it was toward Harrison. "Then tell her, darling. A woman wants to be reassured that she's the most beautiful woman in the room, especially when she's at one of Bunny and Peter's parties." To Gracie, she added, "Bunny Dewitt is one of New York's biggest fashion icons. She's always being written up in the style section. Every woman here is worried that she's underdressed or overdressed or wearing something so five-minutes-ago."

Then Gracie had nothing to worry about. Her dress wasn't so five-minutes-ago. It was so five-decades-ago. She felt *so* much better now.

Harrison threw his mother a "thanks a lot, Mom" smile at her admonishment, but said, "You look beautiful, Grace."

He was looking right at her when he spoke, and for once, his expression wasn't inscrutable. In fact, it was totally, uh, scrutable. His blue eyes were fairly glowing with admiration, and his mouth was curled into the sort of half smile that overcame men when they were enjoying something sublime. Like a flawlessly executed Hail Mary pass. Or a perfectly grilled rib eye. Or a genuinely beautiful woman.

Then the *Grace* at the end of the sentiment hit her.

Nobody had ever called her Grace. Except for Devon, who'd told her she was too classy to be called Gracie—then turned out to be the most déclassé person on the planet. But she wasn't going to think about Devon tonight, so he didn't count.

And even if Harrison didn't think she was beautiful—or classy, for that matter—the fact that he was making an effort to…well, whatever he was making an effort to do…was a welcome development.

So she replied, "Thank you. And call me Gracie. No one calls me Grace." Well, except for the aforementioned—

Dammit, why did Devon keep popping into her head tonight? With no small effort, she pushed thoughts of the past to the back of her brain again, where they belonged. *And stay there.*

Harrison looked like he wanted to balk at calling her Gracie, but he dipped his head in acknowledgement that he had at least heard her.

"Ms. Sumner!"

Gracie was surprised—and delighted—to hear another familiar voice, and smiled when she turned to greet Gus Fiver, the second-in-command at Tarrant, Fiver & Twigg. He was dressed as conservatively as all the other suits at the party, but there was something about his blond good looks that made him seem far more relaxed. Instead of the briefcase she'd always seen him armed with before, this time he held a cut-crystal tumbler with what looked to Gracie's trained eye like two fingers of very good single-malt Scotch.

"Mr. Fiver," she greeted him. "What are you doing here?"

"Mr. and Mrs. Dewitt's son Elliot is one of my best

friends," he said. "Our families go way back. And please call me Gus."

Gracie turned to include Harrison and Vivian in the conversation, and then realized she had no idea how to do that. Although everyone in the small group knew each other already, it wasn't like the Sages and Tarrant, Fiver & Twigg were exactly best friends. "You, um, you remember the Sages, I'm sure."

Although there was a bit of a temperature drop not unlike the one she'd experienced in the Sages' library a few days ago, Harrison and Gus managed to exchange civil greetings. Vivian was a bit warmer, but she, too, was reserved. Gracie supposed it was the best any of them could manage, having been on opposite sides of a very contentious case for two years.

"I'm surprised to see you here," Gus said. Somehow, though, Gracie couldn't help thinking that the subtext of his sentence was something along the lines of "I thought by now one of the Sages would have suffocated you in your sleep." "I hope you've been enjoying your stay in the Hamptons."

"I have," she said, surprised to realize it was true. In spite of the weirdness of the situation and the wariness of the sort-of truce that seemed to have developed between her and Harrison—at least for now—her stay had been reasonably pleasant and abundantly enlightening. "Long Island is beautiful, and I'm learning all kinds of things about Harry I never knew before. Vivian and Harrison have been very accommodating."

"Vivian and Harrison." Gus echoed her use of their first names in the kind of speculative tone he might have used if he were conjecturing about the identity of Jack the Ripper. "I see."

Gracie supposed it was only natural that he would be skeptical. After all, the last time she'd seen him, Harrison had been accusing her of giving his father an STD and robbing him blind. Now that she thought about it, she, too, wondered why she wasn't still mad at Harrison.

In a word, hmm.

"I'm glad to hear it," Gus said. "And you'll be glad to know—as will you, Mrs. Sage—that the paperwork on the Long Island house and the Manhattan penthouse is in progress. We should be able to courier the papers to you in Amagansett Thursday or Friday, right on schedule."

"That is wonderful news," Vivian agreed. "Thank you again, Gracie."

"No thanks are necessary, Vivian. I'm sure Harry knew I would return the houses to you and that it's what he wanted."

"Yes, well, that makes one of us, darling. Oh, look, there's Bunny," Vivian said, lifting a hand in greeting to their hostess. "You'll all excuse me."

She hurried off without awaiting a reply, leaving Gracie to be the buffer between her son and the law firm that was her son's biggest antagonist.

"So, Gus," she said, grappling for some benign subject to jump-start the conversation. "How did you get into the long-lost-relative business?"

"Tarrant and Twigg recruited me when I was still at Georgetown law school. I was in my last year of probate law and wrote a paper on how to better employ the internet for heir hunting for one of my classes. My professor was a friend of Bennett's and thought he'd find it interesting so he passed it along to him. The next time Bennett was in DC, he and I met for lunch, and he offered me an associate position."

"So have you guys reunited lots of families?" she asked.

"Or split a lot of them up?" Harrison interjected.

Gracie threw him an irritated look, but Gus only chuckled.

"No, it's a fair question," he said. "Family estates can be very contentious, especially when they're large. Fortunately for us, we most often deal with single heirs to estates. Ones who are the last in a line, so there's no one to contest the terms."

"Well then," Harrison said, "aren't my mother and I lucky to be among the few, the proud, the contested."

Again, Gus smiled. "Well, we do seem to have had an unusual run lately of clients who could be wandering into some potential conflict. Once we find them, of course."

"And I'm sure you'll find them," Gracie said.

"We always do," Gus assured her. Then his expression changed. "Well, except for that once."

Gracie was about to ask him more about that, but someone hailed him from the other side of the room. So Gus bid her and Harrison a hasty farewell and made his way in that direction, leaving the two of them alone. And although they had been alone together pretty much all day with fairly little uneasiness, Gus's departure left Gracie feeling very uneasy indeed.

Harrison seemed to share her discomfort, because the moment his gaze met hers, he quickly glanced off to the right, and then turned his entire body in that direction. In response, Gracie turned away and shot her gaze in the opposite direction. Then both of them looked back at each other again, turning their bodies back a little, then a little more, until they were standing face-to-face again. For one long moment, they just stood that way, their gazes locked, their tongues tied. And then...

Then something really weird happened. It was as if some kind of gauzy curtain descended around them on all sides, separating them from everyone else in the room. Everyone else in the world. The clamor of the chattering people tapered to a purr of something faint and almost melodic. The gleam of the chandelier mellowed to a blush of pink. The chill of the air conditioning ebbed to a caress of awareness. And everything else seemed to recede until it was nothing but shadows and murmurs.

Gracie had no idea if Harrison felt it, too, but he stood as still and silent as she, as if he was just as transfixed and didn't want to move or speak for fear of ruining the moment, either. Time seemed to have stopped, too, as if nothing but that moment mattered. Then a woman somewhere in the room barked raucously with laughter, and the entire impression was gone.

Leaving Gracie—and possibly Harrison—feeling more awkward than ever.

"I'll go get us a drink," he said suddenly, sounding almost panicky. Yep, he felt the awkwardness, too. "What would you like?"

Like? she echoed to herself. How was she supposed to answer that? Her brain was so scrambled at the moment, she barely knew her own name, and he was asking her what she wanted? Well, okay, maybe she had an idea of what she, you know, *wanted* at the moment, but there was no way she was going to tell Harrison she wanted *that*. And how could she want *that* from him in the first place? Not only had she known him a mere matter of days, but she also wasn't even sure she liked him enough for *that*. And she was pretty sure he didn't like her, either, even if he was sharing weird, gauzy-curtain, shadow-and-murmur moments with her.

"Um, whatever you're having is fine," she said. "That will be fine. It's fine."

It was all Gracie could do not to slap a hand over her mouth to keep herself from further babbling. For one terrifying second, she honestly thought she was going to tell him that what she wanted was him. Then for another even more terrifying second she thought he was going to tell her that that was good, because he intended to have her. There was just something about the expression on his face just then that—

Thankfully, after one more panicky look, he bolted toward a bar in the far corner of the room, where a group of people had congregated, leaving Gracie alone to collect her thoughts. Unfortunately, her thoughts had wandered so far off that she was going to need an intergalactic mode of transportation to bring them all back.

By the time Harrison returned with their drinks, she had managed to gather herself together enough that her brain and other body parts were reasonably under control. At least until she went to remove her right glove so she could accept her cocktail, because that was when her fingers suddenly wanted to fumble all over the place. Possibly because he seemed unable to peel his gaze away from hers, and then seemed unable to peel it away from her fumbling fingers. After she finally wrestled off the glove, she made a tight fist to halt the trembling of her hand before accepting her drink. But it still trembled when she took the glass from him, enough that he cupped his hand over hers for a moment after transferring the drink to her, to make sure she didn't drop it.

And damned if that weird gauzy-curtain thing didn't happen again. This time, though, they were making contact when it did. She was able to feel how gently he was touching her, and how warm his hand was over hers, and how she wished more than anything he would never let her go. But he did let her go, finally, and up went the curtain again. Somehow, she was able to mumble her thanks, though whether her gratitude was for the drink, the way he touched her or the fact that the strange episode had come to an end, she couldn't have said.

Harrison's gaze met hers again, and he was smiling the same sort of smile he'd smiled when he'd told the butler she was with him. She lifted her drink for a sip and—

Wait. What? The import of that finally struck her. Harrison had been smiling when he told the butler "she's with me." Therefore something about her arrival at the party had made him happy. And something about telling Ballantine she was *with him* had made him happy, too.

Now he was smiling that same smile again, which must mean that he was viewing her less as an enemy. But that was good, right? It meant he was starting to believe Harry left his fortune to her for philanthropic reasons, not because she took advantage of him. So why did Gracie suddenly feel worried again, and for entirely different reasons?

For a moment, they only sipped their drinks in

silence—bourbon, not Gracie's favorite, but it was okay—and looked around the room. Then Harrison fixed his gaze—that blue, blue, good God, his eyes were blue gaze—on hers.

And very softly, he asked, "Earlier tonight, why did you ask if you should leave?"

It took her a moment to remember what he was talking about. Back when she first arrived at the party, when it was obvious he didn't like what she was wearing. "I thought you wanted me to leave because I was going to embarrass you and Vivian."

He looked surprised. "Why would you think that?"

She was surprised by his surprise. Wasn't it obvious why she would think that?

"Because I'm not...sophisticated," she said. "I'm not...elegant. I'm not..." Now she made an exasperated sound. "I don't know how to act around people like this, in situations like this. I don't *belong* here. Not that it ever mattered before, you know? I never needed to be sophisticated or elegant. I never wanted to be. But tonight..."

She trailed off without finishing, and Harrison looked as if he had no more idea what to say than she did. So Gracie sipped her drink again, finding the smoky flavor a little less disagreeable this time. See? People could learn to like things they didn't like before. They just had to give them a chance.

She looked at Harrison again. Harrison, who was so far out of her league, even intergalactic modes of transportation couldn't connect them. No way would he ever consider her sophisticated or elegant or think she belonged in a place like this. She wished she didn't care about that. She wished it didn't matter. She wished...

The irony of the situation was staggering, really. For the first time in her life, Gracie could—technically—afford anything she wanted. And the one thing she was beginning to think she might want was the only thing she would never be able to have.

Seven

The morning after the Dewitts' party, Harrison lay in bed with barely four hours of sleep under his belt, staring at the ceiling and wondering why he couldn't stop thinking about Gracie, who for some reason now seemed exactly suited to that name. Mostly, he couldn't stop thinking about the moment he'd glanced past Ballantine to see her standing at the front door, looking like something that should have been under glass in a pastry shop.

He still didn't know what the hell had happened to him in that moment. He only knew that his stomach had pitched, his mouth had gone dry, his brain had fizzled and his…well, never mind what some of his other body parts had done.

And there had been nothing about her to warrant such a blatantly sexual reaction, which was all his reaction to her had been, he assured himself. Sexual. Even if it had felt like something different. Something more. It couldn't have been anything *but* sexual. She'd just looked so... She'd just seemed so... And he'd felt so... And he'd really wanted to...

He turned onto his side, toward the open window, and glanced at the chair draped with his discarded clothing of the night before. Ah, dammit. He didn't know what he'd wanted when he saw her standing there. Okay, yes, he did know that. What he didn't know was why. Okay, maybe he knew that, too. It had been a while since he'd acted on a sexual attraction. Probably because it had been a while since he'd felt a sexual attraction. All the women he knew were women he *knew*, and once he got to *know* a woman, he pretty much stopped being sexually attracted to her. There wasn't much point in continuing with something once you knew what it was like, and it stopped being challenging. Or interesting. So although Harrison knew *why* he found Gracie attractive, what he didn't know was why he found *Gracie* attractive.

Why her? He'd seen a million pretty girls in a million party dresses in his life. Hell, he'd helped a million pretty girls *out* of a million party dresses in his life. And Gracie wasn't even the kind of party girl he normally went for—the kind who wore lots of makeup and little clothing. What makeup she'd worn last night had whispered, not screamed, and there'd been nothing revealing about her dress. For God's sake, she'd even worn gloves.

Although, now that he thought about it—not for the first time since the night before—her collarbone had looked pretty damned lickable. As had the nape of her neck. And the line of her jaw. And her earlobes…

Really, all of her had looked pretty damned lickable.

He tossed to his other side, punched his pillow, closed his eyes and commanded his brain to grab another hour of sleep. Instead, his brain etched another vision of Gracie on the insides of his eyelids, this one of her looking dashed and asking him, "Should I leave?" He'd been stunned later when she told him she'd asked the question because she thought she was embarrassing him. Because she wasn't sophisticated or elegant and didn't belong in high society.

And all the while Harrison had been thinking how she was more elegant and sophisticated than any of them.

Just who was Gracie Sumner? *Was* she a con artist? Or was she something else?

Harrison bit back a groan. Why was he doubting her? Why was he doubting himself? She *couldn't* be anything other than what he'd suspected since he'd heard the particulars of his father's will. Okay, maybe she wasn't as predatory as he'd first thought, but his father had had too deep an appreciation for money— too deep an obsession with money—to give it all to a stranger and insist that she give it to even more strangers. Harrison Sage, Jr. had been the most calculating, close-fisted man Harrison III had ever known. Philanthropy was the last thing he'd thought about when he was alive. He wouldn't have felt any differently when thinking about his inevitable death. He would have made sure his fortune stayed with the family, where it would grow more obscene, even after he was gone. So what had happened to him to change that?

His father couldn't have been in his right mind when he put Gracie in charge of his personal estate. He had to have been mentally diminished, and she must have taken advantage of that. Maybe she'd convinced him to give his money to charity, and to put her in charge of the funds. And the moment the spotlight was off of her, she was going to take the money and run.

That had to be it. It was the only explanation that made sense.

He was through being enchanted by Gracie Sumner. *Grace* Sumner, he corrected himself. And he wouldn't be swayed by her again.

Gracie was the first to come downstairs the next morning, a not unexpected development, since Vivian had still been at the party last night when she and Harrison left, and Harrison had opted for a nightcap before he went to bed himself. No breakfast had been set up on the patio yet, so Gracie headed back into the house...mansion...palace...most gigantic residence she'd ever seen...to forage in the kitchen herself. She would at least start the coffee, since, as far as she was concerned, a day without caffeine was like a day without precious, life-giving oxygen. As she entered the hall she was pretty sure would lead to the kitchen, however, she crashed into the most gigantic man's chest she'd ever seen. *Oops.*

"Whoa," Harrison said as he wrapped his hands around her upper arms and moved her back a few steps. "What's the hurry? Are we planning to take advantage of everyone's absence to fill our pockets with anything that's not nailed down?"

Ignoring, for now, that neither her red-and-yellow

plaid pants nor her red short-sleeved blouse had pockets—and even if they did, no way could she stuff a
Louis Quatorze buffet into one—Gracie frowned at
Harrison. When they'd parted ways last night, they'd
been on pretty good terms. In spite of some of the
weirdness that had arced between them at the party,
they'd eventually fallen into a reasonably comfortable
fellowship that had lasted all the way through the ride
home.

This morning, though, he seemed to want to return
to the antagonism she'd thought had vanished. Or at
least diminished to the point where he had stopped
thinking of her as a thief. She took a step backward,
removing herself from his grasp, and frowned harder.
Not as easy to do as it should have been, because he
looked even yummier than usual in casual dark-wash
jeans and a white oxford shirt, the sleeves rolled to
his elbows.

Instead of rising to the bait he was so clearly dan-
gling in front of her, she said, "And good morning to
you, too."

He deflated a little at her greeting. But he didn't
wish her a good-morning in return. Instead, he told
her, "The servants get the weekend off. Everyone's on
their own for breakfast."

"Which isn't a problem," she said, "except that I
don't know where the kitchen is."

He tilted his head in the direction she'd been headed.
"You were on the right track. It's this way."

Gracie may have been on the right track, she thought
as she followed him through a warren of rooms, but if
he hadn't shown up when he did, they would have had
to send a search-and-rescue team after her. It struck

her again as she absorbed her grand surroundings just how rich Harry had been, just how much he'd turned his back on when he ran away to Cincinnati and just how out-of-place the man she'd known would have been in these surroundings.

Even the kitchen reeked of excess, massive as it was with state-of-the-art appliances—some of them things Gracie didn't recognize even with her restaurant experience.

"Coffee," she said, hoping the word sounded more like a desire than a demand, thinking it came off more as a decree. "Um, I mean, if you'll tell me where it is, I'll make it."

"I set it up last night. Just push the button."

She looked around for a Mr. Coffee, and then reminded herself she was in the home of a billionaire, so switched gears for a Bonavita or Bunn. But she didn't see one of those, either. When Harrison noted her confusion, he pointed behind her. She turned, but all she saw was something that looked like a giant chrome insect. She looked at him again, her expression puzzled.

"The Kees van der Westen?" he said helpfully.

Well, *he* probably thought it was helpful. To Gracie, a Kees van der Westen sounded like something that should be hanging in the Metropolitan Museum of Art. When she continued to gaze at him in stumped silence, he moved past her to the big metal bug, placed a coffee cup beneath one of its limbs, and pushed a button. Immediately, the machine began to hum, and a beautiful stream of fragrant mahogany brew began to stream into the cup.

"Wow," she said. "That's more impressive than the espresso machine we have at Café Destiné." Then, because she hadn't had her coffee yet so couldn't be held responsible for her indiscretion, she asked, "How much did that set you back?"

Harrison didn't seem to think the question odd, however. He just shrugged and said. "I don't know. Six or seven thousand, I think."

She couldn't help how her mouth dropped open at that. "Seven thousand dollars? For a coffeemaker?"

"Well, it does espresso and cappuccino, too," he said. "Besides, you get what you pay for."

"You know what else you can get for seven thousand dollars?" she asked, telling herself it was still because she hadn't had her coffee, but knowing more that it was because she wanted to prove a point.

He thought for a minute. "Not a lot, really."

"There are some cities where seven thousand dollars will pay for two years of community college," she said. "What you think of as a coffeemaker is a higher education for some people."

His expression went inscrutable again. "Imagine that."

"I don't have to imagine it," she said. "I've done a lot of research. Do you have any idea how many lives your father's fourteen billion dollars will change? Any concept at all? Do you even know what *one* billion dollars could buy?"

Instead of waiting for him to answer, she continued, "One billion dollars can send more than twenty-five thousand kids to a public university for four years. Twenty-five thousand! A billion dollars can put two million laptops in public schools. A billion dollars can buy decent housing for six thousand families in some places. A billion dollars can run seven thousand shelters for battered women for a year. You add up how many lives would be improved. And that's only the first four billion."

Harrison's expression remained fixed, but something flickered in his eyes that made her think she was getting through to him.

So she added, "Your father's money can bring libraries to communities that don't have one. It can put musical instruments in schools that can't afford them. It can build playgrounds in neighborhoods that are covered with asphalt. It can send kids to camp. It can build health clinics. It can fill food banks. Maybe that was why Harry changed his mind late in life about what he wanted to do with his money. So he'd be remembered for changing the world, one human life at a time."

At this, Harrison's expression finally changed. Though not exactly for the better. "And what about his family?" he asked. "Did my father have to completely shut us out? You keep talking about him as if he were this paragon of altruism in Cincinnati, conveniently forgetting about how he turned his back on his family here. Not just me and my mother, but my half sisters and their mothers, too. My father spent his life here taking whatever he wanted whenever he wanted it, often from people he claimed to love. Now he wants to give it all back to strangers? Where's the logic in that? Where's the commitment? Where's the obligation? Where's the… Dammit, where's the love?"

His eruption stunned Gracie into silence. Not because of the eruption itself, but because she realized he was right. She'd been thinking of Harry's fortune as an all-or-nothing behemoth, something that either went to charity or to the Sages, and neither the twain should meet. But Harry could have left something to his family. Not just to Harrison and Vivian, but to his ex-wives and other children, too. So why hadn't he?

"I'm sorry," Gracie said, knowing the words were inadequate, but having no idea what else to say. She didn't know why Harry had excluded his family from his will. Maybe he'd figured Harrison would be fine on his own and capable of taking care of Vivian. Maybe he'd assumed his divorce settlements with his exes were enough for all of them and his other children to have good lives. And probably, that was true. But he still could have left each of them *some*thing. Something to show them he remembered them, to let them know he had loved them, even if he hadn't done that in life.

Because one thing Gracie did know. As rough-around-the-edges and irascible as Harry could be, he *had* been able to love. She'd seen him express it every day. Maybe not in his words, but in his actions. He'd loved his parents and little brother once upon a time, too. And if he'd been able to love a family as fractured as his had been when he was a boy, then he *must* have loved Harrison and Vivian, too, even if he'd never been any good at showing it. Maybe if Harrison had known him the way Gracie did, he would be able to see that, too.

If only she could take Harrison back in time a few years and introduce him to the version of his father she knew. If only he could see Harry in his flannel bathrobe, shuffling around his apartment in his old-man slippers and Reds cap, watering his plants, his favorite team on TV in the background, his four-alarm chili bubbling on the stove. If only he could see Harry's patience when he taught her to fox-trot or his compassion when he filled trays at the shelter or his gentleness showing some kid how to hold a bat.

And that was when it hit her. There was a way she *could* show Harrison those things. Harry wouldn't be there physically, of course, but he'd be there in spirit. Harrison had shown her his version of his father in New York yesterday. So why couldn't Gracie show him her version of Harry in Cincinnati? They could fly there tomorrow and spend a couple of days. She could take Harrison to the storage unit to go through his father's things. They could watch the Little League team Harry coached. She could show Harrison the hospital and shelter where Harry volunteered and introduce him to some of the people who knew him. She could even take him dancing at the Moondrop Ballroom.

Harrison had never known that side of his father. Maybe if they went to Cincinnati, he'd see that Harry wasn't the cold, rapacious man he remembered. And maybe, between the two of them, they could figure Harry out, once and for all.

"Harrison," she said decisively, "we need to go to Cincinnati."

His expression would have been the same if she had just smacked him with a big, wet fish. "Why do we need to go to Cincinnati?"

"So you can meet Harry."

"You've already told me all about him."

"And you don't seem to believe any of it."

He said nothing in response to that. What could he say? He *didn't* believe anything she'd told him about Harry. Not really. He was the kind of person who needed to see stuff with his own eyes to be convinced.

"I have to go back to work next week," he said,

lamely enough that Gracie knew that wasn't the reason he was balking.

"You can give yourself a couple more days off," she said. "You're the boss."

He said nothing again, but that only encouraged her. "Look, you took me on the Harrison Sage, Jr. tour of New York City. So now let me take you on the Harry Sagalowsky tour of Cincinnati."

"And did the Harrison Sage, Jr. tour change your mind about your friend Harry?" he asked.

Gracie hesitated before replying. "Not really," she admitted. But she quickly declared, "But it's given me a lot to think about. It's added a lot to my picture of Harry, and even if the things I learned don't paint him in the greatest light, I'm still glad to have learned them. I want to do the same for your picture of Harrison, Jr.," she added more gently. "So you'll have more to think about, too."

This time, Harrison was the one to hesitate. Finally, he told her, "It won't make any difference in the way I feel. About my father or you."

Something in the way he said it, though, made Gracie think he was at least willing to give it a chance. Where his father was concerned, anyway. Although maybe he meant—

"It doesn't matter how you feel about me," she said before her thoughts could go any further, wishing that were true. Wondering why it wasn't. She really shouldn't care about how Harrison felt about her. Her only goal at the moment was to help him move past his resentment toward his father. But she couldn't quite forget those few moments the night before when things had seemed…different between them. And she couldn't forget the way he'd looked when she told him all the things he hadn't known about his father's past. Like a hurt little kid who was just trying to make sense of things and couldn't.

Let me help you make sense of it, Gracie silently bid him. *Of your father and of me. And let me try to make sense of you, too.* Because somehow, it was beginning to feel just as important for her and Harrison to understand each other as it was for them to understand Harry.

Harrison hesitated again. Long enough this time that Gracie feared he would decline once and for all. Finally, reluctantly, he told her, "Okay. I'll go."

She expelled a breath she hadn't been aware of holding. "Great. How long will it take you to pack?"

Eight

Gracie couldn't have ordered a better day for a baseball game. June was the kindest of the summer months in the Ohio Valley, the skies blue and perfect and the breezes warm and playful. The park where Harry's Little League team, the Woodhaven Rockets, played had four baseball diamonds and every one of them was filled. She and Harrison had arrived early enough to find a bleacher seat in the shade, up on the very top bench, where they could see all the action. She'd instructed him to wear the team colors, so he'd complied with gray cargo shorts and a pale blue polo that made his blue, blue eyes even bluer. She'd opted for white capris and a powder-blue sleeveless shirt for herself.

They'd arrived in Cincinnati the evening before, late enough that there hadn't been time to do much more than say good-night and turn in. Harrison had wanted to have lunch before the game today, but Gracie told him that until she presented the league with a check from Harry's estate, concessions were where they made most of their money for uniforms and equipment, so the least she and Harrison could do was plunk down a few bucks for a couple of hot dogs and sodas. Not to mention if Dylan Mendelson was still on the team, there might be some of his mom's red velvet cupcakes.

The Rockets were leading in the seventh inning four to zip, their pitcher barreling ball after ball over home plate without a single crack of the bat. If this kept up, it was going to be a no-hitter.

"Way to go, Roxanne!" Gracie shouted to the pitcher at the end of the inning as the teams were switching places. "Keep it up, girlfriend!"

When she sat back down, Harrison said, "That's a *girl* pitching?"

"Damn straight. Don't sound so surprised. Girls are great ballplayers."

"No, it's not that. It's that she must not have been on the team when my father coached it."

"Your father was the first one to recognize what a good arm she has. Making her the Rockets' pitcher was one of the last things he did before he died." She brightened. "Now there's a legacy for you. Thanks to Harry, Roxanne Bailey might be the first woman to play in the Majors."

Judging by his expression, Harrison was doubtful. Or maybe it was his father's actions he was doubting.

"What?" she asked.

He hesitated, as if he were looking for the right words. "My father never…cared much…for women."

He seemed to realize Gracie was about to object, so he held up a hand and hurried on. "Oh, he liked women. A lot. My mother would tell you he liked them too much. But he only hired them for clerical positions and never promoted any to executive. He just didn't think women could do anything more than be pretty and type."

"Wow," Gracie said. "That is so *not* the Harry I knew. He put up with a lot of crap from some of the dads for making Roxanne the pitcher, but he didn't back down. And I never saw him speak to a woman any differently than he spoke to a man."

Harrison looked out at the field, but his expression suggested he was seeing something other than a bunch of kids playing baseball.

"Gracie?" a woman called out from behind the bleachers. "Gracie Sumner, is that you?"

She turned to see Sarah Denham, the mother of the Rockets' catcher, standing below them. She, too, was dressed in the team colors, a Rockets ball cap perched backward on her head, hot dogs in each hand.

"Hi, Sarah!" Gracie greeted her, happy to see a familiar face.

"I thought that was you," Sarah said. With a smile, she added, "It's strange to see you without Harry. What are you doing back in town?"

At the mention of Harry's name, Harrison turned around, too, clearly interested in meeting someone else who knew his father in this world. So Gracie introduced the two of them.

"I am so sorry for your loss," Sarah told him. "Your father was one of the nicest men I ever met. He was so great with these kids."

Harrison was clearly surprised by the statement, in spite of Gracie having already told him the same thing.

Sarah continued with a smile, "And his jokes! He kept these kids in stitches."

"My father told jokes?" Harrison asked, startled.

"Oh, my gosh, yes," Sarah said. "What did one mushroom say to the other mushroom?"

Harrison smiled. "I don't know."

Sarah smiled back. "You're a fun guy. Get it? Fungi?"

Harrison groaned. "That's a terrible joke."

"I know," Sarah agreed with a laugh. "They were all like that. The kids loved them." She turned to Gracie. "So where are you living now?"

Gracie's back went up almost literally at the question. Her own past in Cincinnati was the last thing she wanted to revisit, especially in front of Harrison. "Seattle," she said, hoping Sarah left it at that.

But of course, she didn't. "So far away? I mean, I knew things with Devon got bad—"

At this, Harrison snapped his attention to Gracie.

"—but I didn't know you went all the way across the country," Sarah said.

"That's all in the past," Gracie said. Then she rushed to change the subject. "Hey, did Trudy bring any of her red velvet cupcakes?"

"She did," Sarah said. "But they're going fast."

The perfect excuse to escape. "You want a cupcake?" she asked Harrison as she stood. "My treat. I'll be right back."

Before he could reply, she was trundling down the bleachers toward the concession stand. And just as she tried to do whenever Devon Braun intruded into her life, she didn't look back once.

* * *

Gracie hadn't visited the self-storage unit with Harry's things since snapping on the padlock two years ago, so she braced herself for the discovery that everything might be a little musty. And dusty. And rusty. Fortunately, both she and Harrison were dressed for such a development: he in a pair of khaki cargo shorts and a black, V-neck T-shirt, she in a pair of baggy plaid shorts and an even baggier white T-shirt. Each was armed with a box cutter, and they'd brought additional boxes in which to pack anything Harrison might want to ship back to New York right away.

She had deliberately saved the storage shed for the last day of their trip, because it held what was left of the heart and soul of Harry Sagalowsky. After yesterday's game, they'd visited the shelter and hospital where Harry had volunteered, and where many of the people remembered both him and Gracie. Then she and Harrison had had dinner at her and Harry's favorite hole-in-the-wall barbecue joint, where the owner-chef had come out to regale Harrison with stories about how he and Harry had always argued good-naturedly over whose sauce was best. The chef had finally admitted—but only to the two of them—that there was something about Harry's chili he had never been able to duplicate and he was pretty sure it had something to do with the cumin.

Gracie and Harrison had ended the day by retiring to his hotel room with a rented DVD of *The African Queen*, Harry's favorite movie, something that also surprised Harrison because, even though it was kind of a war movie, it had a romance in it, too, and his father had thought the idea of romance was foolish.

Gracie wondered if Harrison thought that, too. For the most part, he didn't seem any more of a romantic than he claimed his father had been, but there had been times over the last couple of days—and times when they'd been in New York, too—when she'd caught him looking at her in a way that was… Or else he'd said something in a way that was… Or the air around the two of them had just seemed kind of… Well. Gracie wasn't sure if the right word for those occasions was *romantic*. Then again, she wasn't sure it was the wrong word, either. Because something about those occasions, especially over the last couple of days, sure had felt kind of…romantic.

That wasn't likely to change tonight, since the last leg of their tour would be at the Moondrop Ballroom, the epitome of old Hollywood romance, where Gracie would try to teach Harrison to dance the way Harry had once taught her.

If, after all that, Harrison still saw his father as a coldhearted, cold-blooded cold fish who hadn't cared about anything but money, then he was a lost cause, and Gracie didn't know what to do. Of course, she still hadn't accepted the coldhearted, cold-blooded cold fish who'd only cared about money that Harrison kept insisting Harry was, so maybe she was a lost cause, too. At least they could be lost causes together.

She had to wrestle with the storage-unit padlock for a few seconds until it finally gave. Then it took both Harrison and her to haul up the big, garage-type metal door. It groaned like a dying mammoth when they did, and the storage unit belched an odor that was a mix of old books, old socks and old man. Gracie gazed into the belly of the beast, a cinderblock room about twenty feet wide by twenty feet deep, wondering where to begin.

"I probably should have tried to find Harry's family as soon as he passed away," she said when she realized how musty, dusty and rusty everything was. "But I truly didn't think he had anyone."

"Was no one at his funeral?" Harrison asked, the question touched with something almost melancholy.

Maybe there was part of him that still had the capacity to forgive, and even love, his father—or, at least, think fondly of him from time to time. Although he might never fully grieve the loss of a man he hadn't seen in half a lifetime, and hadn't really ever known, maybe he was beginning to entertain the possibility that his father wasn't the villain he'd thought him to be.

In spite of his somber tone, Gracie couldn't help but smile at the question. "There were lots of people. His visitation was three days long so that everyone could have a chance to pay their respects. Even after that, there were still hundreds of people who attended the funeral."

"But no one from his family," Harrison said, still sounding pensive. "Not from any of his families."

"In a way, he had family here," Gracie said, hoping Harrison wouldn't take it the wrong way. She didn't want to diminish his and Vivian's ties to Harry. She just wanted to comfort him, and make him realize his father hadn't been without loved ones when he died.

But Harrison didn't seem to take offense. "That's not the same," he said. "Someone from his real family should have been here."

Gracie extended a hand to touch him, waffled for a moment and then placed her palm gently against his shoulder. Harrison looked over at the contact, his gaze falling first on her hand, then on her face, but he didn't move away.

"Your father touched a lot of lives, Harrison," she said softly. "He made a difference for a lot of people when he lived here. And he'll make a difference for a lot more when his fortune is given away."

Harrison inhaled a breath and released it. Then, not even seeming to realize he was doing it, he covered her hand with his. "I just don't understand why he felt like he could only do that for strangers."

Gracie didn't understand that, either. There had to be a reason. But they might never know what it was. She looked into the storage unit again. Maybe they could start looking for an explanation here.

She had taken care to organize Harry's things when she stowed them. Furniture on the left, boxes on the right, clothes and miscellaneous in the middle, with two narrow aisles separating everything to enable access. Nearly half the boxes held books and his record collection, mostly jazz and big band. Many of the rest held his accumulation of Cincinnati Reds memorabilia. It was the boxes in front, though, that Gracie wanted to open first. They were the ones that contained Harry's personal items, including the photographs Harrison needed to see.

She strode to the one closest to the front, pressed her blade to the packing tape seam and slid it along the length of the box with a quick *z-z-zip*. Harrison took a few steps into the unit as Gracie finished opening the box and removed a couple of layers of cedar-scented tissue paper. The first thing she encountered underneath was a beer stein from the last Oktoberfest she and Harry attended. She smiled as she lifted it up for Harrison to see.

"Zee?" she said, affecting her best German accent—which, okay, wasn't all that good. "Your papa luffed hiss *Schwarzbier und leberwurst.* He *vas* a real *Feinschmecker."*

Harrison chuckled at that. He even took a few more steps toward her. But all he said was, "Um, *Feinschmecker?"*

"Ja," Gracie replied. Then, returning to her normal voice, she said, "I wanted to slap him the first time he called me that. German isn't the easiest language to figure out."

"So what's a *Feinschmecker?"*

"A connoisseur of fine foods. Okay, maybe beer and liverwurst don't qualify as such. Suffice to say he enjoyed good *Hausmannskost."*

Harrison nodded. And came a few steps closer. "I never knew my father spoke German."

"Very well, in fact," she said. "He grew up in one of the German neighborhoods here."

Gracie held out the beer stein for Harrison to take. It was stoneware and decorated with a dachshund wearing lederhosen and playing an accordion. Gingerly, he closed the last few feet between them and took it from her.

"Harry was good at the chicken dance, too," she said as she released it.

"No," Harrison said adamantly, finally meeting her gaze. He set the beer stein on top of another still-closed box. "You will never convince me my father did the chicken dance."

Gracie picked through some of the other items in

the box. "If you're ever in Seattle, look me up. I have photographic evidence. Oh, look!" she cried as she picked up something else, cutting Harrison off from commenting on the "if you're ever in Seattle" thing. What was she thinking to say something like that? "I gave Harry this for Christmas!"

She withdrew a plastic electronic device the size of a toothbrush that, when its buttons were pushed, lit up, made funny noises and was generally annoying. She handed it to Harrison.

"What is it?" he asked.

"A sonic screwdriver like the one Doctor Who uses."

"But Doctor Who is science fiction. My father hated science fiction."

"Your father loved science fiction." She gestured toward the boxes in back. "There's a ton of Ray Bradbury, Isaac Asimov and Harlan Ellison books in those. You'll see."

Harrison began pushing the buttons on the sonic screwdriver one by one, the same way Harry had on Christmas morning after unwrapping it. Then he grinned. In exactly the same way his father had.

"Okay, here's what I've been looking for," she said when she uncovered the shoebox with Harry's photographs. She began sorting through them, and then was surprised when Harrison reached in, too, and pulled out a handful to look through himself.

"Here," she said, pausing on one. "This is what I wanted to show you. It's your dad and his brother, Benjy, when they were kids."

She handed the black-and-white photo to Harrison. The edges were frayed, the corners bent, and it was creased down the middle, creating a fine white line between the two boys. They were on the front stoop of the brownstone where the family had rented an apartment. Benjy was sitting on a square box nearly as big as he was. Harry had his arm around his brother, and both were grinning mischievously.

"Your dad is on the left," Gracie said. "He was six in the photo. Benjy was three. The box Benjy's sitting on is where the milkman left the weekly milk deliveries. Harry said the reason they're smiling like that is because they just put the neighbor's cat in the box without telling anyone, and with Benjy sitting on it, the poor thing couldn't get out."

Harrison nodded. "Now *that* sounds more like my father."

"He assured me they let it go right after their neighbor snapped the photo, and he promised it wasn't hurt."

She watched as Harrison studied the photo, but his expression revealed nothing of what he might be thinking or feeling. Finally, he said, "That's my dad, all right." After a moment, he added, "And I guess that's my uncle. Or would have been, had he lived."

Gracie sifted through the photos until she found another one. "And here are your grandparents."

Harrison took it from her, studying it with the same scrutiny he'd given the first photo.

"You look just like your grandfather," she said. "He couldn't have been much older in that picture than you are now."

He considered the photo for another moment. "I can't believe my father never told me about any of this. About where he came from, or his little brother, or what his parents were like." Now he looked at Gracie. "But then, I never asked him about any of it when I had the chance, did I? I never took an interest in where he came from when I was a kid. It never occurred to me that his history was mine, too. I know everything about my mother's family. But they're Park Avenue fixtures. They've been rich since New York was New Amsterdam. My father marrying her was the biggest social coup of his life."

"Maybe that was why he never talked about his past," Gracie said. "Maybe he didn't think it could stand up to Vivian's. Maybe he thought you would be ashamed of an alcoholic grandfather and a grandmother who abandoned her only surviving child."

"The same way he abandoned his family," Harrison said softly.

Gracie sighed. "Yeah. I guess so."

He shook his head. "I wouldn't have been ashamed of any of that. I would have felt bad for him. If I'd known how much he lost when he was a kid… How hard he worked to try to keep his family together… How poor they were all along…"

"What?" she asked when he didn't finish.

"I don't know. Maybe it just would have helped me understand him better or something."

Harrison continued sifting through the photos of his father's family—of his family—lost in thoughts Gracie figured she would probably never be able to understand. Thoughts he would never share with her, anyway, she was sure. Funny, though, how there was a quickly growing part of her that really wished he would.

Sunlight was slanting into the storage unit in a long beam of late-afternoon gold when Harrison finally closed the lid on the box of things he wanted to take back to New York with him. The rest could wait for him to have it moved professionally. There was plenty of room in his mother's attic to store everything. Not that he had any idea why he wanted to store it all. There was nothing of value among his father's things. The furniture was old and scarred. The clothes were old and worn out. The knickknacks were old and kitschy. Even the books and records were run-of-the-mill titles that could be found in a million places. For some reason, though, Harrison didn't want to let go of any of them.

So everything Gracie had said was true. Neither she nor his father had made up any of it. Harrison Sage, Jr. really had had a little brother. He'd really dropped out of school to go to work—one of the things they'd found was his first union card, issued when he would have been fifteen. And he really had lost his parents in terrible ways—they'd also found diaries written by his grandmother describing it all. Harrison had scanned a couple of them, but he wanted to read them all in depth when he got back to New York.

As he gazed upon the boxes and bags that held all his father's worldly possessions—or, at least, all the worldly possessions he had wanted to surround himself with as his life drew to a close—Harrison tried to understand how and why his father had lived his life the way he had. How and why a man who'd had *everything* in New York had preferred to spend his last years in a place where he had had nothing.

Gracie's words echoed through Harrison's head. *There were hundreds of people who attended the funeral.* A lot of them were people Harrison had met yesterday. Kids who loved terrible jokes. A World War

Two veteran whose only visitor most weeks had been Harry Sagalowsky, who brought him a magazine and a cup of coffee, then stayed to talk baseball. A homeless mother he'd helped get a job at a local factory, who was then able to move herself and her kids into their own place and start life anew.

Big damn deal.

There would have been *thousands* of people at his father's funeral if he'd died in New York. And they would have *really* known him. They would have known how much he was worth and recognized his accomplishments in the business and financial worlds. They would have known what companies he'd acquired, which ones he had shed and which ones he had his eye on. They would have known which of his latest ventures had been most profitable. They would have known his favorite drink, his favorite restaurant, the name of his tailor. Hell, they would have known who his current mistresses were and where he was keeping them.

But here? What was the value in delivering a magazine or helping in a job hunt or making kids laugh? What difference did it make if Harry Sagalowsky had shared part of his day with others, supplying simple pleasures and favors to people who needed them? Who cared if one person took time to acknowledge another person's existence in the world and share a little bit of himself in the process? What was so great about making a connection with other people to let them know they were important? Who needed to be remembered as a normal, everyday person who made other normal, everyday people happy when he could be remembered as a titan of commerce who'd made billions of dollars for himself instead?

Thankfully, Harrison's spiel was in his head. Because if he'd said those things out loud, Gracie would have read him the riot act. And he probably wouldn't have blamed her. Okay, maybe he was starting to see why his father had wanted to spend his final years here. Because here, with people who didn't know him as Billionaire Harrison Sage, Jr., he could live a life free of that image and be…well, some guy named Harry who did nice things for other people. Things that maybe didn't change the world, but things that made a difference on a smaller scale. Things that would maybe make up for some of the stuff Billionaire Harrison Sage, Jr. did during his lifetime, like putting money ahead of everything else.

Like turning his back on his family.

Not that Harrison thought what his father had done here in Cincinnati would ever make up for that. But he could see where his father might think it would.

"Did you get everything you want?" Gracie asked.

Her question registered on some level, but Harrison didn't know how to answer it. No, he didn't get everything he wanted. There were still answers to some questions about his father. There was still his father's estate. There was still fifteen years of his life that his father could have been a part of but wasn't. And the other fifteen years when his father was around, but not really part of his life, either. And then there was still the most maddening thing of all that he wanted.

There was still Gracie Sumner.

The trip to Cincinnati had been as eye-opening for him where she was concerned as it had been where his father was concerned. A lot of the kids on the base-ball team had responded to her with genuine affec-tion, even begging her to do an impression of a rival coach they must have seen a dozen times before, but still left them rolling with laughter. She'd stopped for five dozen doughnuts before they'd hit the veterans' hospital, and the staff had received them with thanks in a way that indicated it was something she'd done all the time when she lived here. At the homeless shelter, she'd shared fist bumps with a half-dozen men and asked them how things were going. More to the point, she'd listened to each of them when they replied.

And tonight, she wanted to take Harrison to a place called the Moondrop Ballroom. Somehow, he was cer-tain she would know people there, too. And that they would love her the same way everyone else in this city seemed to.

All of these things made him wonder again about this Devon person whose name had come up more than once today—never in a good way. And every time, Gracie's reply had been the same before she'd changed the subject: *that's all in the past.* But how could it be in the past when everyone kept bringing it up?

"Harrison?" she asked.

Only then did he realize he hadn't answered her question about having everything he wanted from the storage unit. "For now," he said. "I'll get the rest of it as soon as I can."

He turned around in time to see her struggling to lift a box that was too wide for her to carry. When she began to pitch backward with it, Harrison lurched to-ward her, grabbing the box from the side nearest him. For a moment, they grappled to stabilize it, and then, as one, they set it down where she had been aiming. That, however, left the two of them standing literally shoulder-to-shoulder, something that each seemed to notice at once, and something that left them both speechless. They were also unable to make eye contact, since every time their gazes met, they glanced away from each other.

Where before the air in the storage unit had just been uncomfortably warm, it suddenly felt like a sauna. It was a really bad analogy, Harrison decided, since it also brought to mind naked, sweaty bodies wrapped in towels. Towels that could be removed with the simple flick of a wrist, thereby allowing lots of other, infinitely more interesting ways for naked bodies to get sweaty.

"Well, that was close," he said. Not that he was talking about the box they'd just saved, but Gracie didn't have to know that.

"Yeah," she said breathlessly.

A little too breathlessly. Maybe she wasn't talking about the box, either. Maybe she'd been having some sauna ideas, too. As if triggered by such a possibility, a single drop of perspiration materialized from behind her ear, rolled along her jaw, then down the front of her neck, before finally pooling in the delectable divot at the base of her throat. Harrison watched its journey with the same single-minded fascination a cheetah might show toward a wildebeest, wanting to pounce the moment the time was right. Like right now, for instance. But Gracie lifted a hand to swipe the drop away before he had the chance. Dammit.

But when his gaze met hers again, he saw that the reason for her reaction wasn't because she'd felt the perspiration running down her neck. It was because she had noticed his preoccupation with it. Their gazes locked for a minute more, and the temperature ratcheted higher. A single strand of damp blond hair clung to her temple, and it was all he could do not to reach for it and skim it back, and then follow his fingers and brush his lips over her damp skin.

"We, uh, we should get going," she said roughly, the words seeming to echo into his very soul. "We have to…to get cleaned up before going to the Moondrop. And we need to have, um…" She hesitated just a tiny, telling moment before finally concluding, "Dinner. We need to have dinner."

Dinner, he echoed to himself. Yes, they would definitely have that before going to the Moondrop. But maybe later, if the stars were aligned—and if they were both still having sauna thoughts—they could have something else, too.

After all, dancing could really work up a sweat.

Nine

Having known the Moondrop Ballroom was one of the places where she would take Harrison, Gracie had packed the dress and accessories she'd bought for the Dewitts' party and instructed Harrison to bring a suit. So it was a surprise when she answered his knock on her hotel room door to find him on the other side wearing a tuxedo. He even had a white silk scarf draped around his neck. She battled the wave of heat that wound through her at the sight of him, so dashing and Hollywood handsome, and the feeling was not unlike the one she'd experienced in the storage unit that afternoon.

And what the hell had that been about? One minute, she'd been about to drop a box on her toe, and the next, Harrison had been staring at her neck as if he wanted to devour her. His damp T-shirt had been clinging to him like a second skin, delineating every bump of muscle on his torso. His dark hair had been falling rakishly over his forehead, his blue eyes had been hot with wanting, and…and… And, well, suddenly, she'd kind of wanted to devour him, too.

"You look…nice," she finally said.

He smiled. "You look beautiful."

"Thanks," she replied, the heat in her belly nearly swamping her.

"So what time does this thing start?"

When Harry was alive, he and Gracie had been regulars at the Moondrop for Fox-trot Fridays, with an occasional appearance for Samba Saturdays and Waltz Wednesdays. Her favorite nights, however, had been Tango Tuesdays, which, as luck would have it, was tonight.

"There's a beginner's hour at seven," she said, "which is where the instructors give some basic lessons for people who've never been dancing before. The main event is at eight. If you want to go early for the first hour, though, we can," she added, thinking Harrison might not be comfortable jumping in with both feet, especially with the tango, since that was probably the hardest dance to know where to put both feet.

"You know what you're doing, right?" he asked. "I mean you said you and my father did this sort of thing on a regular basis."

"Yeah, but Tango Tuesdays tend to be tricky."

He smiled at her unintended alliteration. "But aren't you trained in tango? A tip-top tango teacher I can trust?"

Gracie smiled back. "Totally top-notch."

His eyes twinkled. "Terrific."

Another moment passed where they did nothing but smile and twinkle at each other. Then Harrison, at least, seemed to recall that they had something to do.

"So…do we have time for dinner?"

"Sure."

She gathered her purse and exited, pulling the door closed behind them. When Harrison proffered his arm with all the elegance of Cary Grant, it somehow felt totally natural to tuck her hand into the crook of his elbow. The warmth in her midsection sparked hotter, simmering parts of her that had no business simmering this early in the evening.

Or ever, she hastened to correct herself. At least where Harrison was concerned. That way lay madness.

Maybe this part of his Harry tour hadn't been such a good idea. If this was the way her body reacted when it was just hand-to-elbow contact, what was going to happen when they got into dance mode? Sure, ballroom dancing in its purest form allowed for space between the bodies, but there were still a lot of parts touching. Not just hands and elbows, but shoulders and backs. Waists. Hips.

Yikes.

Then she remembered this was tango Tuesday. Uh-oh. That meant leg contact. Torso contact. Damn. Why hadn't they been in town for open dance night instead, where she could have insisted they do the bunny hop or something? And now she'd gone and told him she would be his top-notch tango teacher. Tsk, tsk.

Note to self, Gracie, she thought as they waited for the elevator—and her stomach did a little cha cha cha. *It's a treacherous tactic, teaching tango to a tempting, um, guy.*

* * *

Stepping into the Moondrop Ballroom was like stepping back in time. Not just because it had been beautifully preserved in all its postwar elegance since opening in the 1940s, but because the people who came here did their best to dress as if they'd been preserved from that period, too. Most of the regulars were elderly, people who remembered coming here or to ballrooms like it when they were young. That was why Harry had liked the Moondrop so much. But many were Gracie's age or younger, newcomers to ballroom dancing who loved the period and wanted to experience the manners and styles of the time, if for just one evening. Even the orchestra dressed the part. The ceiling was painted the colors of twilight with twinkling white lights that looked like stars. Each wall had a silhouette of the 1940s Cincinnati skyline, topped with more stars. Between the décor and the music—the band never played anything written after 1955—it was easy to forget there was another world beyond the front doors.

"Wow, this place is like something out of a movie," Harrison said when they entered, clearly having fallen under the spell of the ballroom as quickly as Gracie had the first time she was here.

"Isn't it wonderful? It's exactly like I remember."

"How long has it been since you were in town?"

She stiffened at his question, even though it was one she'd fielded in one way or another ever since her arrival. "I left six months after Harry's funeral," she told him. "I haven't been back since."

"But you have so many friends here," he said. "I mean, all those people yesterday obviously knew you pretty well. But it sounded like you haven't stayed in touch with any of them."

"That's because I haven't."

"Why not?"

He didn't seem to be asking out of idle curiosity. But she told herself she was imagining things. She was just hypersensitive because of all the questions she'd fielded about Devon since she'd come back.

All she said was "It's complicated, Harrison."

He looked as if he might let it go, but then said, "Because of Devon."

For some reason, hearing that name spoken in Harrison's voice was far worse than hearing it in anyone else's.

"Yes," she said. "Because of him."

"Do you want to talk about it?"

She shook her head. And she told Harrison what she'd told everyone else, what she told herself whenever Devon invaded her thoughts. "That's all in the past."

Harrison looked like he was going to say more, but the band saved her, striking up the first notes of "La cumparsita."

"Well, aren't you lucky?" she said. "You're going to wet your tango feet with the mother of all tango tunes."

He listened for a moment. "I recognize this song. This is in *Some Like It Hot* when Jack Lemmon is tangoing with Joe E. Brown."

And when Tony Curtis was making out with Marilyn Monroe, she thought, but hopefully neither of them would mention that part. Judging by Harrison's expression, though, he was definitely thinking about it. And also judging by his expression, he knew she was thinking about it, too. Damn.

"Shall we?" he asked, tilting his head toward the dance floor, where a number of people were already in full tango mode.

She smiled in a way she hoped was flirtatious. Not that she was flirting with him or anything. She was just keeping in the spirit of the Moondrop Ballroom, that was all. "If you think you're ready for it."

He smiled back in a way that went way beyond flirtatious and zoomed right into bewitching. "I'm ready for anything."

As if to prove it, he extended his left hand, palm up. The moment she placed her right hand against it, he closed his fingers over hers, drew her close and lifted their hands to chin height—his chin, not hers—so her arm was higher. Then he pressed his other hand to the small of her back and drew her body, very firmly, against his. There was nothing tentative in his hold. His confidence was absolute. Her own body's response was just as fierce. In every single place they touched, little explosions detonated under her skin, rushing heat to every other part of her body.

The moment she was in his arms, he assumed a flawless tango stance, placing his right leg between hers and his left alongside her right. Then he began to guide her forward. Well, for her it was backward, since—obviously—he intended to lead. His first step was with his left foot, all fine and good—except for how Gracie's insides were turning to steaming lava— and his next was with his right, which would have also been fine if Gracie had reacted the way she was supposed to and stepped backward.

But thanks to the little-explosions-of-heat thing, not to mention the steaming-lava thing, she wasn't exactly

on her game. So his step forward pressed his thigh
into the juncture of her legs, and *wow*, talk about an
explosion of heat *and* steaming lava. Her entire torso
seemed to catch fire and melt into his. Even though
she was pretty good at the tango, she stumbled those
first few steps, something that made Harrison splay
his fingers wide on her back and pull her closer still,
and— *Oh. My. God. She was going to spontaneously
combust!* After that, it was all Gracie could do to just
try and keep up with him.

He led her deeper into the crowd of other dancers
with a few perfectly executed *barridas*, sweeping his
feet along the floor in a way that made hers move that
way, too. Then he spun them in a perfect *boleo*, punc-
tuating the move with a beautiful *gancho*, wrapping
his leg briefly around hers before turning her again.
Then he threw in a *lápiz,* tracing a circle on the floor
with his free foot—he was just showing off now—and
followed with a *parada*, where he suddenly stopped,
literally toe-to-toe with her, to perform a really delicious *caricia*. He drew his leg slowly up along hers,
then pushed it slowly back down again, generating a
luscious friction. She wished he would do it again, and
he did. Then he did it again. And again. And—holy
mother of mackerel—again.

By now Gracie's heart was hammering hard inside
her chest, even though they'd only been dancing a matter of minutes, and he'd been doing most of the work.
Harrison had to feel the pounding of her pulse, too—
their bodies were so close, in so many places—but he
didn't say a word. He only held her gaze tight with his
and began to dance again, with all the grace and style
of a *vaquero*. As the final notes of the song came to a

close, he pulled her close one last time, and then—of course—he tilted her back until her head was nearly touching the floor, in a dip that was nothing short of spectacular.

At that point, they were both breathing heavily, a combination of both the dance and their heightened awareness of each other. They'd also earned an audience, Gracie realized, when she heard applause. Or maybe that was just in her own brain, acknowledging his skill at…oh, so many things, because she honestly wasn't even conscious of anyone in that moment but him.

Still poised in the dip, her free arm looped around his neck, she said breathlessly, "You've been holding out on me."

He grinned. But he didn't let her up. Instead he only roped his arm more possessively around her waist and pulled her closer to him. He, too, was out of breath, his voice quiet when he spoke. "My mother made me take cotillion classes when I was in middle school. I hated it until I realized how many points knowing how to dance earned me with girls. Knowing the tango multiplied those points by about a thousand."

"I can see how that would work in a guy's favor."

Still, he didn't let her up, and still, Gracie didn't care. For one interminable moment, it almost seemed as if he were bending his head closer to hers, as if his mouth were hovering over hers, as if he actually intended to—

She closed her eyes, and for the merest, faintest, most exquisite millisecond, she thought she felt the brush of his lips over hers. But when she opened her eyes, he was levering her to a standing position, so she told herself she'd only imagined it.

The crowd had dispersed, caught up in another song, another dance, another moment. But Gracie couldn't quite let this moment go. Their fingers were still curled together, her other hand still curved around his nape while his was still pressing into the small of her back. Although they'd stopped moving, she couldn't seem to catch her breath. And in spite of the music that still swirled around them, she couldn't seem to make herself move.

But neither, did it seem, could he. His breathing was as erratic as hers, and he wasn't any more inclined to move than she was. And that maybe-imaginary, maybe-not kiss still had her brain so muddled, she wasn't sure what to do. Even when he began to lower his head toward hers—there was no mistaking his intention this time—she didn't know how to react. Not until his mouth covered hers completely. After that, she knew exactly what to do.

She kissed him back.

The feel of his mouth on hers was extraordinary, at once entreating and demanding, tender and rough, soft and firm. He kissed her as if he had done it a million times and never before, confident of his effect on her and tentative in his reception. Gracie kept her hand cupped over his nape, and with the other, threaded her fingers into his hair. It had been so long since she had been this close to a man, so long since she had allowed herself to get lost in the sensation of two bodies struggling to become one. She didn't want it to stop. She wanted to stay here in this spot, with this man, forever.

By the time he pulled back, her brain was so rattled,

her body so incited, her senses so aroused, all she could do was say the first thing that popped into her head. "I thought you didn't like me."

He nuzzled the curve where her neck joined her shoulder. "Oh, I like you very much."

"You think I took advantage of your father."

He nipped her earlobe. Gracie tried not to swoon. "I don't think that at all."

"Since when?" she asked, her voice barely audible.

Instead of answering, he skimmed his lips lightly along her throat, her jaw, her temple. But just when she thought she would melt into a puddle of ruined womanhood at his feet, he straightened. And then he began to lead her in the tango again, as if nothing had happened.

Well, nothing except a major tilt of the earth's axis that had just changed *every*thing for Gracie.

It was that damned dress.

That was what Harrison told himself as he and Gracie sat on opposite sides of a cab as it sped down Hamilton Avenue, back toward their hotel. Someone somewhere had put a spell on that dress that made men's brains turn to pudding whenever they got within fifteen feet of it. And when it was on someone like Gracie, with creamy skin and silky hair and eyes dark enough for a man to lose himself in for days, well... It was amazing all he'd done on that dance floor was kiss her.

But he had kissed her. And he'd told her he liked her. Very much. But he hadn't been able to answer her question about "since when." Probably because he didn't know "since when."

When had that happened? Today at the storage unit?

Yesterday at the baseball game? That morning at the stock exchange? He honestly didn't know. He only knew he had been wrong about her. She really had been his father's friend and nothing more. She really was a decent person. She really was a girl next door.

Now he just had to figure out what to do. Almost since the moment they met, he'd been suspicious of her. But he'd also been attracted to her. He'd wanted to expose her as a fraud, but he'd also wanted to have sex with her. He'd been sure every word she said about his father was untrue, but he'd learned things about his father from her that he'd never known before.

Hell, no wonder he didn't know what to do.

Bottom line, he told himself. That was what everything came down to in life. What was the bottom line?

The bottom line was he liked Gracie. The bottom line was he wanted her. The bottom line was she'd kissed him back on that dance floor. The bottom line was she wanted him, too.

So why not do what he always did when he was attracted to a woman, and she was attracted to him? Once they got back to the hotel, they could have a nightcap and then hop into bed and enjoy themselves. No harm, no foul, a good time had by all. There was nothing in this encounter that was any different from any other encounter he'd had with a woman. Maybe the circumstances of their meeting were a little weirder, but the essentials were the same. Man, woman. Hormones, pheromones. Foreplay, play, replay. He'd done it a million times, a million ways, with a million women. So what was the problem?

He looked at Gracie again. She was staring out the window, the passing streetlights throwing her beautiful face into light, then dark, then light, then dark. Maybe that was the problem. All this time, he'd been trying to focus on her dark side. Now he was seeing the light. And he... Hell, there were times when he wondered if he even had a light side.

What would happen if his dark side mingled with Gracie's light side? Would it leave them both more balanced? Or would it just turn everything gray?

As if he'd uttered the question out loud, she turned to look at him. She really was beautiful, whether in light or dark. And he really did want her. He just wished he knew what the fallout of having her would be. And that thought was strange, because he'd never worried about fallout before.

Clearly, girls next door were a lot more dangerous than con artists.

When they arrived back at Gracie's hotel room and she turned to tell Harrison good-night, she could see he was no more ready to say the words than she was. In fact, the way he was looking at her now was a lot like the way he'd looked just before he'd kissed her at the Moondrop Ballroom. So it really didn't come as a surprise when he took a step closer and dipped his head to hers. Nor was it surprising when she took a step forward and tilted her head back to meet him.

The kiss was even better this time. Maybe because Gracie played an equal part in it from the beginning, or maybe because she had time to enjoy it from the very start. Something about the feel of Harrison's mouth on hers felt like coming home. But to a home where she didn't have to live all by herself.

Reluctantly, she ended the kiss. "Do you… Um, do you want to come inside?"

He met her gaze intently. "Yeah. Are you sure you want me to?"

She nodded.

"Because if I come inside, Gracie, I won't leave until morning."

Actually, she was kind of hoping he wouldn't want to leave at all. But morning was good for a start. "That's okay," she told him. "I don't want you to leave." There. Let him make of that what he would.

He dipped his head forward in silent acknowledgment. Then he followed her into the room and closed the door behind them, taking care to tuck the Do Not Disturb notice into the key slot as he did.

She started to ask him if he wanted to order something from room service, a snack or a bottle of wine or a game of Jenga or anything that might slow this thing down. But he obviously didn't want to slow down, because he pulled her close, looped his arms around her waist and kissed her again. He brushed his lips lightly over hers, and then skimmed them along her jaw, her cheek, her temple. With each new caress, her pulse leaped higher. When she splayed her fingers open on his chest, she felt his heart thumping against her palm, every bit as ragged and rapid as her own. When his lips found hers again, he deepened the kiss, and she opened her mouth to invite him in.

As he kissed her, he scooted one hand from her waist to the top of her dress. He pulled the zipper down down down, until it stopped at the base of her fanny, and the dress fell completely open. Then she felt his warm hand on her naked skin, his fingers pressing into her, pushing her more closely against him. He traced the outline of her mouth with the tip of his tongue, and then darted it inside to explore more thoroughly. His fingers went exploring, too, down to the waistband of her panties, dipping lower until his palms were pressing into the tender flesh beneath.

Gracie tore her mouth from his at the contact, gasping for breath, wondering again if this was such a good idea. But when her gaze met his, when she saw how dark his eyes were with wanting, how ruddy his cheeks were with his desire, how damp his mouth was from her own, she moved her fingers to his shirt, carefully slipping the buttons from their fastenings, one by one.

Harrison watched, his own breath shallow and warm against her temple, his hands still where he'd left them, curving over her bare bottom. Her fingers began to tremble after the third button, but she managed to undo them all. He released her long enough to shrug out of his shirt and jacket at once, leaving him bare above the waist, an absolute feast for her eyes.

His torso was long and lean, his shoulders wide and rugged, all of him corded with muscle. Her hands were on him before she even made the decision to touch him, her palms flattening against his smooth flesh, her fingertips raking gentle lines along each salient ridge until she reached his shoulders. Then she ran her hands down over the bumps of biceps, triceps and everything that came after.

When she reached his wrists, he turned his hands so they were grasping hers, and then urged her arms down to her sides. With one deft move, he hooked his fingers in the sleeves of her dress and nudged them over her shoulders, tugging on the garment until it pooled in a heap of frothy mint at her feet. Beneath it, she wore only white lace panties and a strapless bra. His gaze flew to the latter, followed by his hands. Without hesitation, he cupped one over each breast, making his claim to her absolute. Gracie fairly purred at the contact, and then lifted her hands to his torso again, touching him just as intimately. After squeezing her breasts gently, he moved his hands to her back, unhooking her bra to let it fall to the floor before pulling her body flush against his.

The sensation of finally touching him, flesh to flesh, heat to heat, was breathtaking…literally. Gracie's breath caught in her throat at the contact. He lowered his head and kissed her again, driving a hand between their bodies to grasp her breast once more. He moved his thumb over her nipple several times, before cradling her fully in his hand. She felt him swell to life against her, getting harder with each touch, until he was straining against his zipper. When she lowered her hand to his fly, he began backing her toward the bed. The action moved her hand more intimately against him, making him harder still.

By the time they reached the bed, his pants were open, and she was stroking him over the silk of his boxers. He growled something unintelligible against her mouth, and then sat down on the edge of the mattress, bringing her down on his lap to face him, her legs straddling his. For a moment, he only held her there with a hand on each hip, kissing her and kissing her and kissing her. Then he moved his mouth to her breast and kissed her there, too. First one, then the other, licking her, sucking her, driving her mad. Gracie twined her fingers in his hair and held him there, relishing each new touch of his tongue. Then she felt his hand between her legs, pressing into her over her panties, gently rubbing her with one finger, then two, creating a delicious friction that nearly drove her mad.

And then he was pulling the fabric aside, pushing his fingers into the damp folds of her flesh, slipping one finger easily, deeply into her. Gracie cried out at the contact and instinctively tried to close her legs. But Harrison pushed his own wider, opening her more, making her even more accessible to him. For a long time, he fingered her, until she thought she would explode with wanting him. Only when her entire body shuddered with her orgasm did he slow his movements. And only when her body relaxed in her release did he let her rest.

For all of a minute.

Then he was rolling her onto her back on the bed and pulling down her panties, until she lay blissfully and wantonly naked. She sighed with much contentment and threw her arms above her head, dissolving into a pool of something sweet and hot. The sensation doubled when she opened her eyes and saw Harrison shedding his trousers, his cock fully erect and ready for…oh, anything.

When he lay down beside her, she closed her hand over him, dragging her fingers slowly down his heavy length and up again, palming the damp head before repeating her actions. He closed his eyes as she caressed him for long moments, his breathing deep and ragged, his body hard and tense. When she sensed he was close to coming, he grabbed her hand and stilled her motions, and then opened his eyes.

"Not yet," he murmured.

She started to object—she certainly hadn't stopped him—but he sat up and rolled on a condom. Then he pulled her up beside him, grabbed her by the waist and set her astride him again. As she draped her arms over his shoulders, he rubbed his cock against the wet flesh between her legs until he was as damp as she. Then he pushed himself inside her—deep, *deep* inside her. So deep, she wasn't sure where his body ended and hers began. Still gripping her hips, he pushed her up until he almost withdrew, and then urged her back downward. Over and over he entered her, seeming to go deeper with each stroke. Then he withdrew and levered both their bodies onto the mattress until Gracie was on her knees with her shoulders pressed to the mattress, and he was entering her again from behind.

She clutched the sheet in both hands, hanging on for dear life, knowing they were both close to coming now. Harrison rose up on his knees and held her hips, pulling her back toward him as he thrust forward, until finally, finally, both of them came.

For one long, lingering moment, it seemed as if neither of them would ever move again. Then he rolled onto his back beside her, and she straightened until her belly and breasts were flat against the bed. She felt his hand on her bottom, gently stroking her sensitive skin, and she somehow managed to move her own hand to his chest. The skin she encountered was hot and wet, his chest rising and falling with his patchy respiration. She turned her head to look at him, only to find him staring intently at her.

Neither of them said a word. For Gracie, that was because she had no idea what to say. Never, ever had it been like this with a man. No one had made her feel so desirable and so desired. She'd never felt the things Harrison made her feel and would never feel them with anyone else. She didn't know how she knew that, but she did. There was something between them, right here, right now, that was different from anything she'd ever known before. Anything she would ever know again. And she just wasn't sure how she felt about that.

Until he smiled. And she knew he felt it, too.

Only then could Gracie close her eyes and let sleep take her. For a little while, anyway. Because she knew she hadn't had nearly enough of Harrison. Not tonight. Not forever. She only hoped he felt that part, too.

Ten

Harrison awoke to a buzzing sound, and wasn't sure at first what it was. A hum of satisfaction after a night of unbelievably good sex? The fizzing of his brain when he recalled some of the finer moments of that sex? The thrum of his heart at the sight of Gracie, naked and rosy beside him?

She lay on her stomach, the sheet dipped low enough to reveal the expanse of her tantalizing back and the soft indention of the two perfect dimples over her ass. He stirred to life at the sight of them, and it was all he could do not to run his tongue down the length of her spine. He wanted to hear her make that sound again, that little gasp of delight when he moved his hand between her legs and dragged his little finger higher, inserting it softly and gently fingering the more sensitive, sultry part of her.

He bit back a groan at the memory and did his best to stifle the response of his erection. *Later*, he promised himself. After she was awake. They could both probably use a little more sleep. Even if he knew his body and brain both were done sleeping for a while.

He couldn't remember a morning after with a woman when he didn't want to race out of her bed or chase her out of his. Normally, at a moment like this, he was considering the scenario in the same way a jewel thief plans a heist, tracing his route from leaving the bed without waking his companion to completing his escape without setting off an alarm. At this point, he probably could be a jewel thief, so expert had he become at vanishing without detection.

But he didn't want to vanish this morning. And he kinda did want to wake his companion. And not just so they could have another round of riotous lovemaking, either. He was actually looking forward to having breakfast with her. Just the two of them, sharing coffee and toast and quiet conversation. And that, probably, was the weirdest thing of all. That he wanted more from Gracie than sex. He never wanted anything from a woman but sex. And once he'd had sex he seldom wanted a woman again. And breakfast? Conversation? Ah, no.

It finally dawned on him that the buzzing that had awoken him had come from his phone, lying on the nightstand beside him. He palmed it and held it up where he could see it. A text from a number he didn't recognize, one with a New York City area code. He thumbed the prompt and found a message from the private investigator his attorney had hired after the reading of his father's will. The one who was supposed to prove Gracie was the gold-digging con artist they'd all been so sure she was.

Damn, what a waste of money that turned out to be.

The text was short and to the point: Check your email.

In spite of Harrison's certainty that his original opinion about Gracie was wrong, something pinched in his chest when he read the message. He told himself that a terse direction to check his email meant nothing. The PI's initial report probably said something like "You're an idiot, Sage. The woman you hired me to expose as a predator is actually one of the nicest, most decent people in the world."

So why the pang in his chest? Why did he suddenly want to check his email? Why did he want to see a report if he already knew what it said?

He looked at Gracie again. She was still asleep. So, with all the stealth of a jewel thief, he eased himself out of bed, slipped on the hotel bathrobe he had shed a couple of hours ago and retreated to the other side of the room. He cracked the curtains enough to allow in a slice of morning sunlight, and then thumbed the email icon on his phone and waited. There were a lot of new messages, since he hadn't checked his mail since yesterday morning. Even so, his gaze flew immediately to the one from the PI. With a subject head of Re: Grace Sumner, the body of the email read, As per agreement, initial report attached. Information gathered to date. Harrison skittered the cursor over the link to the attachment. But something made him hesitate before clicking on it.

Would opening this file after last night constitute a violation of trust? He supposed it depended on what last night was. If it was just sex, then no, this wasn't a violation of trust, since no trust had been established. Sex and trust didn't go hand in hand unless the people having the sex had some kind of agreement. If they were married, for instance. Or if they had made a commitment or developed feelings for each other. Feelings of love, say.

None of those things applied to him and Gracie. Did they? They certainly weren't in love. They'd only known each other a week. And they really hadn't made a commitment to each other. Last night was just…

Well, he still wasn't sure what last night was. But even if he did feel different this morning from the way he usually felt after spending the night with a woman, there was no reason for him to hesitate. And hell, the PI's report probably just confirmed that she was on the up-and-up.

Before he could second-guess himself again, Harrison clicked on the attachment. Immediately, a document opened on his screen. And he began to read.

Gracie awoke slowly and squinted at the bedside clock, startled to discover it was after ten-thirty. She never slept this late. Of course, she'd never spent the night the way she spent last night, either. Harrison Sage was certainly a thorough lover. She stretched languidly and smiled at the pleasant stiffness in her muscles, marveling again at how quickly things between them had changed. Not that she was complaining—she liked this new direction. A lot.

Blame it on the ballroom, she thought with a happy sigh. Or on Harrison's sweet, wistful expression as he sorted through his father's things yesterday. Or on his cheering for Roxanne at the top of the ninth inning and his genuine delight when the Rockets won their game. Or on their intimate conversation at the stock exchange, or even those minutes in the library that first morning, when he'd charmed her out of her anxiety. Those blue, blue eyes. That luscious smile. That wounded soul. How could she not fall for a guy like that?

Any rancor Harrison had shown since meeting her had been the result of hurt and grief. Any chilliness had come from his fear that she was taking advantage of his family. Had the situation been reversed, had Gracie been the one who'd lost her father and felt as if Harrison were threatening her family, she would have behaved the same way. They'd just needed to get to know each other, to understand and trust each other. Anything that had happened before last night didn't matter now. Because all of that had changed. They never could have been as good together as they were last night if they didn't know, understand and trust each other now. If they didn't care about each other.

And Gracie did care about Harrison. She cared about him a lot.

She shrugged into the remaining hotel robe and crossed the room to where he sat with his back to her, reading something on his phone.

"Good morning," she said as she approached him.

He jumped up from the chair and spun around so quickly, she might as well have fired off a shotgun. And when she saw his face, something cool and distressing settled in her belly. Because he didn't look as though he thought it was a good morning at all.

"What's wrong?" she asked.

For a moment, he only stared at her, as if he were

searching for the words he wanted to say but had no idea where to find them. Or maybe he was searching for something else, something just as nebulous and elusive.

Finally, he pulled himself up until he was ramrod-straight and crossed his arms over his midsection as if trying to keep himself that way. "Two words," he said. "Wilson Braun."

Gracie's heart dropped at the mention of Devon's father. How on earth had Harrison heard about him? More to the point, *what* had Harrison heard about him?

"He's Devon's father," she said. "And like I said, anything that happened between me and Devon is in the past. You seemed to be okay with that. What does Wilson have to do with anything?"

Harrison studied her more intently, as if he'd been expecting a different reaction from her. "I was okay with the past when I thought Devon Braun was just an old boyfriend."

"He is just an old boyfriend." Among other things. Things Gracie preferred not to think—or talk—about.

"An old boyfriend you tried to extort a lot of money from."

The accusation washed over Gracie like a wave of polluted water. She closed her eyes in an effort to block it out, but that only made it worse. So that was what he'd heard about Wilson. The same thing a lot of other people had heard. Exactly what Wilson had wanted them to hear.

She opened her eyes again and met Harrison's gaze levelly. "That isn't true," she said, surprised by how calmly the words came out.

"My PI says it is," Harrison told her.

The PI, she remembered. The one his attorney had hired to prove Gracie was a predator who'd seduced an old man and stolen his fortune. The PI she'd been so certain wouldn't be a threat because her life was an open book. She should have realized he would eventually get to the chapter about Devon and his family. The problem was, he'd undoubtedly read a heavily edited version of the story—since Wilson Braun had made sure no one would ever hear the real one—and that was what he'd relayed to Harrison.

She sighed. "And of course you always trust people to tell the truth right off the bat, don't you?" The way he had with Gracie. Hah.

The charge had the desired effect. His brows arrowed downward and he looked less sure of himself. "He has no reason to lie."

"Maybe he's not lying. Maybe he's just misinformed." Hey, Gracie would give the PI the benefit of the doubt. She didn't like to jump to conclusions the way a lot of people obviously did. Even if there was a good chance the PI had been paid a pile of money by Wilson Braun to bury the truth like so many others.

Harrison's expression fell a bit more, as if it hadn't occurred to him that the PI could be wrong. Nevertheless, he said, "This guy doesn't make mistakes. He's one of the best in the business."

Yeah, so was Wilson Braun. At least, when it came to the business of silencing other people or smearing their reputations.

"What did your PI tell you?" she asked.

Harrison hesitated again before replying, "He spoke at length to Wilson Braun about your relationship with his son, and he sent me copies of emails from Wilson to you that indicate you tried to blackmail the family for six figures in exchange for your silence on the matter of an alleged assault Devon committed—a story that you manufactured in the hope of profiting from it."

The first part of Harrison's statement didn't surprise her. Devon's father had always made sure his emails were worded in such a way that they never quite sounded like what he was actually trying to do—bribe Gracie in exchange for recanting what she'd witnessed so the charges against his son would be dropped. It was money Gracie had refused to take. It was the second part of Harrison's statement, the part about him believing she would lie about something like that in order to pocket a pile of cash, that did surprise her. If after everything the two of them had shared, and after the way they had been together last night, he could go back to thinking the worst of her this easily and this quickly…

Very quietly, very evenly, she said, "The story wasn't manufactured. Devon tried to rape a friend of mine at a party. Thankfully, I walked in on it before it became an actual rape, otherwise that's what Devon would have been charged with, and that would have been the story his father would have been trying to suppress."

She paused, letting that sink in. Judging by the way Harrison's expression changed, it did. Some. So Gracie told him the rest of it.

"But Devon had beat her up pretty bad, so I took her to the hospital, and she filed a police report and told the cops what happened. I corroborated her story. Then Wilson Braun tried to bribe both of us to shut up and pretend it never happened. Did your PI find his emails to my friend, too?"

Harrison shook his head, still looking a little torn. "No. He was only interested in information on you."

"Then do you have copies of *my* emails in response to Devon's father?" she asked, already knowing the answer. If he'd read those, they wouldn't be having this conversation, because he'd already know the whole story.

He sounded even more uncertain when he responded, "He's working on it. Your old service provider won't release them without a warrant. Wilson Braun volunteered his."

"Yeah, I bet he did. He was super careful about what he said to me and my friend in his emails. Too bad neither of us was wearing a wire when he spoke to us in person. And he did everything he could to discredit us."

It was why the case had never gone anywhere and the charges were ultimately dismissed. Because the Brauns were one of Cincinnati's oldest and most revered families. They had more money and power than an entire Mount Olympus full of gods. People like that thought the world was at their disposal. They couldn't be bothered with things like the truth if it meant their perspective had to be changed or defended.

And Harrison was just like them, she realized. He'd decided a long time ago that Gracie was someone who couldn't be trusted and only cared about herself. And in spite of everything the two of them had shared, he'd gone right back to thinking that the minute he was given a chance. If his feelings for her were even a fraction of what hers were for him, he would never—could never—suspect her of doing what he was accusing her of now. He would trust her because he knew what kind of person she really was. Instead, when another member of his tribe said Gracie Sumner was a liar, then by all means, she must be a liar.

"You don't believe me, do you?" she asked anyway.

His expression revealed nothing of what he was thinking or feeling. Which probably told Gracie everything she needed to know. If he couldn't trust that she was telling him the truth… If the past few days hadn't changed the opinion he'd originally held of her… If last night had meant nothing to him…

"I don't know what to believe," he said softly.

Yep. That was everything Gracie needed to know.

"You'd rather put your faith in a private investigator who doesn't even have all the facts than in me. You'd rather believe Wilson Braun, a man you've never even met, than me."

"I didn't say that," he said.

She inhaled a deep breath and released it slowly. "Yeah, you did."

How could she have been thinking he had changed? How could she have been thinking she was falling in love with him? Someone who couldn't be trusted and only cared about himself.

"I think you should go," she said.

"But—"

"Now, Harrison."

Reluctantly, he gathered his clothes from the night before and went into the bathroom to change. When he came out again, his white tuxedo shirt hung unbuttoned over his black trousers, and the rest of his clothes were wadded in his hands. Gracie still stood where she'd been before, her arms roped across her chest, feeling colder than she'd ever felt in her life. When Harrison stopped near her on his way to the door, looking as though he wanted to say more, she only pointed toward it silently and turned her back. But when she heard the click of the latch, she called out to him over her shoulder one last time.

"Harrison."

He turned slowly, but said nothing.

"I'll have Mr. Tarrant send the documents to transfer ownership of the houses to Vivian to me in Seattle and return them to him as soon as possible. And I'll ask Vivian to ship anything I left at her house to me at home. There's no reason for me to go back to New York. Or to stay here in Cincinnati."

He paused for another moment, and then closed the door behind himself. Only then did Gracie allow herself to collapse into the chair he'd vacated. And only then did she allow her heart to break.

Harrison felt flummoxed when he got back to his own room, wondering if he'd just screwed up the best thing that ever happened to him.

No, he immediately told himself. There had been nothing to screw up. All he and Gracie had had was a single night of spectacular sex. And lots of good things had happened to him in his life. He had money and professional success. What could be better than those?

Now his PI had information that might just prove Gracie was the financial predator Harrison had suspected her of being from the outset, something that increased his chances of winning back his father's estate. And that was really good.

So why didn't any of that make him feel good? Why did he feel so bad?

The answer came to him immediately, but he didn't

much care for it. Maybe because, on some level, he actually wasn't convinced that Gracie was a financial predator. Maybe he'd been too quick to come to the conclusions he had.

He tossed his wadded-up clothing onto the still-made bed and fell onto the mattress. Then he pulled up his web browser on his phone and typed the name *Devon Braun* in quotations, along with the word *Cincinnati*.

The first hits that came up were for his Twitter and Facebook accounts. Harrison saw photographs of an innocuous-looking guy of above-average appearance who talked mostly about sports and a band Harrison hated. No red flags. Just some guy whose family happened to have a lot of money.

Scrolling down, he saw a link to a blog that covered Cincinnati crime called "Word on the Street." It was written by a local resident unaffiliated with law enforcement and clearly stated that it reported gossip, rumor and innuendo. Not exactly something that instilled great confidence.

But still interesting.

The piece was more than a year old and described a rape charge filed against the member of a prominent local family, indicating that it came after sexual assault and battery charges against him in another incident were dismissed. Neither of the victims was named. Nor was the perpetrator. So why had this item come up in a search for Devon Braun?

Maybe because the author of the piece had hidden his name on the site somewhere so that it would still appear in searches for Devon but avoid the wrath of Wilson Braun?

If that was the case, if Devon Braun had committed these crimes and the charges against him had been buried, then there was still a criminal on the loose in Cincinnati, which was a scary enough thought in itself. But somehow even scarier was the thought that maybe Gracie had been telling the truth all along and really was the best thing that had ever happened to him.

And scariest of all was the thought that Harrison had screwed that up. Bad.

The feeling only grew stronger when he was back in his Flatiron District high-rise with the boxes from the storage shed he'd brought with him. The cartons were dented and misshapen from the trip, and each bore numerous Sharpie markings, in different colors and handwriting—his father's, Gracie's and his own.

They looked completely out of place in Harrison's bedroom, with its wall of windows offering spectacular views of the nighttime skyline, its sleek, tailored furnishings and monochromatic taupe decor. They didn't look anything like Harrison or the man he remembered as his father. They looked a lot like Gracie, actually, offbeat and colorful and full of character. They looked as if they belonged to someone who had spent their life, well, living. Yet they were set against the backdrop of a room that looked as if it belonged to someone who hadn't lived at all.

Was that how he seemed? Like someone who had never lived? Sure, he spent the majority of his days— and sometimes his evenings—in his office or someone else's. And okay, most of his socializing had something to do with work. But that was what a person had to do to build a successful life. All Harrison had required of his home was that it look like it belonged to a successful, wealthy man, because those were the adjectives he'd wanted attached to himself. His place had always reinforced that desire.

So why did he suddenly feel kind of useless and needy?

The boxes, he decided, could wait. Unfortunately, he couldn't find enough space in any of his closets to stow them. So he shoved them into the corner of his bedroom, where they'd be—mostly—out of view. Funny, though, how his gaze kept straying to them all the same.

Work, he reminded himself. He had a ton of it to catch up on before he went back to the office tomorrow.

He started a pot of coffee, headed to his office and pulled up his email. Then he scrolled to the one he'd received from his PI this morning. Then he hit Reply and started typing. But he didn't ask for more information about Gracie. Instead, Harrison asked for more information about Devon and Wilson Braun. And he made sure, before he hit Send, that he tagged it "highest priority."

It was nearly two weeks before he received a reply—at 8:13 on a Tuesday night, thirteen days, eight hours and thirty-seven minutes after calling Gracie Sumner a liar in Cincinnati.

Not that he was counting or anything.

And not that he hadn't replayed nearly every minute the two of them spent together during that time—like Gracie's shy smile that first day in the library, and how the wind played with her hair during breakfast, and her chirpy "batter, batter, batter, suh-wing, batter" support of the Rockets, and their chaste but mind-scrambling kiss in the Moondrop Ballroom. And not that, with each passing day, he'd become more convinced that he'd had something with her he would never find again and had completely, irrevocably screwed it up.

Because even before emailing his PI, on some primal level, Harrison had known he was wrong about Gracie and should never have accused her of lying. Especially after the night they'd spent together. He'd just been so stunned—and, okay, kind of terrified—by the speed and intensity of his response to her. So he'd looked for the quickest, easiest way to escape. The PI's report had offered the perfect excuse to put Gracie at arm's length again. Hell, arm's length? He'd sent her to the other side of the planet.

And then he began to worry that there was nothing he could say or do to repair things. That even if he did, Gracie might not forgive him or take him back. That he'd spend the rest of his life thinking about how happy they could have been together. How happy *he* could have been. If only he hadn't jumped to some stupid conclusion that ruined everything.

In spite of all that, Harrison clicked on the file from his PI. And immediately realized that yep, he was a first-class, numero-uno, see-exhibit-A jerk. Because Gracie had indeed told him the truth about Devon Braun. All of it. The assault on her friend, the police report, Wilson Braun's bribes to suppress it. And Gracie Sumner's refusal of the money he'd offered her.

Harrison grabbed a sharp knife from the kitchen and headed for his bedroom. He pushed a chair into the corner where he'd stacked the boxes from Cincinnati, and stabbed the packing tape seam of one to open it. He wasn't sure why he suddenly wanted—needed—to go through his father's things. Maybe because they were the only link he had to Gracie, and he just wanted to touch something she had touched herself.

His grandmother's five journals sat on top. She'd written the first entry the day his grandfather proposed to her and the last the day she abandoned her family in Cincinnati. Harrison had skimmed the first two diaries that day in the storage unit, so he picked up the third, opening it and riffling through the pages to check the dates at the top of each. Toward the end, he found an envelope shoved between two pages.

There was no writing on the outside, and the flap wasn't sealed. Inside was a letter written in his father's hand, dated two years before his death. It started off "Dear Vivian…"

Harrison stopped reading there, telling himself he should give it to his mother. But he wasn't sure his mother would even want to read it. Still, he should probably let her decide. Then again, maybe he should read a little of it first, to make sure its contents wouldn't make her feel even worse about his father's behavior than she already did.

Dear Vivian, I hope you and Harrison are doing well.

Oh, sure, he thought. His father had been out of their lives for more than a decade, and they'd had no idea what made him leave or if they'd ever see him again. Why wouldn't they be doing well? He made himself read more.

I suppose that was a ridiculous sentiment, wasn't it? How could you and Harrison be doing well in the situation I created for you? Please, first, let me apologize for that. Then let me try to explain.

Harrison had never heard his father apologize for anything. Whenever he was wrong about something, Harrison Sage, Jr. had only made excuses. And he'd never felt the need to justify anything, either. Harrison kept reading.

And, wow, did he learn a lot.

The letter was long, chronicling everything his father had done since leaving New York and his reasons for doing so in the first place. How he'd begun to feel as if he didn't know himself anymore. How there was nothing left in him of the boy who had hoped to become a major-league baseball player. How his intention when he came to New York as a teenager was to make enough money to support himself and the family he hoped to have someday but how, once he'd started making money, he'd fallen under its spell, and had wanted to make more. And then more. And then more. How it had become something of an addiction that motivated every decision he made and eclipsed everything else in his life.

He'd thought the only way to break the addiction was to remove himself from its temptation. He hadn't meant to stay away from New York—or his family— for as long as he had. But with each passing week, then month, then year, it became harder for him to figure out how he could ever apologize and atone for his behavior. Eventually, he had come to the conclusion that it was too late to even try, and his wife and son would never take him back. He knew by then that Harrison had built a successful business and was outearning his father, so he'd be able to care for himself and his mother. They couldn't possibly need—or want—Harrison, Jr. after all this time.

That was why he had decided to leave his money to Gracie. Because he'd known that Vivian and Harrison wouldn't want anything he'd earned after he shunted them aside. He'd known Gracie would disperse the funds charitably, but, even more importantly, she would also give a sizable chunk of it to Vivian and Harrison. That was the only way he'd been sure they would accept any of his wealth. If it came from someone else. Someone like Gracie, who was the kindest, fairest, most generous person he'd ever met. In fact—

The letter ended there, midsentence, suggesting his father had wanted to say more. Why hadn't he finished the letter? More to the point, why hadn't he mailed it?

The answer to both questions was right there in the letter. His father had been convinced Harrison and his mother wanted nothing to do with him. He'd convinced himself that he couldn't make up for what he'd done, so there was no point in even trying.

And that kind of thinking was crazy. Harrison and his mother would have absolutely welcomed him back into their lives. It would have taken time—and, possibly, professional counseling—to put things back to rights, but hell, his father could have at least tried. It was never too late to ask for—or obtain—forgiveness or make amends. It was never too late to start over.

Harrison halted when he realized that so much of what his father had said in his letter mirrored what he himself had begun to fear about Gracie. His father had been sure he'd irreparably botched his relationship with the people he loved, so he hadn't even tried to fix it and lived the rest of his life alone.

Gracie was right. There really was a lot of his father in Harrison. The question was, did he want to end up the same way?

Eleven

"That should do it," Gracie said as she lifted her pen from the last of a dozen checks she had signed in a row. "For today, anyway."

Cassandra Nelson, the financial advisor Gracie had hired to help her distribute Harry's money, smiled. She reminded Gracie of Vivian Sage, with her always perfect silver hair and chic suits. Gracie was wearing a suit, too, a new one—well, new to her, anyway. It was a lavender Givenchy from the 1950s. A real Givenchy, not a knockoff, one of the few things she'd let herself purchase with some of the money Harry had insisted she spend on herself.

It had been nearly a month since she'd returned to Seattle, and she hadn't heard a word from Harrison. Vivian had written to thank Gracie for transferring the deeds to the Sage homes along with a sizable share of

Harry's estate, closing with her hope that Gracie would "come and visit us when you're in New York again." *Us*, not *me*, clearly including Harrison in the invitation.

Not that Harrison had had any part in doing the inviting, Gracie was certain. Vivian was just being polite. She clearly didn't know that her son still clung to the idea that Gracie was a crook even after she'd given away so much of Harry's money. It was only natural Vivian would include Harrison in an invitation to visit. And it was only natural for Gracie to decline.

Even if she still thought about him every day. Even if—she might as well admit it—she still cared for him.

"Philanthropy isn't for sissies," Cassandra said, jarring Gracie out of her thoughts. "People think all you do is throw around money. But there's a lot of work and paperwork that goes into it. Especially with an estate as large as Mr. Sage's."

"So I'm learning," Gracie replied.

Boy, was she learning. Not just about money and how to use it, but about how people reacted to you when you had access to that money. She'd received enough invitations to functions over the last few weeks to keep an army of billionaires busy. Already, she'd put three of Harry's billions to good use, for everything from endowing university chairs to bailing out failing mom-and-pop businesses.

"Now then," Cassandra said, "do you want to talk about your own future? Please?"

Ever since Gracie's first visit to the office, Cassandra had been badgering her about how much of Harry's money she was going to put aside for herself, to make sure she was covered for the rest of her life. But Gracie always stalled. Naturally, she did want to be covered for life, but she wasn't sure Cassandra's idea of what that meant mirrored her own.

Cassandra's focus would be on Gracie's financial needs, where Gracie was more concerned about intangible needs. Personal needs. Emotional needs. No amount of money could guarantee those. Harry's money hadn't exactly brought her any happiness so far. On the contrary. Not that she wouldn't keep some—Harry had insisted, after all—but tallying a specific amount wasn't something she wanted to think about. Not yet.

Before Harry's fortune, all Gracie had ever wanted was a job she enjoyed, friends to have her back, a decent place to live and a man who would love her till the end of time, the same way she would love him. Seriously, what more could anyone want or need beyond that?

But now, when she looked down the road to the future, there was only a curve around which she could see nothing. She told herself she must still have a destination, but she just didn't know what it was anymore. Or who it was with. If anyone.

Gracie bit back a sigh. "Cassandra, I promise I'll get to it before all this is done, okay?"

They made an appointment for their next meeting, and then Gracie left, to go…somewhere. She had no idea where. She'd quit her job at Café Destiné since Harry's generosity meant she could return to school full-time in the fall and earn her degree by December. So job hunting could wait until then. In the meantime, there was still most of summer to get through, and little to fill the weeks.

Her days since returning to Seattle had mostly been

filled with internet searches for places to donate Harry's money, reading and discovering British TV shows on Netflix. Maybe she should get a cat…

Finally, she decided to return to her apartment. Maybe she could check out the next episode of *Call the Midwife* or something. She was sorting through her mail when she topped the last stair to her floor, so she wasn't looking where she was going as she ambled forward. That was why she didn't notice the guy waiting by her front door until he'd placed his hands on her shoulders to prevent her from running into him. She leaped backward at the contact, her entire body on alert. Just as quickly, Harrison lifted his hands in surrender mode and apologized.

"I'm sorry," he said. But the expression on his face seemed to suggest he was sorry for a lot more than just startling her.

It was as if he'd been conjured by all the thinking she'd been doing about him, as if he were here because she'd somehow wished for it strongly enough. In spite of how things had ended between them, she'd found it impossible to stay angry with him. Harrison Sage III was a product of the world in which he'd grown up, one of deep wealth and shallow feeling, where people viewed each other as opportunities and commodities instead of human beings. Mostly, she was just sad. Not only about how things had turned out between them, but also about how he had to live in that world and didn't seem to know how to leave it.

"What are you doing here?" she asked.

He said nothing at first, only scanned her up and down, as if refreshing his memory of her. Then he said, "You cut your hair."

Her fingers flew to her slightly shorter tresses. "Just a trim."

"I like it."

"Thanks."

She studied him in return and realized he'd changed some, too. Not his expensive, tailored, dark-wash jeans or his crisp, white oxford shirt. But the fatigue in his eyes that hadn't been there before, and the shadow of uncertainty in his expression. Harrison Sage had been many things since Gracie had met him—from antagonistic and suspicious to adorable and sweet—but he'd never been uncertain. To see him that way now made her feel…

Well, actually, seeing him looking uncertain made her feel a little more sure of herself.

"So…what are you doing here?" she asked again.

He hesitated, then replied, "I finally had all of my father's things shipped to New York from Cincinnati."

That was good, Gracie thought. But she wasn't sure why he'd had to come all the way to Seattle to tell her that.

"And as I was unpacking everything in my mother's attic," he continued, "I realized there might be something in there that you wanted to keep for yourself. I mean, you never asked for anything—"

It was nice to hear him finally say what he should have known all along. Gracie really had never asked for anything. Not from the storage unit. Not from Harry's estate. Not from Harrison. Even though it would have been nice if Harrison had given her a little something—like his trust or his appreciation or…or his love.

"But I thought you might want a keepsake," he continued. "Something that would remind you of him. Of your time with him."

"Thanks, but I don't need any reminders," she said. She pointed to her forehead. "Everything I need to remember Harry is right here."

"Wow. You really didn't want anything from him, did you?"

"Only his friendship," she said. "Thanks for finally noticing."

He said nothing in response to that.

So Gracie asked again, a little more wearily this time, "What are you doing here, Harrison?"

He studied her again. "I came for you. If you'll have me."

She felt the same tingle of pleasure that wound through her that night at the Dewitts' party, when he told the butler that she was with him. Because this time, he said it in a way that was even more romantic and intimate. She said nothing in response, however. She wasn't *with him* now any more than she had been that night.

When she remained silent, he began to look even more fatigued and uncertain. And more panicky. "Gracie, I am so sorry about what happened in Cincinnati."

The apology surprised her. Even with him standing here, having traveled more than two thousand miles to offer it, she was amazed he didn't try to stall or use a "sorry, not sorry" euphemism. Then again, maybe he wasn't apologizing for their last conversation. An awful lot had happened when they were in Cincinnati. Maybe he was sorry the two of them had shared that delicious tango. Maybe he was sorry the two of them had made love. Maybe he was sorry for those three red velvet cupcakes at the Rockets game.

"I'm sorry I ever doubted you," he went on.

Oh. Okay. Well, that was a start.

"I'm sorry I thought… I'm sorry I made you feel like a—a…"

"A trashy, scheming, manipulative gold digger?" she supplied helpfully, harkening back to their first meeting.

"Yeah," he said sheepishly. "Like that. I'm sorry I was such a colossal jerk."

Better. But he wasn't quite done yet.

"I'm sorry I jumped to conclusions after reading the PI's report," he continued. "I never should have read the damned thing to begin with. Not after we—"

He halted before finishing. Not that she needed him to finish, since she knew perfectly well what he was referring to now. He shouldn't have read the report after the night the two of them spent together. After everything they'd experienced together. He should have trusted her instead. He was right about that and everything else. But the fact remained that he did do all those things, and that he didn't trust her. It was nice of him to apologize for that now, but…

"But you did doubt," she said. "Even after—" Gracie couldn't quite put that night into words, either. So she hurriedly said, "And you did jump to—and cling to—conclusions. And you were a colossal jerk."

"I know. I'm sorry."

She didn't want to make him grovel—well, okay, she *did*, but she wouldn't, because that was the kind of thing people did in his world, not hers—so she told him, "Okay. I appreciate the apologies. Thank you."

He looked even more surprised by her capitulation than she'd been by his apology. "So you forgive me?"

She inhaled deeply and released the breath slowly. That was a tricky one. *Did* she forgive him? In spite of all of her thinking about him over the last month, the idea of forgiving him had never come up. Then she realized the reason for that. It was because she already had forgiven him. She wasn't sure when or why. Maybe she just hadn't wanted to be the kind of person who held a grudge. Nobody was perfect. Imperfection was part of being human.

"Yeah," she said. "I forgive you."

It didn't mean that everything was okay between them. It just meant that she was willing to listen to what he had to say.

So she asked one more time, "Why are you here, Harrison? If all you wanted to do was apologize, you could have texted me from New York and saved yourself a lot of money on plane fare. I know how important money is to you, after all."

He winced. "Gracie, that's not… It's just… I mean…" He expelled a frustrated sound. "Look, can we talk? Can I come in?"

She would have told herself there was no point in either of them saying anything else, but he had gone to some trouble and expense to get here. The least she could do was hear him out.

"Okay," she said. "We can talk."

She unlocked the door and entered her apartment, and then swept a hand toward the interior to silently invite Harrison in, too. He entered quickly, as if he feared she might slam the door in his face, and she told him to sit wherever he wanted.

She was reminded again of the day they met on Long Island and thought about how different things were here in her world. The view beyond her window wasn't of the ocean, but of another building across the street. Where the Sages' library had been filled with expensive collector's editions of books, her shelves were crammed with well-thumbed paperbacks. Instead of leather furniture, her sofa and lone chair were upholstered in a chintz floral long past being fashionable, and her coffee table was an old steamer trunk placed horizontally. Instead of lush, jewel-toned Aubussons, her hardwood floor sported a rubber-backed polyester area rug.

Harrison seated himself on the sofa, close enough to one side that it was clear he was making room for her on the other. Deliberately, Gracie chose the chair. His expression indicated he understood her decision and was resigned to it—for now. Even though he was the one who had asked if they could talk, the moment they were both seated, he fell silent.

So Gracie said, "What did you want to talk about?"

He threw her a look that indicated she should already know. And, of course, she did. But just because she didn't want to make him grovel didn't mean she was going to make this easy for him.

"Oh, I don't know," he said. "Maybe about developments in the Middle East? Or why we have to learn trigonometry in high school when we never actually use it in real life? Or how the music these kids listen to today is nothing but crap?"

Dammit, he was trying to be funny and charming like he was that first day in the library. She had to stop him before she started falling for him the way she did then.

"I choose trigonometry," she said. Because there was nothing funny or charming about math.

"Okay," he agreed. "But first, I want to talk about me and you."

Again he'd opted not to stall. How was she supposed to stay cool when he kept trying to get to the heart of things? To the heart of her?

"There is no me and you," she told him.

"There was," he retorted. "Before I screwed it all up."

She still wasn't prepared for him to go there so swiftly and candidly. She said nothing in response to his statement, but met his gaze levelly in a silent bid to go on.

"A couple of things," he began. "First, when I got back to New York, I had my PI look into Devon and Wilson Braun."

"Because you still didn't believe me," she said.

He shook his head. "That was what I told myself in Cincinnati, but I knew I was wrong to have mistrusted you before I even left your hotel room. I was just too stubborn and too stupid to admit it—to you or to myself. But we'll get to that. The reason I had my PI look into the Brauns was because I just wanted to make sure those guys got what was coming to them. And they will. My PI collected enough info on both Brauns—they're even worse than you thought—to cause them a lot of trouble for a long time. With the law, with their friends, with their jobs, you name it. Those guys are going to spend the rest of their lives in disgrace and dishonor, and, more than likely, prison. I told my guy to get all the info to whomever he could trust will do the right thing with it."

"Wow," she said. "Thank you, Harrison."

"Now then," he said. "About that morning in Cincinnati."

She couldn't quite stop herself, and replied, "The morning you called me a liar."

He started to deny it, and then seemed to realize it would be pointless. "There's something you have to understand about me, Gracie."

"What?"

He didn't hesitate at all this time. "I've never met anyone like you before."

That comment, too, surprised her. "But I'm a totally normal person. There are millions of people like me."

"Number one, no, there aren't. There's no one like you. And number two," he continued before she had a chance to say anything, "until you came along, I thought everyone in the world was like me. Because everyone I met *was* like me. Selfish, greedy takers who looked at every new opportunity, experience and acquaintance with the same question—what's in it for me? There was no reason for me to think you weren't like that, too. It never occurred to me that there were people in the world who wanted to help other people and make a difference. People like you and my father. Selflessness was an alien concept to me. To me, it made more sense that you would steal from my father than it did that he or you would give money to people who needed it."

She remembered how his father had taught him when he was still a child that money was more important than anything else. She remembered how he'd gone to a school for thirteen years that stressed financial success over any other kind of success. Lessons learned in childhood went deep, she knew. People could talk all they wanted about how when adults made stupid choices, they had to live with the consequences, never taking into account that those adult choices were based on childhood experiences. If someone was taught early on to choose money over happiness, then no one should be surprised when, as an adult, that person chose money over happiness.

"So when you told me you were going to give away my father's money," Harrison continued, "I didn't believe you. That didn't make sense to me. At least, it didn't until you took me to Cincinnati, and I saw how much my father meant to so many people. That's when I started to understand why he would want to give something back."

Dammit, he was doing it again. Being that sweet guy who made her fall in lo— Who had made her fall for him.

"That morning in Cincinnati, after we…" He hesitated again, but his gaze locked with hers. "I'd never felt the way I felt that morning, Gracie. Ever. Always before with women, I wanted to be gone before they woke up. But with you…" He smiled halfheartedly. "With you, I realized I never wanted to be with anyone else again."

There went the happy humming in her blood again. It was nice, having that back.

He continued, "And I guess I kind of panicked, when I understood what that meant. That I…had feelings for you…that I'd never had for anyone before.

That I wanted to see you again. Probably forever. That scared the hell out of me."

The humming thrummed louder. Faster.

"When I got the PI's report, and I read the lopsided version of what happened, it was easy for me to jump to the conclusion I did, because it meant I had an excuse for not wanting to wake up next to you every morning. It meant I didn't have to be in… It meant I didn't have to…care for you…the way I did. It gave me an excuse for going back to being the guy I was before. The one who didn't have to feel things. Life's a lot easier when you don't have to feel. Feeling is hard. And exhausting. And scary."

Oh, Harrison…

"But even after you were gone, I kept feeling. Every day. Every night. I couldn't stop thinking about you. But I didn't know what to say or do that would make up for what I did. I was afraid you'd never want to see me again after that. And I didn't blame you. I worried it would be pointless to apologize or to try to make up for it, figured you wouldn't talk to me if I tried. I started envisioning a horrible life without you. Then I found this."

He reached into his back pocket and withdrew an envelope. "It's a letter from my father I found in one of my grandmother's diaries. He wrote it to my mother two years before he died but never mailed it. You should read it, too."

Gracie balked. "But if it was meant for Vivian…"

"Mom's read it and doesn't mind my sharing it with you. It's important, Gracie."

Gingerly, she took the letter and read it in its entirety. When she looked up at Harrison again, it was with a heavy heart. "I can't believe he didn't think you and Vivian would forgive him."

"I can," Harrison said. "Because I thought you'd be the same way."

"But that's crazy."

"I know that now. But, clearly, I had a lot to learn about people. I still do. I just hope it's not too late. Because I don't want to end up like my father." He smiled. "Except for the part about where he got to spend the rest of his life with you."

Okay, that did it. Her heart was fully melted. Harrison must have realized that, because he smiled and scooted down to the other side of the couch. Close to Gracie, where his knee could gently touch hers. And even that tiny little contact made her feel better than she had in weeks. Four weeks, in fact. Four weeks, one day, three hours and twenty-seven minutes.

Not that she was counting or anything.

He lifted a hand and, after only a moment's hesitation, cupped it over her jaw. Unable to help herself, Gracie turned her head until his fingers were threaded in her hair, and then moved her hand to his cheek, too, loving the warmth under her palm. Her heart hammered faster when she remembered what happened the last time she touched him this way. His pupils expanded, his lips parted, his breath stilled. But he didn't move an inch.

So Gracie did.

She stood and took his hand in hers, and then led him to her bedroom. It was all the encouragement Harrison needed, because the moment she turned to look at him, he pulled her into his arms and covered her mouth with his. He kissed her lovingly, deeply, and for a very long time, cupping her jaws in both hands. Gracie splayed her fingers open on his chest, loving the feel of his heart racing against her hand, as rapidly as her own. After a moment, she moved her hands to the buttons of his shirt and began to unfasten them, her fingers sure and steady this time. He, in turn, dropped one of his hands to the single, oversized button on her jacket, freeing it and spreading the lapels open. He looked surprised to discover she wore only a bra beneath.

He was also more than a little aroused to discover that. Because he immediately freed his mouth from hers and skimmed the jacket over her shoulders to look at her. To help him in that respect, she reached behind herself to unzip her skirt, and let that, too, fall to the floor. The pale lavender lace bra and panties she wore were nearly transparent, leaving nothing to the imagination. When Harrison saw her effectively naked, he sucked in a deep breath and released it slowly.

"Is this the kind of thing you always have on under your clothes?"

He obviously remembered the lacy ensemble she'd been wearing in Cincinnati, and it was actually one of her more conservative sets. She nodded.

"This is the kind of thing you were wearing all those times I was with you in New York and Cincinnati?"

"Yeah," she said. "Except sometimes a little more revealing than this."

His eyes went wide at that. "You're not really much of a girl next door, are you?"

The question confused Gracie. "What do you mean?"

He only smiled and shook his head. "Nothing. Just…"

But he didn't finish. At least, not with words. Instead, he went back to unbuttoning his shirt and shrugged out of it, and then pulled Gracie close again… in a perfect tango hold, which meant really close, really intimate and really, really arousing. He danced her the few steps to her bed, and then spun her and dipped her deeply. As he nuzzled the place where her neck met her shoulder, he dragged a hand down the outside of her bare leg, lighting little fires all along the way. When he reached her calf, he moved his hand to the inside of her leg and drew it upward again, halting scant inches away from the hot, damp core of her.

Although Gracie caught her breath in anticipation of his touch there, she still gasped at the contact, so sure and steady were his fingers over the sheer fabric. Slowly, carefully, he righted them both to standing again, but he caressed her though her panties the entire time, and she was in no way steady on her feet. So he maneuvered their bodies until they were lying on the bed facing each other. He kissed her as he continued to stroke her, this time dipping his hand inside her panties, but Gracie somehow found the presence of mind to unfasten his belt and zipper. Then she tucked her hand inside his jeans and boxers to grasp him in her hand, rubbing him slowly up and down, too.

For long moments, they kissed and pleasured each other manually, their tongues darting in much the same way as their fingers. But when Gracie felt herself nearing an orgasm, she circled his wrist and withdrew his hand in an effort to slow the pace. He seemed to understand and used the opportunity to rise and shed what was left of his clothing. Gracie did likewise, and then bent over the bed to turn it down. Harrison was behind her naked body in a heartbeat, covering her breasts with his hands and moving his cock, already sheathed in a condom, between her legs to wreak havoc where his fingers had been before. She sighed as he caressed her breasts and thumbed her ripe nipples, guiding his hips forward and back to create a delicious friction for their bodies. When she bent forward more, he gripped her hips and entered her from behind, slow and slick and deep, again and again and again. But once more, he stopped before Gracie or he could climax, urging both of their bodies onto the bed.

When he turned to lie on his back, she sat astride him and began to move backward so that he could enter her again. But he halted her and instead pushed her body forward, more and more, until the heated core of her was poised above his head. Just as she realized his intent—and before she could prepare herself—he lowered her onto his mouth, pressing his tongue to the damp folds of flesh he had already incited to riot. Gracie was washed away to a place where her thoughts evaporated, and she could do nothing but feel...exquisitely, outrageously euphorically.

As his tongue lapped at her, he moved his hands to her bottom, curling his fingers into the cleft that bisected it, stroking her sensitive skin up and down, circling the delicate aureole at its base before darting away again. The sensations that rocked her every time he came close wound the hot coil inside her ever tighter. When he finally slipped a finger inside her there, moving his tongue inside her at the same time, she cried out. Never had she felt such a rush of heat or exhilaration. But as the cataclysms began to slow, Harrison tasted her again, deeper this time, and penetrated her again, deeper this time, and set off the waves of pleasure a second time.

She cried out again at the sensations rocking her. Harrison rolled her onto her back, gripping her ankles to spread her legs wide and drape them over his shoulders. Then he lifted her from the bed to drive himself deep inside her once more.

A third wave began to build inside Gracie as he bucked against her, climbing higher and higher, hotter and hotter, until she was crashing to the ground, and Harrison was right there with her. As they lay beside each other afterward, panting for breath and groping for coherent thought, she wondered if it would always be this way with them. If there would ever come a time when their lovemaking wasn't explosive and fierce, when they didn't feel so urgent and intense.

But all the thought did was make her smile. Somehow, she knew they would have lots of time together to discover each other. They would have lots of lovemaking. Lots of feelings. Lots of chances.

She looked at Harrison, lying beside her with his eyes closed, his hair damp, his chest rising and falling raggedly. A chance was all she'd wanted from him. And it was all she'd needed to give him in return.

"I love you, Harrison Sage," she said softly.

He opened his eyes and smiled. "I love you, Gracie Sumner."

Okay, maybe there was one other thing she'd wanted from him. Now she had that, too. And when it came to love, not even fourteen billion—yes, *billion* with a *b*—dollars stood a chance.

Epilogue

It was snowing on Roosevelt Avenue in the borough of Queens. The fat, frilly flakes danced to and fro around Gracie as she stood at the edge of a vacant lot that would soon be a pediatric clinic. Although it was early April, and the snow wasn't supposed to last for more than a day—a good thing in light of this afternoon's ground-breaking ceremony—Gracie liked seeing it. There was something promising about snow. Something clean. Something genuine. Something hopeful. Something that said everything was going to be just fine.

And everything was fine. The clinic was the last recipient of Harry Sagalowsky's billions. In the last ten months, she had spent his money on hundreds of projects and thousands of institutions that would affect millions of people. She'd traveled all over the country to participate in not only ground-breaking ceremonies, but also ribbon-cutting ceremonies. She'd visited preschools, elementary schools, high schools and colleges, attended meetings in churches and synagogues, temples and mosques. She'd even been invited to a couple of weddings and a barn-raising that had been facilitated by Harry's estate.

She had seen firsthand the good things money could do when it was placed in the right hands. Harry had been wrong about money causing the world's problems. Greed did that. Money properly spent could create a utopia. She hoped Harry was resting easily now, wherever he was.

"Not the best weather for a ground-breaking," Bennett Tarrant said from his position on her left.

He was elegantly bundled in an exquisitely tailored camel-hair overcoat, a paisley silk scarf tucked beneath the lapels. Gus Fiver was a mirror image of him, his own coat a few shades lighter, and Renny Twigg almost epitomized Gracie's initial impression of her as someone who should be working outdoors in flannel, wrapped as she was in a red-and-black-checked wool coat that was belted at the waist.

Gracie would have felt bland beside her in her own creamy Dior-style coat, circa 1950, if it hadn't been for the luscious way Harrison was looking at her—the same way he'd been looking at her since she'd come out of his bathroom wrapped in a towel this morning. And that was a weird thought, since she'd come out of his bathroom wrapped in a towel lots of times. So why was today any different?

He was another reason the last ten months had been so fine—and so hectic. Bicoastal relationships weren't the easiest thing to maintain. But she'd wanted to finish her degree in Seattle, and his business was in New York, so one of them had flown across the country almost every weekend. Or he'd flown to whatever event she was attending with Harry's money to join her. She sent up another silent thank-you to Harry for making that possible. Yes, he'd wanted her to buy a house on the water or go to Spain with some of his money, but using it to see a man who had become more important to her than anything had given Gracie a lot more happiness.

But she'd had her degree for more than two months and still didn't have a job. Of course, that could be because her work with Harry's money had intensified once her classes concluded. It could also be because her search for work in Seattle had been kind of halfhearted. Then again, her search for work anywhere had been kind of halfhearted. There were probably more positions in a big city like New York—and, truth be told, she'd applied for as many jobs here as she had in Seattle. But as good as things had been between her and Harrison—and as big a pain as it was living thousands of miles apart—neither had brought up the subject of taking things to the next level. Like living in the same city.

"I like the snow," Gracie said in response to Mr. Tarrant. "It's very pretty."

"I like it, too," Renny Twigg said from his other side. "It looks like wrapping paper on this big, beautiful gift that Harrison Sage is giving to the neighborhood."

Gee, Renny Twigg had something of a whimsical streak, Gracie thought. Maybe she really should be doing something besides working for a probate firm.

"I think they're about to begin," Bennett Tarrant said. "Shall we?"

The ground-breaking ceremony went off without a hitch. Gracie and Harrison laughed as they jabbed their shovels into the ground, fighting to get them deeper than a couple of inches into the frozen sod. Gracie even stepped up onto the top of the blade of her own shovel in an effort to drive it deeper. But all that did was send her teetering backward. Thankfully, Harrison was there to catch her. He set her on the ground beside him before returning both their shovels to the community leaders in charge.

Once all the thanks had been made and the farewells uttered, Tarrant, Fiver & Twigg returned to the big black Town Car that had brought them, and Gracie and Harrison headed for his. As they strode across the vacant lot, the snow began to fall harder around them, blurring the rest of the urban landscape, making her feel as if there were no one in the world but them. Harrison seemed to sense it, too, because he entwined his gloved fingers with hers.

"I heard you applied for a teaching position at my old school," he said. "Kindergarten. Starting this fall."

Dang. Busted.

"Well, the listing came up on LinkedIn," she said, "so I thought, what the hey. I mean, I've applied at schools all over the place," she added, fudging the truth a bit, since she hadn't applied for positions in, say, Nauru or Abu Dhabi—or anywhere else that wasn't Seattle or New York. "I probably won't get it, though, since I'm sure they want someone seasoned who feels the same way about education that they do."

She couldn't help adding, not quite under her breath, "More's the pity."

Harrison grinned. "I've spoken to the director about you. Seeing as I'm sitting on the board now and all, I have some pull there."

Gracie grinned back. "So then I guess I really can kiss that position goodbye, since you know the first thing I'd do is rally for art and music classes to be mandatory and for the uniforms to be eighty-sixed."

Harrison's grin grew broader. "You should be getting a call this week, actually. You could really shake things up there. Get 'em while they're young and teach them about the stuff that's really important. Not that I told the director that part. I just told her you're exactly the kind of teacher that place needs. And hey, you'll have an ally on the board."

Gracie chuckled. "Thanks, Harrison." Then she sobered. "Of course, that means I'll be moving to New York. Will that be a problem? For us, I mean?"

Now his expression turned confused. "How could that possibly be a problem for us? We'd finally both be in the same place at the same time for more than a few days."

She shrugged. "I know, but we haven't—"

"Of course, apartments are crazy expensive in Manhattan," he interjected. "Living there on a teacher's salary would be impossible."

Ah. So. Evidently, that "taking things to the next level" discussion was still on hold for a while, since anything she would be able to afford in New York was probably still going to land her in another state like Connecticut or New Jersey. Still, they'd at least be closer.

"Yeah, crazy expensive," he reiterated. "So it would probably be better if you move in with me."

Oh. Okay. So maybe they *were* going to talk about it?

"Or we could look for a new place together," he continued.

Wow. *Really* going to talk about it. At least, they would be, if Gracie wanted to jump in. At the moment, though, she wasn't sure what to say. Harrison clearly was, though.

"But you know," he said, "the school where you'll be working is pretty traditional. For now, anyway. They might frown on one of their kindergarten teachers living in sin."

So then maybe they *weren't* going to talk about it. Or take it to the next level. Never mind.

Harrison sighed with resignation. "So it might be best if you just marry me."

Before Gracie could say a word—he'd just skipped every level there was!—he withdrew a small velvet box from inside his coat and opened it. Nestled inside was a diamond ring. An old diamond ring. A modest diamond ring. An absolutely beautiful diamond ring. It was probably about a third of a carat, mounted on a white gold, filigreed setting, and it was dazzling amid the falling snow.

"It was my grandmother's," he said. "I found it in one of the shoe boxes where my dad stowed stuff. The minute I saw it, I thought of you. If anyone could make this represent happy memories instead of sad ones, it's you."

That, finally, made Gracie break her silence. "You

told me you finished going through your dad's things back in October."

"Yeah, I did."

"So you've been thinking about giving me this since then?"

"No, I found this in August. But you were so busy with school and my dad's estate, I didn't want to overwhelm you."

Overwhelm her? He'd overwhelmed her the minute she saw him.

He smiled again, a little less certainly this time. "So what do you say, Gracie? Will you marry me? Or should I have asked you sooner?"

Well, he could have asked her sooner, she supposed. But it was never too late for something like this. Then again, with Harry's money no longer a strain on her time, and with her starting a new job in a few months, and with Harrison just looking so gorgeous and being so wonderful...

"Your timing is perfect," she said.

Just like you, she thought.

"Just like you," he said.

"Just like us," she amended.

He smiled at that. As he removed the ring from the box, Gracie tugged the glove off her left hand. And when he slipped it over her third finger, it was... Well, it was perfect, too.

"I love you, Gracie Sumner," he said softly, pressing his forehead against hers.

"I love you, Harrison Sage," she replied.

As the snow continued to swirl around them, and as he covered her mouth with his, Gracie couldn't help thinking she'd been wrong about the clinic for which they'd just broken ground. It wasn't the last recipient of all that Harry left behind. Because she'd just received the last—and best—part of that herself.

* * * * *